MURDER ON KAANAPALI BEACH

A Leila Kahana Mystery

R. BARRI FLOWERS

Murder on Kaanapali Beach is a work of fiction. Names, characters, places, and incidents are either the product of the author's imagination or are used fictitiously. Any resemblance to actual events, locales, business establishments, or persons, living or dead, is entirely coincidental.

MURDER ON KAANAPALI BEACH
A Leila Kahana Mystery
Copyright © 2015 by R. Barri Flowers

ISBN: 1519458428
ISBN-13: 978-1519458421

Aloha to everyone who loves the Hawaiian Islands and appreciates their breathtaking beauty.

And to the many fans of my Hawaii mystery, suspense, and thriller fiction who inspire me to continue writing in the spirit of Aloha. Mahalo!

* * *

CRIME & THRILLER NOVELS
BY R. BARRI FLOWERS

Dark Streets of Whitechapel
Dead in Pukalani
Dead in the Rose City
Fractured Trust
Justice Served
Killer Connection
Killer Evidence Legal Thriller 4-Book Bundle
Killer in The Woods
Murder in Honolulu
Murder in Hawaii Mysteries
Murder in Maui
Murder on Kaanapali Beach
Murdered in the Man Cave
Persuasive Evidence
Private Eye Bestselling Mysteries 2-Book Bundle
Seduced To Kill in Kauai
Serial Killer Thrillers 5-Book Bundle
State's Evidence

* * *

PRAISE FOR R. BARRI FLOWERS

"Flowers delivers the goods. An exotic setting, winning characters, and realistic procedural details make MURDER IN MAUI a sure hit with crime-fiction readers." — Bill Crider, Edgar winner and author

"MURDER IN MAUI is a steamy, non-stop thrill-ride through the seamy underbelly of Hawaii." — Allison Leotta, Federal Sex Crimes Prosecutor and author

"Vivid details of police procedure one would expect from top criminologist. A gripping novel in what promises to be an outstanding series." — Douglas Preston, New York Times bestselling author on MURDER IN MAUI

"Gripping, tightly woven tale you won't want to put down. The author neatly contrasts the natural beauty of tropical paradise with the ugliness of murder and its aftermath." — John Lutz, Edgar winner and bestselling author on MURDER IN MAUI

"MURDER IN HONOLULU is an exquisitely rich and masterfully constructed mystery. R. Barri Flowers now lays fitting claim to the beautiful island paradise as his territory.... A savvy, smooth, and sumptuous read that's as hot as Waikiki beach sand." — Jon Land, bestselling author

"Infidelity and murder in paradise lead to a one of a kind case for PI Skye McKenzie Delaney, and an enjoyable ride for the reader. Definitely put this one on your list." — John Lutz, Edgar winner and bestselling author on MURDER IN HONOLULU

"Flowers once again has written a page-turner legal thriller that begins with a bang and rapidly moves along to its final page. He has filled the novel with believable characters and situations." — Midwest Book Review on STATE'S EVIDENCE

"A clever mystery with many suspects.... Vividly written, this book holds the reader's attention and speeds along." — Romantic Times on JUSTICE SERVED

"A model of crime fiction.... Flowers may be a new voice in modern mystery writing, but he is already one of its best voices." — Statesman Journal on JUSTICE SERVED

"An excellent look at the jurisprudence system....will appeal to fans of John Grisham and Linda Fairstein." — Harriet Klausner on PERSUASIVE EVIDENCE

STATE'S EVIDENCE will make the top sellers list because it's fast-paced, intriguing, satisfying, and I highly recommend it to you." — Romance Reader At Heart

"A rocket of a read. Not only a heart-thumping thriller, this is that rare novel that is downright scary." — John Lutz, Edgar winner and bestselling author on BEFORE HE KILLS AGAIN

"It gets no better than this! R. Barri Flowers has written another thriller guaranteed to hold onto its readers!" — Huntress Reviews on DARK STREETS OF WHITECHAPEL

"Selected as one of Suspense Magazine's Best Books." — John Raab, CEO/Publisher on THE SEX SLAVE MURDERS

* * *

PROLOGUE

On Tuesday, Joyce Yashiro was up bright and early for her usual morning run on the beach before going to work. In addition to staying fit, it was also her best time to think. There was actually a lot on her mind these days, much of it troubling. Clearly, some serious changes needed to be made in her life. Or had she already made too many changes, angering more than one person in the world she had not so carefully constructed?

After putting her medium length black hair into a ponytail, Joyce did her pre-run warmups, stretching her long limber legs and then her arms this way and that before deciding she was ready to head out. She walked through the house that she had once shared with her husband and son until things fell apart, and spotted her dog Seiji in the Great Room. He was resting comfortably in his favorite spot by the sectional, right under the ceiling fan.

She had a mind to wake him, but since he was recovering from a tummy ache, she thought the rest would do him good in spite of the fact that the Staffordshire terrier mix she'd had since he was a puppy loved to run with her.

Not this time, she told herself wisely, certain they would have plenty of other opportunities to run together.

She grabbed her keys and left the house. It was warm and muggy on this February morning; nothing at all like the frigid winters she had spent in New York before returning to her native Hawaii and settling down on Maui.

Joyce headed down the hill of the golf course in the Kaanapali Beach resort area, and then across the grass en route to the beach. It was quiet aside from the slight swoosh of palm trees that were sprinkled around the property. She spotted a few other runners who were, like her, out and about before the locals and tourists got up.

Taking her usual path between hotels lining the strip, Joyce made her way to the soft, sandy beach. It was still dark, but her eyes had adjusted so she had no trouble seeing where she was going. Honestly, she wished Seiji had been up to the run, as his company was pretty much all that kept her going these days as far as companionship. When it came to love and romance, she had flopped big time. But it wasn't from lack of trying on her part.

Then there was her son. Where had she gone wrong with him? How could his father's influence and irresponsible ways have been stronger than what she could offer him?

Joyce was now in a groove, moving in even strides across the sand. Her legs felt weary and her breathing was slightly labored. She looked forward to a nice soothing shower when she got home. And maybe Seiji would feel well enough to eat something.

So focused on her thoughts, Joyce never even heard the sound of footsteps rapidly approaching her.

Until it was too late.

She was suddenly pushed down hard onto the sand. She tried to move, but someone was on top of her holding her down. She couldn't tell if it was a man or woman, but assumed by the weighty feel that it was a man.

Her mouth and nose were pushed into the sand. She couldn't breathe and was choking on the sand.

Who was doing this and why? A few suspects crossed her mind. But would any of them go this far? For what, to teach her a lesson?

Okay, she got the message. Now it was time to let her go.

But whoever was doing this to her did not seem to want to leave it at that. As she struggled to free herself, Joyce gasped for air, but found none. Her chest felt tight and her lungs burned. She tried coughing, but only got a mouthful of sand with her face held down flush against the beach.

She suddenly felt some type of wire being placed around her neck. Then it tightened, slicing into her neck and constricting her air and the flow of blood to her head.

The person intended to kill her right there on a public beach! But since it was early in the morning, perhaps there would be no witnesses.

She fought hard to breathe, clawing at the sand with her hands, while her legs were pinned down to the point of being virtually unmovable.

As the wire around her neck grew tighter and tighter, her will to fight and breathe faded as unconsciousness started to seep in. Any dreams she had were about to die with her, and there was nothing she could do about it but pray that her life would be better on the other side. And that her killer would be brought to justice in what was no longer paradise, but a nightmare that she would never wake from.

Joyce saw flashes of light in her head, and then total darkness ensued, as if to let her know time had run out.

* * *

He tightened the zip line around her neck as hard as he could until he was certain she was dead, wanting to take no chances that she could somehow survive this. The last thing he needed was to lose the element of surprise and have her ready for him the next time. She didn't deserve to live and he was left with no other choice than to make sure she had breathed her last breath.

He felt her neck go limp and her head jerk to the right involuntarily, while her face remained buried in the sand.

3

Her body, now lifeless beneath him, became pliable and he wondered if some of the bones might actually break from his weight. Lifting up, he left the zip line embedded around her neck and removed the gloves he wore, stuffing them into his pocket.

He thought he heard someone coming and had to get the hell out of there—fast! He couldn't afford to be spotted, screwing up everything. Gazing in both directions through the darkness, he tried to determine which way the sound had come from. But he saw no one.

Hedging his bet, he ran off in one direction, content in the knowledge that dead people didn't talk. This one certainly wouldn't. That meant he was in the clear. Or he would be, once the dust settled.

* * *

Evan Locklear was vacationing on Maui with his wife, Sara. It was a much deserved break from both their hectic work schedules. If the truth be told, she had insisted they come, indicating that they needed some time away to work on their marriage. He had to admit that there had been some strain with them hardly able to spend any time with each other these days. As a result, the spark had all but disappeared from their love life. But he still loved her and didn't want to lose her.

So he agreed to put things aside at work and try to be the man she had married. At least for a couple of weeks. So far, everything seemed to be clicking. But how long would it last?

Evan's thoughts subsided as he left their beachfront hotel room and went for a run just before five in the morning. That wasn't Sara's thing, so he didn't bother to wake her up. The day had yet to break, but he could still make out the ocean, which seemed relatively calm today. He felt a slight breeze as he took to the beach.

Out of nowhere, a figure seemed to emerge from the darkness, nearly running into Evan. He only got a brief look at the man who whisked past him without so much as uttering a word.

"Asshole," muttered Evan, as he continued to jog. He was about to return to his thoughts when he tripped over something and fell down.

Getting back to his feet, he brushed the sand off his clothes and peered at the object. His heart skipped a beat when he realized it was a person laying there face down and not moving.

His first instinct was to roll the person around, which he did. It was a female. He felt for a pulse. There was none. He tried again. Same result. It left him with a sinking feeling.

Even if he hadn't been a doctor, he would have known she was dead. He called 911, but knew there was nothing they could do for her.

Evan looked in the direction of the man who had nearly run into him. He had apparently murdered this poor woman and was now trying to get away.

CHAPTER 1

Detective Sergeant Leila Kahana had been roused from her sleep by word of an apparent homicide on one of Maui's most popular beaches. It was hardly the way she wanted to begin her day working for the Maui County Police Department. Unfortunately, the crime of murder came with the territory. A Native Hawaiian, she was in her eighth year on the force as an investigator and composite sketch artist, and her fourth year with the Homicide Unit. Being a cop was in her blood. Her grandfather, Ekewaka Kahana, was once the County of Maui police chief and her father, Katsumi Kahana, had been in Internal Affairs. Family heritage aside, at thirty-three, Leila believed she was her own woman with a desire to take on criminality and the bad guys who would dare tarnish paradise and all it stood for in past generations.

She arrived at the crime scene just after six a.m. It was in Kaanapali on the west side of Maui. What had once been land consisting of taro, green sugar cane, and a fresh water spring, had now become a master-planned resort community that featured luxurious homes, world-class ocean front hotels, and posh condominiums along a three-mile stretch of palm trees and pristine white sand. Indeed, Kaanapali Beach had once been given the distinction of being called America's Best Beach.

Leila's brown shoulder length hair with blonde highlights was pulled back into a ponytail. She was comfortable in her own skin at five-foot-four inches tall with a slender build. She flashed her identification at a uniformed officer in an area that had been cordoned off by yellow police tape. She could see the body of a female lying on the sand in what appeared to be jogging attire. Leila tried to imagine what her last moments were like. Or was that even possible?

Just before she could reach her, Leila was cut off by her partner of six months, Detective Jonny Chung.

"Sorry to disturb your beauty rest, but duty called," he told her.

"Maybe you should feel sorry for her," Leila said, glancing at the victim. "I can catch up on my sleep later."

He grinned. "Good point."

Her brown eyes gazed at him. Chinese-American, the former vice cop had tried to hit on her more than once before and after they partnered up. Though he wasn't bad looking and a good fit for her height-wise at just a few inches taller, after her recent involvement with her ex-partner and now boss had ended badly, she was not about to go down that road again.

"So what do we have?" she asked.

"Caucasian female, mid to late thirties," Chung said routinely. "There was no ID on the body, but she did have a house key in her pocket. Based on the zip line left around her neck, I'd say she was strangled—like the others..."

Leila grimaced. Over the past year, three women had been strangled to death by a serial killer dubbed by the press as the "Zip Line Killer" because he used this weapon to kill each of the victims, leaving it behind as his calling card. The first two murders occurred in Spreckelsville, a small beach community on the island's North Shore. Marcia Miyashiro, was the first victim. The thirty-six-year-old clothing store clerk was strangled inside her apartment. Four months later,

Amy Lynn Laseter, a twenty-one-year-old tourist, was missing for three weeks before her remains were found amidst some shrubbery. Then two months ago in Makena, an area in South Maui, the body of twenty-nine-year-old designer Ruth Keomaka was found in the park. In each case, the victim had been clothed and there was no sexual assault.

Leila wondered if that would hold up for what appeared to be the latest victim. She first noticed the sand caked on one side of her face and mouth, as if the victim had been face down during the assault. Based on her attire of a matching sports bra and shorts with sneakers, it was obvious that she had been on the beach running when she was attacked.

It was only when Leila focused more intently on the victim's face that she took a step back in horror.

"What?" Chung asked, glancing at her. "This isn't the first time you've seen a dead body, is it?"

She ignored the question, given that he surely knew it wasn't the case. "I know the victim—"

He cocked a brow. "Really? Who is she?"

"Her name is Joyce Yashiro. She teaches at the College of Maui."

"You took her class?"

"I saw her last year at a seminar," she said. "I can't believe someone killed her. For what reason?"

"To get his kicks," Chung suggested. "It's all about opportunity and satisfying some sick urge to kill while thinking he can keep getting away with it."

Leila knew all too well how serial killers thought. Or at least what they weren't thinking about, which was the police would never rest till they were brought to justice and punished accordingly for their crimes.

"Were there any witnesses?" she asked.

"Not to the murder itself, but just about as important. A doctor not only tripped over the victim, but thinks he may have come face to face with the killer."

"Oh..." Leila gazed at the detective.

"Yeah. He was jogging when he nearly ran into a guy, who apparently couldn't get away from here fast enough."

The notion that they might finally have a solid description of a killer who may have been responsible for several murders on Maui excited Leila.

"Where is he...?"

"Over there waiting patiently. Name's Evan Locklear."

She looked beyond the crime scene and saw a tall, gray-haired man. He was talking on a cell phone. It occurred to her that there were times that the actual killer pretended to be a witness to the crime as part of his or her perverse gratification. Could this be one of those times?

Walking over to him, Leila watched as he hastily ended his call.

"Mr. Locklear—" she began, giving him the benefit of the doubt.

"Yes," he said evenly.

She detected a Southern accent. "I'm Detective Sergeant Kahana of the Maui Police Department. I understand that you called 911 after discovering the body in the sand."

He smoothed a thick brow. "That's right."

"And you're a doctor?"

"Yes."

Right, I've heard that before. Just what have you been up to, Doc? Leila thought sardonically. She asked the man: "What type of doctor are you?"

"I'm a cardiovascular surgeon."

She was impressed. "So when you discovered the body, there were no signs of life?"

"I'm afraid not." He grimaced. "I wish I could've saved her."

That would have been nice, she thought. But her killer had seen to it that she wouldn't live to identify him.

"Are you visiting the island, Dr. Locklear?"

"Yes. My wife and I decided to get out of Charleston, South Carolina for some fun in the sun." He frowned. "But I certainly never expected anything like this."

"I'm sorry it ruined your vacation," Leila said sincerely. "Tell me about the man you saw."

He sighed. "Well, I didn't get a very good look at him. He was just there all of a sudden. I only caught a glimpse of his face before he took off running."

She considered that the man may have been running for some reason other than having just murdered a woman. After all, that was what the good doctor claimed he was doing.

"Was he tall? Short? What about his race?"

"He was about my height," Locklear admitted. "Maybe a bit heavier. Had short hair. Not sure what color."

"Was he Caucasian? Asian? African-American? Something else...?"

"He wasn't African-American," Locklear said. "I can't be sure about any other race or ethnicity."

"How old was he?"

"I'd say early to mid-thirties."

That was a start, Leila mused, though hardly definitive. "Do you think you could provide a description of him to a sketch artist?" That would be her.

He hesitated. "Like I said, I barely saw the guy."

She peered at him. "But you *did* see him, which is all we've got right now for the possible suspect to a murder. Any help you could provide could lead us to the killer—"

"Sure," he said, running a hand across his chin. "I'll do the best I can."

"Mahalo," Leila said, figuring he would get the gist that it meant thank you. "If you could drop by the police department sometime this morning that would be great. It's in Wailuku. Or I could have someone pick you up—"

"I'll be there."

She nodded, willing to give him some time to see his wife and recall the person he saw leaving the area.

Making her way back to Chung, who was chatting with someone from the medical examiner's office, Leila diverted his attention.

"Dr. Locklear will be coming in to provide a description of our possible killer."

"Good. Maybe we can turn the corner on this serial killer—if, in fact, we're dealing with the same killer..."

Leila looked around. She didn't spot any surveillance cameras—as if there would be any right on the beach. But the hotels and condominiums lining it were a different story. "We need to have all these properties pull up their security camera footage for the last few hours—see if we can make out anyone coming or going that may have a taste for murder."

"I'm on it," Chung said.

"Even if we do get lucky with the composite and matching video footage, since we don't know if the killer is a local or a frequent visitor, we still have our work cut out for us nailing him," Leila said.

"Yeah, tell me something I don't know." Chung ran his hand through his short, choppy black hair. "I guess that's why they pay us the big bucks."

She rolled her eyes. "Yeah, right."

Leila thought about the victim, Joyce Yashiro. Had she been targeted? Was her death truly another notch on the Zip Line Killer's belt?

Or could this be a copycat killer with his own agenda?

CHAPTER 2

Renee Bradley woke up in a daze when she heard her cell phone buzzing. She grabbed it off the nightstand and saw that it was eight a.m. The caller was one of her sources at the police department, a cop she used to date. She gathered herself and answered.

"I just thought you'd like to know the body of a female was found this morning on Kaanapali Beach," the caller said. "It looks like she was strangled. Do what you want with the information. Bye."

Renee disconnected. So the Zip Line Killer had struck again, breaking his eerie silence of two months. As a journalist, she had been following this scary story from the start. Meaning, she needed to get any detailed information she could from quotable sources, such as the detective in charge of the investigation, Leila Kahana.

Dragging herself out of bed, Renee brushed her long blonde hair from her face and gazed down at the dark-haired man she'd had several tequila shots with at a local bar before they ended up at her place in Kapalua, a resort area just north of Kaanapali. She and Franco Romalotti were friends with benefits. Neither of them wanted anything serious, content to have sex whenever it suited their fancy while otherwise living their own lives without having to answer to the other.

The fact that their time in bed always took place at her condominium didn't bother her. After all, he was living with his grandmother while going to school and they both agreed that it wasn't the ideal scenario for getting naked and giving one another orgasms. Still, Renee couldn't help but wonder if this was headed anywhere. Or was it only destined to run its course when one of them got tired of the other?

"Hey," Franco muttered, opening his eyes.

"Hey," she said, feeling a tad embarrassed as he stared at her nudity. Never mind that he was also stark naked and very good looking from head to toe and everything in between.

"Where you going?"

"There's been another murder by the Zip Line Killer." She had yet to confirm this, but her source had never led her astray. "I have to stay on top of the story."

He frowned. "Well I hope they catch the son of a bitch, but can't you hold off for a little morning fun?"

She smiled, turned on by his words and expression that told her he wanted her in the worst way. While tempting, she chose to suppress her feelings. "Sorry, but I can't. If the police have the bead on this killer, I need to know. My career could depend on it." She knew that was a little over the top, but the fact that she had been covering the story for the Aloha News meant that if the case was close to being solved, she needed to be the one who broke the story.

Franco sat up, leaning on his elbow, frowning. "Do you want to get together later?"

"We'll see. I'll call you." Her head was killing her. She had obviously had too much to drink last night. "I'm going to hop in the shower. You can show yourself out."

She knew his eyes were studying her firm ass, as she made her way to the bathroom and closed the door.

By the time she opened it again, feeling refreshed, he was gone, as expected. She was already missing him, but had to stay focused on getting to the police department and learning everything she could about the latest murder.

* * *

Leila sat at her desk with pencil in hand as she prepared to sketch what she hoped would be a reasonable facsimile of a serial killer. Or, at the very least, a killer who had set his sights on Joyce Yashiro.

Across from her sat the witness, Doctor Evan Locklear from Charleston. She gave him a brief smile meant to relax him, before asking with more than curiosity: "So how long will you be on Maui?"

He seemed to ponder it. "We have a week left."

"Have you ever been here before?" She thought about the other murders that had occurred over the past year.

Locklear met her eyes. "Only in my dreams." He paused as she peered at him and then said: "This is our first time in Hawaii."

Leila accepted that, knowing it should be easy enough to verify, assuming he had used his own name. She sighed. "Okay, why don't we start with the hair? You mentioned it was short."

"Yes."

"Like really short in a buzz cut kind of way?" she pressed. "Was it tight on the sides? Tapered? Curly?"

"It was pretty dark out there, so I can't be very specific on the style of his haircut."

"Try anyway." Leila had a knack for getting people to remember things they thought they could not. "I know there wasn't much light and you hardly saw him, but even a glimpse can usually be retained. Take a breath and focus..."

She watched as he did just that. "I think it was short and a little messed up," he said. "Kind of like a business casual look."

Leila couldn't help but think that he had described his own hairstyle. Was that a Freudian slip? Or was it more endemic of today's look for many men?

She began to scribble on the pad. "Okay. Was it dark hair? Blonde? Gray?"

"It was dark—maybe brown."

"How about his face?" she asked. "Was it roundish? Narrow? Square? Wide-jawed? Long?"

Locklear sighed. "He had a square type face with a long forehead."

Leila drew this. "Did he have a long nose? Short? Thick? Crooked?"

"It looked long," he said.

"How about his mouth?"

"Crooked, but probably because he was scowling as though angry."

"Maybe he was angry that you saw him," Leila suggested.

"Could be." Locklear leaned back in the chair. "Except that I hardly saw enough of him to pose a threat. At least I probably wouldn't have thought that were I in his shoes."

Maybe you were, she mused, and a perfect fit at that.

"Did he have any facial hair?"

"Maybe a day's growth on his chin and neck."

Leila noted that the doctor was clean-shaven. Was he trying to steer them in a different direction? "Did his ears stick out? Were they large? Small?"

Locklear wrinkled his nose. "I honestly couldn't tell you that."

Was he really being honest? Leila continued sketching in using his description. While doing so, she asked for a better mental picture of the suspect to see if she might trip him up. "How tall was he? Shorter or taller than you?" She recalled him saying earlier that they were around the same height.

"Close to my height," he answered calmly. "And a little on the heavy side."

"And his race?" she asked again. "White? Hawaiian? Black? What...?"

Locklear chewed on his lower lip. "I think he was white. But I guess he could have been Hawaiian..."

Leila met his eyes. Had she just implanted Hawaiian in his head, giving him a perfect means for misdirection? In her mind, there was no comparison, physically speaking, between a white man and a Hawaiian man. But since it was dark and he only had a moment to glimpse the suspect, she supposed such uncertainty was possible.

"What was he wearing?" she asked, for the record.

"I think maybe a tee shirt and shorts."

Made sense, she thought. That would make it easy to move around on a beach, while fitting in at the same time.

"Could he have been wearing long-sleeved clothing?" she asked, in case the memory of the witness needed to be shaken up a bit.

"No, I don't think so."

She accepted that and finished the composite, showing him. "Does the man you saw look something like this?"

Locklear held the pad, studying it closely. "Yeah, it looks like him—or at least what I remember of him with only a moment to see his face."

"Then that will have to be good enough," she said, taking the sketch back. "We'll put it out there and see if we can find him."

"Wish I could do more," Locklear said.

Leila believed him. "Yeah, don't we all," she said humorlessly. "I hope you and your wife can make the most of the time you have left on the island."

Locklear smiled. "Me too."

She suddenly found herself wondering what type of marriage he had. Was this vacation meant to fortify something good or to salvage something bad?

Leila couldn't help but think about her ex-lover, Blake Seymour, now a lieutenant and the one she answered to. He had gone back to his wife and mother of their little girl, deciding he was no longer interested in having an affair with his partner. Leila had taken it hard initially, before realizing they weren't meant to be together. Meaning she had to forget about him and wait for someone more suitable to come along.

She walked with Evan Locklear away from her desk, hoping that his description of the suspect would lead to an arrest. The doctor might be called upon to make a house call if they needed more from him.

* * *

Renee found the one she was looking for. Detective Kahana had been talking to a gray-haired man when she shook his hand and said Aloha. Then the detective headed back toward her desk.

Now was the time to pounce on her, thought Renee.

"Detective Kahana," she said, getting her attention. "Can I have a word with you?"

Leila eyed her with a frown. "All updates on cases go through our spokesperson."

Renee was not deterred. "I know, but I'd just like a brief statement from the lead detective on the case involving the dead woman found on Kaanapali Beach."

Leila frowned. "You don't know when to quit, do you?"

"Do you?" Renee challenged her. "I'm just doing my job, like you are. With a serial killer on the loose and another woman strangled, the public deserves to be kept up to date."

Leila peered at her. "No one said anything about a person being strangled. Where did you get that information?"

Oops, Renee chided herself. She hadn't meant to let that detail slip, having been given a head's up by her source. She had to think fast.

"You just confirmed it, more or less," she said smartly. "I took a wild—or maybe not so wild—guess, considering the victim was a female and the circumstances eerily similar to the other victims of the so-called Zip Line Killer." She paused. "So am I right?"

Leila pursed her lips thoughtfully. "All right, yes, the victim does appear to have been strangled, though it will be up to the medical examiner to determine the exact cause of death."

Renee took mental notes. "What can you tell me about the victim?"

"Not much," Leila responded evasively, "other than it looks like she was on the beach for an early morning run when she was accosted by her attacker."

"Were there any witnesses?"

Leila hesitated. "Yes. Someone saw what could be the killer fleeing the scene."

Renee wondered if the witness was the man who just left. "Can you describe the possible killer?"

"We'll be releasing a sketch of the suspect shortly. That's all I can say for the time being."

Renee furrowed her brow. "Can you at least tell me if the victim has been identified?"

"Yes," Leila told her. "However, there has not been a positive identification, per se. Pending notification of the next of kin, the victim's identity will remain off limits to the press. Now, if you'll excuse me, I have work to do."

"Of course." Renee decided she better quit while she was ahead. "Mahalo for your time."

"Have a nice day," Leila said stiffly and walked away.

Renee watched her for a moment, before heading in the opposite direction. She wondered if she might be able to get more information from the witness. Who was he? She knew just who to ask to find out.

* * *

Leila went back to her desk, wishing they could keep the press at bay while working on cases. Realistically, she knew that in the Internet and cell phone age, it was hard, if not impossible to keep crimes bottled up until they were solved—especially when murder was involved with a serial killer on the prowl. Still, reporters such as Renee Bradley could be a pain in the ass, even if she was just doing her job.

"Hey," Leila heard as she sat at her desk.

She looked up into the slightly tanned, handsome face of her former partner Blake Seymour. He had short gray hair, was over six feet tall, and fit. He had been promoted to lieutenant six months ago following the retirement of Paul Ortega, which had made things a bit weird between them initially, partly due to the fact that they were no longer sleeping together. But as time went by, the more normal things became and she learned to accept things as they were.

"Hey," she said, straightening some papers on her desk, as though they needed it.

"Did you get a good composite of the suspect in the beach murder?"

"The witness seemed to believe so." Leila handed him the sketch.

Seymour gazed at it. "Hmm... So this could be the Zip Line Killer?"

"If not, he's certainly a person of interest in the murder of Joyce Yashiro," she told him.

"Chung said you knew her from a seminar."

"Yes, she gave a lecture on Hawaiian history. Guess I wanted to brush up on my knowledge and add to it."

"Has her family been notified?"

"Not yet. We'll be heading over to her house shortly." For Leila, this was perhaps the most painful part of dealing with homicides.

Seymour nodded. "Well, once we get the composite sketch out there, maybe someone will recognize him."

"That's the hope," Leila said, trying hard not to let their history dictate their relationship today. "Maybe we'll get lucky and someone matching the description will show up on the Kaanapali Beach hotel and condo security cameras that we've gained access to."

"Yeah, we could sure use that type of break." He paused, gazing at her. "If there's anything I can do for you, let me know."

Leila wasn't sure if he meant professionally or personally. She assumed it was the former, as the last thing either of them needed was to slip back into anything personal.

"Will do," she said tonelessly, then turned back to the papers on her desk while waiting for him to leave. He did and she found herself wondering how his nine-year-old daughter was doing. She had been the love of Seymour's life and, by virtue, a brief part of Leila's life. She would welcome being updated about the cute little girl every now and then, even if she was perfectly content otherwise maintaining a business-like relationship with Seymour as her boss.

CHAPTER 3

Leila drove the department-issued sedan onto Hakui Place, cruising down the palm tree-lined road with expensive homes atop a hill in Kaanapali.

"Looks like Joyce Yashiro was living the good life before disaster struck," Chung said. "If I could live in one of these places, I think I'd put in for retirement in a heartbeat."

"Dream on," Leila told him. "This area is way outside of both our pay grades."

"Tell me about it," he grumbled. "Apparently the victim didn't have such a problem."

"Maybe not," she said.

Leila had done a cursory search of the victim on the Internet. Apart from teaching Hawaiian Studies at the College of Maui, she was married and had a son. Obviously, the family had done well for themselves, since they resided in one of West Maui's most exclusive communities. Which would make it all the more difficult to have to reveal her passing to her loved ones.

But it was the job she had signed up for, meaning Leila would do it professionally and with respect for both the dead and the living.

They pulled up in front of a large Mediterranean style, two-story residence that included several palm trees. A tall male about nineteen or twenty with black hair in a short ponytail came out of the house. He glanced at them and continued walking toward a black pickup truck in the driveway.

Leila got out of the car, along with Chung, and approached him. "Excuse me," she said, "I'm Leila Kahana with the Maui Police Department. And this is Detective Jonny Chung."

The young man seemed nervous. "Okay..."

"We're looking for Verlin Yashiro," Leila said.

"He's my father."

"And you are...?"

"Ayato Yashiro. So what did he do this time?"

Leila glanced at Chung and back, wondering what the elder Yashiro had previously done. "We just need to talk to him."

"He doesn't live here anymore—at least not right now. My mother kicked him out. You can ask him why."

"Where can we find him?" Chung asked tersely.

Ayato shrugged. "Probably at work."

"And where is that?"

"The Aloha Architectural Group in Kahului. He's the director."

Chung nodded. "Okay, we'll catch him there then."

Ayato narrowed his eyes. "So what's going on?"

Leila hesitated. They usually preferred to give such news to the spouse first as a courtesy, even if they were apparently estranged. "We're not at liberty to say," she told him simply.

He rubbed his nose. "Did my mother send you after him?"

"Why would you say that?"

"Because she has before—"

"Why?" Leila pressed.

"Forget it. I probably already said too much." He sighed. "I have to go."

Leila studied him. She could tell by his bloodshot eyes and reddish nose that he was high on something—maybe meth. "Do you live here?" she asked curiously.

He looked away. "No. I have my own place. I just came over to feed the dog while my mother's at work."

Leila eyed Chung, while wondering if that was his only reason for being there. "Does anyone else live here besides your mother?"

"No."

"Well, we won't keep you any longer," she said, and thought, *for now anyway.*

He nodded and got inside the pickup, but seemed content to wait there till they left.

* * *

Detective Jonny Chung looked at Leila as they drove off, leaving the pickup truck and Ayato Yashiro behind.

"So what did you make of him?" Chung asked her.

"He's not exactly someone I would've wanted to bring home to mom when I was his age," she said. "He was high as a kite."

"Yeah, I was thinking the same thing." Chung thought back to his days with the vice squad. He had dealt with his fair share of druggies and dealers, with the two often interchangeable. He wondered if the kid was dealing too. The drug business had proven to be lucrative on the Hawaiian Islands, in spite of the best efforts of local and federal law enforcement. Chung had skillfully managed to get in on the action and slowly build up his retirement fund, even as he switched to the homicide division in partnering up with Leila Kahana. He wouldn't mind if things got personal between them. But she didn't seem interested and he wouldn't push it, especially when there were so many other attractive women on Maui to play around with.

"Did you buy his story that he just came over to feed the dog?" Leila asked him.

"Not really," Chung said. "With the father staying elsewhere, the kid is probably taking advantage of the situation by stealing whatever he can from his mother."

Leila frowned. "Unfortunately, with her now dead, it could be open season on what he claims for himself."

Chung faced her. "You think he could have had anything to do with her murder?"

"He certainly isn't the person in the composite sketch," she said, "so maybe he gets off the hook there. We'll see what the father's story is."

"Yeah. From what the kid implied, part of his story is he's a wife abuser with the cops being called at least once."

"I got that impression, too."

"You think that's why they're separated?" he asked.

Leila glanced at him from behind the wheel. "Isn't that reason enough?"

"Yeah, definitely. I just wondered if it might have been something else."

"Maybe we'll take the son's advice and ask him."

"Even if the man beats up on his wife, it doesn't mean he killed her," Chung pointed out.

She nodded. "I agree. If he's not the man the witness saw, hopefully we'll be able to match the sketch with someone on the surveillance video."

"Right, and if he turned out to be the Zip Line Killer, it would solve all our problems."

"Or at least an immediate problem," Leila said.

Chung heard his cell phone chime. He took it out of his pocket and saw that he had a text message from Renee Bradley, the reporter he had been banging a few months back. Ever since then, she had been hitting him up for information. He had gladly leaked just enough info to keep her happy, while keeping his own options open should he need her services in the future—either personally or professionally.

She wanted to speak to the witness in the Joyce Yashiro murder investigation. He glanced at Leila, who was focused on the road, then texted Renee the name of the hotel where Doctor Evan Locklear was staying along with his room number.

* * *

Renee was glad to get Jonny Chung's text, letting her know that the witness was named Evan Locklear and he and his wife were vacationing at a hotel right on Kaanapali Beach. It just so happened that she was in the area, so she might as well see if he would talk to her about what he saw.

She stepped inside the massive lobby of the Kaanapali Seas Hotel and basically ignored a bellhop who was hitting on her. Finding the elevator, she went up to the sixth floor and down the hall till she arrived at Evan Locklear's room.

What should I say to him? she asked herself in preparation. It was more about what he said to her in trying to gather as many details as possible in this latest chapter of the Zip Line Killer investigation, which people she'd talked to seemed to believe fit the M.O. of the serial killer terrorizing the island to perfection.

Renee knocked on the door. It was opened by a striking blonde-haired woman in her late thirties.

"Aloha," Renee said sweetly, assuming she was his wife. "I'm looking for Doctor Locklear."

"And you are?" the woman asked suspiciously.

"Renee Bradley. I'm a reporter for the Aloha News. I'm doing a story on the woman who was discovered on the beach early this morning. I was hoping to have a word with the doctor, since he's the only witness to come forward thus far..."

Hope I didn't let the cat out of the bag, thought Renee, not knowing if Locklear had bothered to share the news with his roommate.

The woman nodded. "Come in."

Renee flashed a little smile.

"I'm Sara, Evan's wife. He's getting dressed. He'll be out in a moment."

"All right." *Hope he doesn't to take too long*, she thought. She still had a few other stops on her schedule and possibly a repeat performance tonight with Franco.

"Have a seat," Sara offered.

"Thanks." Renee sat in one of several plush chairs in the suite. There were two empty glasses and a half filled bottle of wine on the table. She suspected the couple needed a drink after what he had witnessed. Who wouldn't?

She watched as a man came out of the bedroom. He was gray-haired, tall, tanned, and trim, wearing casual clothing.

"I didn't know we had company," he said, eyeing her.

"This is Renee Bradley. She's writing about that poor woman you found on the beach."

Evan regarded her warily. "How did you find me?"

Play it cool, Renee thought, glancing at the iPad on her lap. She responded: "It's what I do—ask around and get answers." She decided not to mention her source with the police department, Detective Chung. "I promise not to take up too much of your time. I just wanted to hear in your own words what you saw."

He sighed. "There's not much to tell really. I was jogging on the beach and saw a man. A moment later, I tripped over something that turned out to be a woman. She was dead...and there was nothing I could do to save her."

Renee could tell that it had hit him hard. "Do you think the man you saw was her killer?"

"Yes, I think so, especially considering the way he tore out of there."

She took notes. "Is it all right if I quote you?"

He shrugged. "Sure, why not. I saw what I saw and the police know it, so it's not exactly a secret. And there is a sketch."

"Sketch?" Renee asked.

"The police did a composite sketch of the guy, based on what limited description I had of him."

She recalled the doctor talking to Detective Kahana, who doubled as a sketch artist for the police department. "Can you describe the man to me?"

Evan did just that, and she got him to describe the woman too, while establishing that the low light had made it difficult to be too accurate.

"Did this man say anything to you?" Renee asked.

"No, he didn't say a word."

"Maybe it was a good thing that you didn't exchange words with him," she said. "There have been several similar killings on Maui recently—all believed to be the work of a serial killer."

Sara put a hand up to her mouth and said, "That's terrible!"

Much worse for the victims, Renee thought, but said: "The police are doing their best to get this guy. If he is the same person your husband came face to face with, then hopefully the composite will get people talking and result in an arrest."

"We hope so," Evan said. "We came here to get away from bad stuff—not have to deal with it on an ongoing basis..."

Renee suspected they were having second thoughts about choosing Maui as their vacation destination. "No place is perfect," she told them. "Not even Hawaii. But it is true paradise much of the time." She stood up. "Mahalo for talking to me."

Evan smiled crookedly. "If your story can help the police nail this killer or serial killer, then I'm all for it."

"So am I," Sara added.

Renee smiled at them. "Aloha."

She left, feeling she had gained enough information to write something compelling. Of course, it would be even better once the victim was identified and her killer revealed.

CHAPTER 4

Kahului was in central Maui and included the island's main airport, a commercial harbor and seaport, a wildlife sanctuary, and several major shopping centers. Unlike some other parts of Maui County, it was not a big attraction for tourists, but was popular among the locals.

The Aloha Architectural Group was on East Ka'ahumanu Avenue, near the Maui Mall. Leila and Chung went inside the building and walked up to the receptionist.

"Aloha," the woman said cheerfully.

Leila flashed her badge. "We need to speak to Verlin Yashiro."

"He's on a conference call right now."

"He'll want to see us," she said, knowing that likely wasn't the case, under the circumstances.

"Just a moment," the receptionist said.

As they waited, Chung spoke lowly: "Since they weren't together anymore, Yashiro might not be all that broken up about her death."

Leila disagreed. "No matter what their troubles were, I doubt he wanted his wife dead."

"Unless, of course, he actually did want her dead," Chung said half-joking.

"We'll see about that." As far as she was concerned, even a spouse abuser had to be given the benefit of the doubt when it came to cold-blooded murder—until the evidence suggested otherwise. Especially for a case that had all the earmarks of being linked to a serial killer.

They were approached by a forty-something Hawaiian man wearing glasses. His black hair was parted on the right side and he was dressed professionally in a blue suit.

"I'm Verlin Yashiro," he said. "You wanted to see me...?"

Leila tried to imagine him as a wife beater and found it hard to picture—not that abusers came in any particular shape or size. He didn't look at all like the person she had sketched either. "I'm Detective Sergeant Kahana and this is Detective Chung. Is there some place we can talk in private?"

He met her eyes uneasily. "Yes, my office. Follow me..."

Leila walked behind him next to Chung. They went down a long hallway and turned right, before entering a large office with an interesting design and ergonomic furnishings.

Yashiro faced them. "What's this all about?"

Leila swallowed. "It's about your wife..."

"Is she all right?"

Leila paused. "I'm afraid your wife is dead."

"What—?" He looked from one detective to the other. "Was she in a car accident or something?"

Or something, Leila thought sadly. "No, she was murdered."

"Murdered—?" Yashiro looked visibly shaken. "By who...?"

Leila deferred this to Chung, who responded: "We don't know yet. Her body was found on the beach this morning and it looks like she was strangled."

Yashiro's shoulders slumped. "I can't believe it! Joyce is dead... Murdered..."

"I'm sorry for your loss," Leila told him respectfully. "We need you to come to the morgue to identify the body."

"I have to call my son..."

29

"Of course." She looked at Chung and back. "Maybe you should tell him in person—after you've confirmed that it is, in fact, your wife."

He nodded. "Yes, okay, I'll do that."

A couple of minutes later, they were in the police car, with Leila again behind the wheel and Verlin Yashiro in the back seat.

After a moment or two, she said casually: "We actually went to your wife's house first and spoke to your son, without telling him what happened, believing it would be best if it came from you."

"Thank you."

Chung jumped into the conversation. "We understand that you and your wife were separated..."

"Yes, we were dealing with some issues."

"You mean like domestic violence?" he asked bluntly. "Were you beating up your wife?"

"No, it wasn't like that."

"So what was it like?" Chung asked.

Yashiro paused. "It was actually my wife who got violent at times, acting out without cause. After a while, it just got to be too much."

Chung glanced at Leila with a healthy dose of skepticism. "You mind telling us where you were at five o'clock this morning?"

"In bed asleep. If you're implying that I killed my wife—"

"I'm not implying anything," Chung said. "It's just routine questioning."

Leila glanced at her partner knowing that he was building the foundation, should it be proven later that Yashiro was somehow involved in his wife's death. For now, she was willing to at least give him the courtesy of confirming what she already knew—Joyce Yashiro was dead and possibly the victim of a serial killer.

* * *

Leila and Chung accompanied Verlin Yashiro to the Maui Forensic Facility in Wailuku, the county seat in central Maui.

They headed into the walk-in refrigerator unit, where the deceased were kept for identification, preservation, and autopsies. Leila stepped inside the viewing room with Yashiro. Behind a glass partition, the body was lying on a slab, covered with a sheet.

"Are you ready?" Leila asked delicately.

Yashiro touched his glasses and sucked in a deep breath. "Yes."

She nodded to a morgue attendant, who lifted the sheet up enough to show the face.

Watching his reaction to the face of death that was unmistakable, Leila waited for his response.

"It's Joyce," he muttered.

"You're sure?" she had to ask routinely.

"Yes, that's my wife."

Leila gave the morgue attendant, who was standing beside Detective Chung, permission to pull the sheet back up. She turned to the widower. "I'm very sorry."

"She didn't deserve to go like that," Yashiro said sadly.

Leila gazed at him earnestly. "You're right, she didn't. And we're going to do everything in our power to identify her killer and see that justice is served."

"I appreciate that."

She could only hope he meant it and wanted his wife's murderer brought to justice as much as she did. Only time would tell, along with a deeper investigation.

* * *

Leila was glad to be home after another difficult day on the job, where murder always took center stage. Her two-bedroom plantation cottage was on Wainee Street in Lahaina, the second largest area in West Maui. The onetime Kingdom of Hawaii capital and 19th century whaling village, Lahaina was previously called Lele, meaning in Hawaiian, "relentless sun." Now it was one of Maui's hottest spots, with numerous art galleries, restaurants, and shops.

It was the one place where Leila could get away from it all and be normal instead of a homicide cop. The modest

31

house was built in 1934 and previously owned and lived in by her grandfather, who then passed it down to her parents. She had taken possession of it nearly six years ago after her mother had gone to live on the Big Island of Hawaii. Though the cottage had retained its original wood frame windows and hardwood flooring, Leila had renovated the kitchen, bathrooms, and her bedroom.

No sooner had she kicked off her shoes and poured herself a glass of wine, intending to enjoy a nice hot bath, when the phone rang. She didn't even have to look at the caller ID to know who it was. Almost like clockwork every few days at around this time, her mother called to talk, snoop, and basically try to run her life from afar.

And, as was usually the case, Leila did her best to stay deferential to a conservative and often set-in-her-ways Hawaiian mother with Polynesian roots. But that didn't always work, especially where it concerned her professional life, which she found herself constantly defending as something that a modern day woman was fully capable of handling. Even if her mother accepted this, irrespective of the fact that her own father and husband were in law enforcement, she still believed that Leila belonged in a more traditional occupation, such as nursing or secretarial work.

Then there was her love life—or lack thereof these days. Her mother fully expected her to uphold tradition, as she had, and marry a Hawaiian man. Though Leila didn't reject this outright, she didn't exactly embrace it either. She was not ready to marry anyone right now with her busy life. When such time came, it had to be based on mutual love and respect, not the race or ethnicity of her partner.

But since there was currently no one in the picture, she had no reason to share this opinion with her mother only to have to defend it, especially when she knew her mother was not very open-minded on this front.

Leila answered just before it went to voicemail. "Hi, Mom."

"I was hoping I didn't have to leave you a message," Rena Kahana said.

"Is everything all right?" Leila asked, though she had no reason to believe otherwise.

"Maika'i no au," came the curt response.

Leila knew this meant she was fine in Hawaiian, which her mother chose to use whenever it suited her, as if to turn her back on English in favor of the language of their ancestors.

"I was happy to hear that the lava flow from the Kilauea volcano had subsided," Leila said, referring to the most active of the island of Hawaii's five volcanoes, "and no longer posed a threat to the people in the town of Pahoa."

"The threat is always there for those who choose to live in that area," Rena remarked. "The sacred mountains are always speaking to us and we must listen."

Leila thought about the legends associated with the island's volcanoes. The summits were regarded by many, including her mother, as holy and were an important part of Hawaiian mythology.

"Maybe we do," she allowed.

"So what are you doing right now?" her mother asked.

"I just got home and was about to take a bath."

Rena made a grunting noise. "I suppose you're working on another big case."

"All cases are big, Mom." Leila thought it best not to shy away from the truth. "I always treat each case the same and try to solve it if I can."

"I hope you don't end up getting hurt one of these days. Crime is a dirty business, you know."

That much Leila couldn't argue with, but she did anyway. "Right, and it's my job to clean it up, just like Makuakāne and Tūtū," she said of her father and grandfather when they were in law enforcement.

"It's never that simple," Rena said. "They both learned the hard way. Maybe you will too."

Leila decided to put a different spin on this, rather than irritate her further. "Well, I believe that with their blood running richly through my veins, I'm up to the task of doing my job effectively, even if it's challenging at times."

Her mother sighed. "Okay, well I guess I'll let you take your bath now."

To Leila, this was her way of pausing on the subject matter until the next time. "Okay. Aloha au ia 'oe," she added.

"Love you too," her mother said and then hung up.

Leila wondered if all daughters had to constantly battle to live up to the expectations of their mothers. Or was it just her?

She ran the water in the bath, adding some Japanese cherry bubble bath. After testing it with a toe and deciding the temperature was perfect, she got in. Her body relaxed almost instantly and the stresses of the day that had left it tightly wound faded away. She grabbed her wine glass and took a sip of the white wine.

Closing her eyes, Leila inadvertently found herself thinking about Blake Seymour. She hadn't been with a man since they broke up. She wasn't sure why. Maybe she wasn't eager to have her heart broken again. Or maybe she was content at the moment to go it alone. Or maybe she just hadn't met anyone who captured her fancy.

I'm not going to freak out about it, she told herself.

Leila sipped more wine and turned her thoughts to her current case and the prospects that a serial killer had struck again.

CHAPTER 5

It was just after six p.m. and Parker Breslin was eager to get home from his job as a landscaper. He and his business partner, Vincente Miyake, operated the company with a crew of ten. Jobs were lined up all over the island, sometimes in conjunction with the Aloha Architectural Group and properties they developed. The current main project the landscaping company was working on involved consultation and design work for a new condominium complex in Wailea, a resort community in South Maui.

In spite of their success, Parker didn't always see eye to eye with Vincente. They sometimes clashed over everything from work assignments to crew misbehavior to money, which caused strain in their relationship. But as far as Parker was concerned, they would simply have to agree to disagree and look at the big picture. He realized it was easier said than done. But what choice did they have? Neither of them wanted to see the company go under. Or was it possible that Vincente was willing to sink his own investment purely out of spite?

As he drove down South Kihei Road in a new black Chevrolet Colorado, Parker's thoughts shifted to an equally pressing matter: the fate of his little girl Marie. He was currently in a nasty custody fight with his ex-wife Willa. She had gone out of her way to paint him as an alcohol abusing, workaholic jerk who neglected his daughter the way he had her during their marriage.

At the end of the day, he doubted the judge would believe her. He loved his daughter more than anything in the world, and would never hurt her. He wasn't an alcoholic and never put his work ahead of his little girl.

Surely the judge would see this and award him full custody of Marie, since he was the major bread winner and most stable parent.

Parker sighed, trying hard not to get himself all worked up. He pulled into the driveway of his home on Keonekai Road in Kihei on the island's southwestern shore. He grabbed a bag of snacks he had picked up at noon in anticipation of Marie's stay for the next week. His ex was due to drop her off any time now. He hoped they could at least remain civil, if only for Marie's sake.

After exiting the pickup, Parker headed for the house when his periphery spotted a figure moving his way from the sidewalk. His first thought was that it was a neighbor he had become friends with. But when he turned to look, he realized the person was a complete stranger.

And he was holding a gun, aiming it straight at him.

For an instant, Parker was frozen with fear. But the thought of never seeing his daughter again scared him even more. So he bolted for the house.

He didn't get very far, as a bullet ripped into his back. He immediately fell to the ground flat on his face and the bag flew from his hands, landing nearby. Searing pain from the bullet coursed throughout his body.

He could hear the shooter move closer. Then another shot rang out. Parker felt it explode into his head, just before he blacked out. He never knew what hit him when a third shot lodged inside the back of his head, shattering everything in its path.

The shooter immediately took off on foot, leaving Parker Breslin mortally wounded.

* * *

He glanced back at the dude he'd just taken out. Breslin was sprawled out on the ground like a frog, blood oozing out of him. No question about it, the man was no longer amongst the living. And he never even saw it coming, not till it was too damn late to stop it from happening.

With long, lean legs, he ran briskly down the block, keeping his head bent down and his collar up. He made sure not to make eye contact with anyone along the way or say anything that could come back to haunt him. Fortunately, he hadn't run into anyone who could identify him. Mindful of home security cameras, he used his hands to shield his face so there would be no clear image the police could use to come after him.

Turning the corner, he moved onto another street and slowed down, not wanting to draw any undue attention as though he were in a hurry to get away from something. Or someone. His car was waiting for him at the end of the block. He slipped into it, took a deep breath, and drove off. Mission accomplished.

Or just about. There was still one more thing that needed to be settled and then the Parker Breslin kill would be behind him for good.

* * *

Officer Natalie Yuen was patrolling the streets of District VI, which included Kihei. It had been a quiet evening, giving her time to consider if she should stay with her boyfriend. The relationship had grown stale of late and she wondered if they had simply grown tired of each other and should just cut their losses now before things got any worse.

Those thoughts were put on hold when a report of a shooting on Keonekai Road came in. Since it was only a couple of blocks away from where she was, Natalie wasted no time getting there.

The moment she pulled up to the address, she could see what appeared to be a man's body sprawled out on the walkway in a pool of blood. She got out of her car and immediately took out her Glock semi-automatic pistol, though there was no sign of a shooter—assuming the shooting wasn't self-inflicted.

Moving carefully toward the victim, Natalie winced as she realized that half of his face had been blown off and there seemed to be at least one shot in his back. Still, she had to check and see if he might somehow still be alive.

No such luck. Someone had clearly wanted the man dead. But who?

She would leave that to the detectives to determine. Since she was the first responder, her duty right now was to secure the crime scene and try to preserve any evidence that could point toward a killer.

* * *

Lieutenant Blake Seymour was in his department-issued sedan en route to the scene of a murder in Kihei. It marked the second homicide in less than twenty-four hours in Maui County, which was somewhat unusual, but not unheard of. Still, it was troubling for both the Maui Police Department and the Hawaii Tourism Authority. For the former, any crimes were too many crimes, with murder the worst of the worst, that couldn't be tolerated. For the latter, perception meant everything. Maui was viewed as one of the top destinations for tourists and places to settle down and enjoy paradise. If people believed it was more akin to an episode of Hawaii Five-O, it could spook them into looking elsewhere.

As he drove down South Kihei Road, Seymour's primary focus was dealing head on with any homicide investigations under his watch. It was, after all, what he had signed up for when he was promoted to lieutenant in the Homicide Unit six months ago, following the retirement of Paul Ortega. He had learned a lot from the man and wanted to measure up to the standard he set with the department as a no nonsense, finish what you started type person.

In the process, that meant he had to end his relationship with his former partner Detective Sergeant Leila Kahana, with whom Seymour had embarked on a brief affair while separated from his wife Mele, and by extension, their daughter Akela. He was now back with his family and doing what he needed to do to make it work this time around at age forty-seven.

At first, Leila hadn't taken their breakup too well. She blamed him for leading her on, sending mixed messages, and more. He took full responsibility for that and had been working ever since to try to smooth things over. They now seemed to be at a place where they could coexist professionally, while still maintaining some semblance of friendship with no sexual overtones. As far as he knew, she wasn't dating anyone. He wondered if she was somehow hoping they might get back together again. Or was that his ego getting the best of him?

Maybe Leila was simply waiting for the right unattached man to come along and be the person she had bargained for. If so, he wished her all the luck in the world, as she deserved to be happy in a relationship. Just as he did. Only time would tell if that would hold up now that he and Mele were back together.

Seymour parked just down the street from the cordoned off crime scene on Keonekai Road and headed there. He flashed his ID at Officer Yuen and she allowed him through.

"Be sure no neighbors find their way inside the crime scene," he told her.

"Yes, sir."

He headed toward the investigators on the case, Detectives Trent Ferguson and Rachel Lancaster. Both were experienced and more than capable of getting to the bottom of this killing.

"So was it a robbery gone sour or what?" Seymour asked as he stood between the two, just inches away from the bloody corpse of a male who looked to be in his mid to late thirties. Some food items were scattered about on the ground and grass near a bag.

"I'd say it was more like an execution," Ferguson said, scratching his pate. "I count three bullet wounds."

Seymour winced. "What do we know about the victim?"

"According to his driver's license, his name is Parker Breslin," Rachel answered, holding the license up while wearing a latex glove. "He's thirty-eight years old and lives at the address where he was dropped by an as yet unknown assailant."

Seymour studied the positioning of the victim's body, knowing that once the medical examiner took it away, things would never be the same again insofar as establishing the scenario of the crime.

"It looks like he was trying to make a run for it when the killer shot him—probably first in the back, before finishing him off with two clean shots to the head."

"Yeah, I was thinking the same thing," said Ferguson.

"The killer probably caught him by surprise," Rachel surmised, "and may have been someone he knew."

"Not necessarily," Seymour said. "If it was a hit, a professional could have done the job."

"After a preliminary search of the victim's person as well as his vehicle, there was no cell phone located," she noted. "Who doesn't carry a cell phone these days? That suggests to me the killer might have taken it for one reason or another."

Seymour could think of a few reasons, none of which was good—starting with a clear attempt to cover up evidence of a crime, which prompted him to say: "Okay, then let's try to locate his phone and see if it's in the hands of a killer." They would use the Stingray phone tracking device, which was the latest surveillance tool in the law enforcement arsenal.

"I'm on it," Ferguson told him.

Seymour looked up at the house. "Anyone inside?"

"No, it's empty," Ferguson said. "But judging by the cookies and candy Breslin brought home and never got to take inside, I'd say he was expecting company. Maybe a wife and kids."

Seymour couldn't help but think about his own daughter, now nine. He hated the thought of someone having to tell her he was dead, the victim of violence. Yet his life as a cop made anything possible. The same was true for others such as Parker Breslin, who died a tragic death, leaving others to pick up the pieces.

"Any witnesses?" Seymour asked.

"We're checking that out," Rachel said, looking down the street. "Someone must have seen something."

"If not, security cameras on some of the homes may have picked up the killer leaving the scene," he suggested.

"We'll go door to door if we have to and see what we come up with," Ferguson told him. "Breslin was gunned down right in front of his house for crying out loud. Apart from the shell casings the shooter left behind, hopefully forensics can come up with fingerprints or DNA that will identify the person or persons involved in this..."

"I'm counting on that," Seymour said, even if he wasn't prepared to bet his pension on it. Outdoor assassinations often left less identifying markers than indoor killings, where perpetrators needed to touch more things and move around in an enclosed space. That said, he was confident they would find out who murdered Parker Breslin at the end of the day. And why.

* * *

Detective Rachel Lancaster had seen far too many homicides and other crimes of violence during her time with the Maui County Police Department. But no death had affected her like the death of her husband, Greg, nearly three years ago while serving his country in Iraq as an Army veteran. Being a widow at thirty-four made life in Hawaii less than paradise. Pouring herself into the job had helped to the extent that it took her mind off of being lonely and the realization that she had become an alcoholic.

But it was times like these when it hit her that life was too short, and even shorter when someone decided to end yours as a criminal action. That was the case with Parker Breslin, who had been gunned down by an unknown assailant, ending his time on earth prematurely. Now she had the unpleasant task of notifying the next of kin of his passing.

Trouble was that person was a seven-year-old girl named Marie. So they would have to notify Breslin's ex-wife, Willa Breslin, of his departure to then pass on to his daughter. It was something Rachel wouldn't wish on anyone, much less a little girl whose father would miss out on her first date, prom, marriage, children, becoming a grandfather, and more.

But this was something Rachel knew she must separate herself from, to the extent possible. Right now, a man was dead and there were no suspects. This meant no one could be excluded yet. That included the ex-wife who, as she understood it from information found in Breslin's home, had been in a child custody battle with him while staying with her mother. Of course, seeking custody of a child, no matter how nasty it got, was a far cry from an execution-style murder. But it wasn't unheard of either.

We'll see where it leads, thought Rachel. Until then, she had to give the ex the benefit of the doubt and respect that she would truly be grieved and shocked upon learning of Breslin's death.

Rachel drove to a Kihei subdivision on Kawailani Circle, arriving at the single family home owned by Lynnette Takeyama a few moments later. There was a red Honda and a blue Buick in the driveway.

Rachel glanced at the rocking chair on the lanai and ran a hand through her shoulder length blonde hair, before ringing the bell.

A short Hawaiian woman, perhaps in her late fifties to early sixties with graying hair, opened the door but said nothing.

"Hi," Rachel said. "I'm Detective Lancaster with the Maui Police Department. I need to speak with Willa Breslin."

"I'm her mother," she said coolly. "May I ask what this is about?"

Yes you may, but I'd rather not tell you, Rachel thought. "I think it's best if I just talk to your daughter."

She nodded. "All right. I'll get her."

Rachel's impression of the mother was that she was a no nonsense type of person who probably dictated her daughter's life now that she was no longer married and back under her roof.

A tall, slender woman in her mid thirties with short black hair came to the door. "I'm Willa. How can I help you?"

"Are you Parker Breslin's ex-wife?"

"Yes," she said calmly. "What's this about?"

Rachel thought she might have spotted a little girl with long dark hair through the door opening. It wasn't the type of news she should overhear. "Can you step outside for a moment?" she asked Willa.

"Yes."

Rachel waited till she closed the door and faced her before saying: "I'm afraid I have some bad news—"

"Did something happen to Parker?" Willa asked with trepidation.

Rachel wondered why those were the first words from her mouth. Did she know something about his death? "He was murdered this evening..." she told her straightforwardly.

Willa put her hands to her mouth. "Oh no... How?"

"He was shot to death in front of his house," Rachel answered, observing her demeanor.

Willa shook her head. "I can't believe it! Parker was supposed to pick up our daughter, Marie."

"What time was that?" asked Rachel.

"Seven o'clock."

Rachel realized that was around the time the 911 call came in, reporting the shooting. Coincidence? She regarded the ex-wife thoughtfully. "And he was picking her up for—" she cut it off there to see what the response was.

"The rest of the week," Willa said with watery eyes. "We're divorced and share custody of Marie. It was his turn to have her—"

But that opportunity was cut short at the worst possible time, thought Rachel. Could the ex have had anything to do with it? "Do you know of anyone who would have wanted your ex-husband dead?"

Willa stared at the question. "No. As far as I'm aware, Parker had no enemies."

"Well, someone wanted him dead," Rachel said bluntly. "He was shot three times at pointblank range."

Willa wiped tears from her face. "I need to tell my daughter—"

"I understand." She expected no less, considering Willa was now the only parent the girl had left. "I need you to come to the morgue to identify the body. If you'd like to do that a little later—"

"No, I'll do it now," Willa said flatly. "I want to see for myself that Parker is really dead before I have to break this news to our daughter..."

Rachel found her wording odd, but reasoned that each person reacted differently to such tragic news.

Half an hour later, she stood with Willa Breslin at the Maui morgue, where the ex-wife of Parker Breslin formally identified his remains before breaking down in tears. Rachel felt appropriate sympathy for her, fully understanding loss as well as anyone. But as a homicide detective, she also had to consider that the grieving former wife of a murdered man could be playing her while going through the motions as a party to murder.

CHAPTER 6

On Tuesday night, Renee went for a drink at the Coconut Club on Front Street in Lahaina. She had learned over the course of the day that the victim of the Kaanapali Beach murder was Joyce Yashiro, a thirty-nine-year-old Native Hawaiian and lecturer at the College of Maui. She was believed to have been jogging when attacked. What Renee didn't know yet was whether or not Joyce knew her attacker or vice versa.

According to Detective Jonny Chung, there were no indications that a sexual assault had taken place. That fit the pattern of the earlier victims of the Zip Line Killer. But did that mean they were looking at the same killer? Or was someone intent on making it look that way?

Renee looked around the club hoping to find Franco, as this was his favorite watering hole. She spotted him. Only he wasn't alone. There were two shapely young women commanding his attention. Or was it the other way around?

Maybe this wasn't such a good idea after all, she thought. Though they weren't exclusive, a tinge of jealously crept through her otherwise calm appearance. What did she expect when she decided to sleep with him? That they would suddenly go from friends with occasional sex benefits to girlfriend and boyfriend. She wasn't sure she wanted that any more than he did. And clearly, he did not.

"What's up?" She heard the voice say over her shoulder.

Renee turned away from Franco and looked into the handsome face of another guy. "I'm good," she said.

He flashed a smile. "Same here. Buy you a drink?"

She glanced back at Franco, who was so wrapped up with his company that he hadn't even realized she was there.

"Sure, why not," she told the man.

"I'm Todd," he said.

"Renee."

"Nice to meet you, Renee." He stuck out his hand for her to shake.

She did so, while sizing him up further. He was over six feet tall and in good shape, with thick dark hair and gray-blue eyes.

He flagged down a waitress and then asked: "What would you like?"

"I'll have a Lava Flow."

Todd ordered it, and himself a Mai Tai. "So are you a tourist?" he asked, eyeing her curiously.

"Are you?" She turned the question around, since she hadn't seen him there before.

"Not exactly. I'm here on business. How about you?"

"I live on Maui."

He grinned. "Lucky you."

She smiled, but thought about Joyce Yashiro, whose luck had run out. "All that glitters is not gold," she told him. "Not even in the paradise of Hawaii."

"I suppose you're right. Fantasy and reality don't always go hand in hand."

The drinks came and Renee noticed that Franco and the two women were gone. She couldn't imagine them hooking up at his grandmother's house. But that didn't mean he hadn't taken them elsewhere. Renee knew there was little chance he would end up in her bed tonight.

So maybe she would have to settle for someone else.

"What do you on Maui?" Todd asked, getting her attention.

"I'm a journalist."

"What do you write about?"

Renee had a feeling he wasn't really that interested and was just making small talk while hoping to get into her pants. She would save him and herself the trouble.

"Do you want to get out of here?" she asked bluntly.

He cocked a brow. "Yeah, sure. Where to?"

"Your hotel room," she suggested, preferring not to go to her place for a change.

"Sounds good to me."

Twenty minutes later, Renee was in bed with a total stranger, while fantasizing that he was Franco. Maybe next time it would be. Or not.

For the moment, she fully intended to make the most of the situation at hand before getting back to the grind tomorrow of chasing another island murder, wherever it might lead.

* * *

On Wednesday, Leila was up at five-thirty a.m. for a quick jog while getting the sleepiness out of her. She had been jogging for years now, enjoying the way it made her feel. She imagined Joyce Yashiro felt the same way, not expecting that she would run smackdab into a killer.

As such, Leila was on guard for anything or anyone suspicious. She resisted the urge to carry her personal handgun, not wanting to give in to fear with one or more killers on the loose. She was well schooled in self-defense techniques and would not hesitate to use them if necessary. She ran down Front Street, which was currently empty compared to later in the day when tourists and locals would vie for space. Forty-five minutes later, she headed home to get ready for another day on the job.

When she got to work, Leila was greeted by Detective Jonny Chung, who had a strange grin on his face.

"What's up?" she asked curiously.

"I think we may have a hit on the sketch."

"Really?"

"Yeah. I looked at surveillance footage we retrieved from the closest hotel to where the victim was found and, in accordance with the time line, I saw a man moving across the lobby, clearly in a hurry. He looks like the one in the composite. You can see for yourself..."

"All right." Leila contained her enthusiasm that they might have a solid lead on Joyce Yashiro's killer, knowing how composite sketches, for all their strengths, could still be off the mark. Especially if the witness had provided an inaccurate description or, even worse, was purposely misleading.

They went to the crime lab, where their resident Certified Forensic Video Technician David Lovato was doing what he does best, analyzing data fed to him from the various divisions of the police department.

"We need you to pull up that footage again we looked at from the Kaanapali Seas Hotel," Chung ordered him.

"Ahh yes, the chunky white guy who looked like he was doing his best to avoid being seen," Lovato said, and touched his glasses. "Unfortunately for him, it didn't work."

"Let's take a look," Leila said anxiously over the shoulder of the lanky, twenty-something technician.

"Just a sec," he said, and pulled up the digital video, advancing it to the right spot. "This was taken a little after five a.m. Here goes..."

She watched with interest as the suspect walked into the lobby. He appeared to be in his thirties, medium build, with curly short hair and some hair on his face. He was wearing what looked to be a maintenance uniform. She recalled the witness had said he was wearing a tee shirt and shorts. Had he changed outfits between then and when this footage was taken? Or were they looking at two different men?

"What do you think?" Chung asked her, holding up a copy of the composite sketch.

Leila had to admit that it bore a pretty good resemblance to the man on the video, who looked a little flustered. Did he have good reason to be?

"I think we need to find out who he is," she responded. "And fast!"

"I'm with you there," he agreed. "I'm guessing he works at the hotel, or at a nearby one."

Lovato adjusted his glasses. "Hope you guys get him, assuming he's the one who murdered that poor lady."

There's only one way to find out, Leila thought. If he was their man, there was a good chance he would recognize himself in the composite that had been circulated to the media, and make a run for it. The thought of a possible serial killer slipping from their grasp was more than she wanted to bear.

* * *

Jonny Chung thought about his old gig with the vice squad as Leila drove them to Kaanapali. If the truth be told, he missed the good old days when he dealt with drug dealers, addicts, and whores. He worked the system as he saw fit, while establishing a good track record for arrests and cases solved. But working homicide was a step up the ladder. And it didn't hurt to have a hot partner, even if he was smart enough not to step over the line she had set. Then there was the fact that he got to play a role in getting cold-blooded killers off the street and behind bars where they belonged.

Putting the screws to the Zip Line Killer would certainly be a major coup and a feather in his cap. Especially since this asshole had been picking off vulnerable women and strangling them before he was transferred to the unit. He was ready to bring him down and get the respect he felt had always been lacking with vice.

Were they on the right track in catching the elusive killer? Or were they barking up the wrong tree in pinning down the person responsible for the death of Joyce Yashiro?

"If this killer does turn out to be an employee at a Kaanapali Beach hotel," Leila said, "it stands to reason that if he is our serial killer, he must be moving around from job to job, given the location of the other murders."

"I was thinking the same thing," Chung muttered, though he was looking at it from a slightly different angle. "But the guy wasn't expecting to be seen by the good doctor, who was able to give us a description of him."

"Which makes him all the more dangerous," she noted.

"Yeah, and that's why if the guy in the footage is the Zip Line Killer, or even a single event killer, we have to get to him now when he's caught off guard."

"Exactly."

Leila turned off the Honoapiilani Highway and onto Kaanapali Parkway. A couple of minutes later, they were entering the Kaanapali Seas Hotel.

Chung quickly spotted a male supervisor who was directing someone from the maintenance crew. After he was through, the worker walked away. They moved to the supervisor.

Showing his badge, Chung wasted little time getting right to it. "We're detectives with the Maui Police Department."

"How can I help you?"

"We're looking for a man who may work at this hotel in maintenance."

"No problem. Do you know his name?"

"We only have a picture of him, taken from video surveillance in this lobby," Leila said. She removed the still shot and handed it to him.

The supervisor reacted. "It looks like Bradley Sawyer, one of our custodial workers."

Chung and Leila exchanged glances, optimistic that they were onto something. "Take another look to be sure," Chung said.

"Yeah, that has to be him," he reiterated.

"What can you tell us about Mr. Sawyer?" asked Leila.

"He's only worked here for three months. Mostly keeps to himself, but hasn't had any problems that I know of. What did he do?"

Chung did not hold back. "We're investigating him as a possible murder suspect."

The supervisor was clearly shocked. "What—?"

"Does he happen to be here right now?" Leila asked hopefully.

"Yes, he should be on the lower level buffing the floor."

Chung noted the sprawling nature of the hotel. He didn't want to give Sawyer any extra time to escape. "What's the quickest way to get there?"

* * *

Bradley Sawyer went through the motions as he buffed the floor. It wasn't exactly the ideal job on the island, but he'd had worse. Moving to Hawaii definitely had its ups and downs. Same was true when he lived in Boston, Atlanta, and Portland along the way. In the latter instance, he'd made the mistake of getting a woman pregnant who told him she couldn't get pregnant. He never stuck around to see what her plans were. All he knew was that he could barely afford to take care of himself, much less another mouth to feed.

He did the best he could to roll with the punches and try to keep his head above water. Maybe when things went south on Maui he'd try his hand on the Big Island. He'd heard they were hiring there and it was also a good place to lay low.

Sawyer was just about to go over a spot he missed and then go for a smoke on his break, when he spotted an Asian man coming his way. There was something about the man's demeanor that rubbed him the wrong way. He looked like a cop, including the cheap suit. Or was it his imagination? He'd had a few run-ins with cops and feared that they were onto him and his latest criminal activity. He didn't want to go to jail again.

He pretended not to notice the man while continuing to buff the floor. Once he turned away, Sawyer bolted for the exit that he knew was nearby. It would take him out the back way and he could disappear. He heard the man in hot pursuit yell: "Stop!"

Sawyer ignored him and continued to run. As he approached the exit, a Hawaiian woman appeared. She pulled out a gun and pointed it at his head.

"Going somewhere?" she asked sarcastically as he stopped in his tracks.

Sawyer was surrounded by the two people, both aiming weapons at him.

"Put your hands up where we can see them," ordered the male.

Sawyer obeyed, raising his arms. He tried to play innocent. "What's this all about?"

"Are you Bradley Sawyer?" the male asked in a tough voice, as if he already knew the answer.

"Yeah, so what?" he responded brusquely.

"Detective Chung of the Maui Police Department," the man said, "and this is Detective Sergeant Kahana."

Sawyer knew he was screwed, but still hoped he could somehow worm his way out of it. "Look, you've got the wrong guy, whatever he did."

"Is that why you ran?" Chung tossed back at him.

Sawyer felt his armpits perspiring. "I didn't know you were cops," he claimed lamely.

"Well now you do," Leila said while removing handcuffs. She folded his right arm back, cuffed his wrist, and did the same with the other, before saying: "Bradley Sawyer, you're under arrest on suspicion of murdering Joyce Yashiro. You have the right to remain silent. Anything you say can and will be used against you in a court of law..."

He listened as she droned on with the rights thing, and wondered why they were treating him like Public Enemy Number One for passing some bad checks.

CHAPTER 7

Leila looked through the one-way glass as Bradley Sawyer sat restlessly in the interrogation room, still handcuffed, having possibly seen his last taste of freedom in this lifetime. He had a deep tan, which might have explained why the witness, Evan Locklear, was unsure if the man he saw leaving the murder scene was Caucasian or Hawaiian. Other than that, the doctor was pretty much spot on in his description of the suspect.

"So you think we've got our man?" Lieutenant Seymour asked her.

"I hope so," she responded noncommittally. "Whether he's a single killer or serial killer remains to be seen." She had to admit that in either instance, Sawyer didn't exactly put up a fight when arrested. Most killers wanted to prove their toughness to the very end. But this one seemed resigned to his fate.

Leila wouldn't try to get into his head on that. At least not yet. She was just happy that they were able to get him off the streets alive so they could interrogate him.

"Well, get what you can out of him," Seymour directed. "Just be sure to cut it off the moment he asks for a lawyer. The last thing we need is for any of this to be inadmissible."

"Got it!" she told him, and thought briefly about their time together. It suddenly seemed so long ago. Maybe because it had been. Or maybe it was because she didn't want to think that he could still be in her system in any way, romantically speaking.

"Good luck," he offered.

Leila gave a little smile. "Mahalo, but I don't think I'll need it. We already have Sawyer right where we want him. The rest will be a piece of cake." She wasn't sure she really believed that, but it sounded good anyway.

Leila stepped inside the room with a bottle of water the suspect had requested. It was the least she could do, considering she wanted his cooperation in their investigation into one or more crimes.

Sliding the bottle across the table, she sat on the other side and waited for him to take a drink before saying, "You've been a busy man, Sawyer."

He cocked a thick brow. "Yeah, if you mean working my ass off at the hotel."

"Actually, I mean strangling women to death," she countered bluntly.

His eyes grew wide. "Look, I don't know what you're talking about."

She wasn't buying it. Not that she expected him to say otherwise. Opening a folder, she removed the composite sketch and passed it to him.

He looked at it as if it were an alien being. "What's this?"

"It's called a composite sketch. The person in it was seen leaving the scene of a murder early yesterday on Kaanapali Beach. Does the image look familiar to you...?"

He rubbed his nose nervously. "It isn't me."

She had expected him to say that. Removing the image from the hotel security video, she showed it to the suspect. "This picture was taken at the Kaanapali Seas Hotel just after five a.m. yesterday, which is close to the time and spot where a woman was murdered on the beach. Your supervisor at the hotel identified you as the man in the picture. Are you denying it?"

Sawyer licked his lips nervously. "Yeah, so it's me in the picture. But that doesn't mean I'm the one in that sketch—"

"Cut the crap!" Leila said, peering at him. "We both know it is you in the composite. I can get the witness who saw you down here to pick you out of a lineup. Why don't you just save us both some trouble?"

"All right, all right... I was on the beach and saw a guy, but that's it. I don't know anything about anyone being murdered."

Leila rolled her eyes. She'd heard the totally innocent and baffled claims before. More often than not, they proved worthless. Maybe that was true this time too. She kept the pressure on. "You killed that woman, admit it. And you killed several others too. You're the Zip Line Killer..."

Sawyer furrowed his brow. "Hey, now wait just a minute. If you're trying to make me out to be that serial killer, it won't work. I didn't kill anyone!"

Leila glanced at the one-way mirror and back, knowing that for the moment they had nothing to tie the suspect to the Zip Line Killer and not nearly enough to charge him with the murder of Joyce Yashiro.

"For an innocent man, you wasted no time running when we came after you," she pointed out.

"I thought you were after me for something else," he said tensely.

"What?" Leila was still waiting to hear from Chung on the suspect's criminal record.

Sawyer sighed. "Okay, I wrote some bad checks and I've been trying to stay ahead of it. When I saw you, I panicked. I didn't want to go to jail."

She let that sink in. Maybe he was into fraud. But that didn't mean he wasn't a killer, too. Most psychopaths were good at multitasking.

"What were you doing on the beach at that time of morning?"

He sipped some water. "I couldn't sleep, so I thought I'd go out for a walk before work. There's no crime in that."

Leila narrowed her eyes. "It's what you did afterwards— or prior—that is the crime of murder."

"I'm not a murderer!" Sawyer exclaimed. "You've got the wrong man. I never even saw this woman. At one point, I nearly ran into a guy. I was in a hurry because I was running late, and I had to get to the hotel for work."

She regarded him skeptically. "The sketch of the suspect—you—was released yesterday, including at the Kaanapali Seas Hotel. If you're so innocent, why didn't you come forward, admit it was you, and be on your way?"

"I never saw the sketch till you showed it to me," Sawyer claimed. "I don't watch much TV or read the paper. No one ever came up to me and asked if I was the one in the sketch."

Leila was still far from convinced that they had the wrong man. However, she was not exactly rock solid certain that he was the right man either. She pressed him for his whereabouts on the earlier murders attributed to the Zip Line Killer. His answers were sketchy, but they were alibis nevertheless that needed to be checked out.

Chung stuck his head in the room. "Can I see you for a moment?"

She nodded. "Be right back," she told Sawyer.

He simply twisted his mouth.

Once outside the interview room, Leila eyed Chung. "What did you find out about our suspect?"

Chung frowned. "Not exactly what we wanted to hear. He's been arrested and served time for fraud and other property offenses and DUIs—but no crimes of violence. Of course, that doesn't mean he couldn't have still operated under the radar and been responsible for the death of Joyce Yashiro or others."

Leila gazed at the suspect fidgeting in the room. She wasn't sure what she had expected the Zip Line Killer to look like or the killer of Joyce Yashiro, for that matter, if not one and the same. Sawyer probably fit the bill. Or maybe not.

"He says he was just taking a walk before work when he passed the doctor," she told Chung, "but otherwise was not even been privy to Yashiro's corpse lying in the sand nearby."

Chung peered at her. "And you believe him?"

"I don't want to," Leila admitted. "But right now, we don't have enough to hold him—at least not for murder. He's confessed to writing bad checks. We can turn him over to the Fraud Unit while we check out his alibis and see what the crime lab and autopsy report turn up."

"Good idea."

She heard the buzz of her cell phone and saw a text that indicated almost on cue that the autopsy had been completed on Joyce Yashiro.

* * *

Leila and Chung stood in the morgue in front of a slab holding the remains of Joyce Yashiro. The decedent was visible down to just below her shoulders. Leila noted the paleness of her face and discoloration of her mouth, along with the obvious signs of trauma to her neck. She could only imagine what the victim had gone through at the end before peace came in death. But to put finality to her ending, they needed to know precisely how it came about, the time frame, and who was responsible.

Leila looked at the other side of the table at her friend Doctor Patricia Lee, a coroner's physician who conducted the post-mortem of Joyce Yashiro. Lee belonged to the Hawaii Pathologists organization and rotated between the islands, performing her duties as called for. The Maui Police Department picked up the tab for all Maui County autopsies involving homicide cases.

Patricia, who was petite with long black hair that was in a loose ponytail, wore glasses, which she adjusted while saying to the detectives: "Sorry to have to take you away from your busy schedules."

Leila smiled at her. "We're all pretty busy these days trying our best to deal with these dead people."

"Sad, but true," she agreed.

"So what do you have for us, Doc?" Chung asked impatiently.

"The victim's death was a homicide," she made clear. "This came as a result of asphyxia."

"Meaning...?"

"She was suffocated. This happened due to her face being pressed into the sand for a time, cutting off her breathing, thereby depriving her of oxygen."

"Are you saying she wasn't strangled?" Leila asked, glancing at the victim's traumatized throat.

"Actually, she was strangled," Patricia responded matter-of-factly. "But only after she was asphyxiated, which is what killed her."

Chung frowned. "So are you saying she didn't die the same way the others did, who we all agree were strangled to death probably by the same person?"

"I can't say for sure if this is a different killer or not, Detective, but if I had to make an educated guess as a pathologist, I'd say that what we have here is a copycat killer who wanted to make it seem like he or she was the so-called Zip Line Killer. Right down to making sure a zip line was left behind, wrapped firmly around the victim's neck."

Leila had considered that they might have two different killers on their hands, but had assumed that one killer was responsible for the deaths of Joyce Yashiro, Marcia Miyashiro, Amy Lynn Laseter, and Ruth Keomaka. She wondered who wanted Joyce dead, while hoping to throw the police off course by using a zip line on the victim. The first thought that came to mind was the person they currently had in custody on suspicion of killing her.

"What was the time of death?" she asked.

"Based on all the information at my disposal, I believe the victim was killed between four a.m. and five a.m. Tuesday morning," Patricia said.

Leila recalled that Evan Locklear had indicated it was around five when he ran into Bradley Sawyer near the spot where Joyce Yashiro's body was found. The hotel video showed Sawyer entering the lobby just after five. The proximity of the hotel and crime scene made it more than possible that Sawyer had time to commit the crime and get from point A to point B. But it also left nearly an hour for someone else to have murdered the victim and get away with time to spare.

"Guess we've still got our work cut out for us," muttered Chung.

"Don't we all," Patricia said. "And we wouldn't have it any other way because it's what we do."

Leila reluctantly agreed, while saying with a catch to her voice: "If the dead could speak, it would make the process a little more palatable."

"They do speak, Leila," she said, "through me, you, and everyone else left behind in our business who wants to see the case through, no matter where it takes us."

"Well said," Leila admitted. She was already turning her thoughts to what direction they needed to go in now in order to solve this case, since it appeared it was not the work of the so-called Zip Line Killer.

* * *

As far as Jonny Chung was concerned, Bradley Sawyer was not out of the woods as the person who murdered Joyce Yashiro. The case for him being the Zip Line Killer had lessened though, after getting the autopsy report. The thought that this asshole might still be on the loose instead of behind bars was unsettling. But if it wasn't Sawyer, they would get him sooner or later, as he was bound to slip up. They always did.

In the meantime, there still the murder of Joyce Yashiro to solve. Chung and Leila left the morgue for the crime lab, looking for more pieces of the puzzle. They approached Gil Delfino, a forensic examiner.

"Tell us you've found something useful," Chung said.

Delfino, who was tall, lanky, and losing his dark blond hair, put down a turkey sandwich and responded. "I guess it all depends on what you call useful..."

"Anything that can incriminate the killer of Joyce Yashiro would be nice," Leila told him.

"Afraid I can't help you there. But what I can tell you is that we collected several different sizes of footprints in the sand, which you may or may not be able to eventually match to a suspect."

Chung eyed him. "What about DNA?"

"No DNA was collected, aside from the victim's," Delfino responded. "No fingerprints either. Considering the type of crime and the location, it's not too surprising."

"Were you able to get anything from the zip line?" Leila asked.

"Just the usual fibers left behind on and around the victim, which are consistent with those we tested from the victims of the serial killer. But, truthfully, since those zip lines are pretty standard stuff in their construction, it would be hard to link them to one individual user. On the other hand, if you can find the killer in possession of such, we can use the forensic similarities of the zip lines to make the case that this is your killer."

"Thanks for telling us that, Sherlock," quipped Chung.

Delfino grabbed his sandwich and took a bite. "Hey, I'm just trying to help any way I can, guys."

"If you come up with anything else, let us know," Leila told him.

"Will do."

She smiled. "Enjoy the sandwich."

Outside in the muggy air, Chung sighed. "It looks like we're going to have to do this the old fashioned way."

"Don't give up on Delfino or modern technology just yet," Leila said. "The investigation into Joyce Yashiro's death is still new. We'll take each step as it comes—starting with the suspect in custody."

"Think we've got the wrong guy?" Chung asked.

"Maybe. We're checking out his alibis for the zip line murders, just to eliminate him there. As far as the murder of Yashiro, at the very least, Sawyer could have seen the killer while he was on the beach."

Chung raised a brow. "You mean like the good doctor who was so helpful?"

"I was thinking more like someone else who may have finished his business before Locklear reached the scene— and unintentionally crossed paths with Sawyer without giving it much thought at the time or since."

"Guess we better check it out," Chung said, knowing neither of them could afford to leave one stone unturned with a murderer possibly still at large.

CHAPTER 8

"Parker Breslin's death can definitely be ruled a homicide," coroner's physician Patricia Lee told Detectives Rachel Lancaster and Trent Ferguson routinely, having completed the autopsy.

Even if this almost went without saying, Rachel still felt badly for the victim in that moment, as murder was the worst of the worst ways to die in civilian life. The fact that he left behind a young child made it even more unsettling.

"What else did the post-mortem show?" she asked her.

"The victim died as a result of a single gunshot to the head, which tore through his brain. Mr. Breslin was already dead by the time the second bullet went into the back of his head. The initial bullet lodged in the victim's back, severing his spine."

"Thanks for spelling it out," Ferguson said wryly, standing erect at over six feet tall. He frowned. "It was a nasty execution."

Patricia looked up at him. "Is there really any other kind?"

He shrugged. "I suppose not."

Rachel sighed. "What about the bullets?"

"I believe they were .45-caliber," said Patricia. "I turned them over to the crime lab for further analysis."

They listened as she ran through the victim's height, weight, hair color, and other identifying marks for the record.

Patricia made a face. "I hope you get whoever did this."

"So do we," Rachel said, knowing no case was ever a slam dunk.

"Count on it," Ferguson stated. "This was definitely personal for someone. We'll get to the bottom of it and make one or more arrests."

Patricia batted her lashes. "You seem pretty confident about that."

"What can I say—this is serious business."

"Tell me about it," she said. "Playing with dead homicide victims like this and one from the other day—Joyce Yashiro, who was suffocated—is no laughing matter."

"We hear you," Rachel chimed in, knowing that Leila Kahana and Jonny Chung were trying to solve that case. "No funny business here. Just the task at hand."

"Don't let me keep you from it," Patricia told them. "And it's time for me to get back to work, too."

"Aloha," Rachel said dryly.

Ferguson saluted. "Later."

The crime lab was their next stop in the building.

"So what do you think?" Ferguson asked on the way. "Are we talking domestic violence or another type of homicide?"

Rachel had to move her short legs that much quicker to keep up with his long strides. "Could be either," she responded diplomatically. "I need more to go on."

"That's a cop-out," he said.

"No, there are just too many possibilities to speculate." She grinned humorlessly, while knowing some possibilities had, in fact, crossed her mind. But they were more standard, based on what they were aware of thus far. "Ask me again after we see what forensics has to say."

Ferguson seemed content with this. "You're on."

* * *

Forensic examiner Gil Delfino had been expecting the detectives handling the latest homicide to hit the island. Though he was damn good at his job, he took no pleasure doing it at the expense of innocent victims, when that was the case.

"What's the news?" Rachel asked him pointblank.

Delfino, who thought she was hot with the prettiest blue-green eyes, decided not to mince words. "There were three .45-caliber shell casings found at the scene of the crime. As such, the killer is in possession of a .45-caliber pistol—assuming he was stupid enough to hold onto it."

"We may not need him to lead us to his identity and the weapon," Ferguson said confidently. "The shell casings can be entered into the Integrated Ballistic Identification System and compared with bullet casings from other guns put into the national database."

Delfino grinned crookedly. "You took the words right out of my mouth, Detective. I was just about to say that."

"Didn't mean to rain on your parade, Delfino—but we're all working together here toward a common goal—catching a killer."

"Can't argue with you there," Delfino said. But he decided to add his own two cents nevertheless. "The system, run by the ATF, will allow us to hone in on each shell casing's fingerprint and any identifying marks that can lead to the weapon used to fire it."

"We get the picture," Rachel teased. "I can't wait to see if our killer's name or a weapon surfaces as a result. What other forensic results do you have?"

He smiled at her. "I'm glad you asked. We were able to extract some DNA from a piece of chewing gum found not far from the body, as well as a half smoked marijuana cigarette located on the grass. With any luck, either or both may have been dumped by the killer and his DNA will show up in CODIS." When he gave forensic science seminars on college campuses, Delfino loved to talk about the FBI's Combined DNA Index System, which contained DNA profiles that were put in by forensic laboratories on the federal, state, and local levels. But that didn't mean the detectives shared his enthusiasm.

"That's good news," Rachel told him. "Now if only we can get some positive results."

"I wouldn't hold my breath on that," Ferguson said. "Chances are whoever killed Parker Breslin probably watches *CSI* or Investigation Discovery's plethora of crime shows at least some of the time. Leaving DNA behind so carelessly, while managing to get away scot free for now, somehow doesn't add up."

"Things rarely do with criminals," Delfino couldn't help but say. "And that's why the jails and prisons are filled with them."

Rachel smiled. "Even Ferguson would have a hard time contradicting that."

Ferguson grinned crookedly. "Okay, so not all criminals are the brightest bulbs in the chandelier. We'll see if this one gets a passing grade."

"Or not," Delfino said, firmly believing that all killers leave something forensically behind that eventually leads to their downfall.

* * *

Detective Trent Ferguson and his partner Rachel Lancaster, along with Lieutenant Blake Seymour, watched through the one-way glass as Willa Breslin sat patiently in the interrogation room. She had voluntarily come in when asked and seemed to be cooperative in the investigation into her ex-husband's murder. But it had come to light that she and Breslin were not on the best of terms at the time of his death. Both had thrown accusations at one another, some wild, others plausible, as each sought sole custody of their daughter Marie. Did that mean Willa might have had something to do with Breslin's murder? That's what they intended to find out.

"Do you think we've given her enough time to sweat it out?" Rachel asked.

"Yeah," said Ferguson, looking down at the petite but muscular detective. "Let's see what she has to say."

"For her sake, I hope she didn't play a role in leaving her daughter fatherless," Lieutenant Seymour said.

Ferguson scratched his square jaw. "I was thinking the same thing. Some people will go to any lengths to get their children. Or to protect them from some perceived threat."

Seymour wrinkled his nose thoughtfully. "Murder is never the answer, no matter the reason."

Ferguson was sure he was thinking about his own daughter and how close he came to possibly being embroiled in a child custody case himself, before patching things up and getting back together with his wife. "We'll see if she understands that."

"What about the shooter?" Seymour asked.

"We know he was a male between thirty and forty and quick afoot, but not much else at this point," Rachel responded. "Apparently no one got a good look at his face. Or at least nobody has been willing to come forward."

Ferguson chipped in: "We're still talking to neighbors and asking for security videos from homes on the block and the next couple of blocks over where the shooter could have left his getaway vehicle."

Seymour pursed his lips. "You think it was a hit?"

"Damn sure looks that way," Ferguson said. "Question is: who ordered it and why?"

All three looked at the ex-wife, who had to be considered the chief suspect at this point, though the investigation was just getting started.

Ferguson stepped inside the room. He gave the suspect a weak but friendly smile. He would play the nice guy routine and see how that went. Rachel would take over later, if necessary.

"Thanks for coming in," he told her.

Willa smoothed an eyebrow. "I wanted to do whatever I could to help."

Glad you're being so accommodating, he thought. *Let's see if it continues.*

He sat across from her. "I appreciate your assistance, knowing how difficult this has to be with your husband, er ex-husband, being the victim of a homicide—"

She reacted. "In spite of everything, I still loved Parker, and would never have wanted him to be murdered."

No one has accused you of wanting that, Ferguson mused suspiciously. At least not yet.

"Unfortunately, someone out there felt otherwise." He met her eyes. "Do you have any idea who that might be?" He was aware that she had told Rachel that Breslin had no enemies that she knew of. Would she stand by that?

Willa stared at the question thoughtfully before responding evenly: "I know Parker did not always get along well with his business partner, Vincente Miyake. But I find it hard to imagine that Vincente would do something like this—"

Ferguson gazed at the one-way mirror, certain that Rachel was taking notes. "Breslin was a landscaper, right?" he asked, though he'd already established this.

"Yes. He's been in the business for the past decade."

"What type of problems was he having with Miyake?"

"Mostly money problems," she said. "Sometimes they would argue over silly things."

"Such as...?"

"Hiring crews or what jobs to take or pass on."

Ferguson did not necessarily consider those issues silly. Nor did they necessarily rise to the level of murder.

"Is there anyone else you can think of who might have wanted your ex dead?"

"No," Willa said. "Parker seemed to get along well with most people. Why anyone would do this is beyond me."

Ferguson leaned forward. "Let's talk about your relationship with your ex-husband..."

She tensed. "What do you want to know?"

"How long have you been divorced?"

"Two years."

"Why did you get divorced?"

"Why does anyone?" Her lashes fluttered. "We grew out of love and simply decided to go our separate ways."

This seemed reasonable to Ferguson, considering that he too was recently divorced after his wife left him for another man. Though it hurt like hell, he didn't want to see her dead because of it. Quite the contrary, he just wanted her to be happy. If not with him, then someone else.

Could Willa Breslin say the same when her marriage ended?

Ferguson met her eyes. "Tell me about the custody battle you and Breslin were engaged in for your daughter."

Willa swallowed musingly. "Not much to tell. We both thought we could be the better parent for her and hoped to convince a judge of that."

"Did you consider Breslin to be a bad parent?"

"Not really. But I was still better able to care for her."

Ferguson glanced at an information sheet. "According to records in your child custody petition, you accused your ex of being an alcoholic, workaholic, and neglectful of his child. Do you still stand by that?"

She flinched. "Yes." Her eyes watered. "It's why our marriage broke up. And why I felt Marie was better off with me."

Ferguson considered what appeared to be shifting reasons for her marital failure and custody battle. Did it mean she was lying? If so, could her deceptiveness extend to being involved in Breslin's murder?

Just then, the door opened and Rachel walked in. She gave him the eye, signaling that she wanted to question the suspect. He was happy to oblige, as he tried to read Willa Breslin.

Rachel remained standing as she said tonelessly: "Just a few more questions and you can be on your way—"

Willa eyed her warily. "Ask me whatever you want. I have nothing to hide."

"All right." Rachel glanced at Ferguson and back. "Was it you or your ex-husband who decided he was going to pick up your daughter at seven p.m. that day?"

"We both decided it," she answered. "It worked out for Parker with his work schedule and it gave me time to get Marie ready."

"Have you lived with your mother since the divorce?"

Willa lowered her eyes for an instant. "I lived briefly with another man. When that didn't work out, my mother offered to take us in."

"So your daughter has been living with you since the divorce?"

Willa nodded. "For the most part. Parker had her one day a week and some weekends. But then he decided he wanted more time, in spite of his busy schedule."

"And you resented this?"

"I wasn't very happy about it," she admitted. "But I wouldn't have killed him to keep Marie all to myself."

"Do you have an alibi for the time of his death?" Rachel asked bluntly.

Willa did not hesitate. "Yes, I was at home with my mother and Marie, waiting for Parker to pick her up."

Ferguson wasn't particularly surprised with the alibi, which he assumed the mother would corroborate, considering that the actual killer was believed to be a male. That didn't mean he hadn't conspired with the ex or someone else to do the dirty deed.

"Thanks for coming in," Rachel told her equably.

Willa fixed her with an uncertain look. "I can go now?"

Rachel offered her a forced smile. "Yes, I think we have all we need from you for now."

Willa stood, smoothing some wrinkles on her print dress. She turned toward Ferguson. "I really hope you catch the person who took away my daughter's dad. We both need that for closure."

"We'll do our best," he said, standing. "We'll keep you informed."

"Mahalo," she told him, and he saw her to the door and out.

When he and Rachel were alone, she said: "Am I mistaken, or was a possible suspect in the murder of her ex actually hitting on you?"

Ferguson wondered the same thing, but responded sarcastically: "You're definitely mistaken. I doubt I'm her type."

"You mean the type that ends up dead?"

He chuckled. "More like the type who's not easily conned."

Rachel cocked a brow. "Are you saying her story had the same holes that I picked up?"

The thought had crossed Ferguson's mind. He still wasn't prepared to indict the lady just yet. "I think we need to confirm her alibi, see what else she's been up to and who with, and check out Breslin's partner and anyone else who might have had it in for him."

"So let's do it," she said flatly.

He nodded, wanting to wrap this one up as quickly as she did, knowing that there were always more investigations to come.

But first, they needed to put the Parker Breslin case to rest—and that meant eliminating and adding suspects, including Willa Breslin, wherever she fit on the scale when all was said and done.

CHAPTER 9

Renee slipped into the passenger side of the detective's sedan. She was surprised when Jonny Chung sent her a text asking to meet. It was clear that this was about his latest case and not a booty call, for which she was thankful. Since she was still involved with Franco, more or less, that would have been a problem.

"You're late," Chung said.

"I got here as soon as I could," she countered. "I do have a life, you know."

"Yeah." He started to drive off. "Buckle up."

Renee pulled the seatbelt across her and snapped it, then gazed at him. "Where are we headed?"

"Just for a drive while we talk. I wouldn't want any snoops catching us."

She agreed, more than happy to keep her official sources all to herself. "So what do you have for me?"

"The man we arrested for Joyce Yashiro's murder, Bradley Sawyer, probably didn't kill her after all."

"Really?" Renee cocked a brow. When Chung had texted her with the scoop on Sawyer, it seemed like a done deal. So what changed?

"The estimated time of death and the time we estimate Sawyer was at the crime scene isn't a comfortable fit," Chung said, turning the corner. "He's still a crook, but probably not our crook."

"Are you saying he's no longer a suspect in the Zip Line Killer murders either?" she asked.

"No, he's not a serial killer either. His alibis during the times those women were believed to have been killed checked out. We now think Yashiro's murder was committed by someone trying to pin the wrap on the Zip Line Killer."

"Wow," Renee said, feeling a little disappointed. She really wanted to see both cases solved in one fell swoop. "Do you think it was Evan Locklear?"

"We can't eliminate him altogether, but I suspect it was someone closer to Yashiro, like her estranged husband or drug using son, something like that. Just don't quote me on it—yet."

"I won't," she promised, not about to bite the hand that was feeding her some juicy information. Even if what he'd given her about the alleged murderer of Joyce Yashiro was apparently a false lead.

"Good." He planted his free hand on her knee. "So, if you're not doing anything later, I thought I might drop by so we can play."

She removed his hand. "No can do. I'm seeing someone and I don't want to mess it up."

Chung frowned. "Relax, it's cool. Can't hurt to ask, right?"

"I guess." Renee wanted to quickly take his mind off of her, so she asked: "Is there anything else going on in your unit that I should know about?"

"I'm sure you heard about that landscaper who was gunned down in front of his house."

She nodded, and also knew it had been assigned to another reporter. "He must have rubbed someone the wrong way."

"Yeah and paid for it with his life," Chung said.

"Anything else to share with me?" she asked. "I mean, other than yourself."

Chung laughed. "Funny. It's all on a need-to-know basis, as always." He came to a stop, right where they started. "I'll be in touch."

"You know how to reach me," she told him and got out. "Aloha!"

"Aloha," he said and drove off.

Renee watched the back of his car momentarily, before heading to her own car while pondering her next move as a journalist.

* * *

Leila was sitting at her desk while Bradley Sawyer was accompanied by two uniformed officers to an interrogation room at her request. She had no idea where Chung was, leaving it up to her to see what, if anything, she could get out of their previous suspect for the murder of Joyce Yashiro and possibly a string of other women. Though some of the pieces of the puzzle seemed to fit, more did not—making it unlikely that Sawyer was guilty of anything beyond the crimes to which he'd confessed. But maybe he knew something that could help them track down the real killer of the lecturer.

Taking her cup of coffee with her, along with a sketchpad and pencil, Leila made her way to the room, saying a few words of encouragement to some of her fellow homicide detectives—all of whom were, like her, involved to one degree or another in trying to solve one or more murders without driving themselves crazy in the process.

She stepped inside the interrogation room where a handcuffed Sawyer sat, a dour look on his face.

"If you're here to try to pin a murder rap on me—"

"I'm not," she wanted to make clear. She sat across from him. "Your alibis check out for the murders attributed to the so-called Zip Line Killer."

He seemed to breathe a sigh of relief. "I didn't hurt that lady on Kaanapali Beach either."

"I believe you." Leila sipped her coffee. Or at least she believed it was more likely than not that someone else had targeted Joyce Yashiro.

"So why am I here then...?"

She almost hated to say this—*almost*—but she wasn't above leaning on someone in custody for information. "I need your help..."

Sawyer scratched his pate and regarded her uneasily. "With what?"

Leila met his gaze. "If you didn't kill that woman on the beach, someone else did. I don't believe it was the same man you nearly ran into who also fingered you. But the timeline of her death indicates that the actual killer had probably just fled the scene. Did you see anyone else during your walk?"

He tilted his head thoughtfully. "Let's say I did—what's in it for me?"

She frowned. "How about helping the police department solve a crime?"

Sawyer twisted his lips musingly. "How about helping me get some charges to go away?"

She wasn't surprised that he was playing hardball. Most people facing jail time did just that. "I'm not a lawyer," she told him. "I can't simply make your confession and the follow-up that confirmed your crimes disappear like magic."

His nostrils flared. "I don't want to go to jail. You find a way to help me, and maybe I can do the same."

Leila flashed him a suspicious look. "How do I know you won't say anything just to save your own neck?"

"I'm not that type of person," he maintained with a straight face.

She almost laughed at his declaration, considering his present situation. "This isn't a game, Sawyer. Did you see anyone else or not?" she demanded, before they went any further. "If not, you're just wasting my time."

"Yeah, there was someone else..."

Leila peered at him, not sure if he was telling the truth or, for that matter, if the information would prove to be useful.

Given the fact that he might have actually laid eyes on a killer, she had no choice but to play ball—only to a certain extent.

She tasted the now stale coffee and grimaced. "Tell me about this person. If I believe you're being straight with me, then I'll talk to the detective handling your case about possibly reducing the charges. Helping solve a murder would certainly be viewed favorably by both the police department and the Prosecuting Attorney's office. I can't promise anything, but that's the best I can do."

Sawyer needed only a moment to consider this before saying: "A couple of minutes before I nearly collided with one dude I saw another guy. He wasn't that close, but he was running across the beach like he was in a big hurry to get out of there. I never gave it much thought. Maybe I should have—"

Given the early morning hours, Leila was skeptical. "How far would you say this man was from you?"

"I don't know, maybe ten feet at one point..."

"Did he see you?"

"I doubt it. It looked like he was only interested in getting where he was going."

"How do you know it was a man?"

Sawyer shrugged. "I could just tell by his body type and height."

Leila gave him the benefit of the doubt. "Can you describe him?"

"Tall, solid build, I think his hair may have been dark. I couldn't really make out his face."

She opened up her sketchpad and picked up the pencil, figuring that any type of description he could give them was better than nothing in trying to locate this man, who may or may not be the one who suffocated Joyce Yashiro.

"Tell me everything you can remember about him," Leila demanded. "And don't leave anything out, no matter how small it may seem. We've got all the time in the world..."

In reality, she knew that the clock was ticking. The longer their killer remained on the loose, the harder it would be to track him down or prevent him from possibly killing again.

* * *

Seymour sat at the head of the table in the conference room located on the second floor of the police department. His homicide detectives sat on either side for the daily meeting, shooting the breeze, comparing notes, and what not. He focused on Leila Kahana, who was conferring with her partner, Jonny Chung. Leila seemed pretty content these days—at least on the job. Since things ended between them romantically months ago, he didn't know much about her private life. This, in spite of the fact that they were still on friendly terms and his door was always open to her in that regard.

He wondered if anything could be going on between her and Chung. Detective Chung had a reputation as being somewhat of a player and he seemed okay with that. But would Leila actually allow herself to fall into that trap?

I'm sure she can take care of herself, Seymour thought. She certainly didn't need him to tell her who to watch out for. All things considered, he was probably the last person she wanted advice from on her love life. And he had to respect that, for better or worse.

He called the meeting to order. They had two current homicide cases on the agenda, a serial killer still at large, and other hot, warm, and cold cases that remained unsolved. As lieutenant, it was his job to keep morale high and everyone's eye on the ball as their performance and success ratio reflected not only on their jobs, but on the entire department.

He eyed Leila and said evenly: "What's happening with your investigation in the murder of Joyce Yashiro?"

Leila licked her lips and responded: "Well, we're in the process of getting a search warrant for her house. Our first serious suspect appears to be off the hook. However, he did provide a description of a new possible suspect that we're looking into. We're trying to match that up with the men in her personal and professional life and any forensic evidence that can point us in the right direction."

"What's your take on where things stand, Chung?" Seymour asked interestedly.

"Right now, I think she could have been killed by the husband, son, or some other man in her life with a beef against her. But I wouldn't rule out the stranger danger trap that she might have fallen into by being at the wrong beach at the wrong time."

Seymour sat up straight. "So there's no connection with the Zip Line Killer case?" he asked knowingly.

"Doesn't look like it," Leila told him for the benefit of others in the room. "Someone appears to have made a concerted effort to mislead us. It failed. Whoever wanted Mrs. Yashiro dead was after her alone."

"I see." Seymour was already on top of this, but wanted the detectives in the unit to learn from each other as they investigated their respective cases. "Well, do whatever you need to without crossing any lines—including going door to door on her block, if needed, till you get this son of a bitch!"

"Believe me whoever killed her won't get away with it," Chung said.

Seymour grinned contentedly. Chung was proving to be a real asset to the Homicide Unit, if only for his grit and determination. And having Leila's back wasn't a bad thing either.

He faced Detectives Trent Ferguson and Rachel Lancaster, sitting beside one another, to get an update on their investigation into the execution style murder of Parker Breslin.

"We know someone definitely had it in for the victim," offered Ferguson, "be it the ex-wife or someone else. We're trying to track down the victim's stolen phone and we're also contacting everyone in Breslin's life so we can interview them. And we're also waiting to get more information on some possible DNA evidence the killer may have left behind."

"Apart from being in the middle of a nasty custody battle," Rachel said, "Breslin was also apparently having issues with his partner in the a landscaping business. That gives us two directions to go in right off the bat."

Seymour nodded. "Sounds like Parker Breslin had his fair share of people who weren't very happy with him. Almost like a powder keg waiting to explode."

"Only he may have been the last person to know just how much he pissed someone off," Ferguson said.

"Which makes him the only person so far," added Rachel, "who may have gotten a close look at his assailant before trying in vain to get away from him."

Ferguson eyed Seymour and said: "We have a vague description of the suspect, which happens to fit many of the men living on Maui. We're trying to narrow it down through security cameras that may have caught him leaving the crime scene as well as jogging a few memories in the neighborhood—"

"Stay on top of it," Seymour pressed. "Breslin left behind a daughter, not much younger than mine. If anything happened to me, I sure as hell could not rest in my grave till the case was solved—if only to allow my daughter to live her life in peace, to the degree possible. I'm sure Breslin would feel the same way."

Seymour could see that he had struck a nerve throughout the room. He exchanged glances with Leila and felt regret that she was no longer part of his daughter's life. Maybe someday that could change.

He reviewed several other cases and general department information before ending the meeting and sending everyone on their way.

CHAPTER 10

That evening, Leila got together with her good friend and artist, Jan Monroe, at a new Japanese restaurant on Kaahumanu Avenue in Kahului called Island House. She loved hanging out with Jan, as it was a chance to unwind and just be herself without having to wear her badge and department-issued firearm.

But Jan, who was tall and thin with long, blonde hair and green eyes, did not always differentiate between the two.

"So tell me, which killer are you after this time?" she asked curiously, fluttering her lashes.

Rather than bore her with details, Leila answered succinctly, hoping to leave it at that: "Well, I'm after more than one killer, but right now we're trying to catch a guy who killed a woman on the beach in Kaanapali."

"I heard about that. It really freaked me out because the night before it happened, Erik and I went to a restaurant there."

Erik Hollander was her fiancé and a high-end real estate agent. After moving from one man to another at the drop of a hat, Jan had finally settled on one guy and Leila couldn't be happier for her—even if her own love life had become all but nonexistent at the moment.

"As it is, we believe the victim was specifically targeted," Leila told her, as she nibbled on sukiyaki steak. "So I doubt you would have been in any danger. Still, it's nice to know that Erik was there to act as your protector, just in case."

"I guess you're right about that," she said. "He's so sweet and he hates to let me out of his sight."

Leila made herself smile. "Lucky you."

"Yes, lucky me." Jan put down her fork and peered at Leila. "Who's got your back these days with Blake out of the picture? And please don't tell me you're too busy catching the bad guys to enjoy a little loving..."

Leila chuckled and glanced at her plate. "No one at the moment," she hated to admit. "But, hey, maybe Mr. Right is right around the corner."

"He could be!" Jan smiled and sipped Japanese plum wine. "After all, that's pretty much how Erik and I became an item."

Just then, a tall, handsome Asian man with nicely trimmed black hair, wearing a dark suit, walked up to their table. Leila noted he was holding a tray with several things on it.

"Aloha, ladies," he said formally. "My name is Maxwell Kishimoto. I'm the owner of the restaurant. I trust the food has been to your liking?"

"It was excellent," Jan told him, flashing her teeth.

When he eyed her for a reaction with incredibly deep brown eyes, Leila agreed. "Yes, it was marvelous."

"That's good to hear." He smiled brightly. "I have taken the liberty of bringing you dessert on the house." He put a plate down for each of them. "First we have Aloha apple pie, which has a delicious brownie crust, macadamia nut ice cream topped with bananas, chocolate, and whipped cream."

"Sounds delicious," Jan cooed.

"It does," Leila had to admit.

"And it tastes even better," Maxwell said confidently. "Try it, and then wash it down with our mint chocolate chip martini, consisting of Mozart gold chocolate cream liqueur, peppermint liqueur, and vanilla vodka."

Leila did as he suggested, sampling the pie and tasting the martini. As both melted on her tongue, all she could think to say was: "Wow!"

Maxwell chuckled richly. "Then you approve?"

"Absolutely," she said.

"Me too," Jan agreed.

"Excellent." He showed his teeth, which were perfectly white. "In that case, I will leave you ladies to continue to enjoy your meal. If you need anything, please let me know. I'm here to serve you."

"Mahalo," Leila told him.

He walked away and she eyed Jan, who had a strange look on her face. "What...?"

"He couldn't take his eyes off you," Jan said.

"I don't think so," Leila claimed, though she had noticed him staring, but gave it little thought other than simply being courteous to a patron.

"I *know* so." Jan sliced into the apple pie. "He likes you."

"Let's not get carried away, Jan. He doesn't even know me and I don't know him."

"That's what dating is all about, girlfriend," Jan persisted. "You're single and—"

"And he's probably married with at least three kids," Leila broke in. Yes, she was attracted to him and it didn't hurt that he owned a classy restaurant. But she was realistic enough not to believe in fairytales, especially based on a brief encounter.

"Yes, there is always that," Jan said, frowning. "Well, you can't blame me for trying. You deserve to find someone decent to hang out with other than your best friend."

Leila smiled. "Thanks for looking after me, but I'm fine with things the way they are. When I'm meant to be with someone, I will be. Simple as that." She doubted romance and timing were ever simple, but it sounded good anyway.

"Okay, I'll shut up about it." Jan tasted her drink thoughtfully.

Leila did the same and broke the awkward silence by saying: "So tell me about your next showing—"

This seemed to be something Jan was only too happy to discuss, which suited her just fine.

* * *

The following morning, Leila and Chung, along with three uniformed officers and a crime scene investigator, went to the home of Joyce Yashiro armed with a search warrant. Given the fact that her killer was no longer believed to be Bradley Sawyer, the prevailing wisdom was that the killer was much closer to home or work. The victim's home was the first place to look for any evidence that might lead to her murderer.

Leila saw the familiar black pickup truck in the driveway, indicating that Joyce's son, Ayato, was there. She wondered if he had taken up residence at the house now that his mother was dead.

Chung was thinking the same thing. "Looks like it didn't take long for the son to make himself at home."

"Or maybe he's here to deal with his mother's affairs," Leila said, giving him the benefit of the doubt. "Especially if her estranged husband isn't carrying his weight."

"Let's find out," Chung said, and rang the bell.

Momentarily, the door opened. Ayato Yashiro stood there barefoot, wearing nothing but jeans. He rubbed his eyes as though having been awakened. "What's going on...?"

"We have a search warrant as part of the investigation into your mother's death," Leila said, handing it to him.

He glanced at it and faced her. "What are you looking for?"

"Any and everything that might point to a killer," she said flatly, wondering if that would prove to be him. She remembered the dog he had supposedly come to feed on the morning of his mother's death. "Where is your mother's dog?"

"Inside. He hasn't been feeling too good lately."

"Sorry to hear that." Leila wondered if that was a coincidence. "Go get it, put it on a leash, and step outside with it until we finish our business."

He rolled his eyes. "Whatever you say..."

They waited, not wanting to come inside only to be attacked by a sick dog. Or worse, have to defend themselves against an aggressive animal.

"He better not be destroying evidence," Chung grumbled, as the door remained open, giving them a partial view of the interior.

The thought had crossed Leila's mind. They had already lost precious time, having been thrown off by Sawyer's arrest, giving Ayato, Verlin Yashiro, or someone else the opportunity to impede the investigation.

Just when she felt they couldn't wait any longer, Ayato came around a corner with a chocolate Staffordshire terrier on a leash. It seemed pretty tame. Almost too tame.

"What's wrong with it?" Leila asked.

"I think it was something he ate," Ayato muttered, unconcerned. "So how long will this take?"

"As long as it does," Chung answered tersely.

Everyone stepped aside as he and the dog came out onto the lanai.

"Stay with them," Leila ordered one officer.

They went from room to room, combing through the victim's personal belongings and a home office. At a glance, there were no obvious signs pointing to anything suspicious, a crime, or evidence thereof. Wearing latex gloves, Leila supervised and handled items herself in assessing their value as potentially incriminating.

In the kitchen, beneath the sink, she noticed a box of rat and mouse poison. There were occasional mice infestations on the island, so that rang no alarms bells in and of itself. However, she couldn't help but wonder if the dog could have been poisoned, perhaps deliberately by someone who didn't want it to be with Joyce Yashiro during her run. That would have made it easier to attack her, which would then suggest it was an inside job.

Chung entered the room wearing gloves. He was holding a backpack.

"What's inside?" Leila asked curiously.

"Looks like what amounts to an active meth lab. It appears to belong to the son. I'd say he's got some explaining to do."

"And it may go well beyond illegal drug possession," she said, lifting the box. "Rat poison. I think the victim's dog may have ingested some, but not by accident. What better way to keep it home while she went for her morning run?"

"That's jumping the gun a bit, don't you think? The dog didn't seem that out of it to suggest it had been poisoned."

"Just a gut feeling," she admitted. "We'll have him tested for poisoning and go from there."

"You think the son could have done this?"

"All things considered, I certainly wouldn't rule it out. Or someone else with access to the house, given there are no signs of breaking and entering."

"Like her estranged husband?" Chung deduced.

"He's the next logical person to come to mind," Leila said. "Why don't we wait and see what else we come up with."

"Sounds good to me."

"In the meantime," Leila said, "I think we need to have a talk with the son about what he knows, if anything, pertaining to Joyce Yashiro's death—especially since he seems to have made himself right at home here."

"Yeah, complete with his own mini drug lab," Chung said. "Hopefully the home's security video will show us who's been coming and going before and after Yashiro's untimely demise."

"That would be nice, along with anything incriminating we might find on the victim's computer." As far as Leila was concerned, everything in the house could potentially provide clues in the murder investigation and lead to a suspect. But she certainly wasn't prepared to make any hard assumptions at this point, knowing it was still possible the killer had no connection to the victim and her household.

But given no solid evidence that the crime was random, Leila's best guess at this point was that Joyce Yashiro knew her killer, which may have been much too close to home for her comfort. Or she was unable to recognize the danger till it was too late.

CHAPTER 11

It was just after one p.m. when Officers Natalie Yuen and Conrad Spinelli spotted the suspect near a cream-colored Nissan Altima in the motel parking lot on South Kihei Road. He matched the description of a tall, stocky, bald man wearing jeans and a print shirt, who had brazenly perpetrated a home invasion on Mahina Street in Kihei two hours earlier.

"That has to be him," Natalie said, bringing the vehicle to a stop, while thinking: *Hope he does us a favor and gives up without a fight.*

"Yeah," Spinelli concurred. "Let's go get him!"

They exited the car and, with guns drawn, approached the suspect, who seemed to be caught completely off guard.

"Put your hands up!" Spinelli demanded.

The suspect started to make a run for it, but anticipating this, Natalie had cut off his best escape route and now had her Glock pointed within inches of his face. "Don't even think about it!" she said, lowering her voice an octave.

Sensing that he had nowhere to go other than an early grave, the suspect raised his hands in defeat.

As Spinelli roughly handcuffed him, Natalie put on gloves and checked the man for any weapons and also for a cell phone. She found a .38-caliber pistol on his person and a phone. Using her department-issued phone, she dialed the number of murder victim Parker Breslin. The phone rang, just as expected.

Bingo!

In fact, they had used Stingray to track the victim's stolen cell phone, pinpointing the location and possibly catching his killer and home invader in the process.

Ignoring his scowl, Natalie read the suspect his rights.

* * *

Lieutenant Seymour shepherded the handcuffed suspect named Aaron Gifford into the interrogation room, sitting him down. It was during the initial interrogation—before the suspect had time to devise a strategy, ask for representation, and otherwise be of limited use—that they needed to go at him hard for some answers.

It was up to him to get the ball rolling, and hopefully elicit a murder confession, before he let the detectives from the robbery unit have their crack at the suspect.

Sitting across from him, Seymour peered at the suspect and said: "You're in a lot of trouble, Gifford, there's no way around that."

"I didn't do anything," he hissed.

"Right," Seymour said sarcastically, "and the sun didn't rise this morning either. We have the items you stole from the house with your prints all over them, and the victims have positively identified you—so your words don't carry much weight."

Gifford frowned. "So why am I here?"

Seymour paused, and then grabbed the evidence bag containing Parker Breslin's cell phone and slid it toward the suspect. "I want to talk about this."

"What about it?"

"Why don't you tell me where you got it?"

Gifford wrinkled his nose. "What difference does it make?"

"Actually, quite a bit," Seymour said. "It was stolen from a man who was shot to death in front of his home. You wouldn't happen to know anything about that, would you?"

His demeanor instantly changed. "Hey, I didn't have anything to do with a murder! I *found* the cell phone."

Yeah, that's what they all say, Seymour thought, especially when facing a murder charge. "Where?" he asked, unconvinced.

"In a dumpster."

"You expect me to believe that you went dumpster diving and just happened to find a smart phone for your trouble?"

"It's the truth! I was tossing something when I spotted it. I figured since the phone worked, I might as well use it."

"Where is this dumpster?" Seymour pressed.

"Behind some stores at the Kihei Town Shopping Center," Gifford said. "I swear."

"Excuse me if I have trouble believing your story." Seymour flashed him a nasty look. "Why don't you just man up and admit that you pumped three bullets into Parker Breslin—then tell me why you did it. Was it another home invasion gone wrong because the home owner showed up?"

"It wasn't me!" Gifford maintained. "I have no idea who he is and I never broke into his house!"

"Where's the gun you shot Breslin with?" Seymour kept the pressure on, hoping he would buckle. Never mind the fact that a search of his vehicle and apartment had failed to locate the .45-caliber handgun used to murder Parker Breslin.

"I didn't shoot the dude!" Gifford insisted, raising his voice. "I'm not going down for something I didn't do. That ain't my cell phone. Or at least it wasn't till I found it in that dumpster. Someone else killed him."

Seymour sucked in a deep breath. "Are you willing to take a lie detector test?"

Gifford didn't hesitate. "Yeah, I'll take it."

Seymour wondered if he was that arrogant. Or could he be telling the truth?

An hour later, Seymour and Detectives Ferguson and Lancaster watched through the one-way window as the test was administered to Aaron Gifford by the department's polygraph examiner, Zack Poouahi.

When it was finished, he came out and said: "He passed it. Gifford did not murder Parker Breslin."

Seymour was disappointed, as were the two detectives, for it meant the true killer had likely dumped the cell phone with apparently no intention of using it. Or could Breslin have tossed his phone in the trash for his own reasons?

Whatever the case, the search would continue to find his killer, as their job demanded.

CHAPTER 12

Detective Ferguson studied the suspect, Vincente Miyake, as he sat across from him in the interrogation room. He looked to be in his late forties and was short with black hair combed backwards that was starting to recede. Ferguson always wondered early in an investigation who would prove to be a distraction and who would wind up having the cuffs put on them as a killer. He wasn't sure which way it would go with Parker Breslin's business partner, but would keep an open mind.

"Thanks for coming," Ferguson said evenly. "I just have a few questions and then you can be on your way."

"No problem, though I'm not sure I can provide you with much regarding Parker's death."

"You'd be surprised," Ferguson said, pausing for a moment to let that notion sink in. "Why don't you start by telling me about the nature of the business you co-owned with Breslin?"

"Sure. It's a landscaping company. We do everything, including architecture, consulting, design, lighting, maintenance, and hardscape services."

Ferguson met his eyes. "From what I understand, you and Breslin didn't always get along."

Miyake winced. "Do you always get along with your partner, Detective? It comes with the territory."

"You're right, it does," Ferguson allowed. "Unfortunately, murder doesn't."

"Are you suggesting that I had something to do with Parker's death?"

"Did you?"

"Absolutely not!" Miyake insisted. "Parker was not only my business partner, he was a good friend. I had no reason to want him dead."

"How about money? That's usually a powerful motive, especially if a company was struggling and better off with only one captain to steer the ship."

Miyake's thick brows knitted. "We were not struggling financially," he claimed. "Yes, things were tight from time to time, but we worked our way out of it."

Ferguson knew it would be easy enough to check out, if it came to that. "Tell me about your crew. Did any of them have a problem with Breslin?"

"Nothing that couldn't be talked through. Most of them believe in an honest day's work for an honest day's pay."

"Had anyone been let go recently?"

Miyake paused and then nodded. "Yes, come to think of it, Larry Stolberg was fired a couple of weeks ago for drinking on the job. He didn't take it very well."

Ferguson wondered if his anger rose to the level of murder. "What about people you worked for? Did any of them have a beef with Breslin or the company?"

"Nothing that jumps out at me. We take pride in our work and usually come away with pleased customers." Miyake took a breath. "We do some jobs for the Aloha Architectural Group. At times, we've clashed with their management over everything from work performance to expectations. Parker was often the point man in our dealings, so he took the brunt of any disagreements. If he was threatened with bodily harm from them or anyone else, he never told me about it."

"Maybe he chose to keep it to himself," suggested Ferguson, "figuring he could work it out."

"I guess it's possible."

Ferguson propped his arms on the table. "Did Breslin ever talk to you about his personal life and custody battle?" If they really were good friends, this seemed a given.

"Yeah, we talked. He dated, but he wasn't serious about anyone right now, as far as I know. Regarding the custody battle, he was determined to win full custody of his daughter, believing his ex-wife was incapable of caring for her properly."

"You mean financially?"

"I mean in every way. Parker thought she was a bad role model and felt his daughter deserved better."

Ferguson took note of this. "What did he mean by bad role model?"

Miyake shrugged. "He didn't like the company she kept. That's all I know."

Ferguson mused over that, wondering if someone the ex-wife was involved with could have taken him out on her behalf. It was certainly worth looking into. He gazed at Miyake. "I need an address for Larry Stolberg and the names and addresses of everyone on your crew, along with your contacts at the architectural firm."

He nodded. "I can do that."

"Also," added Ferguson, "I need to know where you were last Tuesday around six p.m."

Miyake cocked a brow. "That's easy. I was having dinner with a client and her husband at a restaurant in Wailea. I'm sure they can vouch for me."

Ferguson took him at his word till proven otherwise and finished the interview. At this point, Vincente Miyake didn't appear to be involved in the death of Parker Breslin. But, as Ferguson knew all too well in his line of work, looks could always be deceiving.

* * *

Larry Stolberg lived in an apartment on Lower Honoapiilani Highway in Lahaina. Rachel stood at the door and looked over her shoulder at Ferguson. He nodded, indicating he had her back in case there was trouble.

With that reassurance in mind, she knocked on the door, eager to size up the possible suspect in Parker Breslin's murder.

The door opened and a man in his late twenties with dirty blond hair and a goatee stood there. "Yeah?" he said lazily.

"Are you Larry Stolberg?"

"Who's asking?"

"Detective Lancaster, Maui PD." She flashed her identification. "And this is Detective Ferguson. We'd like to talk to you about Parker Breslin."

"What about him?"

"Mind if we come in?" Ferguson asked in a tough voice.

Stolberg eyed them suspiciously, but relented. "Why not? I have nothing to hide..."

The moment they stepped inside a messy living room, Rachel detected the distinct odor of marijuana. She glanced at Ferguson. They were not interested in drug crimes, but it could be a factor in committing other crimes, such as murder.

"I have a prescription for medical marijuana," Stolberg said defensively. "To control my severe muscle spasms."

Rachel regarded him skeptically, while at the same time wondering if such a condition could affect his ability to use a firearm effectively. "We're not after you for smoking pot," she told him.

He sighed. "Sorry to hear about what happened to Parker Breslin. But what's it got to do with me?"

"He fired you," Ferguson said bluntly. "According to his partner, Vincente Miyake, you were none too pleased about it."

Stolberg ran his hand over his mouth. "Sure, I was pissed. He let me go without cause."

"I thought you were caught drinking on the job?"

He shrugged. "Yeah, I had a beer. So what? It's not like other crew members weren't doing the same thing. I needed that job."

"So maybe because you felt cheated out of the job, you decided to pay the man back by killing him," Rachel suggested.

"Hey, I'm not stupid. Killing Breslin wouldn't get me my job back. I don't wanna go to prison for murder."

"Few people do," she said. "But it doesn't stop them from committing the crime."

"So go after one of them," Stolberg snapped. "I'm not your man!"

Ferguson peered at him. "In that case, I'm sure you have a solid alibi for last Tuesday between six and seven p.m."

"Yeah, I do," he claimed. "I was at the Sunset Bar just down the street, drinking and playing pool. Plenty of people saw me."

"We'll check it out," Rachel said. She eyed Ferguson as the cue that it was time to leave.

"We'll be in touch," Ferguson told him.

Outside, Rachel commented: "You really expect to be back in touch with him?"

"Probably not—if he's as innocent as he proclaims. In the meantime, it doesn't hurt to ruffle his feathers a little, just in case."

"We need to ruffle some other feathers now..."

"I agree. The question is: who would most want Breslin out of the picture?"

If Rachel had the answer to that, they would be making an arrest right now instead of continuing to track down suspects. But murder investigations were rarely cut and dry. Meaning they would have to play this out one day at a time until the case was solved and Parker Breslin's killer apprehended.

* * *

That afternoon, Ferguson drove to the small bungalow he called home on Kupono Street in Paia on the island's northern coast. It was the last town before heading toward the community of Hana in East Maui. Until five months ago, he had lived there with his wife, Brenda. But that ended when she fell in love with a doctor and decided their marriage wasn't worth trying to save.

Ferguson owned up to his role in her departure. He hadn't been paying much attention to his wife at the time, having developed a predilection for a prostitute named Gina. A couple of months ago, he had gotten her off the streets and moved her into his house as his girlfriend. Though she had initially been reluctant to give up her freedom to be with whomever she wished, the mutual attraction and chance to make something of her life were too much to pass up.

He found her in the master bedroom. She was lying on her stomach on the bed reading a textbook, as she had recently begun taking classes at the College of Maui.

"Hey," he said, getting turned on as he gazed at her long blonde hair, sexy bare legs, and ample chest.

"Hey," she said, smiling at him. "You're home early."

"I needed a break from the routine." *And an excuse to see you*, Ferguson mused, sitting beside her.

Gina eyed him. "Tired of chasing the bad guys, huh?"

He ran a hand along her smooth leg. "Better to chase one good girl."

"You think I'm good?" She licked her full lips. "I thought you preferred the bad girl in me?"

Ferguson grinned lasciviously. "Maybe I like a little of both."

She sat up and caressed his face. "Then that's what you'll get."

He was hoping she would say that. Now it was time to put that into practice, leaning more toward her naughty side at the moment.

CHAPTER 13

"Wake up, sleepyhead," Renee heard through the grogginess of her mind.

She opened her eyes to stare into the face of Franco, who was smiling brightly. They had spent the night together and seemed to be back on the right track though, admittedly, she wasn't sure what that track even was. Officially, they remained friends with great benefits in bed. She didn't want to push it beyond that, fearing that whatever it was they had might end prematurely.

"How long have you been awake?" she asked.

"Long enough to make you breakfast."

Only then did Renee notice the tray he had set on the bed.

"How does pancakes with maple syrup, scrambled eggs, and papaya juice sound?"

"Sounds wonderful," she had to admit. "But you didn't have to—"

"I wanted to," he broke in. "Besides, it gave me a chance to work on my cooking skills."

Renee looked at him. "I didn't realize you had any."

"There's a lot you don't know about me."

"I guess." It made her wonder what other things he was hiding from her. She looked forward to finding out as things continued to develop between them.

Franco flashed his teeth. "So eat up..." He scooped some eggs onto a fork and actually fed it to her.

She giggled, finding it sexy, as no man had ever taken the time to feed her.

"So what are your plans for today?" he asked, licking syrup from his thumb.

"I plan to interview the next door neighbor of the woman murdered on the beach," Renee said, sitting up and bringing the tray closer.

"Do neighbors ever really yield any useful information, other than what they actually witness in a crime?"

She sipped the juice. "Sometimes. You'd be surprised just how much neighbors observe, overhear, and take in. Since the authorities think the victim was probably killed by someone she knew—maybe even a family member—picking the brain of someone close by seems like a good idea to get as much information as I can to write about the crime."

"Good luck with that."

She frowned. "Truthfully, it was a much scarier storyline when it seemed like the murder was committed by the Zip Line Killer."

Franco laughed. "So serial killers make better press than your run-of-the-mill domestic murders?"

Renee chuckled, not meaning to suggest any murder was more unsettling and newsworthy than another, even if that was the case. "Any murders on Maui are newsworthy," she said. "After all, this is supposed to be paradise."

He scooped some syrup onto his finger and smeared it across her lips. "Who says it isn't?"

She tasted the syrup, licking her lips, and suddenly found his mouth on hers, sensual and exciting. *Yes, paradise it is*, she thought.

* * *

Leila and Chung entered the West Maui Animal Care & Services clinic in Lahaina. It was where Joyce Yashiro's dog named Seiji had been taken so they could test him for poisoning. Careful not to tip their hand or suspicions, Joyce's son had simply been told that the dog was being treated for an upset stomach. In the meantime, after confirming it was his backpack, Ayato Yashiro was arrested on suspicion of drug possession.

"Do you still think the dog was poisoned?" Chung asked Leila skeptically.

"Until the vet says otherwise," she told him. "All the signs were there." To her, it would be a potentially strong and incriminating piece of the puzzle, indicating that the dog was intentionally fed rat poisoning by someone close to it as a means to give Joyce Yashiro's murderer the ability to attack her without fear of being attacked by her protector.

After flashing their badges at the front desk, the detectives were taken to a room where the dog was being treated. The veterinarian, Doctor Carolyn Narlikar, was in her forties with short black hair and silver-rimmed glasses. Leila noted that Seiji seemed to be resting, though his eyes were open.

"What's the good word, Doc?" Chung asked impatiently.

She ran a hand across the dog's head and frowned. "I'm afraid tests have confirmed that he was poisoned."

"How?" Leila asked, though she was pretty sure she knew the source.

"Toxic meatballs that were laced with something called brodifacoum, which is the active ingredient in most rat poison."

Leila reacted to the news and glanced at Chung, who said: "This is probably a stupid question, but I'll ask anyway. Is it possible the dog could have somehow accidentally gotten into the box of poison while he was eating the meatballs?"

Carolyn shook her head. "It's highly unlikely. The amount of brodifacoum found in the meatballs was a high enough concentration to indicate that it had been mixed into the hamburger maliciously by someone."

Leila sucked in a deep breath. Aside from gross animal cruelty, the guilty party may well have committed murder. Two suspects immediately came to mind. "Is the dog going to make it?"

For the first time, Carolyn smiled. "Yes. Other than probably feeling nauseous for a bit longer, he'll be fine."

Leila was happy to hear that as she stroked the dog's head. He would obviously need a new and safe home now. At least until it was sorted out who was responsible for this reprehensible act.

* * *

Renee was still thinking about the hot morning sex with Franco as she walked up to the spacious Mediterranean home that was almost indistinguishable from Joyce Yashiro's house, save for the address in front and a different arrangement of palm trees. She rang the bell and watched as a middle-aged, red-haired woman opened the door.

Here goes, Renee told herself, knowing not all people were receptive to the media, especially when it involved crime and neighbors. She gave a friendly smile and said: "Hi. My name is Renee Bradley. I'm a writer for the Aloha News, Crime Beat. I was wondering if I could ask you a few questions about Joyce Yashiro and her family..."

The woman studied her warily, before saying: "Come in."

Renee entered a spacious Great Room with wicker furniture. "You have a lovely home," she said as she glanced about.

"Thank you. I'm Sally Oldham, by the way. Would you like some tea?"

Renee smiled. "That would be great."

"Sugar?"

"No, just plain."

Sally nodded and said: "Have a seat."

Renee sat on a chair and thought about what she wanted to ask, while turning on her iPad.

Sally returned with two cups of tea, handing her one, then sitting. "I was so sad to hear about Joyce's death."

"Were you close to her?" asked Renee, sipping the tea.

"We didn't spend a great deal of time together, but yes, I felt we were friends."

"Were you also friends with her husband Verlin?" Renee wondered.

Sally sighed. "Not really. He was moody, abusive, rude, and not a good fit for someone as sweet and kindhearted as Joyce. When she separated from him, I thought it was the best thing she could do in trying to move on."

Renee peered at her. "Do you think he could have killed her?"

Sally tasted the tea thoughtfully. "Yes, I think he had it in him to murder Joyce, if only to keep her from being happy with anyone else."

"Was she seeing someone else?" Renee asked.

"She dated a few men, but I'm not sure she had settled in on anyone."

Or maybe one of those men turned out to be a killer, Renee mused. "Do you know Joyce's son, Ayato?"

"Yes, I know him, though I haven't seen him very much."

"What can you tell me about him?"

"He used to be a nice young man until he got involved with drugs." She furrowed her brow. "That's when Joyce asked him to leave home. Without Verlin there, Ayato was out of control."

"Could he have murdered her?" Renee asked straightforwardly.

"He could have," Sally asserted, "especially if he was high on something. Joyce was afraid of him. She wanted Ayato to get help, but he didn't seem interested in that."

Renee pondered the ugliness of drug addiction. She'd had friends who got themselves in trouble with drugs or alcohol or both—costing them big time. But none of them had killed someone, much less a family member. Had Ayato Yashiro actually followed his mother to the beach and suffocated her? Could he have hated her that much? Or maybe he was encouraged to commit a homicidal act by someone else—perhaps his father.

The idea that the murder was all in the family intrigued Renee, even if it wasn't quite the splash headline of Joyce Yashiro's death coming at the hands of a vicious serial killer such as the Zip Line Killer.

CHAPTER 14

In the interrogation room, Leila sat across the table from Verlin Yashiro. On the surface, he seemed mild mannered enough and not the type who would murder his wife. But appearances could always be deceiving, especially when it came down to murdering the ones we were supposed to love.

"Thanks for coming in," she told him.

"Whatever it takes to help you with your investigation," he said.

Leila decided not to pull any punches, even as she wondered how many punches he had thrown at Joyce Yashiro. "We've discovered some troubling things lately, Mr. Yashiro, that have me wondering if you killed your wife..."

He cocked a brow. "What things?"

"Well, for one, she had a $500,000 life insurance policy naming you the beneficiary of half of it in the event of her death."

"Actually, we were both insured for the same amount with each being the beneficiary of half, with the other half going to our son," Yashiro said calmly. "I run a successful business and am not hurting for money. Even if I were, I would never kill Joyce for something I would likely never collect or get to spend."

Leila credited him with having a response that made sense, especially if money wasn't the issue, which would still need to be determined. She wondered how he would react to her next line of questioning. "You've come after your wife more than once with your fists, haven't you?"

"It's all a big misunderstanding."

"I don't think so." She removed a sheet with his criminal record and placed it before him. "According to this, you've been arrested two times for felony domestic violence-related charges—including domestic battery and domestic assault, inflicting injury upon a spouse, and making criminal threats. You've also been arrested for domestic violence misdemeanors. Obviously, you've got quite a temper and have directed it toward your late and estranged wife."

"None of those charges resulted in a conviction," he pointed out smugly. "Because they never happened. As I told you before, it was always my wife who initiated physical contact and turned it into violence. I sought only to defend myself. But the police chose to believe Joyce over me."

"So you're claiming innocence for each time you were charged with domestic violence offenses?" she asked, batting her lashes. "Sorry, but I don't buy it." Leila was aware that women could also be the aggressors in domestic violence. However, the criminal justice system had become more understanding of this in recent years and weren't as apt to let female offenders off the hook. Joyce Yashiro had no criminal record. This, in and of itself, didn't prove she had not abused her husband, but it certainly gave him less of a leg to stand on where it concerned credibility. And yet each time the charges against him were dropped or he was acquitted. Did that make him any less capable of killing his wife, in spite of the fact that the bruises on her body were consistent with being forced down onto the sand rather than an aggressive assault?

"I did not kill my wife!" Yashiro stated firmly.

you need to leave the island for any reason, please let us know."

* * *

Chung could tell, as he watched the shifting eyes of Ayato Yashiro, that the suspect was nervous as hell. Did he have good reason to be—like being guilty of murdering his own mother? Or was it because he feared that the drug charges would put him away for a while?

Either way, he wasn't about to go easy on Joyce Yashiro's son, who just may have sent her to an early grave.

After taking a measured breath, Chung leaned forward and said: "You're in a hell of a lot of trouble." He hoped the kid didn't ask for a lawyer—at least not till he could get something useful out of him. "Did you poison the dog?"

"What—?" Ayato's eyes widened.

"That's right, the reason he was sick was because someone put rat poison in his meatballs. Since your mother obviously didn't want to keep her companion from accompanying her on her morning run, someone else did. That leaves you and your father—both of whom showed up on the home's security video on the two days leading up to Joyce Yashiro's murder. My bet is on you as someone who had the greatest access to the dog." He didn't bother to tell him that the video footage showed that another as yet unidentified adult male had visited the house the day before the murder occurred.

"I had nothing to do with poisoning Seiji," Ayato claimed, his voice unsteady.

"So are you saying your old man did the dirty deed?"

"No, he wouldn't have."

"Then who...?"

Ayato sucked in a deep breath. "Maybe it was an accident. The dog gets into things, including the cabinet where the rat poison is kept. He could have—"

Chung cut him off. "This was no accident. The dog was deliberately fed rat poisoning. And I think the culprit was your mother's killer."

106

"It wasn't me," he insisted. "I loved her."

"Some people have a bizarre way of showing that," Chung said. "You couldn't have been too happy that she kicked you out of the house when you let substance abuse take over your life. What better way for you to get back at her than by killing her and reclaiming the house as your own, with no dad around looking over your shoulder. Just admit it and ease your conscience."

"No, I didn't kill my mother!" Ayato practically jumped out of the chair. "And I didn't poison my dog." He paused, looking at Chung. "Yeah, he was mine—I've had him since he was a puppy. When I moved out, I had to leave him there because there was no room for a dog at my new apartment."

Sing me a lullaby, Chung thought unaffectedly. He wasn't convinced of Ayato's innocence regarding the dog or his mother's murder, especially if he had acted impulsively while under the influence of meth. He asked the suspect about his whereabouts during the time of Joyce Yashiro's murder.

"I was at my place sleeping," he said.

"Right. Is there anyone who can verify that?"

"No, I was alone," Ayato told him. "I didn't know I needed a witness to be asleep in the early morning hours."

"Well now you know," Chung said, wrinkling his nose. "Not having anyone to back up your story means you remain a chief suspect in your mother's murder. Chew on that..."

Ayato glared at him. "You can't pin something on me I'm innocent of. I would never hurt my mother physically in any way and I definitely wouldn't take her life like that."

Tell it to the judge, Chung thought humorlessly, knowing full well that all they had at the moment on him pertaining to the murder of Joyce Yashiro were his fingerprints and the security video that placed him at the house the day before the murder and the day of it. Neither were enough for a conviction, or even going to trial. Then there was the fact that no witnesses had placed him at the scene of the crime at the time of the murder.

Chung conceded that Ayato probably wasn't their strongest suspect at the moment, but it still didn't mean his hands were totally clean. He narrowed his eyes at Ayato, deciding to turn up the heat. "Someone suffocated your mother and then strangled her. Who does such a thing and thinks he'll get away with it? I'll tell you who: someone who is overconfident and stupid. Someone who had a beef against her and made damned sure she paid the ultimate price with her life. If it wasn't you, it had to be your father—the guy who didn't mind beating the hell out of her whenever it suited his fancy, and also knew her routine. Don't you agree?"

Ayato sighed, lowering his head. "My father and mother had a difficult relationship. They fought a lot. But killing her, I don't think so. It has to be someone else."

Chung frowned. Clearly, he wasn't going to get a confession out of this one or get his help implicating his father for the murder. Still lacking hard evidence to put the screws to either one of them, he had no choice but to simply keep Ayato Yashiro on the list as a person of interest in the death of his mother.

But he was hardly off the hook altogether, as they had him on charges of possession and manufacturing crystal meth. Chung strongly suspected that he was also guilty of dealing meth. If so, he likely had partners in crime. Chung liked the notion of getting a piece of the pie for himself. Maybe he would investigate this further when he could do so without his boss, Lieutenant Seymour, observing the interrogation from the other side of the window. For now, it was all about solving a murder and getting justice for Joyce Yashiro.

On that note, he looked at the laptop before him and pulled up the still shot of someone Joyce Yashiro's security camera had recorded as he came on to her lanai. Maybe the kid knew who he was.

Chung turned the laptop around and pushed it toward Ayato. "Do you recognize this man?"

He studied the image. "No. Should I?"

"Look again," pressed Chung. "He visited your mother's house the day before her death."

Ayato peered at the screen. "I've never seen him before." He looked at the detective. "Did he kill her?"

"Your guess is as good as mine at this point," Chung admitted, which was not to say that he or his father were off the radar. He looked at the drug-using son and said: "We're through for now. Hope you've got a good lawyer—you're going to need one. Manufacturing meth is a serious crime in this state and you crossed the line."

CHAPTER 15

After work, Leila went to a favorite cop hangout in Kahului on Dairy Road called Drinks. Present were Chung, Blake Seymour, and other detectives from the homicide squad. Though she didn't spend a great deal of time socializing with her colleagues, Leila basically considered them family. With Seymour, in particular, she'd gotten past the romantic vibes that once had them more than friends and was now at ease being around him with others outside the job.

For an hour, they talked about their current cases, the ups and downs of the investigations, the tipping point of solving the crimes, and the inevitable twist or turn that would provide the breakthrough needed to solve the case.

"My money's on the son murdering Joyce Yashiro," Chung said over his mug of beer.

Detective Rachel Lancaster disagreed. "From what I've heard, it's just as likely, if not more so, that her estranged husband did it."

Seymour looked at Leila and said: "Would you like to break the tie?"

Feeling put on the spot but unwilling to commit to one suspect or the other, knowing how easily the evidence could point elsewhere—such as the mysterious man who was seen

on Joyce's security video a day before she was murdered—
Leila couched her words carefully. "Let's just say I'm keeping
all my options on the table, at least until the evidence is more
conclusive."

Detective Trent Ferguson frowned. "That's not fair,
Kahana."

"Look who's talking," she said, cleverly shifting to his
case. "Are you prepared to name a single suspect for Parker
Breslin's murder?"

He laughed, tasting his drink. "Good point. Ask me later
when I'm too wasted to give a damn about what I say."
Turning to his partner, Rachel, he asked: "Care to weigh
in...?"

She sipped a nonalcoholic drink and responded: "My gut
instincts tell me that his ex-wife is up to her neck in his
murder. I can't prove it yet, but she stood to gain the most—
full custody of their daughter."

"Maybe uttering a simple *pretty please* to Breslin in family
court would have done the trick," Chung said, with a laugh.
"Especially since, if she turns out to be behind the murder,
she loses custody as well, leaving neither parent a winner."

"Unfortunately, some parents don't see it that way," Leila
said sadly. "They would rather see the other in the grave—
even if it came at the sacrifice of their own freedom—all in
some misguided attempt to protect the child from a
perceived threat in the form of the other parent."

Seymour lifted his mug, frowning. "Anyone who believes
that murdering their current or former spouse is the best way
to protect a child is the epitome of selfishness and deserves
to rot away in prison."

"We can agree to disagree," Leila said, thinking about his
relationship with his own daughter and the fact that he
would never intentionally do anything to jeopardize it. "I
think it's less about selfishness and more about power—the
power to play judge and jury over someone else's life, damn
the consequences."

"I have to side with Kahana on this one," Chung said. "Sorry Seymour."

He grinned. "Don't apologize. I used to do the same when we were partners. That's the way it should be—you've got each other's back."

Seymour lifted his mug at Leila for a toast. She met his eyes and followed suit, while thinking: *Maybe he does still have my back in the ways that count.*

The conversation drifted to the Zip Line Killer, which most of the homicide detectives had worked on, to one degree or another.

"We're gonna get that son of a bitch sooner or later," barked Chung, his third glass of beer in hand.

"Yeah, but I bet that's not what he's thinking," Ferguson said. "He's stayed on the loose, what, for more than a year now and still running rings around us."

"I think he's coming and going—perhaps from the Mainland," Leila suggested, "picking and choosing his opportunities."

"My sentiments exactly," Seymour echoed. "But I think he might live on the islands, possibly traveling back and forth between them. If he is actually staying on Maui, his job is one that probably takes him elsewhere and away from suspicion."

"He's definitely not through," Rachel muttered. "They never stop till they're caught or dead."

Leila grabbed a pretzel. "Or till they make a mistake. That's when we'll be ready to make him pay."

Chung lifted his mug. "I'll drink to that."

Everyone raised their glasses in agreement. For Leila, the concern was that, until such time, the Zip Line Killer was still a live wire, lying in wait to strike an unsuspecting target again.

* * *

The next morning, Leila was up early for her run. Afterwards, she watered her orchid and bamboo plants before getting ready for work. Just as she slipped into her shoes, her cell phone rang. She grabbed it and saw that it was her mother calling.

"Hey," Leila said in a sweet voice.

"Aloha kakahiaka," her mother said.

"You're up early," Leila responded, noting that her mother was usually a late sleeper.

"Not really," she said. "I get up earlier these days. I guess when you get to be my age you want to be up and at it as often as possible."

"You're not that old."

"Old enough," Rena said. "Anyway, I thought I'd come and visit you for a couple of days."

Leila raised a brow. "When...?"

"Tomorrow."

"This really isn't a good time," Leila hated to say.

"It's never a good time," Rena said. "I know you're busy being a detective and whatever. Don't worry I'll stay out of your hair. I still have friends there to socialize with."

Leila felt a bit guilty, as if she were neglecting her mother for everything else. Or maybe a guilt trip was just what she was hoping for.

"Of course you can come," Leila gave in. "Yes, my workload right now is pretty intense, but what else is new. It'll be good to see you."

"You too," she said. "We can take a walk on the beach the way we used to when you were young."

"That would be nice." Leila had fond memories of her childhood, but they often involved her father too, as family unity was important. She hoped to recreate that sense of togetherness someday in her own life, should she ever get married and have children.

Both seemed a long way off with no man on the horizon and her job pretty much the centerpiece of her life.

She took note of the time her mother was due to arrive tomorrow evening and headed to work.

* * *

Chung and Leila arrived at the outdoor shopping center on Wailea Alanui Drive and found the clothing store they were looking for.

"Think she'll back Yashiro up?" Chung asked, eyeing Leila beneath his shades.

"She better. Otherwise his alibi falls flat and he jumps right back to the top of our list as a suspect in his wife's death."

"So let's see what the lady has to say," he said.

He followed Leila inside the posh designer clothing store where a couple of people were browsing. Chung spotted a tall, attractive, dark-haired Hawaiian woman putting shirts on a shelf.

They walked up to her.

"Are you Willa Takeyama?" Leila asked.

She nodded. "Yes."

Chung flashed his badge. "We're detectives with the Maui Police Department. Wonder if we could ask you a few questions?"

Willa met his eyes coolly. "About what?"

"Verlin Yashiro," he replied.

"What about him?"

Leila moved a step closer. "We're investigating the murder of his wife, Joyce Yashiro. According to Mr. Yashiro, on the morning of her death last Tuesday, he was with you. We need you to verify that."

Willa smoothed a thin brow. "Yes, we were together."

"And where was this?" Chung asked.

"At his condo."

Leila peered at her. "Are you sure you have the right day?"

"Yes. When Verlin learned that Joyce had been killed, he knew he'd be the first suspect, as is usually the case. But since we were in bed till well after seven, we both knew he was innocent."

"You call sleeping with a married man innocent?" Chung asked flippantly.

Willa pursed her lips. "We did nothing wrong, Detective. Verlin was separated and I'm divorced. I'm sorry about his wife's death, but Verlin had nothing to do with it."

Chung realized they were not going to break her. Of course, even with the alibi, it was still possible that Yashiro could have hired someone else to suffocate and strangle his wife.

"Is there anything else?" she asked tersely.

"No, that covers it," he told her.

Leila eyed Willa. "Mahalo for your time."

When they were outside the store, Chung said: "I don't know about you, but I think she seemed a little too pat vouching for Yashiro. It was almost like they had rehearsed this. Think he tipped her off?"

"Perhaps." Leila hand brushed a few strands of hair from the side of her face. "Or, it could be they were together when Joyce Yashiro was murdered, which would mean someone else attacked her on Kaanapali Beach."

"Yeah," he muttered, though he was definitely keeping his options open. His cell phone buzzed and Chung answered. A moment later, he disconnected and looked at Leila. "Ayato Yashiro just made bail."

She frowned. "Why am I not surprised?"

Neither was Chung. "With only the drug charges sticking for the time being, any good lawyer would have been able to get him out."

"For his sake, I hope his problems aren't just beginning," Leila said.

Chung scratched his cheek. "My guess is trouble will follow that kid around wherever he goes."

"What happens to the dog now?" she asked.

"From what I understand, it's been put up for adoption—at least while there's still doubt as to who poisoned him."

Leila sighed. "It's for the best, as neither Yashiro seems very capable of caring for him."

"I was thinking the same thing," Chung said. "Either way, it's out of our hands." *But still very much a part of this investigation*, he told himself, with the killer likely the same one who made the dog sick.

Before going back to the police department, they made a detour to pick up some money Chung claimed he was owed by a friend. Unbeknownst to Leila, it was his cut of drug money as a carryover from his days with vice. If he thought for one moment that she wanted in on the action, he would be happy to make it possible. But knowing Leila was a straight shooter, Chung believed some things were better left unsaid by partners.

* * *

At her desk, Leila reviewed information on her latest case, while debating in her mind if Verlin Yashiro had played a role in the murder of his wife. Or had he been cleared, in effect, thanks to his girlfriend supporting his whereabouts? She wondered if the two had been carrying on an affair even before Yashiro separated from Joyce. Wasn't that often at the root of a marriage ending?

On the other hand, from Leila's own experience, her affair with Blake started after he and his wife had separated. So maybe the same was true with Yashiro and Willa.

Leila considered the still as yet unknown man on the surveillance video who visited Joyce the day before her death. Who was he and could he have killed her?

She put those thoughts on hold when she looked up to see Detective Tony Fujimoto of the Property Crimes and Robbery squad. Beside him was a thirty-something woman with braided dark hair.

"Here to see me, Fujimoto?" Leila asked curiously of the tall, lean detective.

"Actually, I was just passing through to talk to Seymour about a case. This woman said she wanted to talk to an investigator about the Joyce Yashiro murder, so I brought her to you."

Leila glanced at her and back at him. "Mahalo."

He grinned sheepishly. "Anytime."

After he left, Leila stood and eyed the woman, who was around her height. "I'm Detective Sergeant Kahana. And you are?"

"My name is Rosalyn Arbor."

"How can I help you, Ms. Arbor?"

"I'm an instructor at the College of Maui," she said nervously. "I worked with Joyce and have been keeping track of what happened to her in the news." She paused. "I think I might know who killed her—"

That caught Leila's attention. "Please have a seat."

Rosalyn sat beside the desk and Leila sat back down, peering at her.

"Who do you think killed Joyce Yashiro?"

Rosalyn took a breath. "Glenn Diamont. He also teaches at the college."

Leila was intrigued. "Tell me more about your suspicions..."

"Joyce told me that he was stalking her. She said they went out on one date and she made it clear to him that she wasn't interested in pursuing things any further. But he didn't seem to want to leave well enough alone—showing up at her house uninvited and sending harassing texts to her cell phone."

Leila took this in. That was certainly something new that warranted looking into. Could he be the man in the security video?

"Did you happen to witness any stalking behavior by him?" she asked.

"Yes, I saw Glenn acting kind of bizarre around Joyce on campus." Rosalyn made a face. "It was like he became obsessed with her."

"Did Joyce ever report this stalking to the school or the authorities?" Leila asked.

"I don't think she reported it to the police and I'm not sure about the department at school. I think she just wanted it to stop without jeopardizing his job or otherwise getting him in trouble."

Leila batted her lashes. "That may have been a fatal mistake," she said. "Protecting a stalker is the last thing you want to do, as they often see this as encouragement rather than a warning to back off. I'll have a talk with Glenn Diamont and get his side of the story."

"Joyce was a good person," Rosalyn noted. "To die in such a senseless way was terrible."

Leila nodded. "I agree. Once her killer is behind bars, maybe it will prevent some other woman from similar victimization."

For now, Glenn Diamont had just become her chief suspect in the death of Joyce Yashiro.

CHAPTER 16

Ferguson and Rachel entered the Aloha Architectural Group building for a meeting with the manager, Kalena Kimbrough. She greeted them with a smile and led them to a corner office with plenty of windows.

Ferguson waited until Rachel and Kalena sat down, before doing the same. He stared at the forty-something manager with stylishly cut brunette hair who wasn't bad on the eyes.

"So how can I help you, detectives?" she asked evenly.

"We're investigating the murder of Parker Breslin," Rachel informed her. "We understand that his company worked with yours..."

"Yes, we did some projects together," Kalena said. "I'm so sorry about what happened to Parker. He was a great guy and a hard worker, but I'm not sure what his death has to do with us."

"We need to know if anyone on your staff had a problem with Breslin," Ferguson said pointblank. "Or if there was any animosity with him or his company."

"None that I'm aware of. We always maintained a professional relationship with Parker and his partner,

Vincente Miyake. If there were any problems on site, we always worked them out."

Sounds a little too harmonious to me, mused Ferguson. "It's great to hear that everyone got along so well between your companies. I just wish it was that cordial and understanding within my department," he said sarcastically.

Rachel regarded him, suppressing a smile.

"I don't know what to tell you, Detective," Kalena said. "No one here had any reason to harm Parker or want to see him dead."

Ferguson gave her a skeptical look. "All the same, we need a list of the employees who worked directly—or even indirectly—with Parker Breslin and his landscaping company."

She sighed. "Sure, I can get that information for you, but you're not likely to find anything useful."

"You never know what one can find if you dig hard enough," Rachel told her. "In any event, this is strictly routine stuff. No one's pointing any fingers."

Not yet anyway, Ferguson thought. But if there was a connection between Breslin's murder and the Aloha Architectural Group, they intended to find it.

* * *

Rachel sat in the nicely furnished living room of Carly Oshiro, who claimed she had been dating Parker Breslin off and on until his death. Rachel guessed she was about a decade younger than Breslin. Carly showed her several photographs of them together and, by all indications, they appeared to be a happy couple. So what went wrong?

As though reading Rachel's mind, Carly told her: "It was never serious between us, but I did enjoy Parker's company."

For an instant, Rachel choked up as she thought about her beloved late husband, Greg. She would do anything to have him back in her arms again. Instead, she was left to pick up the pieces as he would have wanted—starting with being the best detective she could be.

"Did he have any enemies that you know of?" Rachel asked, holding a cup of herbal tea.

"Yes, I can think of two," Carly said matter-of-factly.

Rachel gazed at her. "Who?"

"Parker's ex-wife Willa and her mother Lynnette. They hated him."

"And why was that?" asked Rachel.

"From what Parker told me, Lynnette didn't like the fact that he married Willa, because she felt he wasn't good enough for her daughter."

Rachel sat back. "Most in-laws feel that way about their children and spouses or spouses to be."

"True, but Willa's mother took it to extremes. She apparently badmouthed Parker every chance she got—often to Willa, who eventually turned against him. Parker also suspected her of cheating on him when they were still married, but she denied it."

"You said they both hated him. Why did Willa hate her husband?" Rachel asked.

"Because he could see right through her and he didn't want his daughter brought up in an environment that he felt wasn't in her best interests. That's what the custody battle was about. Parker just wanted to protect his daughter. But Willa and her mother weren't about to let him have her—even if it meant killing him."

Rachel batted her eyes at the bluntness of the allegation. "Those are strong words."

Carly sighed. "I'm just telling you what I feel and have seen firsthand. One time, Willa actually confronted Parker at a restaurant and accused him of badmouthing her in front of their daughter. She told him she would see to it that he would never get custody of Marie."

"Sounds like she meant business," Rachel said, though she was well aware that people said many things they didn't really mean. Was this one of those cases? Or had Willa Breslin carried out her threat?

"It wouldn't surprise me one bit," maintained Carly.

Rachel sipped her tea musingly. Murder in the family was certainly not a new phenomenon, including a mother and daughter act as co-conspirators. But proving it was a whole different story altogether, if true, considering they were each other's alibi. In the absence of any other strong suspects at the moment, it was time to have another talk with Willa Breslin and Lynnette Takeyama.

* * *

Ferguson had been briefed on Rachel's conversation with Carly Oshiro and her blunt observations where it concerned Parker Breslin's ex-wife and mother-in-law. Both of them had been brought in for questioning about Breslin's death. Ferguson got his crack at the mother-in-law, Lynnette Takeyama. He gazed at her across the table in the interrogation room, giving the cold atmosphere a chance to sink in before finding out what she had to say.

"Can I get you something to drink?" he asked, playing nice.

"I'm fine," she snapped irritably. "Are you ever going to tell me why I've been dragged down here?"

Ferguson narrowed his gaze. "Yes, I'll tell you. We're still investigating the murder of your ex son-in-law and were hoping you could help us out."

She raised a brow. "How could I possibly do that?"

"You could start by telling me how much you despised him."

She leaned back in the chair. "I didn't think Parker was a good fit for my daughter, but I certainly didn't despise him."

"That's not what we heard," Ferguson shot back. "A reliable source told us that you wanted Breslin out of your daughter's life, and your granddaughter's life too—and you would do anything to make that happen."

She batted her lashes nervously. "Are you suggesting that I had someone kill Parker?"

Ferguson peered at her. "You tell me. It wouldn't be the first time a mother-in-law decided to play judge and jury by ending someone's life."

"That may be, but it didn't happen here. I had nothing to do with his death."

"So you say. I'm just not sure you're being straight with me."

Lynnette frowned. "This is ridiculous. I'm not a murderer. Besides, I had an alibi for the time of Parker's murder."

"I know—you were with your daughter." Ferguson paused. "Maybe you were and maybe you weren't. That doesn't mean either or both of you couldn't have hired someone else to take Breslin out. If this was the case, we'll find out sooner or later. Do yourself and your daughter a favor and tell me right now anything you know about your ex son-in-law's death..."

"I have no idea who killed Parker or why someone would. No matter what I thought of him, he was still my granddaughter's father. I would never want to take that away from her."

Ferguson had trouble believing that. But, short of any evidence to the contrary, he had no choice but to let her walk. He glanced at the mirror, knowing Rachel was on the other side. Maybe she'd have better luck with the daughter, Willa Breslin.

* * *

"What do you think?" Lieutenant Seymour asked. He and Rachel were watching through the one-way window as Ferguson interrogated the suspect.

Not mincing words, Rachel responded flatly: "I think she knows more than she's letting on."

"I was thinking the same thing. By all accounts, she and her daughter are pretty tight and were on the same page about wanting full custody of Breslin's daughter. If they did have something to do with killing him, Lynnette Takeyama doesn't seem in any hurry to come clean, as if they can just sweep it under the rug till the dust settles."

Rachel agreed that Lynnette was not a weak link in the mother-daughter bond. It was up to her to go after Willa Breslin and see if she would crack.

"My turn," she told Seymour. "Wish me luck!"

Seymour flashed a half grin. "Since when have you needed luck to break down a suspect? If she's hiding something, I'm sure you'll be able to see right through it, to one degree or another."

Rachel smiled, happy to have his vote of confidence. She was glad that he had made lieutenant, as the job suited him. She was also pleased that he had ironed out things with his wife after a fling with Leila Kahana. Though Rachel liked her fellow detective, she preferred that Leila stick with single men and leave the married ones alone. Having lost her own husband in combat, she would give anything for a chance to work on her marriage again, which wasn't perfect, but something Rachel cherished for what it was and could be no more.

She stepped inside the room where Willa Breslin had waited patiently. "Sorry to keep you waiting," Rachel lied to her. It was a ploy often used in police interrogations to soften up suspects, already stressed out by sitting helplessly between those four walls.

"Are we here to talk about your progress in trying to find out who killed Parker?" Willa asked.

Rachel could barely suppress a laugh while thinking: *She's a real piece of work.* "Yes, you could say that," she told her sardonically. She sat across from Willa and met her eyes squarely. "We have information that leads us to believe you were involved in your ex-husband's murder..."

Willa's eyes popped wide. "Information from who?"

Rachel sidestepped the question, hoping it was enough to lead to a possible confession. "Did you hire someone to kill Parker Breslin?"

"No!" she exclaimed. "I did no such thing. I would never hire a killer to kill anyone."

Rachel tried to read her eyes and expression. Was she really that good? Or was she lying through her teeth?

"Maybe your mother commissioned someone to solve your problem of getting rid of a former husband before he gained full custody of your daughter," Rachel suggested.

Willa sighed, but spoke coolly: "My mother does not go around spending what little money she has to hire assassins. I mean, really—who would do such a thing, knowing the consequences?"

Rachel chuckled humorlessly. "Haven't you been watching Investigation Discovery and other true crime channels? It happens a lot more often than you think."

"I don't watch much TV," she said. "Even if I did, I know that murder is the most serious crime and would only blow back at you. The thought of spending the rest of my life in prison in order to keep my daughter away from my ex makes no sense. Apart from never forgiving me, I'd never get to be a part of the very life I was trying to protect."

Rachel picked up on that last point. "Protect her from what? Breslin was gainfully employed, seemed to dote on his daughter, and there was no record that he had ever abused her. Why don't you enlighten me as to why Marie needed protecting?"

"You wouldn't understand," hissed Willa.

"Try me," Rachel demanded, wishing she and Greg had been blessed to have children before he passed away. The thought of any parent deliberately depriving a child of the other parent really rubbed her the wrong way.

Willa sighed. "Parker wasn't husband or father of the year," she stated. "Behind the scenes, he had no problem criticizing me, even after our marriage ended. And he always put his work ahead of Marie. There were numerous times he didn't show up for the prescheduled time they were supposed to spend together, leaving her in tears. When he was around, his drinking often left my daughter alone to fend for herself while he was passed out—or put her in danger when he drove while intoxicated. So excuse me for not wanting Marie to be part of that. But I wanted to win full custody of her through the courts—not by committing murder. You have to believe that."

I don't have to believe anything, lady, thought Rachel. Yet her mind had to be open to the possibility that Breslin's wife played no role in his death, in spite of her gut feelings to the contrary.

"Maybe a boyfriend acted out on your behalf—or even without your knowledge," she suggested, "to get rid of the problem of an ex-husband who you clearly loathed."

Willa flashed an appalled look at the mere notion. "Detective, I don't have that type of power over any man. If I did, I certainly wouldn't use it. Besides, I'm not seeing anyone at the moment."

"What about before this moment?" Rachel fixed her face with a sharp gaze. "If there was anyone who perhaps could have misinterpreted your—"

"There was no one!" Willa insisted, cutting her off. "I'm not to blame for what happened to Parker and neither is my mother."

We'll see if that's true or not, Rachel mused. "Well, on that note, I guess we're done here. I appreciate your help in clearing this up."

"You asked, and I came." Willa seemed to relax. "Believe it or not, Detective, I want to see justice in this case, if only for my daughter's sake in knowing that someone paid for harming her daddy."

* * *

"I don't think Willa's being straight with us," Rachel declared a few minutes later as she conferred with Ferguson.

"Yeah, neither is her mother," he said. "I'm pretty sure Parker Breslin felt she was the mother-in-law from hell."

Rachel had sensed this unhealthy mother-daughter bond from the moment she met them. But how far had they been willing to take things? "We need to have someone follow Willa and see who she's spending time with, outside of her daughter and mother." Rachel wanted to see if she had a love interest who might hold the key to solving this case.

"Good idea," agreed Ferguson. "Willa Breslin strikes me as someone who doesn't go very long without companionship. Who knows what else she might have wanted from him for her trouble."

Rachel contemplated his words thoughtfully.

Twenty minutes later, she walked into an A.A. meeting in Wailuku. She had been voluntarily attending the meetings for the last two months, hoping to gain control of the drinking problem she'd developed since her husband died. There were about twenty people present. One of them she recognized as a former officer with the police department who had turned to alcohol as a coping mechanism after accidentally killing a woman during a confrontation with a robbery suspect.

Rachel took a seat and listened as a Hispanic man in his thirties spoke from the podium, telling everyone what his alcoholism had cost him both professionally and personally.

When the time came for her to speak, she gathered up the courage, as she had during previous meetings—viewing this as a catharsis in coming to terms with Greg's death and trying to move on with her life, as he would have wanted.

"My name is Rachel," she said evenly, pausing as her eyes panned the audience. "And I'm an alcoholic—"

CHAPTER 17

"You look so skinny," Leila's mother told her bluntly when she picked her up at the airport.

"I weigh the same as the last time you saw me," Leila said, while silently conceding that she might have lost a few pounds between exercise and work. On the other hand, her mother looked a little heavier than when she visited her on the Big Island a few months ago, but she was still comfortable in her own skin at fifty-one.

Leila felt she looked more like her father than her mother, but most people who knew both of them felt she bore a strong resemblance to her mother—especially her eyes and the way she smiled. How could she argue with that?

"Starving yourself isn't the way to go," Rena told her, dismissing Leila's response.

"I didn't know I was," she couldn't help but say; then thought better in not wanting them to get off on the wrong foot. "I was never as good a cook as you are, Mom."

"In that case, it's a good thing I'm here. I can teach you a few things..."

I can hardly wait, Leila thought sarcastically, and grabbed one of her mother's bags.

When they got to her house, Leila wondered if she should have tidied up the place a bit more, knowing that her mother was prone to criticism. But to her surprise, she actually complimented her on the place.

"My, my," Rena said, looking around, "the place is spotless. How do you ever find the time?"

"I just use whatever time I have," she answered. "Do you want to grab a bite to eat?" She wasn't exactly in the mood for cooking lessons right now. On top of that, she hadn't had a chance to go to the grocery store.

Rena shook her head. "No, maybe later. I'm a little tired right now. I think I'll take a short nap."

"Okay." Leila hoped her mother wasn't ill. She assumed she would tell her if there was something wrong with her health. So instead of needlessly speculating, she would try to enjoy this visit as much as possible, though her current investigation into the murder of Joyce Yashiro was never far from her mind.

Leila took her mother's bags to her room and then left her alone. She decided to call Jonny Chung to discuss their current case.

By the time she hit the sack, Leila was exhausted for some reason. For a moment, she thought about her mother sound asleep and wondered if it was a genetic thing. More likely, she believed her own tiredness was the result of a difficult stretch where she was putting in extra hours to solve a murder and keep the Zip Line Killer case from growing too old.

Leila drifted off to sleep almost instantly.

* * *

She was up early the next morning and debated as to whether or not to wake her mother, who had never been an early riser. In the end, Leila decided to let her sleep and get up when she was ready. In spite of Rena clinging to traditional Hawaiian values, ever since Leila's father passed away her mother had become much more independent, which had given her the courage to relocate to the Big Island of Hawaii and make a life for herself there.

With that in mind, Leila was sure her mother would have no trouble being on her own while she was at work. She left her a note, nonetheless, and some money on the kitchen counter in case she needed anything.

Half an hour later, Leila and Chung were making their way across the College of Maui campus in Kahului, passing by palm trees and well-manicured lawns. A few minutes later, they arrived at the Ethnic and Racial Studies Department.

Inside, they headed toward an office with Glenn Diamont's name on the nameplate. Leila could hear conversation within. At the entrance, she saw a young Asian woman doing the talking, sprinkled with a few giggles.

When Leila stepped inside the office, she spotted a tall man with curly black hair and glasses. At a glance, he did not appear to be the man seen on Joyce Yashiro's security video. But he could have changed his appearance then or now.

He chuckled at something the student said, before realizing they had company. "Hope that cleared it up," he said cryptically to her.

She flashed her teeth while offering no comment.

"See you in class," he told her.

She grinned. "Sure, Mr. Diamont."

Leila watched with amusement as Chung appeared to be smitten by the shapely young woman who batted her lashes at him as she left the office. Leila then turned her attention back to the man.

"Glenn Diamont?" she asked, to be sure.

"That's me." He adjusted his glasses. "How can I help you?"

He's not the man in the video, Leila confirmed silently, *but he's still in the hot seat*. She flashed her badge, as did Chung. "I'm Detective Sergeant Kahana and this is Detective Chung of the Maui Police Department. We need to ask you a few questions about your former colleague, Joyce Yashiro."

He tensed. "Yes, I was very sorry to hear about her death. But I'm not sure what I can tell you—"

Chung glared at him. "You can start by telling us about the stalking."

He touched his glasses again. "What stalking?"

"Don't play games, Diamont," Chung snapped. "We know you were stalking the lady—sending her harassing text messages and what not—so spare us the deer in the headlights act."

Leila knew that Chung was baiting the instructor, hoping to elicit a confession to at least the stalking charges.

"Look, I don't know where you got this information, but I wasn't stalking Joyce," argued Diamont.

"We can get a warrant to search your digital content," Leila warned him. "If your texts show you were harassing Mrs. Yashiro, charges can still be filed against you."

Diamont sucked in a deep breath. "Okay, I may have sent her a few texts, but it wasn't stalking or sexual harassment."

"Enlighten us," Chung demanded, glowering at the suspect.

"Joyce and I had been flirting with each other as colleagues, so I finally asked her out on a date. She accepted and it seemed like we were on the same page. Or so I thought. She went from one extreme to the other—going from hot to cold by the time the date ended when I tried to kiss her goodnight. With the texts, I was just acting out of frustration and resentment after being led on by her, only to be rejected when I tried to put the moves on her."

"People get rejected all the time," Leila pointed out, having gone down that road a time or two herself. "It's normal. Stalking isn't and it's not acceptable."

"I know and that's not what it was..." Diamont lowered his head.

"What do you call showing up at her house uninvited? I call it stalking!" Chung said accusingly.

"I just wanted to talk to her—clear the air," stammered Diamont. "When it didn't work, I left her alone."

"But not for long, right?" Chung challenged him. "When she refused to capitulate, you followed her to the beach and murdered her—"

Diamont took an involuntary step backwards. "Wait, you don't think I had anything to do with that?"

"Maybe you had everything to do with it," Leila said, keeping the pressure on. She narrowed her eyes at the suspect. "Did you kill Joyce Yashiro?"

He grimaced. "Absolutely not!"

"In that case, I'm sure you can supply us with an airtight alibi for the morning she died," Chung said, getting up in his face.

Diamont stood his ground. "Yeah, I do have one. I was on Oahu at a symposium that entire day," he stated confidently. "I arrived the day before. Plenty of people saw me. I also have documentation. So you see I couldn't have killed her."

"That remains to be seen." Chung put some space between them nevertheless. "We'll need that documentation, as well as talk to some people who saw you there," he muttered skeptically.

"Okay." Diamont ran a hand across his mouth. "No matter how things turned out for us, I would never have wanted Joyce dead."

Leila gave him the benefit of the doubt for the moment, even if she considered him a slime bag who had stalked Joyce. "We'll check out your alibi when you deliver on it. If there are any holes, you can expect to see us again—at the police station."

* * *

That afternoon, Glenn Diamont was officially cleared as the perpetrator in the murder of Joyce Yashiro. However, given his obsession with the victim, he remained a person of interest insofar as being a possible collaborator in her death.

Leila went to the crime lab after being told that important information had been retrieved from Joyce's computer that was relevant to the investigation. She found Computer Forensic Specialist Andrea Uddipa at her station.

"What have you got for me?" Leila asked her eagerly.

"Well, it took a while to recover data that Joyce Yashiro had either erased or was encrypted. But in the end, I did what I do: outsmarted the computer." Andrea grinned. "What I found that may be of interest to you and Detective Chung is that Joyce was a member of a local online dating service called, Maui Hot Dates."

Leila raised a brow. "Is that so?" She wondered if it was something she might be interested in, aside from the fact that one member might be a murderer.

"Yep. From what I can tell, she actually went on at least one date with two different guys."

"You have their names, photos?" Leila asked, thinking that the photographs might point to one or the other being caught on Joyce's home security video.

"I do have their names and a headshot, along with some other personal and professional information," Andrea told her, "which may or may not be true." She pulled up the information for the first one.

Leila looked at the computer screen and saw the handsome mug of a Caucasian male named Rick Keebler. He was forty-two, divorced, and worked as an electrical inspector. *Could his job give him a reason to use a zip line?* Leila wondered.

The other man was Lawrence Kobayashi, a thirty-eight-year-old Hawaiian, never married, who worked as an information systems analyst.

"What do you think?" asked Andrea. "Either one look like a stone cold killer?"

"Can't say they do," she admitted, knowing that hardly exonerated them. Neither man appeared to be the one in the video who visited Joyce a day before she was killed. This disappointed Leila, but since this unknown man obviously knew the victim, it didn't mean he murdered her.

On the other hand, here were two viable suspects who had gone out with Joyce. Perhaps, like Glenn Diamont, they had been spurned by her. One or the other might have decided to take things further than sending threatening texts by following Joyce to the beach and suffocating her to death, while trying to pass it off as a zip line strangulation to throw the authorities off.

Leila eyed the forensic specialist. "Did you find anything else of note?"

"Well, there were a few heated e-mail exchanges between Joyce and her husband, Verlin Yashiro; as well as with the son, Ayato. None were a smoking gun, so to speak, but clearly indicate the dysfunctional nature of that family."

"Send those to me and I'll take a look," Leila said, wanting to leave no stones unturned in the search for a killer—or anyone who may have been pulling his string. But for the moment, the hunt had shifted from the Yashiros to two men Joyce had met online—either of whom could have become her worst nightmare.

* * *

"What's all this?" Leila asked when she stepped into the kitchen. Her mother was standing over the counter and there were various dishes laid out.

Rena smiled. "What does it look like—it's dinner. I used the money you left me to pick up a few things. I thought I would cook you a real Hawaiian meal."

Though she was admittedly starving, and happy that she had spent the money, Leila still said: "You didn't have to do that."

"I wanted to," Rena told her. "You're my keiki. Clearly, based on what was in your refrigerator and cabinets, cooking hasn't been a priority for you these days."

Sadly, Leila had to concede that was true. Ever since she had put her cooking skills to the test when dating Blake Seymour months ago, she hadn't had much incentive to spend time in the kitchen just for herself. But was that a bad thing? Or merely a sign of the times for a single, unattached woman—especially one who happened to be a homicide detective, where quick meals were an essential part of the job.

"You're right," she told her mother. "I don't have the time to devote to cooking for myself."

Rena batted her lashes. "I can see that. Maybe you need to rethink that. If you're only skin and bones, you won't last very long on the job. Or even when you finally meet the man who may want to take you away from what you're doing."

Leila took a deep breath. Her mother had made it clear that she didn't approve of her career in law enforcement—never mind the fact that she was following in the footsteps of her father and grandfather. But she had begrudgingly accepted it, acknowledging that her mother's stubborn streak nearly matched her own.

And Leila didn't want to disappoint on that score. "No one's going to take me away from what I love, Mom—not even the man of my dreams. As for me being skin and bones, I'm in pretty good shape—or close to my ideal weight—and more than able to hold my own with my heavier colleagues."

"I get it," Rena said, stirring something on the stove. "I don't mean to meddle."

Oh yes you do, mused Leila, *and I have to accept it and not try to change you, any more than I want you to change me.*

"You're fine, Mom," she told her. "We're fine."

Rena grinned. "Mahalo."

"So what's for dinner?"

"Come and see for yourself..."

Leila stepped forward and saw succulent roast pork, poi—a staple of Hawaiian culture made of taro and water, seasoned with soy sauce—baked mahi mahi, squid covered with luau leaves, baked sweet potatoes, papaya slices, and coconut bread.

"Wow, you've been busy," she said, impressed but not surprised. After all, she had grown up with a mother who spent much of her time in the kitchen, feeding a hungry husband, and often several other family members.

"I didn't have anything better to do," voiced Rena. "Besides, it's nice to be home again."

"Can I help with anything?" Leila wanted to feel that she was carrying her own weight here, even if she knew her mother was truly in her element.

"Of course. You can get out the glasses for the guava juice."

Leila smiled. "That I can do."

She washed up and went even further by setting the dining room table and bringing the food out. They ate together like old times and kept the conversation pleasant. Leila even found herself wondering if her mother should move back to Maui so they could be closer to one another.

But she realized that was probably not a good idea. For one, Rena had built a life for herself on the Big Island, with many relatives and friends there to keep her busy. Leila also had her own life to live—one in which she and her mother didn't always see eye to eye. Why rock the cradle?

The next morning, she took Rena to the airport and Leila promised to visit her the next time. Now she just had to find an opening in her life to get away.

For the moment, that wasn't happening with two murder cases on her docket—the most immediate being the suffocation death of Joyce Yashiro, with her killer yet to be apprehended. But maybe that was close to changing.

* * *

Inside the Kahului club, Chung spotted the attractive Asian coed he'd seen in Glenn Diamont's office. She was sitting at the bar all by her lonesome. That worked for him.

"Aloha," he said in a friendly voice.

She looked up at him. "Do I know you?"

It kind of hurt his feelings that she didn't recognize him from earlier in the day. On the other hand, it was best she not associate him with that asshole Diamont and the fact that they were questioning him about a homicide.

"Now's a good time to start," Chung said, flashing his teeth. "I'm Jonny."

She gave a hint of a smile. "Shannon."

"So what's up, Shannon?"

She pouted. "I think I've been stood up."

"What idiot would ever stand up someone as hot as you?" he asked seriously.

"The type of idiot who's more into himself," she moaned.

"Well his loss can be my gain." Chung sat down beside her. "Let me buy you a drink."

Shannon stared at the thought before saying: "Sure, why not. I'll have a Li Hing Mui Rita."

"Cool." He grinned, passing on the margarita himself in favor of a 1944 Mai Tai Original. After ordering, he eyed Shannon and fantasized about getting her into bed. But before he could turn that into reality, he had to go through the motions. "So tell me about yourself..." he said routinely.

She regarded him coquettishly. "What do you want to know?"

He thought: *Where do I start to get to the finish?*

CHAPTER 18

The next day, Leila and Chung went to the home of Lawrence Kobayashi on Liholani Street in Pukalani, an area of the island known by locals as Upcountry for its location on the fertile slopes of Mount Haleakala. A black Mercedes was parked in the driveway.

"Looks like he's home," Chung said, ringing the bell.

Leila thought she saw someone peeking through the wooden mini blinds. "I believe he is."

Momentarily, the door opened. A man stood there. He was tall and trim with short black hair, and pretty much looked like the photograph they had retrieved from Joyce Yashiro's computer.

"Lawrence Kobayashi?" she asked as a formality.

He nodded. "Yes."

She flashed her identification. "Detective Sergeant Kahana with the police department." She listened as Chung identified himself before continuing. "We're looking into the murder of Joyce Yashiro."

Kobayashi reacted. "I heard about that and figured you would probably come to see me sooner or later, but I'm afraid you've wasted your time."

"We'll see about that," she told him. "Mind if we come in?"

He hesitated, and then said: "Not at all."

They stepped inside a spacious, well-furnished living room. Leila pictured Joyce visiting there, perhaps finding out that she had bitten off more than she could chew, and angering him to the point of murder.

"We understand that you met Joyce Yashiro through an online dating service called Maui Hot Dates," Leila said.

"That's right. We seemed to connect online and agreed to go on a date," he said. "We went to a public place—a restaurant in Lahaina. Unfortunately, it wasn't a match made in heaven and we both knew it. So we said our goodbyes there and I never saw her again in person."

"Are you sure about that?" Chung asked tersely.

"Positive."

Chung wasn't convinced. "Maybe you decided that because it was more like a match made in hell, you would kill her for your trouble."

Kobayashi narrowed his eyes. "That's ridiculous. I didn't have any reason to kill Joyce. We didn't part on bad terms or anything. It just wasn't exactly what either of us had hoped for. But hey, it happens. I got over it and met someone else. You've come to the wrong man."

"Can you tell us where you were the morning Joyce Yashiro died?" Leila asked him, adding: "Between five and six a.m."

"I was with my new girlfriend," he responded calmly. "We've been spending most nights together at her place or mine."

"Right," Leila said, glancing at Chung. "What's her name?"

"Lynda Pestana."

"Where can we find her?" Chung asked.

"At work. She's a gynecologist at the Maui Medical Center."

* * *

After Doctor Pestana supported Lawrence Kobayashi's contention that they were together when Joyce Yashiro was murdered, Leila crossed him off the list as the killer, having no reason to believe otherwise.

She was hoping they'd have better luck when visiting Rick Keebler, the other person from the dating service Joyce went out with. While Chung went to Keebler's residence in Lahaina, Leila headed to a building he was said to be inspecting in Wailuku, as an employee of the County of Maui.

When she arrived, Leila asked another worker if Keebler was there, which he confirmed. She was directed to a third story, where she recognized him at the end of a hall. He was tall, solidly built, and wearing a hard hat while talking to a female worker.

Nowhere to run or hide if you're guilty of murder, Leila thought as she approached them.

"Excuse me," he said to the woman and took a couple of steps toward Leila. "Can I help you?"

"Are you Rick Keebler?"

"Yeah, who are you?"

"Detective Sergeant Kahana, Maui PD." She showed her badge. "I need to talk to you about Joyce Yashiro..."

He glanced back at the other woman, who seemed oblivious to the conversation. "Okay, let's go over here to talk—"

Leila followed him, watching carefully, as they headed down the hallway, stopping near a room.

Keebler faced her. "I heard someone killed her, but it wasn't me."

Nothing like being proactive, she mused. That didn't mean he was innocent. "Why don't you tell me about your relationship with her and we'll go from there," Leila told him.

He took his hard hat off and held it. "Not much to tell, really. We met through an online dating site, which I'm sure you already know, went out on two dates, had sex once, and went our separate ways. I got back together with my ex-wife when we realized we had something worth saving. We plan to get married again."

"That's great," Leila said, assuming he was telling the truth. "But I still need to know your whereabouts on the day Joyce was murdered."

"I was in on Kauai in Poipu for the entire week, testing electrical installations and codes for a new condominium complex," Keebler said coolly. "I do some freelance work apart from working for Maui County. You can check it out."

"I will." Leila met his eyes. "Do you know of anyone else Joyce Yashiro dated from Maui Hot Dates?"

He rubbed his chin. "Wish I could help you out there, but we never talked about other people we dated. It would kind of kill the mood, if you know what I mean."

Leila knew all too well, but she wasn't about to go there. After getting some information from Keebler to verify his alibi, she let him get back to work, believing he wasn't the man they were after.

It also meant that Joyce Yashiro's killer was likely still hiding in plain sight and a potential threat to hurt someone else.

* * *

Renee Bradley had taken the lead Detective Jonny Chung had given her and run with it. He had told her that he believed Joyce Yashiro's killer could be a member of the popular dating site, Maui Hot Dates. Though apparently two men she dated had fallen off their list of suspects, it didn't faze Renee. With all the creeps out there, even on Maui, it wouldn't surprise her at all if one of them using the dating site turned out to be a killer.

With that in mind, she had been able to track down the owner of the site, a woman named Bette Shishido. Renee waited for her to come out of the office building on Walaka Street in Kihei before approaching her.

"Bette Shishido," she called out to the shorter woman in her thirties with shoulder length black hair.

She stopped, facing Renee. "Yes."

"I'm Renee Bradley, a journalist. I wonder if I could ask you a few questions."

"You can make an appointment with my secretary."

Renee was not about to be deterred now. "This won't take long. Were you aware that two members of your dating service have been investigated as possible killers in the murder of a local woman named Joyce Yashiro, who also used the service?"

Bette arched a brow. "No, I wasn't aware of that. Even so, we assume no liability for what goes on between consenting adults who passed our criminal background check."

"But aren't you still ultimately responsible if one of your members harms another?" Renee pressed.

Bette sighed. "If the police would like to question me, they're welcome to. We run a reputable service. Now if you'll excuse me..."

"Would you be willing to provide to the press a list of all the men who either dated Joyce Yashiro or wanted to and were maybe turned down?"

Bette's nostrils flared. "Absolutely not! That's privileged information. I'm very sorry about what happened to Joyce. It shouldn't have. But I'm sure none of our members were involved."

"At least one of them was," Renee pointed out. "Joyce Yashiro."

Bette glared at her. "You've taken up enough of my time, Ms. Bradley. This conversation is over!"

"I hope for your sake this doesn't lead right to your front door," Renee called after her as she moved away rapidly. As it was, she had more than enough to write a plausible piece on a possible connection between Joyce's murder and the Maui Hot Dates service.

* * *

In the evening, Leila took a break from work to attend the Lahaina Friday Town Party. Occurring every second

Friday of the month, it was part of the Maui Friday Town Parties, designed to bring together locals and visitors in a celebration of Maui culture, culinary art, and music. She was there to support her friend Jan Monroe's latest showing of some of her artwork, which included Maui landscapes and seascapes, as well as paintings of Maui exotic flowers and locally grown produce. The paintings were on display inside and outside an art gallery on Front Street.

"Nice..." Leila marveled, as she studied the amazing artwork.

Jan frowned. "Only nice? That's the best you can offer?"

Leila chuckled. "Okay, how about totally fabulous!"

Beaming, Jan said: "That's more like it."

"So where is that fiancé of yours?" Leila asked, looking around.

"Erik is coming later," she explained. "As usual, he's busy with a big real estate deal."

"Good for him," Leila said sarcastically. She couldn't help herself, wondering just how supportive Erik was for his girlfriend's career.

Picking up on this, Jan defended him. "Erik loves my art and has actually purchased several pieces to place in homes, increasing their value. If you stick around for a while, he can tell you all about it."

Leila suddenly felt that she may have overreacted. Or maybe she was projecting her own aloneness on her friend. Either way, as long as Jan believed she had met the man of her dreams, who was she to suggest otherwise?

Jan cupped her arm beneath Leila's and guided her into the gallery. "Come and see what else I've put together—"

Leila was again impressed with her friend's talent and the impressive display. She wondered if she should have developed her own art skills beyond composite sketches of criminal suspects and the occasional painting of inanimate objects.

"I'm so jealous," she confessed.

"Don't be," Jan said, smiling at her. "You're doing something good."

"You think?" Leila sneered. "Sometimes I wonder just how much of a difference I'm making in chasing criminals."

"Every little bit counts to keep the island of Maui safe," said Jan. "I feel safer just knowing someone I trust is doing just that."

Leila couldn't help but grin. "Mahalo."

"Besides, there's always room in the art community here if you decide you want an early retirement from law enforcement," Jan told her.

Leila smiled, taking the hint. Maybe she would hang it up sooner than later before she was put out to pasture like some former cops she knew. For now, she was where she needed to be, for better or worse.

As Jan went off to talk to the gallery owner and others, Leila walked around on her own, enjoying the artwork of her amazing friend. She had just settled in on a painting of the Maalaea Harbor, on Maui's southern coast, when she heard the familiar voice say: "I find that one captivating too—"

Looking over her shoulder, Leila recognized the good looking owner of the Japanese restaurant, Island House. Only she couldn't recall his name...

"Maxwell Kishimoto," he said. "We met at—"

"Your restaurant," she broke in.

He grinned. "So you do remember?"

"How could I not? The apple pie and mint chocolate chip martini you brought to our table were incredible."

"I'm so glad you were pleased." He planted his dark eyes on her. "And your name is...?"

"Leila," she said simply, wondering why she was so giddy.

"Nice to meet you, Leila." He stuck out his hand she shook it.

"You too."

He smiled. "Ms. Monroe is a great artist."

"Don't tell her that," joked Leila. "It might go to her head."

Maxwell chuckled. "If you have talent, there's no reason not to flaunt it."

"Maybe you're right."

"So are you here alone?" he asked, glancing about trying to determine if she was with someone.

Leila wasn't sure what it would say about her if she told the truth. "Couldn't find a date," she answered, though in reality, she hadn't tried to find one. Actually, she had briefly considered asking Jonny Chung if he wanted to come, knowing he enjoyed being out and about. But she didn't want him to get the wrong impression, so she scrapped the idea. She certainly would never consider asking Blake Seymour to attend even a platonic outing, now that he seemed to have fit back in so nicely with his family.

"That's very hard to believe," Maxwell said candidly. "You're way too attractive not to be able to find a date, probably anytime you wanted to."

She laughed. *Charming man*, she thought. Did that come from lots of practice? Or was it natural?

"I only wish that were true," Leila told him. "How about you?"

He frowned. "Unfortunately, I'm here to meet an investor. I only came in after I noticed the lovely paintings outside."

Leila hid her disappointment, though she could think of no reason why she should be disappointed over someone she didn't even know. "Don't let me keep you."

"Yes, I better go." Maxwell glanced at his watch and then her. "This may be a bit forward, but would you like to get together sometime for a drink?"

Leila gazed up at him. "You mean like a date?" She hoped she hadn't been too bold there.

"A date sounds good." He grinned. "And it doesn't have to be at my restaurant."

Though her mind said a definite yes, the roadblocks she tended to put up to protect herself said not so fast. "I'm pretty busy these days, so I'll pass on that."

He frowned. "I understand." He sighed before digging out his wallet and removing a card, handing it to her.

Leila looked at as he said: "There's my information in a nutshell, including my business and cell phone numbers. If you find time in your busy schedule, give me a call. Aloha."

She watched him walk away thoughtfully as Jan approached. "Was that who I think it was?"

"Who do you think it was?" asked Leila.

"That gorgeous man who owns the Island House restaurant."

"Yes, it was him."

"I knew he was into you. Tell me you're going to go out with him."

"I'm not," Leila hated to say. "At least not yet..."

Jan narrowed her eyes. "Why not? Did he come on too strong? Not strong enough? What?"

"None of the above. I just want to be extra careful before I put myself out there these days."

"There's careful and there's stupid," Jan said. "Not to say that you're stupid, but he looks like he's got a lot going for him. Why not take a chance?"

"Maybe because I want to check first and make sure this man who has a lot going for him doesn't also have a wife and five kids. Been there, done that, thank you. Well, maybe not the five kids, but you get the point. Then there's the fact that he could be a criminal disguised as a businessman, or worse."

"Or none of the above," Jan said. "Since you're a cop, you can easily check out those things. If he passes the tests, then there should be nothing stopping you from going out with him."

Leila agreed, in theory. Except for one little thing, that was often a big thing with some men. "He doesn't know I'm a cop. Many men can't deal with that, for whatever reason."

"But other men find it sexy," said Jan. "You'll never know, unless you lose the fears and see what happens."

Leila laughed humorlessly. "Thanks, Counselor. We'll see what happens. In the meantime, let's go check out more of the Lahaina Friday Town Party."

Jan smiled. "You're on."

Leila smiled back, and then glanced about to see if Maxwell Kishimoto had decided to stick around.

He hadn't.

CHAPTER 19

On Monday morning, Leila ran the name Maxwell Kishimoto through the system and came up empty. No criminal record. Not so much as a parking ticket. Was he for real or just a figment of her imagination?

She breathed a sigh of relief, knowing that he had at least passed the first test of seeing if he was the right material for her to jump back in the dating game. But she still wanted to know more about him, like was he really single, as implied? The last thing she wanted or needed was to end up with a broken heart again by getting involved with a handsome, successful married man.

As such, she was being overly cautious this time around when it came to romance. Then there was still the matter of how he might feel about dating a cop. Some men wanted to see her gun. Others felt as though it was somehow an affront to their masculinity. Where did he stand on the issue?

These thoughts were put on hold as Leila looked up from her computer screen when a female officer got her attention. "There's someone in the interrogation room I think you'll want to see..."

"Really?" Leila gazed up at Officer Sanchez, who had been with the force for just over a year and seemed to be a good fit.

"Yeah, he says he's got some information on the Joyce Yashiro investigation."

"That's certainly something I can use," Leila quipped, though not expecting miracles. Still, every possible lead had to be taken seriously. She stood up and said: "Mahalo."

On the way, Leila stopped by Chung's desk, informing him of the latest development.

Chung stopped doing some paperwork and stood. "Let's hear what he's got to say..."

The moment they stepped inside the room, Leila recognized the man. Or at least he bore a pretty good resemblance to the unidentified male seen in Joyce Yashiro's security video.

The man, who was seated, was in his late thirties. He was tall and slender, with dark hair that seemed a bit longer than in the video.

"I'm Detective Sergeant Kahana," she told him, "and this is Detective Chung. Who are you?"

"Hal McCann," he said evenly.

Leila glanced at Chung. Before seizing the moment in having a suspect in Joyce's murder right in their lap, she wanted to hear him out.

"How can we help you, Mr. McCann?" she said nicely, while they remained standing.

He licked his lips. "I think I know who murdered Joyce Yashiro."

Chung peered at him. "Is that right?"

"Yes."

"Interesting, but we were thinking it might have been you," Chung told him bluntly. "It just so happens that we have you on video as one of the last people to visit the victim—thereby making you one of the last people to see her alive..."

McCann shifted in the chair. "I would never have harmed Joyce. I only came here to try to help you. But if you're not interested, I'll be going—"

Chung pressed a hand on his shoulder, keeping him from getting up. "You're not going anywhere. Not until we have a little conversation."

Leila took this opportunity to sit across from the suspect. She knew if he was a killer, he was unarmed and not likely to be able to take the two of them on, should he choose to get physical.

She met his eyes. "Why don't you start by telling us what the nature of your relationship was with Joyce Yashiro?"

"We went out on a couple of dates, but it was nothing serious."

"Where did you meet?" She wondered if it was the Maui Hot Dates site.

"At the gym," he said, adding: "The Fitness Paradise Club in Lahaina."

Looks like Joyce got around, thought Leila. And she was clearly open to playing the field while she sorted out her marriage issues. But that was no reason for someone to kill her.

"What were you doing at her house the day before she was murdered?" she asked, peering at him.

"I dropped by to tell her I was on my way back to Las Vegas, where I live," McCann responded calmly. "We became friends and just hung out sometimes—there was no sex involved."

Sounds plausible enough on the surface, Leila thought, but she needed to hear more. "What do you do for a living, Mr. McCann?"

"I'm a dealer at a casino. I keep a condo on Maui for vacation purposes."

"And you just happened to be here just before someone suffocated and strangled Joyce Yashiro?" Chung asked skeptically.

McCann grimaced. "If I'd known that would happen, I would've done whatever I could to try to prevent it. Joyce would have done the same for me. I guess that's why I'm here now, to do right by my friend."

It's a little late for that, mused Leila, but asked: "Who do you think murdered Joyce Yashiro?"

He sighed. "I think that son of a bitch estranged husband of hers did it."

Leila looked up at Chung, who was still hovering over the suspect, and then back. "Why would you say that?"

"Because she was afraid of him and what he might do to her. Verlin has a history of knocking Joyce around. She figured it was only a matter of time before his temper and animosity toward her grew deadly."

"Why would Joyce confide in you about the domestic violence?" Leila asked.

McCann cocked a brow. "Why wouldn't she? We were friends and I guess she needed to get it off her chest."

In spite of Verlin Yashiro's claims to the contrary and insistence that he was the victim rather than offender, Leila had no trouble believing that Joyce had been abused by him—especially with at least two people asserting this was the case, including her son, Ayato. But even if that were the case, had it escalated to murder when they were no longer even living together? And what about Yashiro's alibi that appeared to be solid?

She decided to go with that and see what McCann thought. "Mr. Yashiro has an iron clad alibi as to his whereabouts during the time of his wife's murder. So, as you see, he's not very high on our suspect list. You, on the other hand—"

"He could have gotten someone else to do the job for him," McCann said, cutting her off. "I'm telling you, Verlin is her killer—or the one behind it—not me. If you choose not to believe that, it's your problem. Besides, according to Joyce, her husband was having some money problems—another reason why he might have wanted her dead."

"What kind of money problems?" Chung asked.

"Apparently it was cash flow problems. All I know is Joyce had a bad feeling that he might come after her. I think he did."

Leila stared at the notion thoughtfully. They had explored Yashiro's finances and come up with nothing solid to indicate he was in financial trouble. But he could have found ways to cover it up. Being able to collect on his wife's substantial insurance policy, pending completion of the police investigation, could certainly go a long way toward clearing up his debts.

Leila leaned forward. "Why did it take you so long to come forward with your allegation?"

"I only found out that Joyce had been killed when I got back to town yesterday," McCann explained. "I could barely wrap my mind around it. Then I remembered her fears regarding her husband and knew I had to tell you guys."

Chung narrowed his eyes. "Can you prove you left the island before Joyce Yashiro was killed and didn't come back until yesterday?"

"Yeah," he responded. "The airlines would have the records of my flights and departures. Also, the casino where I work keeps accurate track of workers when they're on duty."

Leila certainly could not dismiss his comments out of hand, considering that the investigation into Joyce's killer was still active. Meaning the killer had not been positively identified or taken into custody.

It would be simple to verify McCann's whereabouts and either remove him from their suspect list or put him front and center.

She stood up. "Thanks for coming in, Mr. McCann. We'll certainly look into everything you've said."

"I hope so." He got to his feet. "Joyce was a decent lady. I'll miss her."

After they saw him out and checked out his story, Leila and Chung brought Seymour up to snuff, including the fact that McCann had been in Las Vegas at the time Joyce Yashiro was murdered so he couldn't be her killer.

"I'd say we need to bring Yashiro back in for questioning," he said. "See what he has to say on the subject."

"Same old, same old," suggested Chung. "The man's not going to confess—not without something to force his hand."

"Unfortunately, we don't have much," Leila said. "We'll just have to lean on him a bit harder and see if he cracks—even while we pursue any other leads that come our way."

"Just get it done, one way or the other, so we can close this case!" Seymour bellowed. "Having two unsolved murders on Maui is not good for me, you, or the public—if you get my drift."

Leila did only too well. He was feeling the heat as lieutenant and making sure they felt it too. And he wasn't cutting her any slack as his ex-lover. Nor would she have it any other way, needing no favors when doing her job.

Now they just needed to follow McCann's lead and Joyce's premonition to see if they were on the right track in finding her killer.

* * *

Chung picked up Verlin Yashiro and brought him in for questioning. He was clearly none too pleased that he had been dragged out of a meeting. But that was his problem. If he had nothing to hide, he could thank them later for being thorough in searching for his estranged wife's killer. If that person happened to be him, or someone acting on his behalf, then no one was going to cut him any slack.

Certainly not me, Chung thought, as he led Yashiro into the interrogation room.

Yashiro sat down, his brow creased. "I'm not quite sure why I'm here, Detective. I thought I already answered all your questions."

Chung sat down in front of him. "I just have a few more for you." He gazed at the suspect, imagining him killing his wife or getting someone else to do it for him. "Let's talk about your relationship with your wife again..."

Yashiro pursed his lips. "What do you want to know?"

"Why did you use her as a punching bag? And, please, don't give me that sad song and dance crap about her knocking you around, because that doesn't fly with me!"

Yashiro sighed. "What I told you was the truth, Detective. It doesn't matter to me if you believe it or not. I never used my wife as a punching bag, as you suggested. I just defended myself from her aggression—but not by retaliating."

Chung glanced at the mirror, knowing Leila was watching on the other side, assessing the suspect's character. He fixed him with a hard stare and said: "We have a witness who says otherwise. According to this person, Joyce Yashiro was scared to death of you and your violence. And she was sure you'd try to kill her sooner or later. Did her hunch prove to be true?"

"No!" Yashiro blared. "Your so-called witness is lying. I never laid a hand on Joyce and you can't prove otherwise. As for her believing I would kill her, that's not possible. My wife and I were separated and both seeing others. I gave her no reason before or after our separation that I wished her harm. Ask my son, if you want. I only wanted to keep things peaceful between Joyce and me, as well as Ayato. Taking away his mother would have only made my son hate me. I could never have lived with that. I also have an alibi for the time of her death—and still cared too much for Joyce to ask someone else to end her life."

Admittedly, Chung had a difficult time believing he was responsible for his estranged wife's death. But, then again, many killers were master manipulators. Was that the case here?

Leila came into the room on cue. Chung nodded at her, standing. "I'm done with him. If you have any more questions, have at it."

She forced a smile at the suspect. "We appreciate your cooperation in this investigation," she said evenly. "Our only objective is to solve the murder of your wife as quickly as possible so we can all move on to something else."

"I understand," Yashiro said. "However, it seems like we keep coming back to the same things over and over. I did not kill my wife and had nothing to do with it."

"The fact that you're standing by your statement makes me inclined to believe you," Leila said, sitting in Chung's chair. "But I do need to ask you about your finances."

He tensed. "What about them?"

"We have information that seems to indicate business is not going as well as you had suggested earlier. Would you care to comment on that?"

"My business is doing fine. I have some cash flow problems from time to time like any successful business, but I'm able to pay my creditors and keep operations running smoothly. I'm not sure what any of this has to do with my wife's death—"

"It speaks of a possible motive—if you decided the insurance on her was more important than her life," Leila said bluntly.

"Nonsense!" barked Yashiro. "No amount of money would have been worth Joyce's life. Apart from that, I'm not in financial trouble." He sighed and glanced at Chung who was leaning against the wall. "Look, unless you plan to charge me with something, I'm afraid I must ask that you stop this harassment."

"Or what?" Chung challenged.

"Or I'll have to come with my attorney from this point on."

"I don't think that will be necessary," Leila offered. "You're free to go, Mr. Yashiro. Mahalo again for coming in."

He got up, glared at them, and left.

Chung shook his head. "If he's behind the death of his wife, he's doing a damned good job of covering his tracks."

"If he's responsible for the murder, he'll slip up," Leila said. "They always do. And that's when we'll nab him—or whoever decided to put Joyce Yashiro into an early grave."

Chung concurred, while wondering if he should put his money on Verlin Yashiro, or even his son Ayato, as being involved in the murder. Or would someone else among their list of suspects emerge as the perp and be taken down?

* * *

That afternoon, Leila stood at the window eyeing the words: Eddie Naku Investigations. She took a breath and went inside the Lahaina based private investigator's office. She had known Naku since he was a homicide detective for the Maui County Police Department a few years ago, before he quit and became a private eye. They had dated once, but ended it shortly thereafter, with both acknowledging they didn't belong together.

Now here she was calling on him out of the blue. Hopefully, he wouldn't turn her away.

"Aloha," the voice said spiritedly. "Can I help you?"

Leila observed the woman she assumed was Naku's assistant. She was in her early forties with short red hair. "I'm looking for Eddie Naku. Is he in or—"

"You found him," she heard the familiar deep, smooth tone of his voice.

She turned and saw him standing in the door frame of an office. Like her, he was a Native Hawaiian, tall and good looking, with long dark hair, parted in the middle.

"Hey," she said awkwardly.

"Back at you." He introduced his assistant, Vanna, then said: "Leila's an old friend from my days on the force." Naku eyed her. "Let's go into my office..."

Leila followed him into the good sized office with a window overlooking the street.

"I wondered how long it would take till you finally showed up to check out my digs," he said.

She chuckled. "You know how it is—between work and everything else..."

"I understand." He gave her the once over and Leila found herself blushing. "I see you're still staying in tip top shape."

"I could say the same for you, Naku."

He grinned. "So what can I do for you? I assume this isn't a social call?"

"It isn't," Leila said. "I'd like to hire you..."

Naku cocked a thick brow. "Uh, okay. Have a seat."

Leila resisted the temptation. "Actually, I have to get back to work, but I wanted to see if you could do a background check on someone."

"Sure, it's what I do. Who?"

"His name is Maxwell Kishimoto," she said. "He owns a local restaurant and I'm thinking about dating him..."

He smiled. "I see. And you want me to find out if he's on the up and up?"

"Yes."

"I assume you already did a criminal background check on him?"

"I did," she replied. "He's clean."

"But you're still not satisfied that he's all he's cracked up to be? Or maybe he's hiding the fact that he's leading a double life? Or forgot to mention the wife and kids?"

"That's pretty much it," Leila admitted. "Guess I just want to err on the side of caution before I let my guard down again."

Naku clutched his chest as though he had been hit. "I hope none of that mistrust comes back to me?"

She smiled. "It doesn't. We were straight about things from the beginning."

"Yeah, I guess we were."

"So will you take the case?" she asked politely. "I can pay whatever your going rate is."

"Yes, I'll take it and there's no charge."

"I don't want any special favors."

"It's not," he insisted. "As I seem to recall, you saved my ass more than once when I was with the Maui PD. The way I see it, I owe you and I'm more than happy to repay my debt."

Leila wasn't sure he owed her anything, but said: "Fine." She took Maxwell's card out of her purse and handed it to him. "Here's his contact info."

Naku studied it. "Okay, this should be more than enough to check him out."

She smiled. "Mahalo."

"Anytime." He met her eyes. "So I've been keeping tabs on the PD and I know you've got a couple of hot button homicide cases going on—"

Not wanting to get into it, even with a former member of the force, Leila simply responded: "Never a dull moment, as I'm sure you remember all too well."

"Yeah, I do."

She sighed. "Well, I better go."

Naku grinned. "I'll let you know what I come up with."

"Okay."

"Aloha!" She saw herself out and immediately began having second thoughts about hiring a private eye to investigate a man she hadn't even gone out with. Was that overdoing it, or what?

She decided that peace of mind, even when dating someone these days, was a good thing. And why not find out in advance if Maxwell Kishimoto was worth her trouble.

If he was, then she would find out how he felt about dating a police detective.

CHAPTER 20

"We've got a match on the DNA from the chewing gum we found in front of Parker Breslin's house," Gil Delfino announced excitedly to Detectives Lancaster and Ferguson in the crime lab.

"Is that so?" Ferguson asked, tempering his delight until he heard more.

"Yeah, CODIS finally came through," he said. "The DNA belongs to a man named Ray Hennesy. He's thirty-eight and has been in and out of trouble for most of his adult life, serving time for armed robbery and multiple weapons violations."

"Sounds like a real piece of work," commented Rachel. "And clearly not too bright if he left behind evidence that could nail him to the wall for the murder of Parker Breslin."

"Of course, it's also possible he was just passing by," warned Delfino, "and is guilty of nothing more than loitering when he decided to spit out his chewing gum."

"Yeah, right," Ferguson said, rolling his eyes. He conceded that the DNA alone wasn't enough to make Hennesy a cold-blooded killer. But the circumstances seemed to indicate much more than just an ex con out for a stroll. "I think we need Ray Hennesy to explain it to us."

Delfino chuckled. "Good luck with that. Assuming he even stuck around on the island, my guess is he'll employ the old deny, deny, deny strategy."

"I wouldn't be too sure about that," Rachel said. "Remember we're talking about the same career criminal who tossed the gum in the first place. You think he's smart enough to dodge the bullet pointing right at him, figuratively speaking?"

"Good point," the forensic examiner said. "Hope he turns out to be your man."

"What about the marijuana cigarette someone dumped on the grass near the victim's home?" Ferguson thought to ask.

"Nothing there," Delfino said. "Sorry. I guess the person was too stoned to leave behind DNA."

"Funny," Ferguson said, but he wasn't laughing. They had to take what they were given and find this Ray Hennesy—and fast!

* * *

They picked up Ray Hennesy at his home on Ulele Street in Makawao, located Upcountry in East Maui. The unemployed construction worker was over six feet tall, solid in build, and had stringy blonde hair. He did not resist or make a run for it, which in Rachel's mind was the mark of a guilty man, in one respect or another.

Once they had him in the interrogation room, she wasted little time going after him, hoping a confession would come sooner than later. "Why don't we start with you telling me what you know about Parker Breslin?"

Handcuffed, Hennesy had a stern look on his face. His lips were bunched together and he played hardball, stating: "I don't know the man."

"Well, let me fill in some blanks for you. He was the co-owner of a landscaping company before he was gunned down right in front of his house." She narrowed her eyes, glaring at him. "You wouldn't happen to know anything about that, would you?"

He tensed. "Why should I?"

"Maybe because you're the one who took him out."

His lower lip quivered. "I didn't kill anyone."

"Your chewing gum says otherwise," Rachel said, fixing him with a firm stare.

"What—?"

Ferguson, who was standing, leaned down and said hotly: "You left behind gum, asshole, and it led us directly to you through something called DNA. So cut the crap. We know you were at Breslin's house that day and shot him to death before taking off like a coward."

Rachel understood that he was just bluffing, at least in part, knowing they needed Hennesy to confess to being there at the right time and doing the dirty deed in order to make it stand up.

As such, she followed up with: "So I advise you to cooperate and tell us why you murdered Breslin and left his seven-year-old daughter without a father."

"It wasn't me!" Hennesy insisted. "I had nothing to do with it."

There was something in his tone that made Rachel believe otherwise. She went with her gut feeling, along with the fact that he had a rap sheet and was prone to violence, and pressed him further. "I think you're lying to us, and I'm sure the prosecuting attorney will feel the same way. You've already got a few strikes against you. Unless you want to go down for a crime you claim you didn't commit, you better give us a damn good reason to look elsewhere!"

"All right, all right," he said. "I didn't kill Breslin, but I was asked to do it..."

Okay, now we're getting somewhere, she thought, and asked: "By who?"

He paused. "Willa Takeyama."

She cocked a brow. "You mean Willa Breslin, Parker Breslin's ex-wife?"

"Yeah, whatever. I guess she went back to using her maiden name."

161

Interesting turn of events, mused Rachel.

Ferguson narrowed his eyes at Hennesy and asked tonelessly: "Are you telling us that Breslin's ex-wife asked you to murder him?"

"Yeah, that's what I'm telling you." Hennesy shifted in the chair. "We were dating for a minute there, when she offered to pay me $20,000 to take him out. Said he was standing in the way of her keeping their kid. She even told me where he'd be, at what time, and that she was supposed to deliver their kid to his house around same time—but would make sure she wasn't anywhere near the house."

Rachel considered that Willa had told them Breslin was scheduled to come to her house to pick up the daughter, rather than the other way around. Clearly, it was a lie to cover her ass while she gloated knowing that Parker Breslin would not be around to get full custody of their daughter Marie.

"So why didn't you do the job?" she asked.

Even with handcuffs on, he managed to wipe sweat from his brow. "I did a practice run the day before—going right up to his front door. But I realized I couldn't go through with it. So I left and I guess I spit the gum out without thinking."

"Lucky us," Rachel said sarcastically. "And lucky you, if you're telling the truth."

"I am," he maintained. "It wasn't me who killed him."

Ferguson kept the pressure on. "If not you, then who?"

"I have no idea, I swear. After that, me and Willa went our separate ways." He paused. "Come to think of it, I had a feeling she was two-timing me when we were hanging out, but she denied it."

"Did you ever see her with anyone else?" Rachel asked.

He stared at the question. "Yeah. One time I saw her talking to some dude in a BMW. Said he was just a friend who did business with her ex."

"What did he look like?" asked Ferguson.

He shrugged. "Hawaiian, forties. Never really got a good look at him."

Rachel glanced at her partner. That certainly gave them something to look into, unless Hennesy was trying to shift suspicion from himself by sending them off on a wild goose chase. In the absence of the murder weapon or other proof that he was the one who pulled the trigger, they had no choice but to give him the benefit of the doubt.

"Would you be willing to do your civic duty and testify in court that Willa Takeyama attempted to hire you to murder Parker Breslin?" Rachel asked.

He didn't hesitate, as if trying to gain a favor for future misconduct. "Yeah, I'll do it."

Rachel nodded. That was about all they could ask from him for the time being.

* * *

Detective Troy Mancuso considered it grunt work as he followed Willa Breslin around like a puppy dog, waiting to see who she talked to and where. As far as he was concerned, she was only leading him around in circles, though he had been very careful to keep from being made. He would much rather be doing some real detective work. That's what he dreamt of when he got his Master's in criminology. But he was a realist. They weren't going to hand him anything, degree or not. He had to pay his dues just like everyone else trying to make the grade.

His thoughts turned to his wife. They were expecting their first child in three months after working at for two years. They didn't know if it was a boy or girl, as they wanted to be surprised. Either one would work for him, though he leaned slightly toward having a boy to carry on his name and rough and tumble with.

Mancuso had watched Willa with her daughter. She seemed to be a loving mother who spoiled the girl rotten. Somehow it didn't square with a woman under suspicion of having something to do with the murder of her ex-husband.

But he knew people did strange things when it came to love, hate, child custody and what not.

He followed Willa's Honda to Kapalua, a resort community on Maui's northwest coast. She parked at a condominium complex on Coconut Grove Lane. He watched as she headed toward a silver BMW. A man got out and the two kissed before heading toward a unit, oblivious to his presence.

Homicide isn't going to believe this, Mancuso thought. He recognized the man. How could he not? He had seen him enough being interrogated and in the news. After all, his wife was the subject of a murder investigation and he was still considered a suspect on some level in her death.

Verlin Yashiro.

Now he was involved with Willa Breslin, a suspect in the murder of her ex-husband. What were the odds?

Apparently, pretty good from where he was sitting. That was good enough for Mancuso as he headed back to his vehicle, ready to phone in this important development.

* * *

Ferguson lay in bed beside his girlfriend Gina, thoroughly exhausted after having sex every which way and then some. It helped take his mind off the demands of dealing with homicides day in and out, as well as the thought that his wife had left him for another man, notwithstanding the fact that the marriage had died well before that. For better or worse, Gina was good for him and he was good for her.

He had no idea what the future held for them. But, for now, he enjoyed her company in and out of bed, though especially the former, where she'd taught him a few things from her former profession that brought him to new heights of sexual satisfaction.

She cozied up to him and cooed: "Can I tell you a secret?"

"Sure," he said, wondering what it might be. Maybe she had a secret lover. He hoped not, as he wanted her all for himself.

"I have a kid."

"Really?" He looked down at her face. Somehow he never pictured her as a mother. Maybe he should have.

"Yes. A girl. She's nine now."

"Where is she?"

"I gave her up for adoption." He detected the pain in her voice. "I got pregnant when I was still in the business. The father, a client and judge, was married with three adult children. I knew he would never claim a child from a whore, and I didn't want to raise her in that environment, so I did what I felt was best for her—gave her up so she could have a normal life."

"Do you regret it?" Ferguson asked.

"Part of me does, of course," Gina said sadly. "She's my flesh and blood. But I know it was the right thing to do."

"I agree, under the circumstances," he muttered, assuming that was what she wanted to hear.

She paused. "I know where she is..."

He cocked a brow. "You do?"

"Yes, I hired a private eye a few years ago to track her down. Her name is Akela and she lives on Maui..."

Ferguson shifted his body. "Have you seen her?"

"Yes, every now and then." Gina licked her lips. "And guess what? You know the man who adopted her with his wife—"

"I do?" He met her eyes curiously. "Who is it?"

"Blake Seymour. I think he's your lieutenant..."

Ferguson's head snapped back in disbelief. He had met Akela at a picnic at Seymour's house. He was surprised he hadn't put two and two together, knowing Blake and his wife Mele had adopted the child after being unable to have children of their own.

Still, it threw Ferguson for a loop. What were the odds that Seymour's kid was Gina's? And vice versa?

"Say something—" Gina said.

"What do want me to say?"

"Anything."

"Okay." He considered his words carefully. "What do you plan to do? Do you want to be part of her life? What?"

"I don't want to do anything to disrupt her life," she told him. "I know Akela is in a good place with people who love her. I just like to see what she's up to from afar, how she's growing up. I hope someday she'll try to find me so I can explain why I gave her up, and then maybe she'll forgive me."

"Maybe that can happen someday and she'll understand," Ferguson said. He breathed a sigh of relief that she wasn't planning to cause trouble right now for Seymour and his wife. *Especially since it would impact me too*, he thought, trying to imagine what Seymour would think if he knew his daughter's mother used to be a prostitute and was now living with a homicide detective under his command. All told, the best Gina could do was keep this information to herself. At least until the day came when Akela took it upon herself to try to find her birth mother.

"Does learning this upset you?" Gina asked.

"No," he responded nicely. "I'm glad you told me."

"Seriously?"

"Yeah, it makes me feel closer to you when everything is out in the open."

She smiled. "Same here."

He found himself getting aroused again. Somehow knowing something about Seymour that he didn't even know himself gave Ferguson a sense of power, even if he never planned to exploit it. But he could never predict the future. Or be responsible for the past.

Leaning his face toward hers, he kissed Gina on the mouth. She reciprocated in kind and they made love again.

CHAPTER 21

"Aloha kakahiaka, Makuakane," Akela Seymour said to her father.

"Good morning to you," Seymour said. He smiled as his nine-year-old daughter ran up to him in their contemporary house in Kahului. She spoke Hawaiian nearly as fluently as she did English, which pleased him in maintaining that part of her heritage. He wished he could say that she looked like her mother, but since he didn't know what her birth mother looked like, that wasn't the case. All he knew was that the Native Hawaiian child he and his wife Mele had adopted when she was not even a month old had blossomed into a beautiful little girl, with long black hair and big bold brown eyes. He couldn't imagine not having her in his life.

"You ready for school?" he asked her.

"Of course." She beamed. "I'm always ready for school."

He laughed. "Glad to hear that. Let's hope you keep that attitude all the way through college."

She giggled. "I'll try."

Mele came out of the kitchen with Akela's lunch. Her long dark hair was pulled back into a ponytail. "We better go before you're late," she told their daughter.

Akela grabbed the brown bag. "Okay."

Mele gazed at Seymour. "What time will you be home tonight?"

He didn't want to lie to her, as that had gotten him into trouble before and contributed to nearly ending their marriage. "Not sure," he replied, knowing that the greater responsibilities of being a lieutenant didn't allow him the luxury of punching out at a given time. Still, he added to soften the blow: "But I shouldn't be too late."

She twisted her lips with resignation. "Okay, we'll see you then."

He gave her a kiss on the mouth and kissed Akela's cheek before seeing them out. He left shortly thereafter.

During the drive to work, Seymour thought about Parker Breslin and the young daughter he'd left behind. She would never get to truly know him or vice versa. It was a fate Seymour wouldn't wish on his worst enemy. That was one reason seeing to it that justice was served in apprehending Breslin's killer was such a priority for him and the department. And it looked like they were beginning to make some headway there. Sadly, it appeared the one calling the shots was far too close to home, even if not especially surprising, all things considered. Intimate homicides were prevalent in society and always came at a terrible price. In this instance, the victim's daughter, Marie, would have to suffer that much more once she was old enough to reconcile the apparent sad truth about her parents.

Seymour was still thinking about the effect it would have on Breslin's daughter if her own mother had orchestrated the hit on him. He was standing outside the interrogation room, alongside the detectives working the case. He gazed through the one-way window as Willa Takeyama sat there staring at the wall.

"The walls are closing in on her," Rachel said confidently.

"Not fast enough, as far as I'm concerned," Leila muttered. "She clearly thinks she's pulled one over on us and isn't likely to blink."

Chung grunted and said: "Maybe she'll rethink that now that her ex-boyfriend is talking."

"My guess is she's sweating bullets right now," Ferguson said.

"I think she's sweated long enough," Seymour said. "Let's go see what the lady has to say for herself, if anything."

"This should be interesting," Leila remarked.

He agreed. Just how interesting it would be depended on the suspect and her willingness to play ball at her own expense.

* * *

Rachel entered the room with Ferguson, knowing that the stakes were high for all parties concerned. They now had a bona fide suspect with Parker Breslin's ex suspected as the one behind his murder. As though that weren't enough, in a disturbing surprise twist, she was now linked to Verlin Yashiro, a suspect in the murder of his estranged wife Joyce. Had the two been in on this all along?

Rachel sat down in front of the suspect and asked tartly: "So do you prefer we call you Willa Takeyama or Willa Breslin?"

Willa blinked uncomfortably. "Whatever you want, though these days I'm going by my maiden name, Takeyama."

"So be it. Well, Ms. Takeyama, there's been an interesting development since we last had you in..."

"Really? What is it?" she asked coolly.

"Do you know a man named Ray Hennesy?"

Willa's eyes widened. "Yes, we used to date."

"According to Hennesy, you did more than just date. He says you tried to recruit him to murder your ex, Parker Breslin."

Willa sighed theatrically. "He told you that?"

Ferguson stepped in, staring down at her. "He told us more than that. Hennesy said you offered to pay him twenty grand to murder Breslin."

169

"I did no such thing," she insisted. "Ray is a consummate liar who would say anything to get back at me."

"Why would he want to get back at you?" he asked.

"Why do you think? Because I broke up with him and it pissed him off."

Rachel peered at her cynically. "You expect us to believe Hennesy would concoct such a story out of revenge all because you ended the relationship?"

"It's the truth! Ray is a control freak. He hated that I wanted to end a volatile relationship and swore he'd make me pay. Now I see how he intended to do that."

Rachel had to hand it to her; she seemed to have an answer for everything and was daring them to prove otherwise. "There's a problem with your version of the story," she told the suspect. "Hennesy actually went to Breslin's house and cased the place. In the process, he happened to spit out some gum. We were able to link it to him through DNA. I seriously doubt he would have been smart enough to count on that if his intention was to set you up for conspiring to murder your ex, especially when he initially denied playing any part in Breslin's death, including your involvement."

"So maybe he's a lot smarter than you give him credit for," Willa suggested. "If he went to Parker's house, it was because he wanted to stick it to me. I had absolutely nothing to do with it. What better way to implicate me than by leaving the gum and waiting for you to figure it out for yourself?"

Rachel narrowed her eyes, hiding her frustration. "You know what I think? I think you're the one lying here. I think you were willing to do anything to get full custody of your daughter. That included using Ray Hennesy to kill your ex. Only Hennesy got cold feet, turning down your offer—even though it meant no longer getting you into bed and missing out on a big payday!"

Willa's thin brows bridged menacingly. "The whole thing is absurd," she maintained. "I do not have $20,000 to spare to hire someone to kill Parker or anyone else. So why would I pretend I did knowing that when it came time to collect, I would risk Ray going to the police?"

"Uh, I don't know," Rachel said sarcastically. "Maybe because you thought we'd pin the entire thing on your boyfriend and you would go free to move on to another man, while keeping custody of your daughter."

"It never happened—none of it!" Willa stated firmly. "Sorry if I won't admit to something that's not true."

Rachel bit her lower lip, aware they didn't have enough to hold her, in spite of what Ray Hennesy had to say. She glanced at Ferguson and moved on to their next angle. "Okay, then let's talk about Verlin Yashiro—"

Willa was clearly taken aback by the mention of his name. "What about him?" she asked unevenly.

"How long have you been dating him?"

Willa paused. "Off and on for a few months."

Rachel looked at her. "So you were seeing him and Ray Hennesy at the same time?"

Another pause. "Is there a law against dating two men at once?"

"Only when you use one or both in a murder for hire scheme," stated Ferguson, taking a seat next to Rachel. "Or did Yashiro offer to do it for the price of being in your bed—or his?"

Willa wrung her hands. "There was no murder plot between me and Verlin, just like there wasn't one with Ray. We've simply been dating like normal people—nothing more."

Rachel leaned forward. "Are you aware that Yashiro is a suspect in the murder of his estranged wife, Joyce Yashiro...?"

Willa sighed. "I knew she had been killed, but I didn't know he was a suspect, especially since we were together at the time she was killed. I told the other detectives that—"

Rachel eyed Ferguson. They had already been updated on this development from Leila and Chung. But that didn't

171

mean it had to be revealed to the woman suspected of masterminding a murder.

"So you were with Yashiro when his wife was killed, huh?" she threw out.

"Yes, the entire night," insisted Willa.

Rachel pressed her hands on the table. "I find it just a little suspicious that you're the alibi for Yashiro in his wife's death, and he just happens to be involved with you while someone was gunning down your ex. Do you see how strange that looks from our perspective?"

"Maybe it does," Willa offered, "but one thing has nothing to do with the other. Verlin and I had nothing to do with the deaths of our spouses or exes—or, for that matter, each other's. I'm sure you would love to make this out to be some sort of weird joint conspiracy, but it never happened, I'm sorry."

So am I, Rachel thought. *Sorry that we can't arrest you on the spot and throw away the key.*

Regrettably, that was the situation they found themselves in. And Willa knew it. All they could do right now was let her know they were onto her and bide their time.

Which, unfortunately, was playing right into her hands.

* * *

"Basically, like it or not, right now it's his word against hers," Seymour said ten minutes later. He was standing outside another interrogation room where Verlin Yashiro sat. Leila and Rachel were waiting to go in.

"And Willa knows that all too well," muttered Rachel. "She's smart and cunning, if nothing else—and she has an ally in Verlin Yashiro."

"They're playing us," Leila said. "More than likely, they're both involved in the murders of Joyce Yashiro and Parker Breslin." She was still reeling from the realization that Breslin's alibi was a suspect in another murder case and she had used her maiden name, perhaps to try to circumvent the connection.

"Yeah, it looks that way," Seymour said. "Unfortunately, they also have alibis, shaky or not. And without something more to go on than Ray Hennesy's unsubstantiated allegation, we may have no choice but to cut Willa Takeyama loose."

Leila sighed. Deep down inside, she knew they were right. A search warrant had been executed in searching Hennesy's residence, but they couldn't find the murder weapon used to pump three bullets into Parker Breslin. This only gave more credence to Hennesy's assertion that he was not the killer.

Now was the time to see if Verlin Yashiro would crack under the pressure of two murders he may have been involved in.

"We'll see if Yashiro tells a different tale than his girlfriend," Leila said.

"I can't wait to get at him," Rachel added eagerly.

"Neither can I," Leila said as they stepped inside the room. She wondered if either of them could break a man who seemed just as callous and calculating as Willa Takeyama.

Rachel took a seat in front of Yashiro, while Leila sat to the side of him.

After taking a breath, Rachel spoke first. "I'm Detective Lancaster. I'm investigating the murder of Parker Breslin— the ex-husband of your girlfriend, Willa Takeyama."

Yashiro winced. "Yes, Willa and I are dating, but what does that have to do with her ex-husband's death?"

Rachel rolled her eyes. "Duh—we believe that Willa got someone to murder Parker Breslin. First, she tried to recruit her last boyfriend, Ray Hennesy—offering him $20,000 to do the dirty deed. Once he refused, it only stands to reason that she would get someone else—like maybe a man already suspected of being involved in his own wife's murder. How am I doing so far?"

His brows twitched. "It's ludicrous to suggest I had anything to do with Breslin's murder," he contended. "As for my wife, I have an alibi—"

"I know, you were supposedly with Ms. Takeyama," Rachel said, cutting him off. "How convenient."

Yashiro maintained his composure. "It's true. I've done nothing wrong being involved with Willa when my wife and I were no longer together. And Willa is divorced. Neither of us had any reason to want either of them dead."

Leila listened patiently; sure that he was feeding them a pack of lies while trying to cover his ass and save his lover's ass at the same time.

"Where were you when Parker Breslin was gunned down?" Rachel asked pointblank, reminding him of the day and time.

As though fully prepared for the question, Yashiro responded without prelude: "I was in a meeting with a group of people at my company, the Aloha Architectural Group. And I can provide you with the names of everyone who was there to verify it."

"You do that," she demanded. "And while you're at it, you can tell me who you and Willa Takeyama Breslin hired to knock off your wife and her ex-husband. Think you can do that for me?"

"That's crazy!" Yashiro made a face. "I hired no one. Neither did Willa. You're grasping at straws and coming up short!"

Rachel sighed and met Leila's eyes, as though conceding defeat. Leila faced Yashiro, determined not to allow him and his lover to get away with murder.

"Seems like we keep meeting, Yashiro," she said humorlessly. "What's up with that?"

He glared at her. "You tell me, Detective Kahana. Seems like you enjoy persecuting an innocent man—and an innocent woman, too!"

Leila held his gaze, disregarding his claims of innocence. Still, she pretended to give him the benefit of the doubt by saying: "Believe me, I wish we didn't have to keep bringing you down here. Maybe you are totally blameless in the murder of your wife and have nothing to do with the murder of your lover's ex-husband. But put yourself in our shoes. The fact that you two are together and two people who were intimates of yours are dead...well, it just doesn't look good."

"Maybe not, but that doesn't make either of us killers." Yashiro crossed his arms petulantly. "It's just the opposite. Willa and I just happened to make a connection under unfortunate circumstances. Neither of us could have known these terrible things would happen. We only want to put this entire ordeal behind us and get on with our lives—if you'll let us."

It was all Leila could do not to burst out laughing from the absurdity of it all. She had to give him credit, along with Willa Takeyama—they were good. Both were practiced storytellers and had managed to stick to their guns, as though believing they were above reproach at the end of the day. But this façade did not work with her and would only last so long before it broke down like a sand castle.

Just as she was about to grill him some more, the door burst open. A thirty-something, attractive Hawaiian woman stormed in, glaring at them.

"Don't say anything else!" she ordered Yashiro, then said to the detectives: "I'm Diane Arakaki, Mr. Yashiro's attorney."

Yashiro reacted, while taking her advice and keeping quiet.

"Ms. Arakaki," Leila acknowledged, glancing at Rachel, while wondering who had contacted the attorney. Perhaps it was Willa Takeyama so she could keep Yashiro from saying something that might implicate one of them in the murders of Joyce Yashiro and Parker Breslin.

Diane flashed Leila a sharp look. "Talking to my client without representation is not cool, Detectives. Not too smart either."

Leila begged to differ. "Your client came here voluntarily," she told her. "We had some questions for him and he never asked for an attorney."

"Be that as it may, his attorney is here now," she hissed. "Unless you plan to arrest my client, this meeting is over."

Rachel frowned. "Mr. Yashiro is free to go. But I wouldn't go very far. It's good to know you've got a lawyer. You're going to need her before this is over."

Yashiro stood and cracked a grin, as if to say: *Catch me if you can.*

Leila accepted the silent challenge. She was determined to see to it that justice was served in the death of his wife and his lover's ex-husband no matter how long it took to wipe that smug look off Yashiro's face.

CHAPTER 22

That evening, Leila took a walk on the beach barefoot, enjoying the feel of the sand between her toes. She was happy to step back from the pressures of the job to enjoy a simple pleasure and take in the beauty of nature all around her. In spite of the unsavory elements of life on Maui, it was a place she wouldn't trade for the world, with all the good things it had to offer. As a Native Hawaiian, she was committed to being part of the culture and following the legacy of her father, grandfather, and those who came before them.

When she got back to her house, Leila took a shower and then sat down with a glass of red wine. She was just about to read a couple of chapters of a novel when her cell phone rang. She saw that it was Eddie Naku seeking a video chat. Had he learned something about Maxwell Kishimoto that might derail their potential romance before it even started?

She took a sip of wine and accepted the call, watching as his face appeared on the small screen. "Hey," she said.

"Hey," Naku said, grinning. "Hope I didn't catch you at a bad time?"

"You didn't." She smiled eagerly. "So, I take it you checked out Maxwell?"

"Yeah, I did."

"What did you find out?" Leila wondered if she really wanted to know.

Naku paused. "I learned quite a bit about him. You already know Kishimoto is clean as far as his criminal record. Well, that extends to the rest of his life too. He came to the United States from Japan with his parents when he was five. He's been a successful restaurateur in San Francisco, Houston, Honolulu, and now Maui. He's never been married and has no children that have surfaced. He's got a ranch up in the West Maui Mountains. Let's see, what else... He rides horses and plays tennis. I can keep digging, if you want, but I'd say he's got a lot of good things going for him. If you want to pursue—"

She flashed her teeth. "I think that's enough. I'll take it from here. Mahalo."

"Anytime," Naku said.

Leila wondered if he really meant that. Not that it mattered. She wasn't interested in taking advantage of his private detective skills any more than she already had.

"Catch you later," she told him, before disconnecting.

Tasting her wine, Leila wondered briefly if she could ever return to the private sector and put her skills to use as a private investigator like Naku had. It didn't seem very likely. When she turned in her gun and badge, there were other less hazardous pursuits that came to mind, such as putting a greater focus on her art.

Her thoughts turned to Maxwell Kishimoto. So he checked out as a decent guy with no skeletons waiting to come out of the closet. What was there not to like? Moreover, he seemed to like her.

All that was left was to build up the courage to call him. It was a tall task for an old fashioned girl who still preferred to be pursued.

* * *

Jonny Chung went to the bar called Moonlights on Hana Highway in Paia to meet covertly with drug dealer Shichiro

Gutierrez. But Gutierrez was late, pissing him off. Chung noticed Renee Bradley, the hot journalist he'd once bedded and was currently feeding information. She was sitting at a table with several tequila shots in front of her.

Since he had a little time to kill, Chung went over to her table and sat down. "Need some company?"

Renee looked surprised to see him. "Actually, I'm waiting for someone."

That's what they all say, he thought. "Me too. But in the meantime, why not hang out together?" He grabbed one of the shots and downed it.

Renee seemed ready to object, but had a change of heart. "Sure, why not?" She glanced around and rested her eyes on him before downing a shot herself. "So do you have anything new to report?"

He grinned. "I thought you'd never ask. There has been a development in the case I'm working on—"

She gave him her full attention. "Tell me..."

Chung paused, knowing that telling her too much would only put him in hot water if it was traced back to him. On the other hand, it didn't hurt to put the squeeze on suspects by sharing little bits and pieces of investigation for public consumption.

He had another shot and said: "We think we're closing in on Joyce Yashiro's killer. At the same time, we might be able to tie it to the murder of Parker Breslin."

Renee's eyes widened with enthusiasm. "Really..."

"Yeah. Looks like our killers are lovers who set out to cut ties permanently with their former spouses—"

"Interesting," Renee sang. "I can't wait for some more details."

Chung looked up and saw Shichiro Gutierrez and two of his cronies enter. It was time to collect hush money the drug dealer owed him for allowing him free reign across the island.

"I'm afraid that will have to wait," Chung told her, downing another shot before standing. "I have some business to attend to." He grinned lasciviously at her. "Later."

He walked away and gestured at Gutierrez to follow him toward the back of the bar and away from prying eyes.

* * *

Renee watched with curiosity as Chung met with another man, before the two disappeared.

"Sorry I'm late," she heard over her shoulder and turned to see Franco standing there.

Though she wished he hadn't been late, Renee fashioned a smile on her lips and said: "It's cool."

He sat down. "So who was that man I saw you talking to?"

She glanced back over to where Chung had disappeared, and then faced Franco thoughtfully. "No one." Lifting up a tequila shot, she poured it down her throat. "I was just waiting for you."

He grabbed a glass, grinning. "Wait no more!" He drank a shot, ignoring the empty glasses.

Renee grinned back. She was starting to feel a little tipsy, but was still up for a few more shots, even as she considered the important news Chung had shared with her, though their conversation had been cut short.

Franco took her mind off that as he ran his hand up and down her thigh, exciting her. When he suggested they continue this at her place, Renee was more than willing.

Twenty minutes later, they were in her condo having sex. Renee must have passed out between orgasms, for when she came to, Franco was gone.

* * *

Rachel Lancaster sat in the living room of her home in Waikapu, a census designated area not far from Kahului. She was flipping through photo album, looking at pictures of her and her late husband Greg. Today would have been their tenth anniversary had his life not been cut short much too soon. She put her fingers to his handsome face, wishing he was here in the flesh to touch, hold, kiss, and make love to.

But all she was left with were the memories of the life they had together. It would have to sustain her, even if at times it seemed as if their marriage was but a figment of her imagination, as she struggled to remember some of the day-to-day moments in their lives. Was this what it meant to lose a loved one—the memories start to fade as time goes by? Would the day come when Greg was extricated from her mind altogether?

Rachel's thoughts turned to her murder investigation, something that was more palpable in her daily life. She was pretty sure that Willa Takeyama and her lover, Verlin Yashiro, were behind the murder of her ex-husband, Parker Breslin. Even if they hadn't pulled the trigger, they almost certainly had blood on their hands in both Breslin's death and the murder of Yashiro's estranged wife, Joyce Yashiro.

Now that she was working in tandem with her fellow detectives, Rachel was sure it was only a matter of time before they took down Takeyama and Yashiro. Until then, they would not let up or give them room to breathe. Parker Breslin's daughter, Marie, would suffer mightily in learning that her mother had orchestrated a plot keep her away from her father forever. But the little girl would suffer even more if the truth never came out and she lived her life under false pretenses.

When her cell phone rang, Rachel grabbed it and saw that it was her sister Arlene calling from Santa Fe, New Mexico. Rachel smiled, knowing that Arlene had remembered this was the anniversary of her wedding day.

* * *

Trent Ferguson sat beside Blake Seymour at the bar in Whaler's Village, a popular beachfront shopping and dining center in Kaanapali. They were talking shop over beers.

"You think they were both in on it from the start, don't you?" Ferguson asked the lieutenant.

"Don't you?" Seymour eyed him over the mug. "Wouldn't be the first time two lovers conspired to murder their spouse or ex-spouses for money, child custody, or some bizarre combination of the two."

"You're right," Ferguson said. "Chances are they were planning this for some time—right down to their hard-to-discredit alibis for each other, giving Takeyama and Yashiro everything they wanted."

"Right, other than to be captured and spend the rest of their lives in prison," muttered Seymour. "Most killers never seem to look that far ahead in their diabolical plans. Problem is we still need to prove their guilt. That means we need to find the shooter of Parker Breslin and the person who suffocated and then strangled Joyce Yashiro—assuming they are not one and the same—along with the deadly weapons used."

Ferguson leaned on the counter, not disagreeing that they had a tall task ahead of them. "Could Takeyama's mother and Yashiro's son also be part of the conspiracy?" he wondered out loud.

Seymour rubbed his nose. "At this point, anything's possible. My guess is the lovers did it alone, believing it was their best chance to get away with it."

But they won't, Ferguson thought. Not if he had anything to do with it. If he was ever going to make it to lieutenant himself, solving cases like these were critical.

He put the suds to his lips and asked casually: "So how are things with the wife these days?"

Seymour drank some beer and wiped his mouth with the back of his hand. "We're hanging in there. The sex isn't what it used to be, but I'm not complaining. We're back together and trying to make it work. I think we can."

"Then you will." In Ferguson's mind, putting forth the effort was three-quarters of the battle. Something he had failed to do in his own marriage.

"How are things with you and Gina?" Seymour asked him.

Ferguson lifted a brow. As far as anyone knew, he had met her at a Maui Friday Town Parties in Kihei and not as a prostitute. He hoped to keep it that way.

"We're good," he responded levelly. "She makes me happy and I try to return the favor. And the sex is great between us."

Seymour laughed. "Happy to hear it. If you last as long as we have, separation aside, it may drop off a bit. Or maybe not."

"Not if I can help it," Ferguson said. "Of course, I used to think the same thing about my ex and... Well, things didn't turn out too good for us."

"That was then and this is now," Seymour said. "Take each day as it is and each partner as she comes."

"Yeah." Ferguson imagined he was also talking about his stint with Leila Kahana. Some experiences die hard. He wondered if Seymour would like to have her back—at least part time. Or had that ship sailed for good?

His thoughts turned to Gina's daughter who had been adopted by Seymour and his wife. "How's Akela?" he asked innocently.

"Growing up way too fast," Seymour said.

"I'll bet." Ferguson paused, before saying: "I know you and Mele adopted her. Have you ever thought about the birth mother trying to track her down someday? Or Akela deciding on her own that she wants to meet her birth mom?"

This ought to be interesting, Ferguson mused.

Seymour tasted more beer thoughtfully. "Yeah, I guess the thought has crossed my mind from time to time. I don't imagine the birth mother, wherever she is, will seek out Akela—given that she gave her away. If she does, Mele and I will have to deal with it then. Same thing, should Akela ever wish to contact her. We wouldn't try to stand in her way, if she felt it would make her whole—assuming the birth mother had any interest in being contacted by Akela."

Ferguson drank beer as he contemplated that response. He hoped to hell that Gina left things alone and did nothing to break up Seymour's home. Keeping things as they were was best for all parties concerned, including him.

"Like you said, it's doubtful you'll ever hear from the birth mother," Ferguson told him. "And from what I've seen, Akela looks like a very well-adjusted little girl who would never want any parents other than the ones who love her and raised her."

Seymour smiled. "Mahalo for saying that."

"Just telling it as I see it, boss." Ferguson grinned and they clinked their glasses to toast on it, even as he understood that there were always two sides to every story. Something that Gina knew all too well.

* * *

At the Westside Tavern on Honoapiilani Highway in Lahaina, Kimiko Keomaka sat at the bar nursing a drink after work. He'd come there alone to collect his thoughts now that he was nearing retirement. Eight months to be exact. He felt that he and his wife were prepared, but the truth was he wasn't sure they had saved enough to make this work to both their satisfaction. What if it didn't? Would he have to go back to work? Would she?

Kimiko tried to ignore the thirty-something man who had sat down beside him and was getting wasted. *Must have had a rough day*, he imagined. Or maybe he was anticipating rough days ahead. Either way, it was none of his business, except when the man tried to make it his business.

"I'm screwed, man," he muttered.

Figuring he needed to say something, Kimiko responded: "Did your wife catch you in bed with another woman or something?"

The man scratched his pate. "I wish that were the case, but I'm not married."

Kimiko noticed a lion tattoo on his forearm.

The man drank more liquor and then wiped his mouth with the back of his hand. "It's a lot worse than that—"

Do I want to hear this? Kimiko asked himself, trying to imagine what could be so bad. "What did you do?" he asked.

The man's lower lip quivered. "Did you hear about the dude who was gunned down outside his house in Kihei?"

Kimiko didn't follow the news too much, but he did recall seeing something about the father of a young girl being shot to death. The news report had suggested it was a drug deal gone bad.

"Yeah, I heard," he told him.

The man took a deep breath and said: "Well, that was me—I shot him..."

Kimiko's heart skipped a beat. Since the man was clearly intoxicated, he wasn't sure if he was on the level or not. "You killed that man?" he asked warily.

"Yeah—I was paid to take him out. Wish I could have a do-over, but what's done is done."

Kimiko was alarmed. Was he really talking to a killer? If so, why was he telling him this?

"Maybe you should go to the police...turn yourself in," he suggested.

The man's brows knitted. "I can't do that. With my history, they'd never let me out." He downed the rest of his drink and peered at Kimiko. "Forget what I just said!"

On that note, he got to his feet and staggered toward the door and out.

Shaken at what he'd just heard, whether true or not, Kimiko didn't hesitate to do what he needed to as a concerned citizen for what seemed to be a growing problem with crimes of violence on the island. He took out his cell phone and called the police.

CHAPTER 23

In the morning, Leila went for her usual run, feeling the wind at her back as she picked up the pace a bit. She couldn't help but think about Joyce Yashiro, who had attempted to do the same thing before someone made sure she never finished her run on Kaanapali Beach. Leila desperately wanted to find Joyce's killer. She felt she owed her that as a fellow runner. Having two prime suspects was a big step in the right direction. But the pieces still needed to be tied together before any arrests could be made, which was frustrating, as she wanted to see justice served swiftly.

Yet she knew that justice often came slowly. All she and the other member of the homicide team could do was go through the motions and stay focused till the tide began to turn. Only then—when arrests were made—could she exhale and know she'd done her job.

Leila headed back home as her thoughts shifted to Maxwell Kishimoto. She wanted to get to know him and see if they clicked. Had she waited too long to contact him? Was he still interested in her?

Maybe I'll give him a call today and invite him to lunch, she told herself. If he said yes, they could go from there. If not, then she had to believe they weren't meant to start dating.

When she got to work, Leila was informed that their Crime Stoppers Program had received a call that could be a break in the Parker Breslin murder case—and by extension, potentially help with the Joyce Yashiro investigation. Given the many such calls that led nowhere, Leila was skeptical. However, she knew all such calls had to be taken seriously, just in case they panned out.

So what made this one different?

"He's here, waiting in the interview room," Rachel told her. "The caller, Kimiko Keomaka, was not only willing to identify himself, but he came in to tell his story."

"And what story is that?" Leila asked.

"According to Mr. Keomaka, he was minding his own business last night, having a drink at the Westside Tavern in Lahaina on Honoapiilani Highway, when the guy next to him confessed to shooting Parker Breslin to death. The man, who had been drinking heavily, then told Keomaka to forget what he'd just heard and left. Apparently, Keomaka was so shaken up that he didn't hesitate to phone it in to the hotline. He left his number so we could contact him."

Leila met her eyes. "Have you spoken to him?"

"Yes, and I have to say his statement was very convincing," Rachel said. "Ferguson thought so too. Of course, it could all turn out to be a false lead. But in the meantime, we have to find this man who may have murdered Parker Breslin."

"Do you want me to do a composite sketch of him?" She assumed that was where this was leading.

Rachel nodded. "The witness got a pretty good look at him, but no name. If we can identify him, it might be the break we've been looking for."

Leila could hardly argue the point. Right now, they could use all the help they could get. "Okay, let's see what type of description your witness can provide."

* * *

Entering the room, Leila gave a tiny smile to the grim-faced man, who was in his mid-sixties with thinning white hair. After identifying herself, she said: "Thanks for coming down, Mr. Keomaka."

"It was my civic duty," he responded.

She sat beside him with her sketchpad. "I'm going to do a composite sketch of the man you saw and spoke to. I'll need you to describe him as closely as you can remember."

He nodded. "I'll do the best I can."

Leila regarded the witness pensively. "But first, I'd like to go over the conversation you had with him—"

He went through the brief exchange he had with the suspect. His memory seemed razor sharp and Leila had no reason to doubt him.

"And he said he was paid to murder this man?" she reiterated.

"Yeah," Keomaka maintained.

"Did he say who it was?"

"No."

"Did he mention the name of the man he was hired to kill?" Leila asked, realizing it would be easier if the suspect had dropped some of these details.

"I'm afraid not," Keomaka muttered. "But he made it clear that he was talking about the man who was gunned down outside his home in Kihei."

That might have to do, she thought. And considering that Parker Breslin was the only one who fit the bill in recent memory, the suspect must have been referring to him. One question remained that had yet to be answered. Was the person Keomaka talked to speaking from personal knowledge or just repeating what he heard from the media?

She opened up her sketchpad and asked some general questions. "Was the man slender? Medium-sized? Heavy?"

"He was slender, but not really thin."

"How tall was he?"

"About six feet or so."

"What was he wearing?"

"Jeans and a print shirt, along with work shoes."

Blue collar worker maybe, Leila thought. Possibly outdoor work. Construction came to mind. Or maybe landscaping, which was Parker Breslin's field. Could this person have worked for him?

She eyed the witness. "Can you describe the shape of his face?"

"It was square and he had a long forehead."

Leila sketched this and asked: "What about his eyes?"

"Blue."

"Were they close set? Or wider?"

"Wider."

She sketched this and turned the pad toward him. "Like that?"

"Yeah," he said.

Leila asked about the nose, mouth, ears, and chin before moving to the suspect's hair. "What color?"

"He was bald," Keomaka responded. "It looked freshly shaven."

Perhaps to circumvent justice, she thought. It did help make her a job a little easier.

"Were there any distinguishing marks on his face or elsewhere that you noticed?"

"Yeah, he had a small mole on his left cheek. And he had a lion tattoo covering half his right arm."

"Interesting," Leila mused out loud. She used everything he said to form an image in her mind and put the finishing touches on the sketch before revealing it. "Does the man you saw look like this?"

"Yeah, that's him!" Keomaka stated excitedly.

"You're sure?"

"Yep, that's definitely the man who told me he killed someone..."

Leila glanced at the one-way mirror, knowing Rachel, Seymour, Chung, and Ferguson were all watching on the other side. She nodded at them, indicating they had what they needed as a definite person of interest

* * *

Back at her desk, Leila could only hope that they could quickly identify the man in the composite sketch and one thing would lead to another in solving one case, or perhaps two, in one fell swoop.

She dribbled her fingers across the desk pad thoughtfully before building up her nerve to give Maxwell Kishimoto a call. Grabbing her cell phone, she decided to put trepidation away and just go for it. The worst he could say was too little, too late, and it would be on her.

She dialed his number. He responded on the second ring. "Aloha, Maxwell," she said.

"Aloha, Leila. I was hoping you'd call."

She smiled in hearing those words. "I was wondering if you were free for lunch today."

She imagined that he would be busy at his restaurant as the owner, but he replied: "As a matter of fact, I am. We can meet here or—"

"There is fine," Leila said, thinking that if things worked out, she could cook him dinner sometime. "How does one o'clock sound?"

"Perfect. I look forward to seeing you then."

"Same here," she said. "Aloha."

When she disconnected, Leila couldn't help but grin. She'd made the first move and now the ball was in his court—literally, considering they were having their initial date at his restaurant.

She just wished it wasn't happening in the middle of her work day. But if anything were to develop between them, it was something he would have to get used to.

CHAPTER 24

"We've got a match," forensic investigator David Lovato told Rachel and Ferguson.

"Oh, really?" Rachel rolled her eyes with surprise. It wasn't that she didn't fully believe in Leila's capabilities as a composite sketch artist; it was just that, more often than not, the system was slow to match images with mugshots of offenders.

"Yeah, really. The FBI's Interstate Photo System did all the work. It was able to successfully cross reference the sketch with a mugshot in its criminal database belonging to Howard McCloskey, a white male, age thirty-six. He's on parole after serving time for nearly beating a man to death that he got into an argument with at a nightclub. See for yourself—"

Rachel looked at the computer screen with Ferguson over her shoulder.

"Damn if it isn't him," Ferguson remarked.

She had to agree. "Now we need to locate McCloskey and see if he'll repeat to us what he told Kimiko Keomaka."

"Good luck with that," Lovato muttered. "If he thinks you're onto him, he could make a run for it."

"There's nowhere to run," she quipped, "unless he's a great swimmer. I'm guessing he'll never see us coming, believing that what he told Keomaka went no further."

They learned from Howard McCloskey's parole officer, Chet Okuni, that he was employed as a shelf stocker at a supermarket in Kahului.

Twenty minutes later, Rachel and Ferguson went to question the suspect at his place of employ.

Flashing her badge at the store manager, Rachel said: "We need to talk to one of your employees, Howard McCloskey."

The manager nodded and said: "Sure—he's in aisle five stocking cereal."

Ferguson said: "Mahalo," without explanation and they split up to approach him in opposite directions.

When Rachel entered the aisle, she spotted the suspect. He spotted her as well and, when she called out his name, he bolted.

"He's making a run for it," she called out to Ferguson, who had yet to reach the aisle.

Rachel went after him. She resisted the temptation to remove her firearm, not wanting to see any innocent people hurt. Not to mention, there was no indication the suspect was armed, though if he was guilty of murder, he still had to be considered dangerous.

She chased him through the store, while Ferguson attempted to cut McCloskey off. But he managed to dart and dodge, tossing items at them, as if to slow them down.

Finally, before he could make it to the exit, Rachel got close enough and literally dove at him, landing on top of the suspect. Before he could make a move, she had twisted his right arm behind his back and placed a cuff on him. The other cuff followed as Ferguson caught up.

"Good job, Lancaster."

"I needed my exercise for today," she quipped, before he helped get McCloskey to his feet.

"What is this?" he asked as if he had no clue.

"Why did you run?" Ferguson asked sharply.

"I didn't do anything," claimed McCloskey.

"Yeah, right." Rachel made a face. "That's not what you said last night when you confessed to killing a man—"

McCloskey lowered his head, as if he knew his own words had come back to haunt him.

Ferguson faced onlookers and said calmly: "This is police business. Go back to your shopping. Everything's okay."

Rachel followed that up by advising the suspect: "We're bringing you in, Howard McCloskey, to question you about a murder..."

* * *

Once they had him in an interrogation room, Ferguson wasted little time grilling Howard McCloskey.

"Why don't you tell us about the murder you committed in Kihei," he said tartly to the cuffed suspect sitting across from him.

McCloskey's head snapped back. "I don't know what you're talking about."

"I think you do. We have a witness who recorded in his mind every nasty detail of your confession. He also described you to a tee, which is why we're here right now."

Rachel, who was standing, took over. "So who did you kill, McCloskey?"

"No one," he insisted, darting his eyes. "This is a mistake..."

"The only one making a mistake here is you," she said sternly. "Not fessing up to what you did will only land you in more hot water. We know the man you killed was Parker Breslin. We have video surveillance that places you at the scene of the crime," she lied. "We also know that you were hired by the victim's ex-wife, Willa Takeyama, to murder him after the first guy she hired changed his mind. Any of this sound familiar? And don't even think about sticking to your play dumb story, as it won't work. It's time to get this off your chest..."

Ferguson watched with interest as McCloskey dropped his head in defeat. Rachel had gotten to him.

McCloskey lifted his head and sighed. "Yeah, I did it."

"Did what?" pressed Ferguson.

He paused. "I killed Breslin."

Ferguson and Rachel exchanged looks, as things finally appeared to be falling into place. But they needed more from the suspect to make it stick.

"How did you kill him?"

"I shot him to death," he admitted.

"With what type of gun?" Ferguson asked, peering at him.

McCloskey didn't hesitate when he responded: "It was a .45."

Rachel leaned forward, demanding: "Where is the weapon now?"

"At my place."

She looked at the mirror, which Ferguson knew was a signal to Lieutenant Seymour to start the process of seeking a search warrant to locate the weapon.

"Why did you do it?" Ferguson asked the suspect. He wanted to hear it in his own words.

"She offered to pay me ten grand. I needed the money."

Ferguson couldn't help but think that his employer had gotten him on the cheap, after being willing to shell out twenty thousand to the first hitman she recruited. "Who is she?" he asked to make sure they were on the same page here.

"Breslin's ex-wife, Willa Takeyama—"

Ferguson eyed Rachel, feeling they had her now—or just about. They also had the killer in custody. Once they had the weapon, things could move forward rapidly.

"Did you receive the money?" Rachel asked.

"Yeah," McCloskey said. "She paid me."

Ferguson stared at him thoughtfully. It shouldn't be too difficult to follow the money trail from Takeyama's bank account, or other sources of money, right into the hands of the man she paid to take out Parker Breslin.

But was he also responsible for the murder of Joyce Yashiro?

Ferguson wanted to find out. "What about the other murder?" he tossed out.

McCloskey cocked a brow. "What other murder?"

"The murder of Joyce Yashiro, the wife of Takeyama's lover, Verlin Yashiro. Did you kill her too for them?"

"I had nothing to do with killing anyone else," he insisted flatly. "Willa only paid me to kill her ex."

"You're sure about that?" pressed Rachel. "If you're lying, it will only get a lot harder for you."

"I'm not lying!" McCloskey insisted. "I don't know anything about another murder. Whoever killed that lady, it wasn't me..."

Ferguson met Rachel's eyes. He was inclined to believe McCloskey, if only because it made sense to separate the two murders in order to keep the police from too easily tying the murders together to the two main suspects. Ferguson suspected that Verlin Yashiro could have killed his own wife, especially since his alibi had now been implicated in a murder-for-hire plot. But before they leaned on Willa Takeyama, they had to connect her to McCloskey directly. And they also needed to gain possession of the murder weapon.

* * *

Leila felt a little nervous as she walked inside the restaurant. This time she wasn't there with Jan. She was all by her lonesome, but not for long, as her date was the place's proprietor. Coming there straight from work, she was wearing her usual business casual detective attire: a sleeveless yellow top with brown pants, an open front black stretch jacket, and dark slip-on flats. She hoped she wasn't underdressed. Or was there such a thing these days with outfits so interchangeable for all occasions?

"Aloha 'auinalā," Maxwell greeted her, looking resplendent in a navy suit.

"Good afternoon to you," Leila responded, happy to mix Hawaiian and English pleasantries with him.

"Nice to see you again," he said, flashing a smile.

She smiled back. "You too."

"Our table is ready."

"That's great," she said, "because I'm starving."

"Then you definitely picked the right place for our date. Our motto here is to never let anyone leave hungry, especially a beautiful woman like you."

Leila blushed. She wasn't sure if he was real or playing the charm game. She supposed she would find out sooner than later.

They sat in an area away from other guests—probably reserved for VIPs, Leila suspected. Or, in this case, first dates.

"I took the liberty to order for us," Maxwell said. "I hope you don't mind?"

A man not afraid to take charge, she mused. Why should she mind? She responded: "Not at all."

"Good. The main dish is chicken teriyaki, deep fried shrimp, and vegetables. It's served with Japanese potato salad and tuna rolls. Dessert will be green tea cheese cake. And you also have your choice of the house lunchtime beverages of banana mango smoothie; Sunny Hawaii, which is a mixture of orange, pineapple, and coconut juices with a splash of lime; or Blue Hawaii punch, which is just blue-colored Kool Aid, club soda, and a little pineapple juice."

Suitably impressed with the forethought he'd obviously given to their meal, Leila said: "I'll go with the Sunny Hawaii and what looks like a delicious meal."

Maxwell chuckled. "Sunny Hawaii is a great choice—for both of us."

"Mahalo," she said, smiling.

"So tell me about yourself," Maxwell said a little later as they began to eat.

Leila met his eyes. "What do want to know?"

"What do you do for a living?"

I knew that was coming, she thought. *It's probably best if I get it over with and hope he's not scared off.*

"I'm a cop..."

His eyes registered clear surprise. "Really?"

"Yes." She tried to detect whether or not this was a deal breaker.

He chuckled. "That's very interesting. What type of cop are you?"

"I work homicide for the Maui PD," she admitted, as if it was something to be ashamed of, when it was really just the opposite. Except when it came to impressing dates. Maybe this one would be different.

"So you help get killers off the street?"

She put a fork into the potato salad. "I try."

"Are you working on anything now?" he asked curiously.

"I'm always working on cases," she told him. "Not all cases are solved overnight. In fact, few are. That means detectives can be at it for years, aside from new cases cropping up."

He furrowed his brow. "Are there that many homicides on Maui?"

She chuckled. "No, thank goodness. But sometimes it seems that way when you're caught up in investigations."

Maxwell took a bite of chicken. "Have you always wanted to be in law enforcement?"

"When I was a little girl, I wanted to be a ballerina," Leila said, smiling playfully. "When I got older, I was fascinated by law and order—especially since my father and grandfather were both cops."

"Yes, I can see why that would intrigue you."

"What about you?" she asked, diverting the conversation away from her. "Have you always been in the restaurant business?"

"Not always. In my teens, I wanted to be a cowboy." He laughed, prompting her to do the same in picturing him riding into town as an Old West gunslinger. "But practicality forced me to put that on hold. I went to college and then started working in restaurants in every capacity from busboy to manager to owner. That pretty much brings me to where I am today."

Leila felt a bit guilty that she had already checked him out. But it was for peace of mind, which brought them to this moment.

"It looks like you chose the right profession," she told him intuitively.

"I'd say the same for you."

She agreed with him, but it didn't mean she wasn't open to changing courses when the time was right.

Maxwell tasted his drink. "So how did your friend's showing go at the Maui Friday Town Party?"

"It went very well. She won some new admirers and continues to wow the old ones."

"Count me in as one of the new admirers." He looked at her. "I admire you even more."

"Why?" she couldn't help but ask.

He grinned. "What's not to admire? You're hot, successful at what you do I'm sure, and you're good company."

She flashed her teeth. "Nice answer all the way around." *I'm starting to like him*, Leila thought. Or was it too soon to feel that way?

"Do you ride horses?" Maxwell asked, wiping his mouth with a napkin.

"Yes. My grandparents on my mother's side lived on a farm with horses and cattle. My granddad taught me how to ride. But I don't get to ride very often these days."

"Maybe we can change that," he said. "I have a few horses on my ranch. We could go riding sometime."

"I'd like that," she told him. The thought of spending time with him in any capacity sounded good, but especially one that put her back in touch with nature. "So it looks like you became a cowboy after all."

He laughed. "Yes, I guess you could say that."

Leila's cell phone rang. She debated whether or not to answer, but saw the caller was Blake Seymour. Since they were no longer seeing each other personally, she was sure it pertained to work. "I have to get this," she apologized.

"Please do," he said.

"Hey," she told Seymour. "What's up?"

"There's been a development in the Parker Breslin investigation, with possible implications for the Joyce Yashiro case."

"I'll be right there," Leila said reluctantly, disconnecting. She looked at her date. "I have to go," she hated to tell him.

He looked disappointed, and then nodded respectfully. "I understand."

"Mahalo for that."

"When can I see you again?" he asked.

Leila didn't want to make any promises she couldn't keep. But she also didn't want him to think she wasn't interested in him.

"How about this weekend?" she suggested. "I'd love to take you up on your horseback riding offer."

Maxwell grinned. "It's a date."

Leila told him she would call to finalize things, determined to not let what seemed promising slip by the wayside.

He walked her to the door and gave her a nice kiss on the cheek. A gentleman too, which drew her to him all the more.

* * *

Armed with a search warrant, Rachel and Ferguson, along with a few uniformed officers, descended upon a plantation home on Vineyard Street in Wailuku.

Rachel did the honors of ringing the bell. She hoped against hope that Howard McCloskey was on the level about holding onto the gun he used to shoot Parker Breslin, even though it wasn't a smart move to keep evidence tied to a murder, incriminating yourself in the process. But this was a way for him to make things right, to some extent, for Breslin's daughter if no one else.

The door was opened by a tall, thin Hispanic woman with short brown hair.

"Maui Police Department," announced Rachel. "We have a warrant to search the premises—"

The woman, who identified herself as Pamela Medeiros, McCloskey's live-in girlfriend, did not stand in the way.

Slipping on latex gloves, Rachel led the way to a back room, where McCloskey claimed he'd hidden the gun. The room was small and cluttered. She spotted a cabinet in a corner and went to it, opening the bottom drawer. Pushing aside some junk, she spotted a dirty cloth obviously wrapped around something. She lifted the object and carefully removed the cloth. It was a .45-caliber handgun.

"This could be the smoking gun, no pun intended," she said.

"And this looks like our box of bullets," Ferguson told her, removing a box from a shelf under a small wooden table. "Ballistics should be able to verify if they are the same lot as the ones pumped into Breslin."

Rachel looked at him. "I can't wait to see if we have a match on these and if we can connect McCloskey to Willa Takeyama through the payoff and phone calls made between the two." For the latter, they had obtained a second warrant to search the cell phone records of Howard McCloskey; while a separate warrant had been issued to search the financial records of Willa Takeyama in association with the murder-for-hire scheme.

"It would be even better if we can tie the murder of Parker Breslin to Joyce Yashiro's murder," remarked Ferguson, "given the relationship between Takeyama and Verlin Yashiro."

"I'm all for killing two murderers with one slingshot," Rachel said. She knew neither suspect would break easily in fingering the other, unless it meant saving his or her own neck. At which point, anything was possible.

CHAPTER 25

Leila looked at the suspect through the one-way window, as she stood beside Seymour and Chung. Howard McCloskey didn't exactly look like a killer for hire. But no one really did, until becoming such.

"So he actually confessed to being hired by Willa Takeyama to take out her ex-husband?" Leila asked.

"Yeah, he broke under pressure," Seymour said. "Even as we speak, his house is being searched for the murder weapon and anything else that can tie him to the crime."

"What about tying him to Takeyama?" Chung asked.

"We're working on that, too. Since she supposedly handed him ten grand to complete the job, it shouldn't be too difficult to uncover the transaction from her financial records. Apart from that, we'll put the squeeze on McCloskey to give us more to nail Takeyama. No reason for him to go down alone."

Leila agreed, but didn't want to see it end there. She gazed up at Seymour. "Can we make the connection between Parker Breslin's murder and the murder of Joyce Yashiro?"

Seymour frowned. "We're still working on that. Right now, McCloskey is sticking to his guns that he played no part in Joyce Yashiro's death. Yet there's every reason to believe that Takeyama and Verlin Yashiro are joined at the hip in the dual murders. If McCloskey didn't kill Yashiro, he damn sure was indirectly involved—if only by virtue of being part of an elaborate plot by Verlin Yashiro and Willa Takeyama to get away with murder."

"I want to talk to him," Leila said of the suspect. "Maybe I can get something out of him that Rachel and Ferguson missed, regarding our own investigation."

"Go right ahead," Seymour said.

"If you need backup, let me know," added Chung.

Leila nodded, but said: "It's probably best if I talk to him alone." It wasn't that she didn't think Chung was more than capable of grilling a suspect. It was just that she was more experienced at it and better equipped to play on McCloskey's weaknesses as someone who had owned up to his own guilt in a murder conspiracy.

She stepped inside the room, where the handcuffed suspect sat sullenly. "I'm Detective Sergeant Kahana," she said, as she sat down in front of him. "I understand that you confessed to the murder of Parker Breslin."

McCloskey grimaced. "Yeah, I did it."

"And you were paid by Willa Takeyama to kill her ex-husband?"

"Yeah," he admitted tonelessly.

Leila sighed, wondering what went on inside a person's head to so cruelly take another person's life. "I'm investigating the murder of Joyce Yashiro," she told him. "She was the estranged wife of Verlin Yashiro, the man Willa Takeyama has been having an affair with. I believe the two conspired to kill Joyce and Parker Breslin. My colleagues tell me you say you weren't involved in Joyce Yashiro's murder. Do you expect me to believe that, all things considered?" she pressed, hoping for a reaction.

McCloskey's eyes narrowed. "I didn't kill her! Whatever went on with Willa and Yashiro was between them."

Leila leaned forward. "Actually, that's not quite true. Here's the deal: as a confessed murderer, you could still end up being charged as an accomplice in the murder of Joyce Yashiro, if we discover you've been holding back on us. If you know more than you're saying, now would be a good time to come clean..."

He drew a deep breath. "All right. When I first met Willa, she was with a dude who drove a BMW. I never asked his name, he never volunteered it."

It has to be Verlin Yashiro, thought Leila, knowing he drove a BMW. "Can you describe him to me?"

McCloskey's description was a close match to Yashiro, which, in Leila's mind, placed him in the company of Willa when she initially approached Howard McCloskey. But that still wasn't enough in and of itself to connect Yashiro to Breslin's murder—much less Joyce's death.

"Did Willa mention anything to you about committing a second murder?" Leila asked McCloskey.

He wavered. "I wasn't a part of that," he reiterated.

She picked up something in his tone and went with it. "I'm not saying you were. But she brought it up anyway, right?"

McCloskey sniffed. "She mentioned something about taking someone else out. I refused. Told her it would be too much heat."

"And how did she react?"

"She said it was all right—her friend would just take care of it himself."

Leila glanced at the mirror, with Chung and Seymour listening in. "When you say *friend*, do you mean the man in the BMW?"

McCloskey shrugged. "Yeah, I guess."

She fixed the suspect's face. "And by *take care of it himself*, you mean kill this person?"

"Yeah, that's what I thought she meant." He paused. "All I know is I only took out Breslin. You have to ask Willa and her dude, Verlin Yashiro or whatever, about that—"

"Oh we intend to," promised Leila, feeling they had turned the corner in nailing their chief suspects in the dual murders. She stood up, looking down at the triggerman in Parker Breslin's murder. "I hope for your sake you continue to cooperate. It won't get you out of this jam altogether, but it might give you a little more peace of mind and a lighter sentence."

She seriously doubted the latter point. The County of Maui Department of the Prosecuting Attorney didn't take too kindly to execution-style murders on the island and, as such, weren't likely to cut him any slack.

But McCloskey didn't have to know that.

* * *

Ferguson and Rachel were in the crime lab as ballistics specialist Gil Delfino had news on the firearm brought in from the home of murder suspect Howard McCloskey.

"It's a positive match!" Delfino declared. "The .45-caliber bullets removed from Parker Breslin's body definitely came from the .45-caliber pistol you removed from the suspect's house."

Though not surprised, Ferguson asked nevertheless: "You're sure about that?"

"Oh yeah, ballistics don't lie. The bullets had five grooves and lands that were a perfect match for several bullets from the box of .45-caliber ammo you retrieved when they were fired from the .45-caliber weapon. In other words, the ejection and firing pin marks were identical—meaning this was the gun used to shoot Parker Breslin. As a bonus, the fingerprints on the weapon belong to Howard McCloskey."

"So we've definitely got our man," Rachel said, breathing a sigh of relief.

"Sure looks that way," stated Delfino. "Between that powerful evidence and a confession, I'd say you've got a slam dunk and a half."

"Yeah, but now we need to get our woman," voiced Ferguson. "And hopefully our other man, who's up to his neck in this murder investigation."

Delfino put his hand on Ferguson's shoulder. "My bet's on you for getting the culprits to pay for their misdeeds."

Ferguson twisted his lips thoughtfully. "It's a bet we fully intend to make pay off for the Maui PD as well as the victims."

A little later, they were back in the interrogation room with Howard McCloskey. They had already updated Leila, Chung, and Seymour with their latest findings. All parties were in agreement that the noose had tightened around McCloskey's neck. But they still needed to get the goods on the masterminds behind the assassination of Parker Breslin and the murder of Joyce Yashiro.

With that in mind, Ferguson gave the suspect a hard look. "I'm not going to beat around the bush, McCloskey. You're in a heap of trouble. We've got the murder weapon that tested positive as the one used to kill Parker Breslin. It also had your prints on it, so we know you pulled the trigger. We also have your cell phone records showing that you called Willa Takeyama shortly before and after the estimated time of death, and twenty other times in the week leading up to the hit."

"Yeah, I know I'm screwed," McCloskey said forlornly.

"That's about the size of it. But you don't have to go down alone. Not when you can bring down the person who hired you. And maybe even her lover and partner in crime, Verlin Yashiro."

McCloskey eyed him warily. "What do I get out of this?" he asked. "I mean, I know Willa shouldn't get away with it, but I'm facing hard time. What can you do about that?"

Why am I not surprised that he wants something as incentive to put his partners in crime behind bars? Ferguson asked himself. He expected as much from a habitually violent offender, but didn't want him to think for one minute that his assistance would lead to something akin to a miracle insofar as not paying the piper for his role in the death of Parker Breslin.

"You're going to have to pay for what you did," Ferguson told the admitted killer quite candidly. "However, if you play ball, I can certainly put in a good word to the prosecutor that you cooperated. I can't offer you anything more than that."

As he waited to see if McCloskey would bite the bait, Ferguson exchanged glances with Rachel.

After a moment or two of contemplation, McCloskey tilted his head and asked: "What do you want me to do?"

Rachel met his eyes and said equably: "We'd like you to wear a wire and see if you can get Willa to open up about hiring you and maybe also her involvement, along with Yashiro's, in the murder of his wife Joyce."

McCloskey stared at the request, before responding shakily: "Okay, I'll do it."

Ferguson nodded and said: "We'll set it up—"

CHAPTER 26

The detectives and a technician were in the police van with the electronic surveillance equipment they would use to monitor the conversation between Howard McCloskey and Willa Takeyama. McCloskey had arranged to meet with Willa in her car in Kihei on Moolio Place.

"Quiet everyone!" Leila ordered as they listened in, hoping McCloskey could get her to talk.

"Why are we meeting?" Willa demanded.

"I just thought we should talk," McCloskey responded coolly.

"We have nothing more to talk about."

"I think we do. The ten grand you gave me to kill your ex isn't enough."

"It's what we agreed on," she spat.

Leila silently applauded the admission to conspiracy to commit murder that Willa Takeyama had unsuspectingly just made on tape.

"Yeah, I know," McCloskey told her, "but the cops have been asking around—looking for Breslin's shooter. I need to get off the island till things settle down."

"I hope you weren't stupid enough to keep the gun," Willa said tartly.

"Of course not," he said convincingly. "I just need another ten grand and then I'm out of here."

"I can't just come up with that kind of money out of thin air," she complained. "I'll need a few days to get it, and then I never want to see you again!"

"Fine." He paused and Leila hoped McCloskey had not forgotten to try to get her to implicate Verlin Yashiro in the murder of his wife. "So did you ever get anyone else to take out your boyfriend's wife?" McCloskey asked casually.

"What's it to you?" Willa asked suspiciously.

"Just asking," he said, trying to cover himself. "I heard about her being killed on the beach and then they showed Verlin Yashiro's picture on TV and said he was the husband and a suspect. I remember you told me he would take care of it himself..."

"Well forget what you heard and mind your own damn business," she warned him.

"Okay, okay," he said unevenly. "You're right it's none of my business. And as soon you get me that ten grand, we'll go our separate ways."

"I'll be in touch," Willa told him.

"Yeah," McCloskey muttered and got out of the car, before they heard it drive off.

Leila glanced around the van. That was a tacit admission from Willa that Yashiro had killed his wife, while conspiring with Willa and using her as his alibi. But would that be enough to have them both arrested, much less indicted?

"Did you get any of that?" asked McCloskey.

"We got it all," Ferguson told him. "Your work is done—for now."

Leila understood that they would still need him to testify against Willa and Yashiro, while owning up to what he did himself, to go with the strong evidence in the case against him.

The signal was given for nearby detectives to re-arrest McCloskey for the murder of Parker Breslin.

Next up was Willa Takeyama.

* * *

Rachel and Leila waited in the police sedan as Willa parked her car in the driveway. They had decided to wait until she got home to make the arrest—but planned to do it before she could get inside and expose her daughter to the trauma. Rachel was less concerned about Willa's mother, Lynnette Takeyama, as mother and daughter seemed to be cut from the same cloth. They were both overprotective of their daughters. Only one took it too far, resorting to murder.

When Willa emerged from the vehicle, Rachel and Leila followed suit, with Ferguson and Chung serving as back up, if needed.

"Willa Takeyama," Rachel said, tempted to add her married name, but she did not, as she no longer deserved to carry the name of the man she had killed.

Willa turned around, startled. "Yes—"

"You're under arrest for conspiracy to commit murder in the death of your ex-husband, Parker Breslin..." Rachel then read Willa her rights as Leila handcuffed her.

Though clearly agitated, Willa did not resist, seemingly more concerned that her daughter Marie did not witness it.

Rachel put her in the back of the police car.

One down, one killer to go...

* * *

Leila sat beside Rachel and across from Willa Takeyama as the handcuffed woman who was suspected of orchestrating the murder of her ex-husband, Parker Breslin, sat mute. While Leila was happy to know that they had a solid case against her for Breslin's murder, she was more interested in tying Willa to the murder of Joyce Yashiro. Or, to put it another way, discrediting Verlin Yashiro's alibi for his wife's murder.

"You're going away for a very long time," Rachel told the suspect bluntly. "You might as well have pulled the trigger yourself and pumped three bullets into your ex-husband's body."

Willa wrinkled her nose. "This is crazy. I had nothing to do with that."

It amazed Leila just how conniving and ridiculous some killers were. Did she really think they would have charged her with conspiracy to commit murder if they could not back it up? Was she that arrogant to believe she would somehow be able to walk away from this?

Not this time.

"Actually, you had everything to do with it," Rachel told her. "We know you lied about waiting for Parker to pick up your daughter the day he was murdered. In reality, you were supposed to deliver her to your ex, but that would have messed up your plan to steer clear of the crime scene you set up."

Willa gave her an outraged look. "I don't know who has been feeding you this nonsense, but—"

"Believe it or not, most of it came directly from you," Rachel said with pleasure. "We have you on tape admitting that you gave Howard McCloskey $10,000 to murder Parker Breslin and agreeing to give him another ten grand as hush money so he could flee Maui."

Willa's nostrils flared. "That bastard!"

"Now now, no name calling please," Rachel said comically. "It was our suggestion that he wear a wire and get you to talk—which McCloskey did shockingly well, considering the gravity of the charges he faces: starting with first degree murder and unlawful use of a weapon by a felon. But what you face is even worse, given that you put this whole thing into motion."

For the first time, Leila detected fear in the suspect's face. Or was it contempt? Probably both.

"Look, I never meant for things to go that far," Willa said shakily.

"Really? Well, just how far did you expect them to go?" Rachel asked.

"He was only supposed to scare Parker, that's all. I just wanted him to back off trying to get custody of our daughter."

"I'm afraid that won't fly," Rachel snapped. "You see, in addition to Howard McCloskey's detailed statement and the murder weapon—which, by the way, he didn't get rid of after all—we have phone records of multiple calls he made to you and vice versa, before, during, and after the deed was done—Parker Breslin gunned down at your bequest. So you see, there is no wiggle room here. What you did is abominable as a mother or even a daughter. Now you're going to pay a very big price for it."

Rachel eyed Leila, and she realized this was her moment to step in. "Detective Lancaster is right. They're going to throw the book at you for taking away the life of your child's father in such a cruel way. But there may be something we can do to help your mother get custody of your daughter, which I'm sure you'd prefer." Leila took a deliberate pause while watching her reaction, before continuing. "We know that you and Verlin Yashiro cooked up this plot together. You admitted to it, more or less, on tape to McCloskey. Yashiro wanted his estranged wife out of the picture for his own reasons as much as you wanted your ex out of your life. But, right now, you're the only one going down, while Yashiro could remain free as a bird. After all, you're his alibi for the morning when Yashiro's wife was suffocated and strangled on Kaanapali Beach. Once you go down, he'll be able to turn his attention to someone else to charm and cuddle up to, while you're rotting away in prison. Is that what you want?"

Willa sucked in a deep breath and muttered: "No."

Leila made eye contact with Rachel and back to the suspect, feeling she was ready to break. "So are you standing by your story that Yashiro was with you that awful morning? Or are you ready to tell the truth?"

"I'll tell the truth...." Willa looked down at the table glumly. "I lied about being with Verlin that morning. It was all part of the plan to make sure we both had alibis for Joyce's murder and Parker's murder—which we planned together from the very beginning." She sighed, raising her face to look at them. "It was Verlin who killed his wife. He poisoned her dog the day before, to keep it at home; then he followed Joyce to the beach that morning, strangled her with the zip line so it looked like the Zip Line Killer had done it, then went back home and told me to come over."

Rachel peered at her. "And this is the truth that you're willing to testify to in a court of law?"

"Yes, it's what happened and I'll testify against Verlin." She paused, her eyes watery. "I doubt he ever truly loved me, or I him, for that matter. We were only fooling ourselves, hoping this whole thing wouldn't somehow blow up in our faces. Now it looks like it has—"

"That's usually the case," Leila told her unsympathetically. "Verlin Yashiro will get what's coming to him, we can promise you that much."

She stood and Rachel did as well. They left Willa sitting there, appearing emotionally exhausted as the reality of her dire situation seemed to dawn on her.

Outside the room, the detectives conferred with their partners and Lieutenant Seymour, who said: "Good job. A warrant has been issued for the arrest of Verlin Yashiro, with another to search his condo. I'm guessing the arrogant son of a bitch probably still has the zip line he used to murder his wife."

Leila nodded hopefully to that effect and, after looking at Chung, said with satisfaction: "Let's go pick up Mr. Yashiro."

"You won't have to tell me twice," he responded eagerly.

And so she didn't.

CHAPTER 27

Leila and Chung went to the Aloha Architectural Group place of business and were stopped by Kalena Kimbrough, the manager.

"Aloha. Can I help you?"

Leila showed her ID. "Detective Sergeant Kahana and Detective Chung. We're here to see Verlin Yashiro."

"I'm afraid he's in a meeting," she said.

"That's too bad," Chung told her. "Where is he?"

Kalena swallowed. "Right this way—"

Leila and Chung followed closely behind her, until they rounded a corner and entered a conference room. A number of people were sitting around a large table, with Yashiro at the head, speaking.

Even as they neared him, he kept talking, as if to get in his last words before all hell broke loose in the world he had established.

At the last moment, Yashiro eyed Leila sharply and asked: "What is this?"

She held his gaze and responded succinctly: "Verlin Yashiro, you're under arrest for the murder of your wife, Joyce Yashiro, and conspiracy to commit murder in the death of Parker Breslin."

"What—?" His face contorted with exaggerated disbelief. "There must be some mistake."

"Yeah and you made it," Chung barked while cuffing him. "And now you're going to pay for your crimes."

"You have the right to remain silent," Leila told him as the others in the room looked on with incredulity. "Anything you say can and will be used against you in a court of law..."

Once she had finished, they led the shell-shocked double murder suspect out of the room and past his former colleagues.

* * *

Armed with a search warrant, Leila, Rachel, and Ferguson, along with two officers, went to Verlin Yashiro's condominium.

His son, Ayato, opened the door. He looked surprised to see them.

"What's going on...?"

To Leila, it looked like he was back on meth. Or maybe he never stopped, apart from when he was in custody. "We have a warrant to search the place."

"What are you looking for?" he asked.

"Any evidence to support your father's arrest for the murder of your mother."

Ayato reacted with denial. "That's impossible!"

"I only wish that were true," Leila told him. "He did it, and more." She slapped the warrant in his hands. "Now stay out of the way while we do our job!"

While an officer kept him from tampering with potential evidence, they put on latex gloves and began to look around.

The place was spacious and immaculate with art deco furniture and Hawaiian tropical plants. Leila imagined Yashiro spending time there with his lover, Willa Takeyama, while they went over their stories and made definitive plans to kill their spouses or exes.

She followed Rachel into the master suite, where both searched through drawers, cabinets, and the closet.

"This guy had a good thing going," remarked Rachel, "and threw it all away for what—a few rolls in the hay and an ill-fated attempt to get away with murder?"

"Isn't that how it usually works?" Leila responded. "In Yashiro's case, I believe it was less about the sex and more about the value of his wife's death—such as insurance, her house, and anything else that could help him overcome financial difficulties."

"See where that gets him now," hissed Rachel.

Leila opened up a trunk that was in the walk-in closet and found what she was looking for. "Well, what do we have here...?"

She opened up a zip line kit and carefully removed the roll of nylon coated steel tape. It had clearly been cut, and Leila had no reason to believe it was for anything other than cold-blooded murder.

"I'd say we have Verlin Yashiro dead to rights," Rachel said gleefully.

Leila smiled in complete agreement.

* * *

"Your alibi has been shot to hell, Yashiro," Seymour told the handcuffed suspect as he sat mute in the interrogation room. "That's right; we know you lied about being with Willa Takeyama while your wife was being murdered on the beach. Takeyama threw you under the bus in order to save her own ass—"

Leila watched her boss and former partner in action and couldn't help but wonder if he missed the daily grind and challenges of detective work.

Yashiro's eyes batted disdainfully behind his glasses. "Whatever Willa is saying now, she's lying."

"I don't think so," Seymour argued. "The proof is in the pudding, as they say. That includes your role in orchestrating the execution of Parker Breslin—your lover's ex-husband and the father of her seven-year-old daughter."

"That's preposterous!" Yashiro exclaimed defiantly. "I had nothing to do with Breslin's death!"

"We both know that's not true," Leila voiced intently, taking her turn at bat in attacking the suspect. "The $10,000 Willa gave to Howard McCloskey to murder Parker Breslin was traced back to guess who—you!" She watched his reaction go from she said, he said confidence to seeming surrender to the facts that were indefensible. "That's what you call conspiracy to commit murder! As if that wasn't enough, we also have solid evidence in the murder of your wife—the zip line kit from which you used a piece of the wire to strangle her, while pretending to be the serial killer known as the Zip Line Killer. The problem is Joyce actually died from suffocation when you forced her face into the sand—meaning your attempt to lay blame on another killer failed miserably. So you see we aren't just blowing smoke to get your attention. *You* did this, Yashiro, along with Willa Takeyama, and there's no more running from it."

Yashiro sneered at her. "I think I'd like to see my lawyer now."

"That's your prerogative," Seymour said. "However, even Ms. Arakaki won't be able to get you out of this mess. Taking out your wife and your lover's ex-husband is serious business. Hope it was worth it, though I don't see how it could be."

"You don't know a damned thing," Yashiro retorted angrily. "Don't you see? There was no other choice. Joyce was bleeding me dry and being a bitch about it. I needed her out of my life and I needed money to keep my business from going under. As for Willa's husband, that asshole was standing between her and her daughter. He needed to go so she could raise her the right way. We were trying to help each other and enjoy some companionship at the same time. The casualties just went along with the program."

"As will the repercussions," Leila said, glaring at him with astonishment that he would try to justify two acts of cold-blooded murder. "Did you ever consider just once what this might do to your son?"

Yashiro sighed deeply as he stared at the question, before responding colorlessly: "Ayato's a big boy and he understands that sometimes things happen. He can take care of himself."

Leila wasn't so sure about that, given the son's drug habit and poor excuse for a father. But that wasn't her problem to solve. "Whatever plans you and Willa Takeyama may have envisioned for the future have gone up in smoke and flames. Try snuffing that out!"

Seymour signaled for a guard to come in. "Take Mr. Yashiro back to his cell till his attorney arrives."

Leila watched as the broken killer was led away. She wasn't sure how much of his last words—when he outlined the conspiracy to murder their former spouses—would be admissible in a court of law once he had requested his lawyer, but Leila was sure it would come out one way or the other. Killers often did themselves in, not with mere words, but dire actions that could not be denied.

"We've got them!" Seymour said, almost with relief a few minutes later in his office.

Leila smiled. "Yes, I'd say so."

"Yashiro and Takeyama are some pieces of work."

Leila concurred. "That's one way to put it."

"Guess that sink or swim philosophy fits those two perfectly," he said.

"No swimming will ever bring them back to the surface," Leila said, in keeping up with the water analogies. "But then, that's what separates the good guys from the bad ones. The latter always tend to err on the side of stupidity and miscalculation—till it catches up to them."

Seymour grinned. "I miss the action, and partnering with you."

Leila lifted a brow, surprised at his admission. But she took it the way she assumed it was intended: strictly a professional observation. Nevertheless, she told him, mindful that she had moved on relationship-wise: "I think you're doing just fine as our lieutenant. Keep up the good work, Seymour."

He chuckled. "I will if you do."

"Deal," she told him, and walked away, literally and figuratively, while feeling grateful that Verlin Yashiro and Willa Takeyama were locked away, not likely to hurt anyone else ever again.

CHAPTER 28

On Saturday morning, Leila went horseback riding with Maxwell. She rode a gorgeous American Quarter Horse named Kosho, which was the Japanese word for pepper. They made their way through lush valleys, pineapple fields, and ironwood forests, while taking in panoramic views of Maui and neighboring islands.

Losing herself in the spectacular surroundings that she knew all too well, Leila said: "It's just so beautiful here."

"I agree," Maxwell said atop his Thoroughbred horse named Koa, Hawaiian for warrior. "I love getting away from the day-to-day stuff up here."

"If only everyone was so fortunate to have this magnificent escape," she said dreamily.

"I know. It was my big dream when I moved to Maui and I found a way to make it happen."

"Lucky you."

He faced her. "I am lucky getting to spend time with you."

"I feel the same way," she told him, flattered by his kind words. Being able to relax with a leisurely ride without murder on her mind was just what she needed.

Maxwell grinned. "Good."

They rode for a while longer and eventually stopped for a picnic he had prepared; feeding each other turkey sandwiches and pineapple coleslaw, washing it down with bottled passion fruit juice.

When they returned to his home, Maxwell gave Leila a tour. Built of cedar, stone, and glass, it was oceanfront and full of character, surrounded by fruit trees and cane grass. She was blown away as they went from room to room, each carefully appointed with modern furnishings and bamboo flooring.

Upon entering the master suite, Maxwell said: "And this is where I sleep."

Leila surveyed the room with a king-sized bed surrounded by Japanese and American furniture. Smiling at him, she asked teasingly: "Are you tired?"

He chuckled, placing his hands around her waist, drawing her near. "Not especially. How about you?"

Feeling aroused by his closeness and good looks, she responded boldly: "I'm wide awake, but I wouldn't mind trying that bed out for size."

"Then, by all means," he said huskily, "don't let me stop you."

He kissed her and Leila welcomed the feel of a man's lips upon hers again. It was clear to her that he was just as turned on as she was, so she seized the moment.

She began removing her clothes and watched as he did the same. Then they kissed some more, enjoying each other's taste and tongues.

By the time they got in bed and Maxwell slipped on protection, Leila was ready to be with him. He didn't disappoint, bringing her satisfaction almost immediately. And, again later, when they each rode the crest of exploration and experienced the fire of intimacy before returning back to earth.

Leila had almost forgotten the pleasure and passion of sexual desire and fulfillment. She was thankful to Maxwell for refreshing her memory and making her feel like a desired woman again.

She suddenly felt tired and rested her head against his chest, falling asleep in his arms, not wanting to be anywhere else.

* * *

For lunch, Renee sat in the café on Alanui Kealii Drive in Kihei with her friend, Sylvia Taniguchi. They were talking about the arrests of Verlin Yashiro and Willa Takeyama.

"Can you believe those two apparently cooked up this scheme and actually thought they would get away with it?" Sylvia asked.

Renee put down her fish burger and responded: "Seems like killers always think they'll get away with it. If they believed they would get caught, most, if not all, might think twice before going down that road. Then again, when it comes to intimate violence, nothing surprises me as to the lengths people will go to get what they want."

"I suppose you're right." Sylvia lifted her fork with coconut shrimp and looked over Renee's shoulder. "Say, isn't that your friend with benefits guy—"

Renee turned to see Franco leaving with an attractive, young Asian woman. Though she wished they didn't have an open relationship, he seemed to be comfortable with it. Meaning she could only grin and bear it at the moment.

"Yeah," she muttered nonchalantly. "So..."

Sylvia shrugged. "Nothing. I just thought you should know."

"It's cool," Renee lied. "He can see who he wants and so can I."

"If you say so."

"I do," Renee insisted, even if she was unsettled at the prospect of sharing Franco.

* * *

Shannon Nguyen always preferred to go to her apartment alone after sex, wanting to cleanse herself of the man and be in her own space. Unless, of course, they were at her place, as was the case this time. So she sent the man away, ignoring his protestations to the contrary.

She was about to take a bath, and then do some studying when the bell rang. *Oh hell, is he back for more?* she mused, already thinking of how to let him down easily without wounding his male ego too much.

"Just a minute," she said, tightening her robe.

She opened the door and immediately knew it was a big mistake. One that was too late to correct.

Didn't mean she couldn't try.

She attempted to close the door, but he blocked it with his foot and forced his way in.

Even then, she was hopeful that she could somehow reason with him to not do anything stupid. She even told him she had kept her mouth shut about what she saw. He didn't have to know that wasn't really the case.

Before she could contemplate her next move, Shannon saw a gloved fist heading directly toward her face. She tried at the last moment to avert it, but it caught her flush on the jaw. She went down like a boxer's opponent, seeing stars and feeling pain in her face. Her robe had come open, exposing her nakedness.

He was suddenly on top of her, his weight sucking the air from her lungs. Shannon was still pretty much out of it when she noticed the zip line he was flexing. She raised her arms, attempting to somehow block him, but he easily cast them aside. The next thing she knew, he had wrapped the zip line around her neck, twisted it violently, and began to strangle her.

As the wire cut through her neck, causing blood to ooze out, Shannon felt the bile rise to her throat. She was going to die and there wasn't anything she could do about it—other than pray the end came quickly.

It did.

* * *

He applied pressure, tightening the zip line to the point where the veins bulged from her throat and his target's eyes

223

practically popped from their sockets. Her chest heaved and her breath grew labored before her eyes shut and her body went limp.

Wanting to be sure she wouldn't somehow come back to life, he kept the zip line secure around her neck for a while longer till satisfied the end had come.

Only then did he climb off the corpse, leaving the wire carved into her throat. He had to get the hell out of there before anyone spotted him.

But first, there was just one thing he needed...

He went to her bedroom and spotted some jewelry on the dresser. He grabbed a nice pair of pearl earrings as a souvenir.

When the dust settled, he might come back later to gloat over his victory as another victim bit the dust.

But, for now, staying ahead of the game was his top priority. He left the same way he came in with no one being the wiser.

CHAPTER 29

The moment they received the call that a dead woman was found in an apartment at 74 Vevau Street in Kahului, Detective Jonny Chung had a bad feeling. He had been to that apartment before. But it was only when he actually saw the decedent lying on the living room hardwood floor—with one side of her face swollen, her breasts and lower extremities exposed through an open robe—that his heart sank.

He looked now at the zip line wrapped severely around her neck—the telltale calling card of the notorious Zip Line Killer. *How the hell could this happen?* Chung asked himself, knowing he had only recently had sex with the victim in that very apartment.

Now she was dead—murdered by some maniac.

"Her name's Shannon Nguyen," Leila announced, holding the victim's driver's license with a latex glove. "She's twenty-one, and apparently lives here alone."

Chung had expected his partner to say that the victim looked familiar. They had both first seen her at the College of Maui when they were there to interview instructor Glenn Diamont, who was once a suspect in the murder of Joyce

Yashiro. But his alibi had held up and the actual killer was the victim's spouse.

Apparently, Leila had not made the connection or detected his interest in the sexy coed, for which he was thankful. Otherwise, he'd have some explaining to do.

The victim had been discovered by her next-door neighbor and fellow coed, Maggie Ellington. In Chung's mind, if she had come a little earlier, she might have become a victim of the serial killer too.

"Since there appears to be no break in," Leila was saying, "I'm guessing she knew her killer."

Chung swallowed thickly. "Yeah, I was thinking the same thing. We need to find out who she's been hanging out with and if she got on someone's bad side."

Leila looked at him. "You think the Zip Line Killer could be a student?"

"Why not?" Chung said. "Though not all the victims of the killer were students, if he was a student, he could easily move around the island and associate with young women without casting much suspicion."

"True." Leila wrinkled her nose. "If our serial killer has decided to come out of hiding, he must have either been bored—or did so out of fear of being detected."

"Either of which could give us the upper hand," suggested Chung.

"Why don't we see if the killer left behind any other clues," Leila muttered. "while being careful not to taint any evidence before the CSI unit arrives."

"Good idea." In fact, Chung believed it was a necessity for him to look around, especially in the bedroom, to make sure he didn't leave anything that could tie him to the victim.

He headed to the bedroom before she could. Seeing the twin-sized bed, he remembered making the most of it with Shannon, who was nearly his match when it came to sex and pleasuring. Looking at items on the dresser, which included makeup, jewelry, perfume, and knickknacks, he spotted the card he had given her just before they said their goodbyes—in case Shannon ever wanted a repeat performance.

Chung frowned. Now that was something neither of them would ever get the chance to experience, thanks to the killer snuffing out her life before she could even make it to twenty-two.

He slipped the card into his pocket just as Leila walked in.

"Find anything?" she asked routinely.

Chung glanced again at the dresser. "Nothing unusual," he responded, and opened a couple of drawers for effect. "From the looks of it, I'd say her killer surprised her at the front door, attacked her before she could get away, then left without going anywhere else in the place." Even saying that, he realized the killer could have visited the victim previously, which may have cost Shannon her life.

"Maybe." Leila gave the room the once over. "We'll check with the complex manager to see if there's video surveillance. If lucky, we might be able to see the killer leaving this building and pinpoint the time it occurred."

"Yeah," he agreed thoughtfully, as they both headed out to greet the crime scene technicians arriving.

* * *

Leila recognized the victim right away. How could she not? She had been flirting with college instructor Glenn Diamont when they paid him a visit while investigating Joyce Yashiro's death. Leila could tell that Chung recognized her too. So why did he pretend she was a total stranger to him? Given his obvious attraction to her that day, is it possible he could have followed up by pursuing Shannon Nguyen? She wouldn't put it past him with his track record, at least according to other detectives.

Was it possible he knew more about Shannon's death than he'd let on? *Please don't be involved in this, Chung,* Leila mused, hating to think that he could have accidentally killed the girl perhaps from rough sex, then panicked and tried to make it look like the work of the Zip Line Killer, as Verlin Yashiro had tried unsuccessfully to do.

Admittedly, other than the fact that the victim's body was fully exposed in the front, there was no indication of rough sex, with the exception of the discoloration of her cheek, apparently from being hit.

Leila decided it was best not to approach Chung with her concerns just yet. Or jump to the wrong conclusions without learning more about the victim and the circumstances of her death.

She watched as Patricia Lee, the coroner's physician came in to supervise removal of the body and give her initial assessment of the cause of death.

"Hey," she said glumly.

"I know, it's just the type of thing to suck the life out of your day, no pun intended," Leila said.

"It's certainly not very funny when someone who looks as young as this one winds up dead." Patricia adjusted her glasses as she dropped to one knee to examine the decedent. "Looks like this was personal to a certain extent." With gloves on, she turned the victim's face. "That bruise on her right cheek could only have come from a fist. She must have really pissed someone off."

"How about a serial killer?" Leila asked, glancing at the zip line wrapped around the victim's neck.

"The evidence is certainly there to draw that conclusion," Patricia said, "unlike your last case that turned out to be due to suffocation. Whoever killed this poor girl really did a number on her, as far as using that cord to perfection to get the intended job done. My preliminary belief, based on what I see, including blood seeping from her ears, is that she died from strangulation. There's no indication at this point that a rape occurred. Knowing you'd like a more definitive conclusion, I'll come in tomorrow to conduct the autopsy so you can see if your serial killer is back on the prowl."

"Mahalo," Leila told her, and glanced over at Chung who was talking to the female crime scene photographer.

"It's what I do," Patricia said. "It will be up to you and your unit to run with it."

"We intend to. We might even gallop all the way to the finish line."

Patricia smiled. "That would work."

Leila thought about riding horses, which she'd done again in the afternoon after she and Maxwell made love. Then, before they could make further plans for the day, duty called. Unfortunately, that came with her territory and she hoped it was something he could respect if not support wholeheartedly.

* * *

The next day the official word came in from the coroner's physician. Shannon Nguyen's death was ruled a homicide, with the cause of death strangulation. A sexual assault of the victim was ruled out. Given the stark similarities in the M.O., type of zip line used, and the precise way in which it was left tangled around the victim's neck, as if to rub it in the faces of detectives at the victim's expense, the general opinion among detectives who had worked the case was that it was the work of the Zip Line Killer. There was also a feeling that the serial killer had taken this murder more personally than the previous ones in punching the victim in the face and murdering her when she was naked.

Leila and Seymour, who were the first in the department to investigate this serial killer, went over the case with other members of the division, with Chung also having a vested interest as her new partner. It was agreed that, short of other homicides occurring, this one needed to be a priority, fearing the killer may be becoming brazen and desperate—placing more women at risk.

Afterward, Seymour cornered Leila and asked: "Got a sec?"

"Sure," she responded. "What's up?"

"Let's go to my office," he said cryptically.

"Uh, all right."

Leila followed him, not believing for one moment that he would try to put the moves on her, as had been the case more than once during their brief relationship. She thought about the new man in her life. Though it was hard to compare one man to the next, it was inevitable. As far as she was concerned, things had turned out for the best. She was sure Seymour concurred.

"Have a seat," he said in a serious tone.

Leila's first thought was that Chung had been linked to Shannon Nguyen's murder, leaving her feeling weak.

Instead, Seymour said: "I thought you should know that I've asked an FBI criminal profiler to drop in and lend a helping hand to give us some idea what the hell we're up against with this serial killer who appears to be living and hiding amongst us, sometimes in plain view."

Leila had no problem with outside help, unlike Seymour once did himself before he became lieutenant of the unit. Obviously, he had a different perspective as the level of authority increased. "Sounds good to me," she said. "When is he or she arriving?"

"It's a he. Name's Landon Herridge. He'll be flying in from Quantico tomorrow. I was hoping you could get together with him one-on-one and compare thoughts on the case as someone who probably knows it best—before he gives his profile of the killer to the homicide squad."

If she didn't know better, which she did, Leila might think he was trying to set her up with Herridge. But since he likely wouldn't be on Maui for long and was probably happily married like Seymour presumably was these days, she wasn't interested in going down that road—not when she had Maxwell treating her like a Hawaiian queen.

"I'd be happy to have lunch with him. Maybe he can give me some tips on what makes this killer tick."

Seymour grinned. "From what I've heard about Herridge, he is nothing if not thorough, so I'm sure he can give you something to work with in trying to flush out the Zip Line Killer."

"I look forward to it," she said, leaving at that.

Back at her desk, Chung approached her. "So what did Seymour want?"

Leila almost detected fear in his face. Or was that just her imagination? Did he have something to fear regarding the death of Shannon Nguyen?

"To tell me that an FBI profiler is coming tomorrow," she replied nonchalantly.

He shrugged. "Sounds like fun."

Leila gazed at him, picking up the sarcasm in his tone. "Maybe he'll give us something useful that will help lead to the perp's arrest."

"I'm all ears," Chung insisted.

"So am I," she said, in case there was something he needed to get off his chest.

CHAPTER 30

On Monday morning, Renee sat at her computer staring at the picture of Shannon Nguyen on the screen. She was believed to be the latest strangulation victim of the so-called Zip Line Killer.

A chill ripped through Renee in that moment. She recognized the woman as someone she had seen Franco with the same day she was murdered. And no matter how much Renee tried to convince herself she was mistaken, the journalist in her with a keen eye for memory and observation knew that she wasn't.

Shannon Nguyen was dead and the police were looking for her killer.

Could Franco actually be a serial killer?

Renee thought about the various times he had acted strangely, sometimes even joking about death and violence. Was it some sort of Freudian admission of guilt by him as a killer, just waiting for her to uncover it?

Have I been sleeping with the Zip Line Killer? she asked herself, terrified at the thought. If so, was it only a matter of time before she also became a victim like Shannon Nguyen?

Renee nearly jumped out of her skin when she felt a cold hand on her shoulder, followed by: "What are you doing?"

Realizing it was Franco, already out of the shower, she quickly put the screen in sleep mode, hoping he hadn't connected the dots.

"Nothing, really," she told him, forcing a strained smile.

He was wearing nothing but a towel. "Were you reading about that woman who was murdered yesterday?"

Renee's heart skipped a beat. Had she been caught? Would he need to eliminate her as a witness before and after the fact?

She sucked in a deep breath. "Yeah," she said nonchalantly. "They're saying it looks like the work of the Zip Line Killer and I didn't want to bore you with that."

He gave her a long look before breaking into a grin. "Mahalo for that. I'm sorry for the victim, but it does get to be a drag hearing about these murders and the ineptitude of the police. Especially when I'd rather focus on something more interesting..." He cupped her cheeks and brought their mouths together. "Like this—"

Renee let him kiss her and felt his arousal. But she wasn't about to have sex with him for a second time that morning. The very notion that she may have been sleeping with a serial killer made Renee want to puke.

But she didn't for fear of tipping her hand. She allowed the kiss to go on longer than she wanted before pulling back and standing.

"We'll have to pick up where we left off later," she lied. "I have to go to work."

Franco frowned. "Are you going to write about Shannon's murder?"

Renee met his eyes. He had just basically admitted that he knew the victim. Was that the same thing as confessing to killing her?

"Yeah, I think so," she told him routinely. "After all, it's a plausible connection to the Zip Line Killer murders that I've been working on, so..."

He grinned. "I understand. I'll get dressed and be out of your hair. As you said, we can pick this up later."

She made herself seemed interested. "I'd like that."

The moment he left the room, Renee went back to the computer and got a good look at the attractive face of the woman Franco had walked out of a café with, apparently never to be seen alive again.

As with some of his previous stayovers, Renee let Franco see himself out. She left the condo first, fearing that if he were to suspect anything, she would become his next victim.

* * *

Leila studied Landon Herridge as he sat across from her at the deli on Waiehu Beach Road in Wailuku. He was a tall, handsome man in his forties with wavy gray hair and blue-gray eyes. She wouldn't have pegged him to be an FBI profiler at a glance. But, then again, he would probably say the same thing about her being a homicide detective.

Whether or not he could lend some helpful insight into the characteristics of their serial killer remained to be seen. But she was keeping an open mind, knowing that all avenues had to be explored until he was caught.

"Thanks for taking time out of your busy schedule to meet with me," Herridge said, studying his menu.

Leila shrugged. "I would meet with any FBI agent who came to our island on behalf of the police department."

He grinned. "Fair enough. So do you have any recommendations? There are a lot of interesting choices on the menu."

"You might want to try the pineapple mango chicken," she suggested, "along with grilled mixed vegetables. If you want dessert, the paradise strawberry shortcake is really tasty."

"Done," he said.

She laughed. "That was easy."

"I usually am when it comes to food. But I can be a real hard-ass when it comes to assessing crime and criminals."

"In that case, I'll be ready for whatever comes my way," she half-joked, before deciding on the hot pastrami on rye and garden salad for herself.

After they were served, Herridge said: "So I've been studying your case of the so-called Zip Line Killer."

"What did you come up with?" Leila asked curiously, sipping her tropical fruit smoothie.

"Well, I see the killer as a nomadic sexual deviant who is driven to kill as a power hungry, self-centered, highly motivated individual who thinks he's always in control of the situation and able to keep the police at bay."

Leila rolled her eyes. "How did you reach those conclusions?"

"By being in the business of profiling thousands of criminals, mostly murderers, for more than a decade," he responded bluntly. "I looked over everything Lieutenant Seymour sent my way, and then some. Studying the victims told me a good deal about the likely perpetrator."

Leila was stuck on the sexual deviant part and said: "None of the victims were sexually assaulted. So how do you label him as a sexual offender?"

"Good question." He took a bite of the mixed vegetables. "Sexual deviants are not only those who rape or sodomize their victims, but those who murder them in order to receive sexual gratification. From the pattern of the murders, with the zip line left around the strangled women's throats, I see this as the mark of someone who wanted to be in complete control of the women till they took their dying breaths— giving him something akin to a killing orgasm."

"Okay, if you say so," Leila said, biting into her sandwich. She wasn't sure if she concurred with his explanation. But since he was the expert, she was hardly in a position to challenge it. In this case, she was glad that the sexual sadist part was in the killer's mind and not inflicted upon the women in the form of a sexual assault, adding further indignity to their victimization.

"I also believe that your killer clearly knows his way around the island, given the locations of the victims," Herridge told her. "He's probably a local, but could also be a visitor who is very familiar with Maui. He may have spent time on some of the other Hawaiian Islands too—where he may have also killed, but it has yet to be linked to him."

That sounded plausible enough to Leila. She regarded the profiler. "So how do we catch this person who always seems to stay one step ahead of us?"

Herridge met her eyes. "Well, in many of these cases what you really need is to catch a break. Be it a useful tip, an eyewitness coming forward, or a mistake on the part of the killer." He sliced into his pineapple mango chicken. "Other than that, good old fashioned police work and tracking down every lead in every nook and cranny will usually produce positive results, sooner or later."

It was the "sooner or later" part that concerned Leila. She didn't want another young woman to die at this sadist's hands. So catching him sooner would be much better for all parties concerned.

She gazed at Herridge and said to him: "I'm sure the Homicide Unit will be interested in everything you have to say."

He chuckled. "Well, probably not everything. I know there are always some skeptics when it comes to criminal profiling as a reliable mechanism for investigating crimes. But I'll take one convert at a time—"

Leila couldn't help but smile, figuring he was referring to her. And she was convinced that he did seem to bring something to the table that would help them find out what made the Zip Line Killer tick, which might be just what they needed to bring him down.

* * *

Detective Chung was surprised when Renee asked to meet with him at the Kihei café on Alanui Kealii Drive. He suspected she would try to grill him for information regarding the Shannon Nguyen investigation. And he might give her a snippet or two just to keep her coming back. The truth was they were still in the initial stages of this investigation and pursuing a few leads as they tried to track down the serial killer believed to be responsible for her death.

Chung tasted the espresso while thinking: *I want the asshole who did this to Shannon.* Even if theirs was just a one-night fling, it still burned him that she had her whole life ahead of her. Till someone decided to turn her into a victim, soon to be yesterday's news.

He thought about the FBI profiler Landon Herridge's take on the Zip Line Killer—referring to him as a white male, twenty-five to thirty-five years of age who could easily blend in, a loner and sociable at the same time, from a dysfunctional family, and one who handpicked his victims as much for them fitting certain characteristics that appealed to him as the opportunity presenting itself.

As far as Chung was concerned, he hadn't really told them anything about the man they were looking for that hadn't already been figured out. But if the department wanted to throw away money by bringing in a criminologist to educate them about their killer, who was he to complain? He would leave that to Leila, assuming she was of the same mind, since she was Herridge's point person in the department.

"Hey," he heard and looked up to see Renee standing there.

"Hey." Chung grinned, happy for the good-looking distraction. "I took the liberty of ordering you an espresso." He seemed to recall that was something she drank.

She sat down. "Thanks."

He studied her as she tasted the coffee. Her hand was trembling. Was it him or something else?

"So what's up?" he asked curiously.

Renee eyed him. "I was just wondering how the investigation was coming along regarding the murder of Shannon Nguyen?"

Why am I not surprised? Chung thought, sipping his drink. "It's coming along," he told her.

"Do you have any suspects?"

"No one's been arrested yet, if that's what you're asking." He paused. "Other than that, we're still investigating, so it's open ended."

She looked down into her coffee, as if searching for clues to the universe. When she looked up, Renee said unevenly: "I think I know who killed her—"

"Oh..." This got Chung's attention.

She nodded and said: "My boyfriend..."

Chung thought about the guy he had caught a glimpse of when he bumped into Renee at a club before meeting with Shichiro Gutierrez, a drug dealer.

"What's your boyfriend's name?"

"Franco Romalotti."

"What makes you think he had anything to do with the murder...?"

Renee explained how she and her friend saw Romalotti leave a café with Shannon Nguyen on Saturday, the same day she was killed.

"That doesn't mean he murdered her," Chung said skeptically.

"Doesn't mean he didn't either," she contended. "Doesn't it seem just a little too coincidental that Franco was with her and, hours later, she's found strangled to death?"

Chung had to admit that it was too much to just dismiss out of hand. "Maybe you're right. Did you ask him about it?"

"No way!" Her voice rose an octave. "Like I'm going to tell a possible serial killer that I saw him with his last victim." She paused. "But he did catch me reading about the case online and it seemed to freak him out."

Chung gazed at her contemplatively. "You think?"

"I don't know," she said. "Maybe I was the one freaking out. All I know is that I got a weird feeling when we talked about it. He knows something about this case—I can feel it—probably a lot more than I want to think about. If Franco is the Zip Line Killer, you need to stop him before someone else dies."

"I hear you," Chung said, believing it was worth checking out. If Franco Romalotti turned out to be the killer, it would be a big feather in his cap to be the one who nabbed him. "I'll bring Romalotti in for questioning as a person of interest."

Renee sighed. "Thank you."

"I hope you're wrong about him." He could tell she felt the same way, but believed otherwise.

* * *

Franco Romalotti sat in the interrogation room fidgeting. Chung had picked him up at his grandmother's house in Kaanapali, saying only that it was in regard to a case they were working on.

Now it was up to him to determine if Renee was onto something in pointing the finger at her part-time boyfriend. Then Leila could take a crack at him if she wanted.

Chung studied the suspect while sitting across from him. Romalotti was twenty-eight, dark-haired, tall, slender, and not bad looking. Could he be describing the Zip Line Killer?

Chung got right to the point. "We're investigating the murder of Shannon Nguyen." He watched Romalotti react the way one does when they're unnerved by something.

"What does that have to do with me?" Romalotti asked, as though not a clue.

Chung narrowed his eyes. "You were seen with her on Saturday afternoon, the day she was killed. Does that ring any bells?"

Romalotti tensed. "Yeah, we got together, went to her place, had sex, and then I left."

"You left her dead?" Chung asked tartly.

"No—she was definitely alive when I left her apartment."

"Yet she's dead now and, for the moment, you're our number one suspect." Chung let that sink in and added: "Your girlfriend certainly believes you murdered Ms. Nguyen—"

"Renee—?" Romalotti's left brow rose. "What does she have to do with this?"

Chung thought about backtracking, knowing they had both slept with her and Shannon. But only one of them was sitting there as a murder suspect. And he had Renee to thank for it.

"Her name came up during the investigation in the process of trying to track you down," Chung lied. "When we talked to her, she confessed to seeing you and Ms. Nguyen together at a café in Kihei on Alanui Kealii Drive. Since she's a reporter who was looking into the murder, it didn't take much for her to put two and two together to reach her conclusion. Once the DNA and fingerprint data comes in, I'm sure it will match yours and—"

"I didn't kill her," Romalotti said, cutting him off. "But I might know who did—"

Chung wondered if he was simply trying to throw suspicion off himself. "I'm listening..."

Romalotti rubbed his nose. "Shannon told me that she had been hooking up with one of her instructors. But she broke it off when he tried to use zip line to tie her hands during sex. She accused him, half-jokingly, of being the Zip Line Killer. Though he denied it, she said there was something in his eyes that made her believe otherwise. Then she supposedly read some articles about the victims of the serial killer that scared the hell out of her. The instructor told her if she knew what was good for her, she would keep her mouth shut, but she chose not to."

The whole story sounded way too pat. But did that mean it wasn't true?

"What's the name of this instructor?" Chung asked.

"She didn't say."

Chung frowned. "Too bad. If that's all you've got, it might not be enough to let you off the hook, especially since we can place you at the apartment complex during the time of the crime—"

"Shannon said that he worked in the Ethnic and Racial Studies Department at the College of Maui," Romalotti stated. "That's all I know."

Fortunately, that was more than enough information for Chung to hone in on another suspect—one who had been on their radar before.

CHAPTER 31

Leila sat at her desk looking over the list of names of people Shannon Nguyen knew, any of whom could have killed her. Or knew who did.

One name that wasn't on the list was Jonny Chung. She had no proof that he had been with her and he hadn't volunteered such information. As such, he got a free pass for the moment while she concentrated on more likely suspects.

You won't get away with this, whoever you are, she thought to herself. Shannon and the others deserved a better fate than he gave them. Leila knew it was up to her and the Homicide Unit to complete what they had started. Even if some other cases had managed to slow them down a bit, they were now refocused on this case—which was bad news for the killer, especially now that he had upped his game to hitting his victims. Or at least he'd hit the last one, which was something that might come back to haunt him.

"Detective Kahana..." a voice said, getting Leila's attention.

Leila lifted her face and gazed up at a leggy, thirty-something, blonde-haired, green-eyed woman. She was dressed in business casual clothing and there was a large purse strapped over one shoulder.

"That's me," Leila said. "How can I help you?"

"Actually, I hope I can help you," the woman said. "Or maybe we can help each other. My name's Skye Delaney. I'm a private investigator from Honolulu."

"Nice to meet you." Leila stood and shook her hand while thinking: *What's a PI from Honolulu doing on Maui?* "You're a long way from home, relatively speaking," she said.

"You could say that," Skye conceded. "But it's a short trip back."

Leila smiled. "So what's this about?"

"I was hired by a woman to locate her daughter—twenty-three-year-old Hisako Takumi," Skye informed her. "She went missing on Oahu the day before Joyce Yashiro was murdered here on Maui."

"I'm not sure I follow you," Leila said. "Are you suggesting they're connected?"

"That's what I was hoping you could tell me. Ms. Takumi's remains were found a couple of days ago near Kahala Beach in Honolulu. She'd apparently been dead for a while, having been strangled with a zip line. She was fully clothed and there was no evidence of sexual assault. Also, there were no fingerprints or DNA left by the perpetrator. Ms. Takumi was last seen talking to a man who said he lived on Maui. Claimed he was an instructor at a college. Witnesses were able to provide a pretty good description of the man. One witness thought she heard Hisako call him Glenn. I'm here to see if I can track this Glenn down—with your help."

"Tell me more...." Leila said with interest.

Skye pulled a composite sketch from her pocket and passed it to Leila. "As an ex-cop, I had the Honolulu PD run this through the system for a face recognition match and nothing came up. The official investigation into Hisako Takumi's murder is obviously still active, with several local suspects front and center, which I'm not buying. Maybe this man has come to your attention. I suspect Ms. Takumi's murder is either another copycat killer, like with Joyce

Yashiro, or it's the work of your Zip Line Killer, who I understand has struck again. Given that you've worked both cases, well, here I am..."

Leila peered at the sketch, which she had to admit was every bit as detailed as her sketches were. It only took one good look at the suspect's face, coupled with the name Glenn that the victim had mentioned, for a bell to ring.

Glenn Diamont.

He taught at the College of Maui and had been a suspect in Joyce Yashiro's murder. Ironically, Diamont's alibi was that he had been in Honolulu at the time, which had checked out. It also placed him there around the time Hisako Takumi was killed.

Was he innocent of one murder only to be guilty of another? And possibly several more as the Zip Line Killer?

Leila looked at Skye. "Yes, he was a suspect in Joyce Yashiro's murder."

Skye cocked a brow. "Really...?"

"Yes, and he was cleared when we learned that he had attended a conference in Honolulu at the time."

"Wow!" Skye said. "What are the odds?"

"Not very good, I'm afraid," Leila muttered flatly, wondering if Diamont was actually their guy. "Especially since Joyce Yashiro had accused him of stalking her. It's not a very big jump from stalking to murder and then serial murder."

"This is so weird," Skye said. "But I guess it usually is when dealing with murder."

"It is in my world," agreed Leila.

"I think I'd like to have a talk with Glenn Diamont," Skye told her.

"You and me both," Leila said.

"Make that three of us," they heard a voice say.

Leila turned to see Chung approaching. "Who's this?" he asked, gazing at Skye.

She introduced herself: "Skye Delaney, private detective."

"Nice to meet you," he said.

Leila didn't doubt it. She was happy to see, though, that the search for Shannon Nguyen's killer had moved away from him.

"You too," Skye told him.

"So what's this about going to see Glenn Diamont?" he asked.

Leila ran the whole thing by him, with Skye adding a few details here and there.

"I think he murdered Shannon Nguyen, along with several others," Leila told him bluntly.

Chung was looking at the composite sketch, when he said: "I think you're right about Diamont..." There was an edge to his tone, as though he knew something she didn't.

"What do you have?" she asked instinctively.

"A friend of Nguyen's told me she was involved with an instructor who worked in the College of Maui's Ethnic and Racial Studies Department—and that he liked using zip lines to tie up his partners while having sex. In addition, she reportedly found articles on the Zip Line Killer's victims, scaring the crap out of her. The instructor warned her not to say anything about it—or else."

"And you believe this friend?" questioned Leila.

"Yeah, I think he's on the level," Chung said. "And considering that we saw Shannon Nguyen cozying up to Diamont, the pieces fit—especially with the Honolulu murder Skye brought to the table."

"If the info I've given you can help bring down a serial killer, it's good for everyone on both islands," Skye said.

"True," Leila agreed. Her cell phone buzzed. She answered it and listened to the caller. "We'll be right there," she told him, disconnecting and then turning to Chung. "It was Lovato... He's got something on the apartment surveillance video—"

* * *

In the crime lab, Leila, Chung, and Skye Delaney stood over forensic video tech David Lovato as he sat in front of his equipment.

"What did you find?" Leila asked anxiously.

Lovato scratched his cheek. "Well, as you can imagine, there was a lot of coming and going at the apartment complex and the security cameras could only catch a small part of it. But, based on the estimated time of death, I was able to isolate some footage you might find interesting."

"Get to it, already," Chung barked at him.

"Okay, okay. Here we go..." Lovato started the video. "Now pay close attention. There's this guy coming from the complex..."

Leila noted the image of a man in his late twenties, slim, with black or dark brown hair. It wasn't Glenn Diamont.

"His name is Franco Romalotti," Chung informed her. "He was banging Shannon Nguyen. The two did the nasty just before the murder. I'm guessing the killer waited for Romalotti to leave before catching Nguyen off guard."

Leila frowned at Lovato. "Is that all you've got...?"

"No, I have one more suspect for you—" he said, moving the footage forward.

Leila watched the man move rapidly from the apartment building toward the parking lot. "Can you bring that in closer?"

"No problem."

"Okay, now slow it down," she said.

Lovato followed her instructions. "How's that...?"

"Perfect." Leila's eyes widened as she got a good look at the man who had become their number one suspect in the murder of at least two women, including Shannon Nguyen. "It's Diamont!"

"A dead ringer for the person in the composite sketch," Skye said.

"No kidding," Chung added. "We can now place Glenn Diamont at the scene of the crime clearly trying to sneak away."

Leila concurred. "When you add that to everything else, we've got more than enough circumstantial evidence to get a warrant for his arrest on suspicion of murder in the deaths of Shannon Nguyen and Hisako Takumi, for starters."

"Let's go get the son of a bitch!" Chung said enthusiastically.

"Yeah, let's go," said Leila, equally eager to get him into police custody.

"Mind if I tag along?" Skye asked.

Normally Leila wasn't high on civilians accompanying them on potentially dangerous missions. But she looked like she could take care of herself. Besides, it was Skye Delaney whose private detective skills helped break the case.

"Be our guest," she told her. "Just stay out of the way."

Skye smiled and Leila maintained her nothing-but-business face as they prepared to go after a possible serial killer.

CHAPTER 32

Leila, Chung, and other detectives, along with several uniformed officers, converged on a two-story home on Kopiko Street in Wailuku. A silver Land Rover was parked in a carport.

Armed with her department-issued Glock 23 pistol and wearing a bulletproof vest, Leila motioned for the officers to kick the door open.

They did and Leila led the way in, announcing them as law enforcement. Rushing up the steps, she opened the first door she came to and, with gun drawn and ready to fire, saw Glenn Diamont getting out of bed, half-naked. Still in the bed and attempting to cover up, was a young woman. Leila imagined she was another coed like Shannon Nguyen, who perhaps would end up with a similar fate.

"Stay there!" Leila ordered her.

"What's the meaning of this?" Diamont asked, his face contorted with rancor as he was rushed by officers and quickly handcuffed.

"We have a warrant to search this place," she told him unkindly.

"For what?" He rolled his eyes. "You don't still think I had anything to do with Joyce's death, do you?"

"No, that one's on her bastard husband," Leila hated to say. "Unfortunately, you're in the hot seat again—this time in connection with the death of Shannon Nguyen."

Leila watched the young woman react, prompting her to say: "If you knew Shannon, consider yourself fortunate, as your lover here murdered her—"

Diamont glared at her. "That's ridiculous!"

"I don't think so," Leila argued. "You're going down for this."

"You have no proof of anything," he snorted.

"Maybe more than you think," Chung said, entering the room. In his latex gloved hand was a plastic bag. It contained women's items, including pearl earrings. "Found these stashed away in another room. I'm guessing these belonged to your victims and you took them as trophies of the kills—"

"I've got something else," Officer Marilyn Tamayose said from the doorway while holding a plastic bag. "We found zip line, rope, a cutter, and gloves in a storage room."

Leila walked up to the suspect's smug face. "Has the cat suddenly snatched out your tongue?" He sneered, but remained silent. No matter. She'd heard enough and said with disdain while producing a document: "By the way, in case you hadn't already figured it out... Glenn Diamont, we have a warrant for you arrest for the murder of Shannon Nguyen—"

She read him his rights, while thinking: *That should keep him on ice till we add more murders to his homicide portfolio.*

* * *

Seymour sat before the man now suspected in the murders of at least five women, four of them on Maui. He had beaten around the bush on the death of Shannon Nguyen as if this was a damned game of hide and seek. This was in spite of the strong case they now had against him, including forensic evidence that linked the zip line used to strangle Nguyen to that confiscated from Glenn Diamont's house. And the pearl earrings he had were linked to Nguyen through DNA and photographs.

He wanted this guy so badly, Seymour could almost taste it. And he had no doubt that Leila wanted him just as much. Glancing at her as she sat beside him, he turned back to the suspect.

"All right, enough games, Diamont. You're not getting out of here—not this time."

"You sure about that?" he said arrogantly. "This will never hold up..."

Seymour was not about to swallow the bait and lose his cool. The last thing he needed was to be accused of police brutality or verbal intimidation, especially now that they were so close to nailing this guy's ass to the wall.

"Oh, it will hold," Seymour promised. He tried a different tack to shake things up. Opening a folder, he took out an autopsy photograph of Marcia Miyashiro and slid it across the table. "Do you remember her? You strangled her last year in Spreckelsville."

Diamont simply stared at the picture.

Seymour sensed that he might be getting to him. He showed him an autopsy picture of Amy Lynn Laseter, his second victim; followed by Ruth Keomaka, the third victim of the Zip Line Killer. Finally, Seymour placed before him an autopsy photograph of his fourth victim, Hisako Takumi from Honolulu, which was sent to him by the Honolulu Police Department.

"Witnesses can place you in Honolulu when Ms. Takumi was murdered, and saw you talking to her just before she went missing," Seymour said, keeping the pressure on. "We're tying all the pieces together in one nice neat package that will come raining down on you. Might as well save the taxpayers money and own up to what you did, considering you'll never get the chance to hurt another woman again for as long as you live—"

"Okay, you got me!" Diamont confessed. "Yeah, I'm the Zip Line Killer. I killed them all and a few others you don't even know about..."

Seymour cocked a brow, though not entirely surprised. After all, most serial killers were likely guilty of more crimes than law enforcement was aware of. Why should this one be any different?

"Why don't you tell us about these other victims," Leila said, leaning toward the prisoner.

"What—you want names, places...?"

"That would be a good start," she responded tartly.

Diamont almost seemed to brag as he named four other women he had strangled over the past two years and kept trophies from, amongst those now placed in evidence. The victims ranged in age from eighteen to thirty-two, with one murdered on Kauai, another in Honolulu, and two others on Maui. The latter victims had been buried and were presumed by their families to have left the island. The two killed on the other islands were strangled with a rope, before Diamont changed his weapon of murder to a zip line cord.

Seymour had no doubt he was telling the truth. Though most serial killers tended to exaggerate the number of victims, many wanted credit where it was due and, once captured, were more than happy to spill the beans.

"Why did you kill all these women?" Leila asked him.

Diamont grinned crookedly. "What can I say—it turned me on to catch most of them completely off guard. I liked the power of ending a life and getting away with it. It became addictive."

Leila frowned. "That's sick—you're a certified psychopath!"

He chuckled. "Yeah, I suppose. To tell you the truth, I was a little pissed when I heard that Joyce Yashiro was killed and that it had been linked to the Zip Line Killer. But that bastard husband of hers beat me to the punch, or she would have been mine sooner or later."

Seymour found it ironic that he had planned to kill Joyce Yashiro. That would have given Verlin Yashiro everything he wanted, with someone else doing the dirty work for him, excluding his role in the murder of Parker Breslin.

In any event, Seymour had heard all he needed or wanted to from this serial killer. He signaled for the guard to come in and take him away.

"Hawaii will be a hell of a lot better off when you're behind bars," Seymour said as a parting shot. "Aloha!"

After Diamont was taken away, Seymour asked Leila: "Are you all right?"

She put on a brave face. "I'm fine. I'm just glad we finally got this monster."

"Yeah, me too."

Leila met his eyes. "Sometimes I wonder if I'd be better off walking away from this while I still have my mind intact."

Seymour held her gaze, able to relate. "I think you know the answer to that. If we weren't cut out for this type of work, we both would've known it a long time ago. Take some time off, if you need it, but don't go far. I need my first rate detective here."

She gave him a brief smile. "Mahalo for that. Maybe I'll take you up on the offer to take a little time off. Or maybe not..."

Seymour watched her get up and leave the room, and he followed suit, knowing he needed to put this case behind him, no matter how difficult, with other unsettling homicide investigations to follow.

CHAPTER 33

Leila joined Jan, Rachel, Patricia, and Skye Delaney for a girls' night out after wrapping up several homicide cases in practically one fell swoop. They met up at a club on Kaanapali Beach and were listening to a live band singing torch songs with a Hawaiian twist.

"They're good," Skye remarked. "Better than some of the ones I've heard in Honolulu."

Leila laughed while sipping a Blue Hawaiian. "Clearly you need to get out more, Skye. This band is only average at best."

"Hey, I don't care how good or bad the band is, I'm just glad to take a break from cutting up dead bodies," Patricia told them as she sipped her daiquiri.

"Well, at least they're already dead," quipped Jan, holding a Mai Tai.

Everyone laughed.

Rachel said somberly: "Meanwhile many of the creeps who killed them get to live and spend their days behind bars playing cards and comparing notes on their murderous exploits."

"Yeah, it's definitely a bummer," Leila conceded. It still pained her to think that murder victims like Joyce Yashiro and Parker Breslin were silenced for good by those they once loved and believed would protect them from harm, to the extent possible. Instead, greed, hatred, and ill-advised deadly schemes deprived them of their future. Still Leila refused to let this bring her down. After all, they weren't equipped to stop homicides before they occurred. At the end of the day, detectives could only do their job in solving crimes to the best of their ability. "But not tonight," she told her friends. "Tonight is all about putting our daily lives of chasing criminals, excluding Jan and her wonderful artistry, on pause and letting our hair down, so to speak, but not too much, and having a good time."

"I'm all for that!" Skye declared, sipping her Piña Colada. "I'm glad I came to Maui and got to meet a great group of gals while solving a case, but we won't talk about that."

Jan chuckled. "Mahalo for the praise, Leila, and thanks for inviting me to hang out with you guys."

"We should do it more often," Patricia added, and tossed some chocolate covered macadamia nuts in her mouth.

"Yeah," Rachel agreed, sipping her nonalcoholic drink. "Sisterhood is what I need to get me through the times when I miss my late husband like crazy."

"Then we'll make it happen," declared Leila. "Oh, and you're invited too, Skye, whenever you're on Maui."

Skye smiled. "The same goes for all of you, if you're ever on Oahu!"

"Then it looks like we're all on the same page," Rachel said.

"Or canvas," quipped Jan.

"Aloha!" Leila said as the five women clinked glasses in a toast of friendship.

* * *

After leaving the club, Leila showed up at Maxwell's door. He opened it after one ring.

"Sorry I'm late," she told him. "The girls kept me talking and laughing longer than expected."

"No problem," he said with a smile. "It just gave me a little extra time to work on this dish I cooked up that I hope to add to the menu at the restaurant."

"Really?" She met his eyes. "What is it?"

"It's a chicken and mushroom salad with fresh green leaf lettuce, marinated chicken breasts, sautéed Japanese mushrooms, cucumbers, red peppers and what else...oh yes, a splash of soy dressing."

Leila laughed. "Wow! It sounds wonderful. Can I try it?"

Maxwell chuckled. "I was hoping you would. Follow me."

In the gourmet kitchen, Leila saw the dish on the countertop. She watched with anticipation as he forked some of the salad and put it in her mouth.

"What do you think...?"

She swallowed and said truthfully: "It's incredible. Can I have some more?"

He laughed and pulled her close to his body. "You can have anything you want."

Leila gazed into his eyes longingly. "Anything...?"

"Name it."

She thought about the generous proposition and then the incredibly sexy man himself who she had been spending time with. She whispered something in his ear.

Maxwell's eyes crinkled at the corners. "Now...?"

"Why not," she challenged him. "We can even bring the salad and feed each other."

"You're on," he said smoothly.

Ten minutes later, they were in his hot tub, eating chicken and mushroom salad, sipping white wine, and kissing. For Leila, this was the perfect way to end the day, while looking forward to what would follow into the wee hours of the morning.

# # #

Following is a bonus excerpt from the upcoming
third book in the acclaimed Leila Kahana mysteries
series by R. Barri Flowers

MURDER OF THE HULA DANCERS
A Leila Kahana Mystery

Prologue

Yoshie Akiyama had been a professional hula dancer on
Maui for two years, performing at many different occasions,
including anniversaries, award presentations, birthdays,
celebrations, events, graduations, luaus, weddings, and more.
She loved what she did and knew she did it well. It brought
in enough money for her to own her own home and stash
away a bit for a rainy day, even if those seemed to be few
and far in between on the Hawaiian Islands.

Employed by the Aloha Hula Dance Company, Yoshie
also performed at private clubs, homes, and for individuals
who wished to watch a sexy dancer gyrate and shake her hips
and ass for their pleasure. Though some other hula dancers
she knew took it a step further—actually a few steps—selling
their bodies for extra pay or to get drugs, Yoshie stayed away
from that. Yes, she'd had a drug problem once, but she was
clean today and just wanted to do whatever she needed to
have a bright future.

Tonight she would be doing her thing at a bachelor party. It was being held in a private room at a posh restaurant in Wailea, one of the more affluent parts of Maui.

Wary of horny men who expected more than she was willing to give, as always, Yoshie had made it clear in advance that there would be no hanky panky or extras thrown into the mix. She was strictly professional and wanted that to be respected in the spirit of aloha and her Hawaiian ancestry.

Upon parking her Subaru Crosstrek in the parking lot, Yoshie checked the mirror to make sure her long raven hair and makeup were just right. She wore a plumeria lei headband and orchid lei over her traditional costume that consisted of a pa'u, or wrapped skirt, along with a matching bikini top. The high heels she wore were her own choice. After applying more lip gloss, she stepped out of the car, bringing with her an iPod loaded with a blend of Hawaiian, Samoan, and Tahitian songs.

Once inside, the attractive host said sweetly, "Aloha. Let me show you to the bachelor party."

"Mahalo," Yoshie said. She followed him while trying to suppress the butterflies in her stomach for yet another performance in which she must win over her audience, especially the man of the hour before he made his way into matrimony—something she hoped would come her way one day.

Once inside the room, Yoshie calmed down as she was greeted warmly by those gathered. She fully expected it to be a night to remember for the bachelor, his friends, and her.

* * *

He used a cloth to wipe the bright red blood from his long blade. It would dry completely soon enough and be ready to use again whenever it suited his fancy. Putting the knife back in his duffel bag, he dragged the naked, bloody corpse to his car, tossing it onto the tarpaulin on the back seat. He then climbed in the front, started the engine, and began to drive.

Turning on some music—Ke Kali Nei Au—the Hawaiian wedding song, he sang along, enjoying the adrenalin rush from the fresh kill. He replayed in his mind how he had caught her off guard, then wasted little time going to work on her as he plunged the knife deep within her soft flesh time and time again, until he finished her off by slitting her throat.

She had to die. Just as they all did. It was the only way to punish them properly for stepping over the line. Dancing for an unworthy audience could not be tolerated. He would see to it that they paid the ultimate price for their sins and the sins of those they corrupted.

He sang more of the song and then played it again, which brought great joy to him.

Once he reached the desired destination, he stopped the car and got out. Under the cover of darkness, he pulled the dead dancer out and dumped her onto the field. He doubted she would rest in peace, but that wasn't his problem. Not any longer.

Getting back in the car, he drove off, already turning his thoughts toward the next one who needed to feel the sting of his blade.

* * *

Lloyd Shaughnessy and his wife, Adrianna, had retired to Maui three years ago. After visiting the island many times, they had decided to take the plunge and make it their home. And not a day had gone by that they regretted leaving Portland, Oregon behind. After all, their children were adults now and spread out across the Mainland. Now they and the grandkids had a place to come and visit whenever they wanted.

In between, Lloyd enjoyed the tranquility of a hau'oli lā ho'omaha loa or happy retirement in paradise with its swaying palm trees, ocean breezes, and friendly people. It gave him even greater pleasure to spend time outdoors with his two-year-old Belgian Malinois, named Kolohe, which was Hawaiian for rascal.

Today they were taking their usual morning walk and breathing in the fresh air and scent of fragrant plants from nearby gardens. When Kolohe suddenly tried to break free from his leash, Lloyd wondered what had attracted his attention.

"What is it, boy?"

The dog began to bark and continued to be restless. Seeing nothing but the dry field of tall grass head, Lloyd figured it was nothing more than a gecko lizard. They were common there and Kolohe loved to chase them, but never seemed to catch one.

"All right," Lloyd gave in, "go for it. Just don't go too far."

He released the dog and it quickly made a beeline for a clump of dead grass, where it stopped on a dime and barked repeatedly. It was clear to Lloyd that something other than a gecko had captured his attention.

"What have you found?" he called out.

Lloyd followed him into the field and stopped abruptly when he spotted a human leg. Taking a step closer, he saw the nude body of a young woman lying face up. Her eyes were open but lifeless. Her throat had been cut and, from the looks of the bloody remains, her killer had done plenty of damage elsewhere too.

* * *

Aloha! The entire thrilling third book in the Leila Kahana Mystery series, *Murder of the Hula Dancers*, will be available soon in print, eBook, and audio. Mahalo!

# # #

The following is a bonus Maui mystery novelette
by R. Barri Flowers

KAANAPALI BEACH PARADISE

Prologue

The Hawaiian island of Maui could be seen below, surrounded by some of the clearest, bluest water in the Pacific. As the private plane flew over the area known as Hana, the two people on board were treated to a breathtaking view of the island's magnificent northern coastline with its lush bamboo forests, tropical flowers, and slashing waterfalls.

Within moments, another spectacular landmark came into view—the Kaanapali Palms Hotel. The pilot was particularly interested in the hotel as was the co-pilot, though to a lesser degree. And why wouldn't they be? After all, one was the CEO and majority stockholder of the hotel and the other a minor stockholder who was just an inheritance away from claiming that same title.

"There she is," Ben Crawford said proudly to his daughter, Leigh, beside him as he peered out the window at Maui's newest and, he believed, best luxury hotel.

The Palms, as Ben referred to it, was twelve stories high, and sprawled across thirty acres of lush tropical gardens and waterfalls that tumbled into idyllic pools. It was located within the Kaanapali Beach Resort Area, known for its three-mile long stretch of beautiful white sand beach and clear blue water, and home to Maui's most elegant hotels. The area had become a playground for beautiful, perfect, tanned bodies; tourists from around the globe as well as natives; celebrities and non-celebrities; sexy, sex-seekers; and any combination thereof.

"Oh, Daddy," Leigh gushed, "I love it. Is it really ours?"

"You bet it is, honey." He glanced over at his nineteen-year-old daughter who was too damned pretty for her own good, and his.

She flashed him a devastating smile that left Ben weak in the knees—just as her mother had done before her—and he couldn't help but think what he rarely said out loud to her.

I love you, Leigh. And I love it when I can make you happy. You sure as hell have made me happy. Just like your mother did before she was taken away from us. But now it's just you and me, kid, and I don't want to lose you too. To others, I may be a businessman first, but for you, Leigh, I'm a father first. And what I can't give you, I'll buy you!

At least the hotel was hers to play in whenever she saw fit. It was also a place where he very much wanted his guests to relax and play, hoping it would soon be the "go to" resort on Maui.

* * *

Ben Crawford was fifty-three with slicked back silver hair, intense gray eyes, a cleft that split his chin, and a body that was as sturdy as a tree trunk. His reputation as a ruthless entrepreneur preceded him, passed down the line from his father who had made his own mark as a successful real estate developer in Arizona and Nevada. As a young man, Ben believed nothing was out of reach if you applied yourself.

And he did.

Without his father's help.

If he stepped on someone's toes along the way, so be it; they should have kept their damn feet out of the way, as his father would have said.

By age twenty-three, Ben owned five houses, using other people's money and coming away with plenty of his own.

His flourishing career in real estate was put on hold when he enlisted in the military, deciding to follow in the footsteps of three generations of Crawford men. And maybe to prove to his father that he was just as tough as he was any day of the week, including in the U.S. Air Force, where he made it to Captain.

Four long years stationed in Honolulu was tougher than he'd thought, but it was not without its thrills. He had bedded a number of women, including one who had gotten herself pregnant.

Damn! That stupid bitch!

He offered to pay her to get rid of it, but she refused.

To hell with her.

He had his whole future ahead of him and wasn't about to commit himself to a woman he barely knew, let alone loved.

The best thing that ever happened to him was when his stint ended and he went back to the mainland.

He did not look back.

Ben's career in real estate picked up right where it left off. He acquired property after property, investing and reinvesting, and developing. By age thirty-two, he was a millionaire several times over and the owner of several impressive properties, including a resort hotel in Phoenix.

A year later when he met Melody Sue Harlow, the very lovely twenty-six-year-old former state beauty queen, Ben's priorities shifted. For the first time in his life, he knew what true love was. So did Melody.

Two months later, she became Melody Sue Crawford.

Two years later, she gave birth to Leigh Crawford.

One year later, Melody became ill unexpectedly. The doctors said it was congenital heart failure.

One month later, she was dead.

Ben was left alone to care for his one-year-old daughter.

She, along with his business interests, would have to fill the emptiness that Melody's untimely death left.

Although they did, Ben knew deep down inside that nothing could ever take Melody's place in his heart.

And he was right.

* * *

The plane touched down at Kapalua Airport in West Maui. As usual, the flight had been flawless. Ben had taken up flying as a hobby years ago, and developed it further while in the Air Force.

He'd recently begun teaching Leigh to fly.

Now he wanted to teach her something else that he considered extremely important—how to run a business. After all, one day everything he owned would be hers lock, stock, and barrel. And that included his most recent purchase, the Kaanapali Palms Hotel. She would need to learn how to hang on to her investments. He knew full well that the sharks out there would wrest them from her if she gave them even an inch. If she had been a boy, Ben admittedly would have felt more secure in Leigh's ability to handle anything thrown at her. Of course, he would never tell her that.

Ben shook off his thoughts, realizing he was getting ahead of the game.

Right now, he was still in charge of his holdings and intended to be for many years to come.

He was especially happy to finally get a piece of the action in Hawaii after trying for years. So what if it was not Honolulu. He had a feeling that in no time at all, Maui would be the new economic kingpin of the islands, and he planned to be right in the thick of it.

At the moment, he was here to supervise the last minute preparations before the grand opening of the hotel in two weeks; and, of course, to thank all his friends, investors, and associates for their support by staging a big celebration to mark the occasion.

* * *

A limousine was waiting for them when they got off the plane. The dark-haired Hawaiian chauffeur, who was in his thirties, tall, and superbly built, greeted them.

"This is my daughter, Leigh," Ben said to the man in a condescending tone.

The chauffeur gave her a quick once over and nodded, then smiled. "Nice to meet you, Ms. Crawford."

Leigh displayed a pearly white, toothy smile that she had perfected over the years, and thought: *It's so like Daddy to not even bother to introduce the hot, sexy guy by name, as if it was totally irrelevant.* She was sure that during his many recent trips to Maui he had gotten to know the man's name.

In spite of her attraction to him, she decided with sudden disinterest that maybe it wasn't all that relevant.

The chauffeur grinned at her as he opened the car door. "I'll get your bags."

After he was several feet away from the limo, Leigh blushed and again found herself interested in the man. "Daddy, what's the chauffeur's name?"

"I have no idea," Ben said.

"Oh, Daddy," she said, pouting. "Well, I think he's cute."

Ben regarded her with a slow, less than accommodating smile. "Isn't that what you say about every young man you meet?"

Only if they look like him, she thought mischievously. She could already tell she was going to enjoy her month long stay on Maui.

* * *

Three months shy of her twentieth birthday, Leigh Crawford was already a beauty of stunning proportions. Tall, tan, and lovely, she needed neither makeup nor to be made up to be the envy of most other women—and men. She was the sum of her mother's and father's parts. Her bold, long-lashed, green eyes, small shapely nose, and wide mouth were direct gifts from the mother she never knew. Whereas her broad shoulders, long, lean legs, and chin dimple belonged expressly to her father. The rest of the package was all her own: long, natural blonde hair, burgeoning round breasts, and a shapely figure second to none.

As the only child of a wealthy widower businessman, Leigh had the best and worst of all worlds. She was the beneficiary of enormous generosities including the best clothes, the best cars (her first car at age sixteen was a Jaguar), the best house, the best horse, plenty of money, and the adoration of a loving father—and she basked in every moment of it.

Who wouldn't?

On the flip side, however, were a series of boarding schools, long and frustrating absences by her father, and a considerable amount of loneliness thrown in for bad measure.

How did she offset the price of wealth, a busy father who had a wandering eye, and the lack of maternal care and guidance?

By experimenting with alcohol, drugs, and, sex.

Her first real sexual experience was at age fourteen. The boy, fifteen, was also a product of super-rich parents and he had considerable experience in sexual matters. He taught Leigh the ins and outs of sex during a weekend when they were both supposed to be on a home break from boarding school; but instead they crashed at a five-star hotel where cold hard cash eliminated the need for nosey inquiries.

Leigh loved the experience, if not the teacher.

It was the beginning of a string of relationships that went nowhere. She could never be sure if her lover was more interested in her or her money, and didn't really care. In her eyes, it was only for fun, and the pure enjoyment of making out and hooking up with good-looking guys. It never occurred to her that someone might try to blackmail her with an eye on a big payday from her rich, proud father.

That notwithstanding, she still knew the meaning of statutory rape, or rape as the case may be, and made sure her sex partners knew the same before and after the fact. Aside from being arrested and thrown in jail, incurring the wrath of her powerful and overprotective father would not be a walk in the park.

In truth, although she had never sat down and talked to him about it, Leigh suspected her father knew full well that she was not a virgin, as evidenced by him saying one night totally out of the blue:

"Honey, sex doesn't really have to be messy, as long as you make sure you're protected at all times. Unwanted babies or sexually transmitted diseases can ruin a female for life."

The statement struck Leigh as peculiar. Was he trying to tell her something? Did he and her mother not want her? Was he suggesting that her mother's heart failure was brought on by an STD?

Or maybe she had a sister or brother out there that Leigh knew nothing about.

She decided the answer was no to questions A, B, C, and D. He had never given her any indication that he or her mother did not want her; and had never claimed her mother's untimely death was caused by anything other than what the doctors said.

As for having a sibling, she couldn't rule that out altogether, knowing her father had more than his share of sex partners over the years. Maybe it wouldn't be so bad if she had a sister or brother to hang out with, share secrets, and even fight with.

Leigh thought back to her father's comment. She was sure it was his way of telling her indirectly that what you do behind closed doors is fine as long as you make sure you don't suffer the consequences.

She had made sure.

She had been taking birth control pills from the very start.

If and when she found the right guy to spend her life with, she supposed she would have a child one day.

If not, then she would know it was not meant to be.

Motherhood.

The very idea of being a mother petrified Leigh for some reason and she was not sure why.

Maybe it was because she never had a mother, for all intents and purposes, and wasn't sure if she would be a good mother.

Or maybe it was because she resented the fact that her mother left her at the tender age of one to fend for herself in a male dominated society; and she feared someday she might do the same to her own child.

Invariably Leigh would cry and tell herself she would give up everything: the money...the role she played very well as a spoiled rich girl...the sex...maybe even her father—if she could only have her mother back to comfort her and cuddle up with on rainy nights.

* * *

During the drive, Leigh silently admired the profile of her strong, handsome father who appeared to be deep in thought. As usual, he was wearing an expensive suit—this one dark blue. She was more comfortably dressed in attire befitting the islands: a loose fitting print shirt and jean shorts.

Her father—the wealthy real estate developer.

But what did *she* want out of life? She had tried a year of college and decided it was too boring and unfulfilling. Who needed it anyway when she had more money—or the promise of it—than she could possibly ever use.

Right now she was more than content to be Daddy's little girl as well as her own view of being a big girl, while enjoying all the benefits that accompanied both distinctions.

Suddenly, feeling a bit restless and seeking the type of attention she was used to (both around her father and others), Leigh tucked her arm under his and cooed:

"The first thing I'm going to do is go for a swim. Do you want to join me?" She could see the nameless chauffeur's interested eyes peek at her through the rear view mirror.

Ben's eyes crinkled. "Sounds inviting... There are three pools, you know," he boasted, virtually ignoring the mighty Pacific as the place to go for swimming in Hawaii. His eyes sharpened regrettably and his voice dropped as he said: "But I can't, darling. I've got a meeting to attend damn close to the moment we arrive. But you have some fun. I promise I'll find time to join you later."

She gave him a knowing, disappointed look. "I'm counting on it."

Leigh smiled at the driver and thought: *He might not be a bad substitute.* And from his shifting and desirous eyes, she could tell that he was ready and more than willing.

The drive down the tree-lined Kaanapali Parkway exhibited not only luxury hotel after hotel and a line of cars—many of which seemed to part the way as the limo passed through—but a flock of tan, taut, beautiful bodies walking or jogging by. Leigh was certain now that the fun had only just begun.

The limousine turned onto a street and Leigh looked up in awe. There it stood before them, the hotel her father had bought, renamed, renovated, and dedicated to her: the Kaanapali Palms Hotel. If she knew her father, it was touted as the biggest and best resort hotel on the island. From where she sat, it looked like it.

* * *

The meeting took place in the Sunset Palms Ballroom— one of ten meeting rooms in the Kaanapali Palms Hotel. The seats were set up auditorium style and the hotel staff was perched in them like zombies as they listened to the owner. He stood before a podium, flanked by the hotel's executives, and introduced himself to those who had not met him during his earlier visits. Then he proceeded to tell them what he expected from each and every one of them as employees and how customer satisfaction must always be their number one goal.

Standing at the back of the room, two housekeepers paid particular attention to the monologue—or the man responsible for it.

"I hear he's widowed," Maggie Webb whispered excitedly to the other. "Maybe he's in the market for a forty-year-old who's *all* woman. And she can even clean—a little." She giggled childishly at her fanciful words.

Yoshiko Pelayo, thirty-two, managed a slight smile as she looked at the woman who had befriended her since she joined the staff. She whispered back with unaccustomed candor, along with regret: "I'm sure Mr. Crawford considers himself much too important to be bothered by the likes of us."

Maggie frowned. "Don't sell yourself short," she warned softly. "Certainly don't sell *me* short. No one is so big that they can't be taken down a few pegs, not even Mr. CEO up there—"

But Yoshiko had returned her ears and eyes to Ben Crawford. This was the first time she had seen the great real estate mogul in person.

She had waited a lifetime to do so.

He seemed so eloquent, so in control standing up there—a master before his slaves.

She was not a slave to him or any other man, but especially not to him.

Yoshiko could feel her heartbeat quicken as she peered over the crowd at the one who employed them.

Why am I even here? she asked herself. *I don't belong.*

But then she thought: *Of course I do. I have every right to be here. More than any of these other people do.*

Her eyes started to water.

She hated this man she had never met.

He had taken away everything dear to her.

He was responsible for the rage she felt.

The bastard was her father...

* * *

Nearly thirty-three-years ago, Honolulu native Nahoko Pelayo was an attractive, nineteen-year-old aspiring dancer. Nahoko, who had hoped to someday reach Broadway, worked as a waitress to afford dance lessons and to help her parents supplement their meager earnings. One day while serving a group of soldiers, Nahoko met the enormously handsome Captain Ben Crawford, who immediately wooed her as no man had before.

That was when she made the mistake that would cost her for the rest of her life.

He deflowered her.

She believed she loved him, and he her. So she let him have his way with her again...and again.

Birth control was a foreign word in those days.

Abortion was not.

Both figured into what happened next.

She got pregnant.

She wanted marriage.

And her parents wanted marriage.

But Ben had other ideas.

Her religion forbade abortion. Further, Nahoko loved Ben. She would not destroy his baby's life—not even for him.

He conveniently disassociated himself from responsibility as he returned to the mainland.

Nahoko was left to have her baby alone, which she named Yoshiko after her grandmother.

Her dream of a career on Broadway died along with everything else. Disowned by her parents, abandoned by her community, and disgraced by the father of her baby, Nahoko fled to Maui, where she hoped anonymity would allow her to at least live in peace.

It did not.

A young Hawaiian mother with a half-Hawaiian, half-white illegitimate daughter made life very difficult on the islands, as most native people believed that the white man took their land, their pride, and now their women.

Yet Nahoko could not afford to leave Hawaii. So she worked in the sugar cane fields, then as a waitress, and even a hula dancer, doing whatever she could do to support her daughter.

Dreams died hard. One dream she held onto was the hope that she, Yoshiko, and Ben might someday come together as a family.

Early on, she had followed Ben's career and felt a strange pride for what they once had. She even tried writing him a few times, hoping he would at least acknowledge his child.

The letters always came back, unopened.

When Nahoko learned the only man she ever loved, and still loved, had married, and further, had another child, Nahoko knew she and Yoshiko would never again be a part of Ben Crawford's life.

And yet Nahoko felt her daughter had a right to know who her father was.

She finally got the courage to tell her when she turned ten.

Yoshiko, embittered by her mother's betrayal at the hands of the soldier, nonetheless took up where Nahoko left off and followed from afar the life of her father—a life she should have been a part of—and watched her mother suffer all the while until she went to her grave at the relatively young age of thirty-nine. It hurt even more that Yoshiko was only nineteen at the time—the same age her mother had been when she got pregnant.

For years afterwards, Yoshiko carried the burden of feeling responsible for her mother's ruined life and knowing her father was out there somewhere, having never acknowledged her. Finally, she decided she could not be held accountable for something she had no control over. She had to try to pick up the pieces of her own life as best she could and try to make something of it.

But having grown up poor, she knew the task would be that much harder. She became determined, though, in memory of her mother, and as a knock against her father.

After spending most of her life on Maui, Yoshiko returned to Honolulu, where she worked her way through college, receiving a degree in journalism and graduating with honors. She was also blessed with extraordinary good looks. Yoshiko had the same long black hair, smooth golden skin, and small bosomed slender features of her mother; and as her mother told her often enough, she had the thick eyelashes, straight nose, and full mouth of her father. Her entrancing brown-gray eyes came from both parents.

Yoshiko had little trouble getting a job at a television station, as her homegrown qualities and journalistic instincts made her a natural. She worked her way up from reporter to anchor, with very little social life along the way, although she had been propositioned enough. She decided most men were bad news but, more importantly, Yoshiko knew she never wanted to become vulnerable to a man like her mother had, only to be discarded like garbage. Let some other naive woman fall prey to a man's good looks and bad intentions.

Yoshiko had even managed to suppress the limited memory of her father as she put her life in order. Then, as if a ghost who was not willing to let either her or her mother rest, Ben Crawford once more stabbed at her consciousness.

The article read: BEN CRAWFORD, PROMINENT REAL ESTATE DEVELOPER, SPEARHEADS KAANAPALI BEACH'S LATEST RESORT HOTEL PROJECT.

The accompanying photograph left no doubt in her mind that it was the same Ben Crawford who had abandoned her mother as he went on with his life. Her mother had kept photographs of her former lover, as a means to always keep a part of him for herself.

In gazing at the photo and seeing herself in the process as his progeny, Yoshiko felt anger of indescribable proportions well up inside of her. How dare he come back to Hawaii to throw around his millions on the grave of her mother! Why couldn't he have stayed on the mainland, far enough away so she could forget he ever existed?

For two years, Yoshiko watched and listened with revulsion as the Kaanapali Palms Hotel was renovated with what she considered to be tainted money from the man who basked in riches while she and her mother had drowned in absolute poverty. Yoshiko cried a lot and tried to disassociate herself from Ben Crawford and his interests. After all, what happened between him and her mother happened so long ago it did no good to let it wreak havoc on her life.

Then she would tell herself: *But it has already wreaked havoc on my life.* After all, she was the product of that non-caring bastard, whether she liked it or not; and whether he liked it or not. She could not simply pretend that he didn't exist— especially now—or that he had not destroyed her mother's life and, to some degree, her own.

That was when Yoshiko quit her job and moved back to Maui, where she gained employment at the Kaanapali Palms Hotel as a maid—the same type of job her mother held until the very end of her life. It was there, in her illegitimate father's latest palace, where she hoped to enact her and her mother's vengeance.

Yoshiko felt it was only then that both she and her mother could hope to find peace.

* * *

"In two weeks, we will officially open to the public," Ben Crawford said jubilantly. "Each and every one of you should take great pride knowing that you will be a big part of the Kaanapali Palms Hotel's beginnings..."

Pride! How can you talk about pride? Yoshiko thought with disgust. *What about my mother's pride? Did you care about that?*

"...I do hope that you will all attend our grand opening party, as the people who have worked their asses off to enable us to open on schedule..."

The self-indulgent speech was halted as the speaker became aware of the person entering the room.

All other eyes turned to look at the shapely features of the young woman wearing a halter top and white cropped pants, with long blonde hair cascading over her shoulders. Her mouth curved into a toothy smile and she appeared pleased that she had suddenly become the center of attention.

Ben motioned for her to join him, although she looked as if she needed no enticing, and he produced a wide smile as if he had just become a proud father. It was then that Yoshiko suddenly knew he had.

The woman now stood at Ben's side and was nearly as tall as he was. "For those of you who haven't had the honor," Ben said to the audience, "this is my daughter, Leigh..."

There was a disjointed splatter of alohas and hellos.

Maggie shoved a well-placed elbow into Yoshiko's side and snorted enviously: "Looks like Mr. Crawford isn't too important for one very lucky female."

Yoshiko twisted her nose petulantly, and remarked more saucily than she intended to: "Yes, she certainly is the lucky one."

So that was the daughter she had heard about. Yoshiko sucked in a deep breath, for some reason feeling a tinge of jealousy. But, of course, she knew what the reason was and it had nothing to do with the fact that Leigh was gorgeous and obviously knew it and flaunted it. No. It was that she benefitted from a fairy tale existence as the only *known* daughter of this rich man; while Yoshiko was just his bastard child from a forgotten romance a long time ago.

It should be me up there, Yoshiko thought bitterly, instead of standing in the back of the room as some lowly hotel worker as far as they were concerned.

Her father and half-sister better enjoy the fun of their flashy new hotel and their perfect life while they can.

Yoshiko was going to make Ben Crawford pay for what he had done to her mother, not to mention depriving her of her rightful heritage.

She would see to it that bastard would regret the day he walked out on her mother.

* * *

Standing just a few feet away from Yoshiko, another hotel employee was also hanging on every word of Ben Crawford.

Eugene Keebler was a tall, lanky man of twenty-nine with a freshly shaven head and yellow, uneven teeth. He was a janitor at the Kaanapali Palms Hotel. He was also, by his own description, an opportunist.

And all of a sudden he had come up with an opportunity he felt was too damned good to pass up...

The first time he had come up with an idea to increase his financial worth, Eugene Keebler was thirteen years old. He lived in Hilo on the Big Island of Hawaii with his mother and four sisters. They were so poor and food was so scarce that he decided stealing was the only way they would survive. He started out by stealing fruit and vegetables from the produce market and eventually escalated to breaking into neighbors' homes when they were out and taking any money he could find.

He was fifteen when he got caught and shipped to Honolulu to spend a year in a reformatory. It did not reform him. Instead, he left believing hustling was a far easier way to get ahead in life. He just had to be more careful the next time.

When he returned home, things had changed. Two sisters had married and left the island, one was pregnant, the other hated him, and his mother was ill. He became an outcast in a broken home. He watched his mother die, and then left the island for good to go to the mainland.

With no education past the seventh grade, but street smart, which he believed was the greatest form of education anyhow, Eugene hustled his way around the country doing everything from writing bad checks to stealing cars to robbing old ladies. In between, he worked odd jobs, waiting for the next golden opportunity to present itself.

It did when he and some buddies decided to rob a bank in an Atlanta suburb. Eugene was twenty-one, no longer a kid, and accountable to the adult courts should he be caught.

He was not.

Ever since the year he spent at the reformatory, he managed to stay one step ahead of the law by never staying in one place too long (his longest stint was six months in Chicago) or becoming too chummy with his acquaintances.

So far it had worked like a charm.

He had been on Maui for three months now and had pretty much kept a low profile, particularly after he was nearly apprehended robbing a gas station on a return trip to Honolulu.

He needed a place to cool off and make an honest living for a while. And Maui was the perfect place to do that. After chilling in Lahaina, he had landed the janitorial job at the Kaanapali Palms Hotel a month ago.

He hated it and he hated his supervisor.

But he was thankful that he had acquired the means to put food on the table for a while without constantly having to look over his shoulder.

However, as was the case with all deviant minds, conformity could only last so long, especially when opportunity was staring him right in the face.

* * *

Eugene scratched his chin thoughtfully. This grand opening bash the main man spoke about might be just what the doctor ordered. If he was not mistaken, Ben Crawford and others at the hotel had said that everyone associated with the hotel would be there. That meant investors, the money men and women behind this project, would attend. It seemed like a perfect opportunity for these people to show off their worth. Diamond rings, credit cards, fat money clips, and more... The very idea had Eugene drooling with anticipation.

Why, if enough people showed up, the event could net him a tidy profit. And if he was really lucky, it would be enough to keep him afloat for a while—maybe a good while. The way he saw it, robbing these people would be a piece of cake, and most importantly, he would have the advantage of the unexpected—something that was not always true with established hotels that already had their security well in place.

He would recruit a couple of buddies he had hooked up with who could use some cash.

No one would get hurt, other than those who could most afford it. Those who could not, wouldn't have much to lose anyhow. But he would take what they had anyway, thank you.

He had long since learned that people tended to cooperate real fast if they believed it could mean the difference between living and dying.

Eugene decided he would make them all strip, including Crawford himself. He would really enjoy watching daddy's little girl get naked.

Hmm! Let me see, Eugene mused, *two weeks and counting*. That would be just enough time to work out the details and put his plan into motion.

* * *

Leigh had taken a quick tour of the hotel and the well-manicured grounds. She had come away impressed, but not exactly starry-eyed. And why should she be? After all, her father owned or was a majority stockholder of several hotels and condominiums, most of which were just as nice, if not as expansive.

What she really wanted to do was cool off. So she disengaged herself from the semi boring tour and went up to her private suite. She dug a two-piece swimsuit out of her suitcase.

The orange halter bikini top and bikini bottom fit tightly and accentuated her breasts and firm buttocks. Equipped with a towel, Leigh headed to the pool she liked best: a massive indoor-outdoor fresh water pool designed like a tropical maze with plants, waterfalls, and rock formations. She was well aware that she encountered more than a few roving eyes, and gave as much as she received.

She had just splashed into the water, when Leigh heard the familiar and sexy voice say: "You look like you belong in there—"

Leigh cleared her eyes of water and directed her attention to the person. It was the chauffeur. He was dressed in dark swim trunks, sporting a taut, lean body, and a sensual smile.

She licked her lips and returned the smile coquettishly. "What are you doing here?" Not that she was complaining—not one bit—but still, he was not a hotel guest. Was he?

He gazed at her with amusement. "I work here, remember."

"Not dressed like that you don't," she said sarcastically, finding it hard to keep her eyes off him.

He looked at himself and laughed. "No, not like this. I'm on break. I always try to get in a few laps every day." He paused and then grinned. "Especially today—"

For some reason, Leigh resented him using the pool or any pool at the hotel. Why should he get free privileges when others had to pay for that right? Of course, she too, was taking advantage of her opulent circumstances. But that was different. Wasn't it?

As if reading her mind, he said coolly: "If you're wondering about me swimming here, don't worry, I have permission. All of the staff does, as long as it doesn't take away from a guest's use of the pools."

Leigh accepted the fact that he had a perfectly good excuse for using the pool, especially since he wasn't really interfering with her use of it. She flashed that winning smile of hers again. He was so good looking and she figured he would be a good playmate for her.

She asked sweetly: "So what's your name?"

"Masami."

Masami what? she asked herself, but then realized it didn't matter. What did matter was that he looked like he might be a lot of fun. Might as well get off on the right foot.

Demurely, she cooed: "Masami, would you care to join me?"

Nodding, his velvety brown eyes lit up as if he had struck gold. "You know damn well that I would."

He dove into the pool, causing water to splash in Leigh's face.

They played, teased, bodied up, and made out with Leigh boldly taking the lead, before she decided she was not quite ready to go any further. Not in her first hour of her first day there.

Later, say tonight, would be a different matter altogether.

Leigh left the persuasive lips and burning eyes of super-hot Masami in the pool and departed for her suite alone. She supposed she should make a well-timed appearance at the staff meeting. Daddy had requested she come. Frankly, it sounded like a real bore. On the other hand, she might meet some really gorgeous guy who could keep Masami forever at bay.

* * *

Whaler's Village was located not too far from the Kaanapali Palms Hotel and featured some of the finest restaurants and shops on Maui's west side. Overlooking the beach was arguably the Village's most frequented, most popular, and certainly largest restaurant: The Shoreline Lounge. It had a fountain that meandered through the indoor/outdoor eatery, two levels, live music nightly, and a menu that featured authentic Hawaiian cuisine, as well as good old-fashioned mainland American favorites.

It was happy hour, the sun was still baking the air, and the place was packed with patrons chattering, drinking, perspiring, eavesdropping, dropping by, picking up, and otherwise engaging in fun and frolic.

Known as the Queen of the Village, Rosita Okamura confidently walked around the restaurant like she owned the place, which was not surprising since she did. At least fifty percent anyway. The other fifty percent belonged to her husband Kalani. Together they had opened The Shoreline Lounge twenty-five years ago, or the same year they got married. The restaurant started off slowly, the marriage fast.

A decade later, the trends reversed. A hysterectomy ended their longstanding bid to conceive some new Okamuras, and effectively neutralized their great sex. Meanwhile, tourism on Maui had increased substantially by the turn of the century and business boomed as a result. It was the latter success that became the cornerstone of their relationship, which suited Rosita just fine. She had always had her priorities in order: money, respect, youth, and sex.

The money came rolling in and she loved every moment of it. There was nothing more satisfying than wealth.

Respect. A close second. She took pride in being the Queen of Whaler's Village. It showed that longevity meant something in a business where the failure rate was higher than you could count.

Youth. Now that proved considerably more difficult to manage. At fifty-five, Rosita would be the first to admit that she was no longer the Maui high school beauty queen that wooed men for years after, including Kalani. Gone was the svelte body, replaced by creases and folds that not even her personal trainer and regular exercise could get rid of. What had once been soft laughter lines at the corners of her brown eyes were now deep creases that remained whether she laughed or cried, thanks to too much sun exposure. Her once thick, long black hair was now a short bob, dyed blonde to better hide the gray that had been showing up for the better part of a decade.

But that did not mean she conceded beauty for age. Two face lifts had done wonders to make her look at least ten years younger and considerably more appealing. Her capped teeth gave her a lovely smile.

Then there were her breasts, always and still her most inviting feature. Again, she had called upon the surgeon to put in implants to replace sagging breasts, so they were once again nicely sized, firm, and high.

Sex. Ahh, the way to keep her energy up and the perfect tonic for staying young. Although the lackluster sex she shared with her husband in recent years convinced her as much as anything that their marriage was now just mainly for convenience and the love of money (and neither of them were prepared to give up either of these things), it did not eliminate Rosita's sex drive or, she suspected, Kalani's. In fact, a certain swagger he had exhibited of late suggested he was having an affair.

But with whom?

Did it really matter?

She decided it did not. After all, she herself had found solace in the arms of young studs whose athleticism and libido matched her own.

As long as she and Kalani remained discreet, why should either of them have to deny their urges when neither seemed capable of satisfying the other?

Wearing a figure-flattering Hawaiian dress, a long pearl necklace, and matching earrings, Rosita looked the part of a perfect hostess, which she believed she was, as she smiled appropriately, asked patrons if everything was all right, and chastised employees who were spending too much time fraternizing with customers.

And where on earth was her partner and darling husband?

The hell if she knew—and maybe it was better that she did not.

He had a very distressing habit of sometimes disappearing for hours, leaving the restaurant in her very capable hands.

Not that she minded too much. From the start, she had been the one to make it all work, even though Kalani readily took most of the credit. And she let him. Men needed high powered egos to function. Women did not. What she did need was...

Rosita spotted what she needed. Chad Gibson. He was a waiter in his late twenties and an extremely good looking dark-haired hunk with an incredible six pack, and the latest stud who kept her satisfied under the sheets. And why shouldn't he? She paid him enough.

Right now it was time for him to earn his keep.

Calmly, she sauntered over to him, careful to keep up the soft smile for her audience even though she was already thinking about Chad making love to her.

He had just taken a young couple's order and was headed away from Rosita when she stopped him in his tracks.

"Chad..." Her voice was gentle and level.

He turned as she caught up to him. "What's up, Rosita?" Chad asked innocently as his blue eyes surveyed her.

She peeked devilishly at his crotch, and thought: *You will be soon enough*, but responded coolly: "Have you taken your break yet?"

"Yeah, I just came back," he said.

"I see," she grumbled irritably. But she would not be denied. "Why don't you take another break? I'll get someone to cover for you."

He smiled perceptively. "What did you have in mind?"

She smiled back at him. At least they were on the same wavelength. Rosita glanced around the restaurant before returning her eyes to his. Desperately trying to keep emotion out of her voice and sound professional, she said: "Meet me in my office in five minutes and you'll find out." She winked and they went their separate ways.

* * *

Near Whaler's Village was the very expensive, very luxurious beachfront condominium called Tropical Paradise Place. Its tenants ranged from the super-rich to moderately rich to sufficiently wealthy temporary and full-time occupants. What they shared in common was the love of the ocean, the sun, the beach, the climate, and the company they kept.

"It could be the best damned investment I ever made," Kalani Okamura declared to his bed partner, "short of The Shoreline Lounge."

The investment he was referring to was a stock purchase in the new Kaanapali Palms Hotel.

"What about me?" Genevieve, his young lover, whined as she flaunted her large breasts in his face. "I thought I was the best thing you ever invested in."

He grinned, becoming aroused again by her voluptuous body as much as her attitude. "You are," he told her, "as far as a human investment." In truth, that would probably go to his wife, Rosita, all things considered. But he saw no reason to spoil her fantasy.

Kalani, fifty-seven, with a medium build and thinning black-gray hair, regarded his slimmer girlfriend with loads of curly crimson hair. He leaned over and kissed her.

"Sorry I brought up business," he said softly. "Let me make it up to you."

She seemed to consider the proposition before pouting sexily. "So what are you waiting for?"

He took her advice and climbed on top of her. Peering down at Genevieve with gold-flecked black eyes, Kalani made love to her.

A few minutes later, they were sitting up in bed smoking a joint. That wasn't usually his thing, but it was hers and she had a way of getting him to do things outside of his comfort zone. As long as it didn't interfere with his other life as a successful businessman and husband, he was cool with it.

"Were you serious about trying to help me get a singing gig on Kaanapali Beach?" Genevieve asked.

In fact, Kalani had known from the start that she was an aspiring singer. He had met her while she was performing for free at the Cannery Mall in Lahaina. Kalani had considered letting her sing at the restaurant, but feared that Rosita might put two and two together. No, it was best to separate business from pleasure and save him a lot of grief.

Fortunately, he had another idea. "I was very serious," he said. "I heard they're looking for singers at the Kaanapali Palms Hotel. Since I've got some pull there, I'm sure I could get you an audition."

She beamed. "Would you really?"

"For you, honey, anything."

"Oh thank you," she said enthusiastically.

"Don't thank me just yet," he warned, even if he liked the notion of her being indebted to him. "You'll still have to prove yourself. But I'm sure you can."

"So am I." She licked his lips and then his forehead. "Do you think you've got any gas left in the tank?"

Kalani was instantly turned on again. "More than enough to take you for a ride," he responded anxiously.

Half an hour later, Kalani showered, put on a suit, and left the condo he kept for his side activities. He headed to the restaurant, while wondering what excuse he could come up with this time to explain his absence without arousing his wife's suspicion.

* * *

When Kalani Okamura first arrived in Hawaii thirty-five years ago from his native Japan at the age of twenty-two, he was seeking to put behind him a broken home, an abusive father, and a life that seemed to be spiraling out of control.

He bummed around Honolulu and Hilo that first year working odd jobs and surfing, while trying to decide what the hell he wanted out of life. Or maybe what life wanted out of him.

Nearly a decade later, he met a raven-haired beauty named Rosita Ezaki at a movie theater where she took tickets. It was practically love at first sight.

The following year they got married and moved to Maui. There, they pooled their meager resources and got a bank loan so they could open up a restaurant. Whaler's Village seemed to be a place where growth and profit were inevitable, so they opened The Shoreline Lounge there with high hopes.

And their hopes were fulfilled. Over the years, The Shoreline Lounge became wildly successful and one of the most popular restaurants on Kaanapali Beach.

It was on the personal front where things began to go downhill. Kalani had always wanted a chance to be the father he wished his own father had been. But that aspiration went out the window after years of trying, and ended permanently when Rosita had a hysterectomy. They had considered adopting, but neither of them—particularly Kalani—believed it would be quite the same.

Kalani was surprised when he lost his desire for Rosita after her operation. What had surely been one of the real strengths of their marriage—great sex—suddenly became more or less a duty rather than pleasure. It was as if what had been taken from her was also taken from him, depriving him of his rightful legacy.

Although he did his best to fake it whenever they had sex, Kalani could never recover his former feelings of desire for his wife. And so over the years he began a series of meaningless affairs. He usually felt guilty afterwards because he could not imagine Rosita cheating on him, but not guilty enough to refrain from his adulterous behavior.

He had considered divorce from time to time, but always returned to his senses. Why should he follow his father's footsteps when he had abandoned his mother, ruining her life? He couldn't do the same thing to Rosita.

Then there were the practical considerations. Why the hell would he want to ruin a business partnership made in heaven? Not to mention he had this innate fear that somehow, some way, Rosita would end up taking him to the cleaners. Besides, deep down inside, he still loved her and wanted that to count for something.

That notwithstanding, it was only recently that Kalani had found a new, invigorating pastime to keep him fulfilled, and it both scared and thrilled him. Genevieve was all that in bed and so much more. But he knew that, at his age, he couldn't keep her interested forever. That didn't mean it had to end anytime soon, especially if he continued to help her out in ways he could outside of the bedroom.

For now, it was time to get back to his real life.

* * *

As he headed toward The Shoreline Lounge, Kalani could not help but eye the very noticeable Kaanapali Palms Hotel that seemed to hover over everything else on Kaanapali Beach. Rosita had been reluctant to invest in the hotel, fearing it might take too long before they would see any return.

But Kalani felt differently. He expected to see some return very soon. For one, he respected Ben Crawford as a brilliant businessman, who wasn't afraid to step on toes to get what he wanted. As far as Kalani was concerned, he believed Crawford had a sure-fire winner in that hotel, even if the owners of the previous hotel in that spot had run it into the ground, tainting the entire Kaanapali Beach Resort Area.

Kalani believed another benefit he would gain from his investment in the new hotel was that it would be great advertising for The Shoreline Lounge. Especially if he was able to pull off his bid to stage a sanctioned second grand opening celebration at the restaurant.

He went inside and braced himself for the twenty questions he'd no doubt have to endure from his wife.

* * *

Rosita squeezed her eyes shut tightly and bit down harder than she meant to on her lower lip as she lay on the couch in her office with her young lover on top of her. These afternoon delights with Chad were just what she needed to get through the day—and often the night.

She and Kalani had separate offices in the back of the restaurant, which made it easier to stay out of each other's hair and made it much more convenient for situations such as this. Of course, her door was always locked whenever she did not wish to be disturbed.

It did not take long for either of them to be fully satisfied during their sexual escapade, which was great for her, as she wasn't afforded the time to be away from the restaurant for too long. Especially with Kalani mysteriously absent.

There would be plenty of other times for longer sessions with Chad. This one had more than accomplished its purpose.

They both got up off the couch and quickly put their clothes on.

Rosita kissed her lover. "You almost make me feel like I'm in my twenties again," she murmured.

Chad grinned. "I think you have a lot to do with that."

She touched his lips with her pinkie, appreciating the compliment, whether he truly meant it or not.

It didn't really matter to her, as long as she continued to have a use for him.

Now she mustn't keep the business waiting.

She unlocked the door, mumbled a few waiter instructions to Chad for effect, and let him go out first. Rosita sucked in a deep breath and ran smack dab into her husband.

* * *

Genevieve Roswell smoked another joint after Kalani left the condo, before slipping into a one-piece swimsuit she'd brought along. He had invited her to hang out there as long as she liked so she decided to take him up on it. At least long enough to have a swim and come back to change into her clothes. She didn't want him to take her for granted any more than she wanted to take him for granted.

Besides the age difference, he was married. And it was pretty clear to her that he had no intention of leaving his wife. Not that she would want him to. She was happy being the other woman, and just hoped that, with his connections, Kalani could help make some of her dreams come true.

Genevieve left the condo and made her way to the beach. She knew guys were checking her out and some girls too— with her skimpy bathing suit and abundance of red hair hanging on her shoulders invitingly—but ignored them. Right now, all she wanted to do was jump into the water and work out for a while.

Swimming had always been one of her greatest passions, along with singing and playing the guitar. Living on the island of Maui had given her some opportunities to do them all. But being in paradise had come at a price, one that she would just as soon forget.

* * *

Two years ago, Genevieve, then twenty-one, was living in San Francisco with her boyfriend, Cooper. They were both heavily into the music scene and getting high.

She had gotten kicked out of high school in the eleventh grade when she was involved a fight that another girl started. She never went back to school, feeling it would just be a waste of time. Her folks weren't cool about it and encouraged her to leave home, which she also felt was best all the way around.

After bumming with friends off and on and even being homeless for a while, Genevieve met Cooper at a party. Tall, dark-skinned, muscular, and charming, she fell hard for him. The fact that he was a musician and playing at clubs made him even more attractive.

He helped her land a few gigs and it seemed like they were destined to be together for a long time.

But she hadn't realized he was dealing drugs. Not until it was too late and he was busted.

She wound up testifying against him and, in the process, helped send him to prison, along with a couple of his buddies.

A lot of people weren't happy about that and blamed her. Some even swore vengeance, starting with Cooper. So she had to get out of town. But where? She'd thought about Los Angeles, where she had friends. But Cooper had friends there too.

Moving to Atlanta crossed Genevieve's mind, since she had family there. But she rejected that idea, deciding she didn't really want to live in Georgia.

She ended up in Hawaii, first Oahu and then Maui. The latter seemed like a perfect hideaway. It was laidback, most people tended to mind their own business, and there were opportunities to sing and actually make money from it.

When she started dating Kalani Okamura, Genevieve had no illusions about them living happily thereafter. She knew he was attracted to her looks and sassy personality. She, on the other hand, was turned on mostly by his kind heart and generosity. He was nothing at all like Cooper, for which she was grateful, knowing that her ex and his cronies could be vindictive and scary.

All she wanted was to sing, play the guitar, and live in peace. Maybe things were beginning to fall in place on Maui.

* * *

Genevieve swam to shore and flipped her wet hair to one side. She started to walk across the beach when she spotted a man from afar who seemed to be gazing at her behind sunglasses.

Her heart skipped a beat. She could swear that he was one of Cooper's friends. But how was that possible? She'd gone to great lengths to cover her tracks.

Against her better judgment, Genevieve moved toward him for a closer look. But the man quickly turned and walked away. By the time she got across the sand, he was gone.

Maybe my mind is playing tricks on me, she told herself. No reason to start getting paranoid in paradise, especially when she was an ocean away from San Francisco and those who might seek to do her harm.

She turned her thoughts to the grand opening at the Kaanapali Palms Hotel. She intended to be there, if only to check out the place where she hoped to land a job as a singer.

Genevieve fully expected Kalani to be there too, since he was an investor. She wondered if his wife would accompany him. Or might it be a good opportunity for Kalani to slip away for some time with his mistress?

* * *

Stewart McGann had beaten the sun up and joined a surprisingly large number of joggers in all shapes and sizes meandering their way around a maze of tree-lined boulevards, hilly residential settings, and the seemingly endless white sand of Kaanapali Beach. This was his third day of a two week vacation on Maui, courtesy of Ben Crawford. Stewart, recognizing in a very short time that he had gotten out of shape, decided it was time he made the most of a setting that almost scolded you if you didn't take advantage of its playground. And so, he gave in to the temptations, even if his body would have to work its way back to where he once was.

* * *

It was not so long ago that Stewart was in the best shape of his life. As a detective for the Portland Police Bureau for fourteen years, he was constantly required to use damn near every limb in his body in the pursuit of justice. He also visited the health club regularly, and routinely did one hundred pushups daily, and more.

But that all took an abrupt turn on the day two years ago when, during a stakeout of a suspected drug lab, one of the suspects got wind of it and took counter measures. Those measures included getting into a Chevy pickup, driving through a garage door like it was papier-mâché, and firing at everything that moved.

That included Stewart and his partner, Miles Berry.

Miles was struck head-on by the truck and sent flying like a giant bird with no wings. Stewart flew as well, but with his own thrust, avoiding the vehicle with no time to spare, but meeting the pavement awkwardly and unkindly. He was not aware he had become immobilized until after he had shot and killed the suspect, who had just as swiftly put Miles in the grave.

Stewart considered himself lucky at the time. His diagnosis: a slipped disc and broken back.

Only his luck ran out when it became apparent after a year of therapy and considerable, sometimes never ending pain, that his mobility and back would never again be the same. For his line of work, anything less was insufficient. The department offered him a desk job, or he could retire early with a full pension.

Being a man of immense pride, Stewart considered a desk job a demotion and decided he would rather call it quits; go out knowing he had done his best while he was the best. Instrumental in his decision was the fact that Miles was gone and never coming back. They were a team for nearly ten years. It seemed only fitting that maybe they should end their active duty at the same time.

And thus, at the age of thirty-seven when most detectives were just entering the prime of their careers, Stewart was content to simply collect his pension and do nothing. Alone. He had been married for a short time early on in his career until his wife became fed up with his perilous duty and sporadic work hours and left him for a doctor, whom she later married.

With his back still bothering him off and on, Stewart spent the next year feeling sorry for himself, drinking beer, and getting flabby. He'd gained about fifteen pounds on his previously muscular frame. He shunned get-togethers with members of the force, who would only make him envious. And he couldn't really relate to older retirees who might well have been friends with his father or grandfather.

Then a month ago, Stewart ran into Ben Crawford, a millionaire real estate investor-owner, who he had once done some private investigative work for on the side. He ended up saving Crawford over two million dollars, for which he had been profoundly grateful. Ben told him about his multimillion dollar resort hotel opening in Maui and invited him, all expenses paid, to visit for a couple of weeks.

Ben had told him: "Just consider it a fringe benefit for that job you did for me three years ago, Stewart. I never forget good people."

Initially Stewart declined, not wanting to be looked upon as some sort of charity case. However, Crawford left the offer on the table. And Stewart was glad he did. He decided there was nothing wrong with accepting a trip from a man who probably threw away millions at the blink of an eye.

Maybe that was what he needed: to get away, put some perspective on what he wanted to do with the rest of his life; have some fun in the sun. And really, when Stewart thought about it, what the hell was he doing anyway but taking up space...

After a couple of days on Kaanapali Beach, his back felt better than it had since before the accident. Stewart had little doubt that his first real vacation since going to London, England for a criminal justice seminar as a college student was more than worth the trip.

* * *

By the time he got back to the Kaanapali Palms Hotel, Stewart was dripping with perspiration and huffing and puffing as if he was ready to blow the house down. He went inside and drew in a deep, steadying breath, trying to gather himself. He watched as a group of people—other VIPs who were making use of the hotel before its official opening—passed by heading to the restaurant for breakfast. After catching his breath, Stewart quickly slipped inside an elevator just as it was closing.

There was forty-something woman in the elevator wearing a bright pink jogging suit that stretched across a curvy frame. She displayed a toothy smile and seemed interested, but Stewart was not. He did not come all the way to Hawaii to meet a divorced mother of three from Duluth, Minnesota!

292

He was relieved when his floor—the eighth—came up, and he got off, thinking only about a cold shower. When he got to the door of his room, he realized he had left his key card inside.

Damn!

He looked down the hallway and spotted the housekeeper's cart a few doors down.

Standing in front of the cart, Stewart called out: "Excuse me," as he sought to attract the attention of the housekeeper who was out of his view inside the room.

"Yes," he heard the soft voice say.

Then she stepped into the doorway wearing a brown housekeeper's dress and a stern gaze of resentment, as if he had intruded upon her private time.

Normally on the offensive, for once Stewart found himself on the defensive. At the same time, however, he was struck by the attractive Hawaiian woman. He did not particularly care for the young, deeply tanned, bottle blonde, chesty women he had seen at the beach and elsewhere; and certainly could do without the one he left practically foaming at the mouth on the elevator. But this one—her name tag read Yoshiko—was indeed a pleasant sight with her shoulder length glossy black hair, finely chiseled features, streamlined figure, and grayish brown eyes of fire that were more than a match for his own deep blue eyes. He guessed she was in her early thirties.

When it became apparent he had let his fixation get the better of him, Stewart shifted his eyes, cleared his throat, and said in an apologetic tone: "I left my key card in my room."

The annoyance in her face eased up as she said: "No problem. What's your room number?"

He told her and she looked down at a sheet on her cart. "You are Mr. McGann?"

"Yes, but you can call me Stewart," he told her.

She smiled and he couldn't help but think what a pretty smile it was.

"Do you have some ID?" she asked, no longer smiling.

Stewart cocked a brow, though he knew it made sense to check him out, rather than simply let him enter what could be someone else's room purely on his word. He took out his wallet and removed his driver's license, passing it to her.

Yoshiko studied it and looked at him. "Yes, I'd say that is you, Mr. Mc—I mean, Stewart."

He grinned, taking the license back. "I hope so. I wouldn't want to see anyone else in this skin."

She chuckled as they walked toward his room together. "Are you enjoying your vacation, Stewart?" she asked.

"So far, so good," he said.

"I'm glad to hear that."

They reached the room and she unlocked the door.

She gazed up at him and asked: "Do you need anything else?"

Attracted to her, Stewart could think of a thing or two, but thought better. "No, that should do it. Mahalo."

"Mahalo," she said back, flashing her teeth, before walking away.

Stewart was curious about her, as if there was more to her than met the eye. He couldn't help but think that she seemed out of place here. Or was that just his imagination?

Was she married or involved with anyone? Even then, he didn't want to go there, realizing it was inappropriate to be interested in the staff. Wasn't it?

Stewart watched Yoshiko move lithely away for a moment longer, before going inside his room. He stepped to the window of the ocean front unit and looked beyond the lanai to the beach and the water. It was definitely a perfect setting. He just wished he had someone to share it with.

Stewart's cell phone rang, intruding upon his thoughts. He grabbed it off the counter. "Hello."

"Aloha! Mr. McGann...?"

"Yes."

The woman said she was calling on behalf of Ben Crawford, who was wondering if Stewart could drop by his suite.

"Sure, why not," he said. He had nothing better to do. "When?"

"Nine o'clock."

That was an hour from now. "I'll be there."

"I'll let Mr. Crawford know," she said.

He hung up, curious as to why Crawford had asked to see him. They had only run into each other once since he arrived. At the time, the hotel owner had been passing by with his pretty daughter, who was giving him the eye. Ben, as Crawford insisted he call him, didn't seem to notice. That was fine by Stewart, as she was much too young for his tastes.

Maybe now I'll find out what this all-expense paid trip was really about, Stewart thought.

* * *

Yoshiko Pelayo took a peek back at the handsome hotel guest named Stewart McGann. She was relieved to see that he wasn't still staring at her, as had been the case for most of their brief communication. She wondered why he was here all by himself. At least he was the only one staying in that room. Maybe he was involved in a steamy illicit affair and doing his best to keep it under wraps.

Yoshiko checked her imagination. In spite of her attraction to the man and feeling lonely, she needed to keep her eye on the ball. In this case, it was her father, Ben Crawford, and seeing to it that he got what was coming to him.

"Hey."

The voice startled Yoshiko. She turned and saw Maggie over her shoulder. "Hey."

"How's it going?" Maggie asked.

Yoshiko grabbed some towels from the cart. "I was just about to get back to cleaning this room."

"I couldn't help but notice you were talking to Mr. McGann," Maggie commented.

Yoshiko regarded her with surprise and then realized this was normally Maggie's floor, but she was subbing on another floor right now.

"He left his key card in the room," Yoshiko explained.

"Good thing you were around to help him out."

"If not me, it would have been you," Yoshiko responded with a smile.

"True. Then I would be the one he was indebted to," Maggie said.

Yoshiko chuckled. "I'd hardly say he was indebted to me for doing my job."

"Never underestimate how little things can make a difference, girlfriend," Maggie said. "Especially when the person happens to be a friend of Mr. Crawford."

"He's a friend of Mr. Crawford?" That caught Yoshiko's attention.

"Yeah, before he arrived, Mr. Crawford personally contacted housekeeping to make sure that his room was ready, with a few extras thrown in, like a fully stocked wet bar, some Hawaiian chocolate-covered macadamia nuts, and a complimentary guest pass to dining at any of the hotel's restaurants."

"That's interesting," Yoshiko hummed. For some reason, it didn't seem like Stewart and her father would hang out in the same circles. Maybe they didn't, but shared some business interests or were connected in another way.

"I thought so, too," Maggie said. "I never saw a ring on Mr. McGann's finger, so maybe he's available for some lucky woman."

"Maybe," Yoshiko allowed, "but probably not the hired help."

"Don't sell yourself short. He's a good looking man and you're a gorgeous woman. You just never know what could happen if you play your cards right," Maggie said. "Besides, playtime on Kaanapali Beach stays on Kaanapali Beach."

Yoshiko laughed. "I'll keep that in mind."

Maggie chuckled. "Hey, I'm just saying."

"Well thanks, Ms. Matchmaker. Now if you don't mind, I'd better get this room cleaned or I won't even have a job. And any chance of bumping into Stew—Mr. McGann would be lost forever."

Maggie grinned. "See you later."

Yoshiko waited until she was out of sight, before stepping into the room with the towels.

She wondered exactly what Stewart's connection was to Ben Crawford. Perhaps she might find a clue in his room. She liked Stewart for some reason, and hated the thought of him becoming her enemy too. But if he was just another pawn in her father's dirty dealings, she wanted no part of him—other than perhaps as another means to strike back at the man who refused to acknowledge her existence in his world.

* * *

Stewart, feeling refreshed after a shower and now comfortably dressed, knocked on the door of the top floor suite. He could only imagine what it must look like in there, especially since his room was a cut above a "standard" room, albeit with a nice view.

All in all, he gave Ben Crawford credit for sparing no expense in creating a first class hotel.

The door opened.

"Stewart..." Ben, wearing a gray suit, extended his hand and the two shook. "Glad you could make it."

To the hotel or your room? Stewart wondered, but responded cautiously: "So am I."

"Come on in."

As expected, the suite was immense, superbly and exquisitely furnished, and definitely fitting of the hotel's principal owner. In fact, Stewart speculated that even the President of the United States might be a bit overmatched in here.

He noticed he was not the only visitor. Two other men— one was Asian, fortyish, thin, and wearing a brown suit; the other was taller, huskier, mid-thirties, and wearing a blue suit—approached him.

Ben introduced the shorter one as Rick Chang, the hotel's general manager, and the other as Victor Quail of the security staff.

He shook their hands.

Stewart still wasn't sure what this was all about, particularly with the threesome present, but he had a feeling he was about to find out. Ben offered him something to drink.

"Coffee," he said. He loved beer, but not at nine in the morning.

He joined Rick and Victor at a long glass table for some small talk before Ben handed him a mug of coffee.

"Are you having a good time on the island, Stewart?" Ben asked as he sat down.

"Yeah, it's been great," he admitted. "You've got some hotel here."

"We think so," Ben said proudly, holding a glass that was half-filled with alcohol. He glanced at his employees and back. "Anyway, Stewart, the truth of the matter is my reason for inviting you here was twofold—"

"Oh..." Stewart met his eyes.

Ben laughed—a singularly unpleasant, yet calming laugh. "Don't worry," he said, "I don't think either reason will put you off. First, I wanted you to see our hotel, get a feel for the electric atmosphere on Kaanapali Beach in general, and the Kaanapali Palms Hotel in specific."

Ben paused and tasted the drink, winced, but drank more anyway. "Secondly, I wanted to offer you a job."

"A job?" Stewart lifted his brows with surprise.

"Yes," Ben said. "I'd like you to head my security staff here."

Stewart sipped the coffee in lieu of an immediate response. He honestly never saw this coming.

Ben continued: "I've never forgotten the superb way you handled that investigation for me a few years back. I really think you're the right man for the job here." He paused and sipped his drink. "Victor will be working security with you— or, actually, he'll be working for you."

"I'm flattered," Stewart said honestly, adding with equal candidness, "but I don't know the first thing about the hotel business."

"But you know a hell of a lot about the detective business," Ben told him flatly. "The rest you can learn." He narrowed his eyes and streamlined his pitch. "Look, Stewart...I know about your early retirement from the Portland Police Bureau."

Stewart gazed at him and said: "Then you must also know about my bad back." There was no sense denying it.

Ben confirmed that, but reaffirmed his desire to have Stewart at the helm of his security force. He ran off some of the fringe benefits: more than double Stewart's last pay he made with the Portland Police Bureau, complete charge of the hotel security staff and its functions, room and board at the hotel, and residence in one of the most breathtaking places in the world and its obvious benefits—sun, beaches, palm trees, and beautiful women...

Stewart had to admit the offer was more than tempting. How often could a washed up detective, who had been out of circulation for a year with a bad back subject to flare up at any time, get an opportunity like this?

And yet it was hardly that simple. For a start, he had grown to enjoy being retired—or maybe lazy was more like it. Since the Bureau was footing his life's bill, albeit at a rate that hardly equated to financial independence, he was making due just fine. Why should he end it all by going back to work? No matter what, work was still work.

Then there was the move across the Pacific to Hawaii. Maui was nice, but who could actually live in paradise? And he liked living in the Pacific Northwest. He had grown comfortable there over the years. His life was there.

Then he thought: *What life?*

Still... Why him...? Then again, why the hell not him...?

He needed time to think it over and told Ben as much.

Though Stewart suspected that Ben Crawford was used to getting whatever he wanted, he seemed to understand and invited him to take the rest of the vacation to decide. Even then, Stewart could detect a trifle impatience undercutting his would-be employer's voice.

Stewart believed that was fair, finished his coffee, and left.

He went back to his room thoughtfully, and found it was being cleaned by the housekeeper who had let him in earlier. In this instance, it suited him just fine, for it gave him an excuse to talk to Yoshiko, and he did.

Despite the chip he sensed on her shoulder, she seemed pleasant enough. Yet the exchange of words proved to be awkward—for both parties. *But what the hell*, thought Stewart. There was no rule book that said hotel staff and guests had to limit their contact to towels, sheets, and room service. And he knew for a fact that Yoshiko was a damn sight better looking than anyone else he had seen.

So he asked her what he had wanted to all along. "What time do you break for lunch?"

She regarded him quizzically. "I beg your pardon?"

He sighed, and repeated the question.

"Eleven-thirty," she told him.

"Would you like to join me for lunch?" Stewart almost felt like he was back in high school; and that wasn't necessarily a bad thing, especially if she was his date.

Yoshiko seemed to mull it over, while Stewart wondered if he had overstepped his bounds. Finally, she said evenly, "Okay, why not?"

Stewart smiled and considered that his options seemed to be expanding by the moment on this island, where suddenly all things seemed possible...

* * *

The dramatic and compelling story of Kaanapali Beach Paradise will be continued in the next upcoming episode.

# # #

The following is a bonus excerpt of the exciting new
mystery series by R. Barri Flowers

DEAD IN PUKALANI
An Eddie Naku Maui Mystery

Prologue

Hawaiian music filtered through the speakers on this humid
August evening as Suzette Higuchi-Bordeau sat in the Great
Room of her contemporary home on Hololani Street in
Pukalani, a census-designated region in Maui County,
Hawaii. Located on the slopes of the East Maui Volcano,
Haleakalā, in an area that natives of the island refer to as
Upcountry, the upscale residence was bordered by swaying
palm trees and close to the Pukalani Golf Course and
Country Club.

Suzette sipped a Mai Tai beneath the swirling ceiling
fan as a cool breeze brought forth the aroma of eucalyptus.
She brushed away a strand of curly brunette hair from her
face, barely listening to the conversation in progress. In
truth, her mind was elsewhere. There were many things
going on in her life at once, some of which she had never
meant to happen, others that were beyond her control.
Nonetheless, she had resigned herself to make the best of

302

both worlds, just as her husband Patrick had.

"Can I get you another drink, Suzette?" asked one of the three men she had allowed into their home. He was white, bald, and stocky, with a deep tan, having helped himself to the wet bar, as had the other two men.

"No, I don't think so," she told him. She'd never been able to handle her alcohol very well, and now was not the time to test it, as she'd already had one drink before the men arrived. "But feel free to help yourself to another," she offered. "Patrick should be home any time now."

Her husband, Patrick Bordeau, the successful lawyer. *Right. What a joke*, Suzette thought. He'd called earlier and said he was at the office and would be a bit late, even though he was expecting the visit from his associates. She had no doubt he was busy, but it was not with work. She'd learned long ago to accept his infidelity, along with everything else that was wrong with their marriage. It was all part of the total package she'd become caught up in, mostly due to circumstances. Suzette wasn't sure if she still loved Patrick, or even if she ever truly had, but she was no longer committed to staying with him and pretending to be the dutiful wife who would always look the other way. Not when she now finally had another choice that gave her hope for something that had eluded her for a long time: happiness in a relationship. Or was that even possible? Maybe she was only deluding herself that there really could be a happy ending for two people who loved each other, no matter the obstacles standing in their way.

The ringing of her cell phone jarred Suzette from her thoughts. She pulled out the phone, looked at it for a moment, then glanced toward her visitors. The bald, stocky one had just come back with two drinks in hand, passing one to a white, tall, thinner man with sandy hair. The other man was Asian and small with a short black ponytail, still holding a drink. All three were in their thirties and chattering amongst themselves as though she were invisible. They barely seemed to notice her phone ringing.

"I need to get this," she said anyway, as if she needed an excuse to step away from the men. She moved toward the gourmet kitchen, out of their line of vision. She could hear her Rottweiler named Cherry whimpering behind the door of a spare room, anxious to get out. As soon as her guests were gone, she would let the dog out to roam freely throughout the house.

She engaged in a short conversation with the caller, while peeking out at the men, who were still huddled together, before disconnecting and rejoining them.

The Asian man gazed at her. "Everything all right?"

"I have to go out," she said tersely.

"Where?" asked the tall, thin one.

"To see someone," she responded.

"Tucker Matsumoto?" the bald one asked perceptively.

Suzette cocked a thin brow. How could he have known that? But then she quickly realized they were probably familiar with some of their other business associates through Patrick.

"Yes," she responded, knowing that their interests were indirectly represented here.

"I think we should follow you," he said, "just in case you need back up."

She swallowed thickly. "That really won't be necessary."

"We insist." The bald man's dark eyes narrowed. "Matsumoto's not to be trusted. We wouldn't want anything bad to happen to you."

Reluctantly, Suzette relented, feeling she didn't have much choice. Nor was there time to wait for Patrick to return home from his latest tryst.

Or course, their presence would change the nature of the meeting a bit. But if she was able to accomplish her primary goal, other things could wait till later.

* * *

Suzette drove her gray Lexus through the streets of Pukalani, glancing in the rear view mirror at the three men following her in a red F-150 pickup. She was a bit tense, under the circumstances, but tried to remain calm.

Soon she pulled into a shopping center parking lot on Old Haleakala Highway, well away from the stores, and parked near a light. It was seven fifty-five p.m. She had been told the meeting would take place at eight.

She watched as the pickup truck pulled into a spot a few feet away from her. The men remained inside.

Suzette hoped their presence didn't scare off Matsumoto. Or was that their plan?

She took out her cell phone and called Patrick. It went straight to voicemail. Frustrated, she didn't bother to leave a message.

"Damn you, Patrick," she muttered irritably, jealous that he was likely bedding another woman at that exact moment. She couldn't help herself, in spite of the fact that her own romantic feelings and sexual yearnings lay elsewhere. She took comfort in knowing that soon her life would change for the better and she would no longer need to tolerate the pain Patrick had caused her.

The knock on the partially open driver's side window caused Suzette's heart to skip a beat. She turned and saw Tucker Matsumoto's face. He was Hawaiian and had a thin mustache.

"What the hell are you doing here?" he snapped.

She caught her breath. "I think you know."

Matsumoto cocked a brow. "He sent *you* to bring the money?"

She almost hated to disappoint him. "No, I'm here to *collect* money—from you."

He frowned. "I owe you nothing."

"The merchandise you have says otherwise, Matsumoto," she said boldly. "If you think you can screw us out of payment—"

"You'll do what?" he said, cutting her off. "Go to the cops?" He laughed derisively. "I don't think so."

Suzette was furious at his arrogance and clear intention

to stiff them. Just as she contemplated her next move, a shot rang out, striking Matsumoto, who doubled over. Another shot hit him and he went down.

Fearful that she might be next, Suzette reached in her purse for her gun, which she kept for protection. But it was too late. The crackling sound of gunfire, seemingly louder than ever, rang through her ears. The sudden realization that she'd been shot left her numb, then she felt her head spinning, and suddenly everything was pitch black.

Chapter One

The vibrancy of laughter echoed throughout the bedroom as Eddie Naku playfully nibbled on the neck of his current romantic interest, Gayle Luciano, a flight attendant. They were naked in bed making love on a steamy night. It was one of those on again, off again relationships, where neither was ready to make a real commitment and both were the better for it. Instead, they got together when their conflicting schedules allowed and their bodies lusted for one another.

Now was one of those times as Naku pushed aside his life as a private investigator in favor of a good romp in the sack.

The ringing of his cell phone put a crimp in that. He tried to ignore it, as did his lover.

"Don't answer it," Gayle pleaded. "Remember, this is your day off—and mine."

For a moment, Naku found her incredible powers of persuasion too much to ignore as she claimed his lips with her own.

But the damned phone ringing persisted. Against his better judgment, he decided he better answer it. He pried their mouths apart and hoisted his muscular six-foot-three-inch body from the bed. Seeing the disappointment in Gayle's face, he said, "Don't worry. Whoever it is, I'll get rid of them."

"You better," she said, pouting.

He dug the cell phone out of his jeans that had ended up on the floor. The caller was his secretary, Vanna.

"I hope I didn't catch you at a bad time," she said.

Naku gazed at his lover, ready and waiting. "As a matter of fact, you did."

"Sorry, but there's a lady here, a Ms. Higuchi, who—"

He cut her off. "It's my day off. She can come back tomorrow."

"Well, the thing is, she insisted on seeing you *today*," Vanna told him. "She said it can't wait."

Higuchi. The name had a ring of familiarity to it, and not because it was common on the Hawaiian Islands. He remembered now. A week ago, a Suzette Higuchi-Bordeau was shot to death in Pukalani. The shooter was still at large. Coincidence?

"She says she was referred to you," Vanna said. "She seems really desperate."

He glanced at Gayle, who seemed a bit desperate herself to finish where they left off. But since he was in the business of private detective work and prided himself on never turning down a paying customer, he felt he should at least see what this potential one wanted of him.

"I'll be there as soon as I can," he told Vanna.

"I'll pass that along," she said happily.

Naku disconnected and turned to his bed mate. "I have to go," he said regrettably.

She frowned. "Why am I not surprised?"

"It's work." He ran a hand through his long dark hair. "I'll make it up to you. I promise."

She sprang out of bed, her large breasts bouncing, and her tight ass barely moving. "Don't bother!"

He watched as she started to get dressed. "Where are you going?"

"To work!"

"But I thought you had the day off..."

Gayle sneered. "Yeah, and I thought you did too."

307

Naku was speechless, but understood that their little tit for tat was pretty much par for the course in their relationship. She was pissed at him now, but by the time she got back in town, that would likely pass and they could resume whatever it was they had going on.

For now, he had to take things for what they were between them and get to his office.

* * *

He beat Gayle out the door of her small plantation house in Napilihau, located in West Maui, and got into his Subaru Forester for the short drive to Lahaina, the most populated area of Maui County during the peak tourist season. As a third generation Native Hawaiian, Eddie Naku was happy to carry the torch of his ancestors in being a free spirit and respecting the land. At thirty-six, he had given up a career as a homicide detective for the Maui Police Department two years ago in favor of being his own boss and solving cases that sometimes required working the edges of the law.

Though Maui wasn't exactly New York City or Honolulu for that matter, when it came to criminal activity, there were still enough lawbreakers and other types of investigative work to keep him busy. When that failed, he was more than happy to indulge in his other passions, which included drinking, working out, riding horses, reading thriller fiction, and women. Gayle flew the international routes, mostly to and from Japan, Singapore, New Zealand, and Australia. He had no idea when she'd be back and she was probably in no hurry to see him, but neither of them made any promises to one another, so they could go whichever way the wind guided them.

His thoughts turned to the woman who had taken him away from Gayle at the worst possible time. What was her story? Who referred her to him and why was she so damned intent on seeing him this afternoon?

He'd find out soon enough. He pulled onto Keawe Street and parked in his customary spot in front of his office.

Painted on the window were the words: Eddie Naku Investigations.

Naku stepped inside the dusty, beige-carpeted, white walled place that was divided into three sections: a small waiting area; the office of his dependable secretary, Vanna Dandridge; and his own office. He observed the attractive, slim, long blonde-haired Hawaiian woman in her mid-thirties sitting in the waiting area. She was nicely dressed in a blue dress with high-heeled sandals.

As he met her bold, brown eyes, she stood up.

"I'm Eddie Naku," he introduced himself.

Before she could speak, Vanna bounded out of her office. "You're finally here," she said. "Good."

He grinned while giving her the once over. Vanna was forty, twice divorced, and not bad on the eyes. She was petite and wore her crimson hair in a bob. She had just moved to Maui from Honolulu at the same time he opened up his private investigation business. The timing had worked out well for both of them.

He looked back at the other woman.

"This is—" Vanna started to say.

"Kathryn Higuchi," the woman finished.

Naku extended his arm to shake her hand. "Nice to meet you, Ms. Higuchi."

She proffered a small hand with perfectly manicured nails and they shook. He tried to read her, as he'd done so many other potential clients, but failed miserably.

"Why don't we step into my office so you can tell me why you're here?"

She nodded and he waved Vanna off with eye contact, as if to say he'd take it from there.

His office was pretty nondescript: wooden desk, leather chair, laptop, printer, flat panel television, two stacking guest chairs, and a window with a view of the street.

He invited her to have a seat and he did the same, opting to sit beside her rather than at his desk.

"So how can I help you?" he asked evenly.

"I'd like to hire you."

"To do what?"

"Find out who murdered my sister—" She paused. "Suzette Higuchi-Bordeau. She was shot to death last Friday."

He nodded. "I heard about that and I'm sorry for your loss. But it's an ongoing police investigation."

She frowned. "I don't want to wait until the police get around to solving the crime, if they ever do."

"I can appreciate that you want answers quickly," he told her, "but it doesn't always work that way."

Kathryn frowned. "My sister and I were very close. She didn't deserve to die that way. I need answers. And I think you can give them to me. Money is no object. Please..."

Naku had always had a hard time turning down a pretty face where money was not an issue in paying his fees. It was even more difficult when she was as striking as this one. However, he usually refrained from working on active police cases, so as not to bump heads with his former colleagues.

Of course, there were always exceptions to the rule. Maybe this would be one.

"Tell me about your sister and what you know, if anything, about her death."

He listened as she described Suzette Higuchi-Bordeau as the unhappy wife of a prominent Maui attorney, Patrick Bordeau, and the shooting that took her life and seriously wounded a man named Tucker Matsumoto. Three men were taken into custody briefly in connection with the crime, but were released for lack of evidence.

"There's not much else I can tell you, other than I believe my sister was set up the night she was murdered," Kathryn finished.

Naku regarded her with curiosity. "I take it you have someone in mind who set your sister up?"

She met his eyes. "Yes, her husband, Patrick—"

Naku recalled reading that the husband lawyer had

previously represented two of the men who were taken into custody, and he was also the current attorney for Tucker Matsumoto. Though it was strange for sure, it hardly meant that Bordeau was behind his wife's murder. At the same time, the spouse was often the first suspect in such cases, which surely the police were looking into.

"What makes you think Bordeau had anything to do with this?" Naku asked.

Kathryn sighed. "He may not have been the one to pull the trigger, and even that's suspect, but he certainly had a very good motive for wanting her dead. Suzette often confided in me about what was going on in her life. Patrick's been involved in a gunrunning scheme, which brought in a good deal of money and just as much debt. He had a life insurance policy on Suzette for half a million dollars—an amount that would probably cover his obligations, and then some, if she were out of the picture. I also know that Patrick was having an affair with another woman and Suzette wanted out of the marriage. She was prepared to blow his whole arms trafficking operation wide open, ruining his career and likely sending him to prison."

"Those are certainly some compelling reasons for killing one's spouse," Naku acknowledged, having seen intimates murdered for far less. "Have you told the police any of this?"

"Yes, of course I did. They basically dismissed it as insufficient or hearsay."

He agreed, but also understood that such things would not likely be made public, even to family, until the case could be made one way or the other. Still, something told him that there was more to the story.

"So I take it there's no love lost between you and Bordeau."

She wrinkled her nose. "Why would you say that?"

"Call it instincts."

She paused. "I never thought he was good enough for my sister," she admitted. "Patrick is a control freak and never treated Suzette right. I think he's more than capable of killing her, if he thought he could get away with it."

"We'll see about that," Naku said, keeping an open mind.

"Does that mean you'll take the case?" Kathryn pressed. "I don't want my sister's death to end up as another unsolved homicide while her killer runs free."

Naku didn't have to give it much thought at this point. Since the police hadn't made any arrests yet, and the case was still open, why not look into it. Also, there was something about Kathryn Higuchi that piqued his interest and made him want to keep the connection alive.

"My fee is five hundred dollars an hour, plus any unusual expenses I incur in the course of the investigation," he told her, in the event she had any second thoughts. "I typically require a five thousand dollar retainer to take on a case that looks like it could take a while."

"As I said, I have no problem with your fees, if it means getting to the bottom of why my sister lost her life."

Naku knew he couldn't guarantee results, but he told her sincerely, "I'll do my best to find the answers you're looking for."

Kathryn pulled out her checkbook and wrote a check, handing it to him. "That should cover a week and any added expenses."

"Indeed," Naku told her after gazing at the check. "Mahalo."

"Thank you for taking the case," she told him, then dug in her handbag and pulled out a card containing her address and cell phone number. "Please keep me informed as to what you learn."

"I will," he promised, meeting her lovely eyes.

She stood. "I better go."

Naku rose and walked her to the outer door, when curiosity got the better of him. "By the way, who referred you to me anyway?" He would be sure to thank the person.

Kathryn looked him straight in the eye. "Why it was

Lieutenant Ortega of the Maui Police Department."

Naku nodded with a smile. He and Ortega had worked together during his days on the force and were on good terms. Still, it wasn't every day that the man sent business his way. Why?

He showed Kathryn out just as Vanna stepped out of her office. "Looks like we've got ourselves a client," she said.

"Yeah, I'd say so," Naku responded.

"And she's a hot lady too," Vanna said with a wink. "I hope you'll be able to concentrate on the investigation."

He grinned, conceding that Kathryn was definitely his type. But then, so was Gayle. He wasn't too picky about women, as long as they were energetic and fun loving.

However, Kathryn Higuchi had hired him to do a job and that had to come first.

"I think I can manage," he said, "with your help of course."

"That's what you pay me for," she said dryly.

"You can earn your keep by getting me everything you can find regarding Suzette Higuchi-Bordeau's murder as well as the lady herself."

"Will do." She looked at him. "What are you going to do now?"

"I think I'll pay Lieutenant Ortega a visit to see if he can fill in some blanks for me," Naku told her thoughtfully.

* * *

Read the entire Dead in Pukalani, available in eBook, audio, and print.

# # #

The following is a bonus excerpt from the private
investigator island mystery by R. Barri Flowers

MURDER IN HONOLULU
A Skye Delaney Mystery

Chapter One

The name's Skye McKenzie Delaney. I'm part of the twenty-
first century breed of licensed private investigators who live
by their wits, survive on instincts, and take each case as
though it may be their last. The fact that I double as a
security consultant for companies in and around the city of
Honolulu, where I reside, gives me financial backup not
afforded to all private eyes. This notwithstanding, I take my
work as an investigator of everything from cats stuck in trees
to missing persons to crimes the police can't or won't touch
very seriously. If not, I wouldn't be putting my heart, soul,
and body into this often thankless job.

I also happen to be happily divorced—or at least no
longer pining for my ex—and not afraid to get my hands
dirty if necessary in my business. I get along with most
people, but won't take any crap from anyone should it come
my way.

Before I became a security consultant/private eye, I used to be a homicide cop for the Honolulu Police Department. Stress, fatigue, burnout, and a real desire to get into something that could provide more financial security and flexible hours, without the downside and depression of police work and know-it-all authority figures, convinced me to change careers.

During my six years on the force, I spent my nights earning a Master's Degree in Criminal Justice Administration. I'm hoping to get my Ph.D. someday when I no longer need to work for a living and can devote my time to further educating myself. In the meantime, I'm getting an honorary doctorate in private detectiveology, where every case can be a real learning experience.

On and off the job, I carry a .40 caliber or 9-millimeter pistol Smith and Wesson—depending on my mood. And I'm not afraid to use either one if I have to, as it sure beats the alternative of ending up as just another private dick on a cold slab in the morgue.

If I were to describe myself character-wise, the words that come to mind are feminine, adventurous yet conservative, streetwise though I often rely on intellect to get me over the hump, and kick-ass tough when duty calls.

I've been told on more than one occasion that I'm attractive—even beautiful—and sexy as hell. I leave that for others to decide, but I'm definitely in great shape at five-eight, thanks to a near obsession with running and swimming, along with not overdoing it with calories. I usually wear my long blonde hair in a ponytail. My contacts make my eyes seem greener than they really are.

I recently celebrated my thirty-fifth birthday. All right, in truth, it wasn't much of a celebration. I spent the entire day holed up in my house with my dog, Ollie, contemplating the future and happy to put much of my past behind me. That included my ex-husband, Carter Delaney, whose greatest contribution to my life and times was making me realize that no man was worth sacrificing one's own identity and integrity, even if it meant losing him in the process.

I did lose Carter five years ago, after deciding I had no desire to share him with his mistress (and probably others I didn't know about). It was a decision I firmly stand by today and am definitely the better for.

At least I convinced myself that was the case even as I came face to face with the subject in question on a muggy afternoon at the end of July. I had just filed away some papers when he walked into my office literally out of the blue. It was his first visit to my office since I joined the ranks of private eyes. I had once worked for the man as a security consultant. That turned into lust, sex, love, marriage, and divorce, and now we were little more than distant acquaintances.

The tremulous half-smile that played on Carter's lips told me that he was not entirely comfortable being there. I felt just as awkward for probably the same reason: the *ex-spouse syndrome*, which would forever keep a wall of regrets and painful memories between us, thick as molasses.

Never mind the fact that Carter Delaney was still every bit the physical specimen I had fallen in love with another lifetime ago. Tall, fit, handsome, and perennially tanned with dark hair and gray eyes, he almost looked as if he had just stepped out of the pages of Good Looking Digest. Though it was hotter than hell outside, he was decked out in an Italian navy designer suit and wing-tipped burgundy leather shoes. He glanced at the expensive watch on his wrist as if he needed to be somewhere else.

At thirty-eight, Carter Delaney was a successful businessman. A former Honolulu prosecutor in the career criminal division, Carter had walked away from the job after excelling at it for the lure of cold hard cash in the world of commerce. He had turned his smarts and acumen into a successful Internet-based international trade company.

It was during the early stages of this success that I entered the picture. Carter had hired me, wanting to have the best security devices for both his home and business. The rest, as they say, is history.

At least it was.

We had managed to avoid running into each other for nearly a year now, which suited me just fine. I wasn't looking for history to ever repeat itself, so quite naturally my curiosity was piqued as to why he was here now. Rather than appear too overeager, I decided to wait and let him take the lead.

"Hi," I said tonelessly as I eased back into my chair and scooted it up to my gray workstation desk. I shuffled some papers to at least give the guise of being busy. In fact, I was going through somewhat of a dry spell right now with the sluggish economy and all. This was particularly true on the private eye side of things, where potential clients seemed more willing to go it alone or rely on an overworked criminal justice system to solve their problems.

I wondered if Carter was here for a social call or if he was looking to hire me as a security consultant again.

"Nice office," he said, though the words seemed to squeeze through his tight-lipped smile.

I agreed with his assessment, as I'd paid enough for the roomy one-woman, air-conditioned unit in a high rent downtown office building that had all the tools of the private eye trade.

Carter hadn't taken his eyes off me since entering the office. It made me just a little uncomfortable. I wondered if he was trying to undress me with his penetrating gaze, as if he hadn't seen the merchandise before.

Either way, it was not winning him any brownie points, if there were any left to win.

I glared at him and said dryly: "Glad you like what you see."

He immediately turned his eyes downward, as though searching for something. When he looked at me again, Carter's smile had faded as he said, clearly for my benefit:

"I've been meaning to stop by, see how things were going, but between work and—"

I was only too happy to bail him out in this instance, though I had the feeling he was stalling. For what, I had no earthly idea.

"Don't torture yourself, Carter," I told him. "It's a little late for a guilt trip. Or have you forgotten that we're not married anymore?"

At least not to each other. Six months to the day after our divorce was finalized, he and the mistress tied the knot. Rumor had it she was pregnant at the time. Rarely did I take rumors seriously but, sure enough, the newlyweds did produce a baby girl shortly thereafter. I didn't want kids—at least not until I had done the career thing first. Carter didn't want to wait for me or my career.

To this day, we've never discussed whether that was the beginning of the end or just the beginning of his wandering eyes. Either way, it did little to erase my self-doubts, what might have been, or what had transpired since.

"Like it or not, a part of us will always be married, Skye," he declared, "at least in spirit."

"I don't think so," I said, sneering. "In spirit or otherwise. What's done is done."

"Maybe you're right." He rubbed his chin thoughtfully.

"Do you plan to tell me why the hell you're here?" I decided to be blunt, since he seemed willing to take his own sweet time. And in my business, time was money. He didn't have to know that it was only trickling in at the moment. "Or am I supposed to guess what reason my ex-husband might have for paying me an office visit?" I asked.

I honestly couldn't think of any reason for him to be there. Other than maybe to check out my office digs out of curiosity or get a glimpse of what he'd given up back in the day.

He chuckled. "Still as impatient as ever, I see."

I frowned. "Guess some things never change..."

We eyeballed each other for a moment or two of stubborn reflection. Finally, he asked coolly: "Mind if I sit?"

I indicated either of two brandy-colored cluster armchairs. He sat down and for some reason I was glad that my desk separated us.

Carter sat there staring blankly at me, as though in a trance. I stared back and waited with uneasiness at this unlikely get together.

I suddenly felt compelled to ask: "So how's your wife and...?"

At about the same time he was saying: "I'd like to hire you..."

My question could wait. If I hadn't known better, I thought I just heard Carter Delaney actually say he wanted to hire me! If the notion wasn't so absurd, I might have burst into laughter at that moment. Instead, I forced myself to say: "I'm listening—"

He shifted in the chair unsteadily. "I think Darlene is cheating on me..."

He was referring to wife number two. I'd always detested the idea that someone named Darlene took my place in his life. It was as if her name was *darling*—somehow making her more endearing than I ever was to him.

Apparently, a certain someone must have concurred.

I resisted the urge to say what goes around comes around. *Oh, what the hell*, I thought. *Let's hear what else he has to say.*

"Really?" I said. "Now isn't that a terrible thing to suspect—" I couldn't resist smiling when I said it, in spite of myself.

Carter peered at me beneath thick, dark brows, clearly annoyed and perhaps embarrassed. "I'm not looking for sympathy or amusement," he said.

I got serious again. "Could've fooled me." A well-timed sigh. "Exactly what is it you want from me?" I dared ask, almost afraid of his answer.

He recomposed himself, and after a moment or two said: "I'd like you to follow her around, see where she goes, who she talks to..."

I suddenly found myself laughing, almost hysterically, probably to keep from crying. When I finally stopped, I said: "You can't be serious!" But something told me he was. "You don't really expect me, of all people, to spy on the very bitch-slash-bimbo you left me for, do you?"

His brow furrowed. "Can you lay off the name calling? I was hoping this would be a bit more civilized—"

I was almost enjoying this. *Almost*. "Get real, Carter. You didn't come here for civility. That ended between us the day you decided I wasn't enough for you."

He gave me a quizzical look. "Remember who kicked out who? It's not like I'm asking you to do something illegal. Isn't this the sort of work a private investigator does? Or is my money not green enough for you?"

I leaned toward him; anger building up that I thought had been buried for good. "Don't patronize me! It's not about money. It's about respect! You've got a hell of a lot of nerve showing up in my office and asking me to snoop on your wife. I'm afraid I don't come *that* cheap—" I took satisfaction in making that abundantly clear to him.

He actually seemed shocked by my reaction, and maybe even hurt. "Dammit, Skye, I didn't come here to insult you. I came because I need your help." He batted those charming eyes at me emotionally. "You think it was easy for me to come to you with my, uh, problem? Hell no, it wasn't, but I did because I thought you'd understand."

"Sure, I understand all right," I told him. "You're feeling betrayed, humiliated, and agony over your suspicions. Am I right?" I was sounding like a still bitter ex-wife and found it to be oddly refreshing.

Carter sighed, sounding exhausted. "You're never going to give up the spiteful ex-wife routine, are you? What happened between us is history. Right or wrong, I can't do a damned thing about it now." He hoisted to his feet so fast he nearly toppled over. "I guess it was a mistake coming here. I thought you were professional enough to take on *any* case without letting your personal feelings get in the way. Obviously I was wrong." He turned his back to me and headed for the door.

Carter always had an incredible way of being able to manipulate people—especially me—into seeing things his way. Not this time! I was not about to be conned into feeling guilty or unprofessional because I refused to take a case that was far too personal and could only stir up feelings that I would just as soon forget, if that was possible.

I stood and asked what seemed like a legitimate question under the circumstances. "Why me? Surely you could have found some other private eye in Honolulu to follow your wife around—one who didn't happen to be your ex-wife."

He turned around and gave me a look that implied the answer should have been as obvious to me as it was to him.

"Do you even have to ask why?" He clenched his jaw. "The last thing I want or need is to make public to already jittery investors *my* private business...or the fact that I think my wife—the mother of my three-year-old little girl—is cheating on me. You're the only private detective I felt I could count on for a *discreet* investigation that wouldn't come back to haunt me." He lowered his head. "I guess in some ways it already has—"

I suppose I took it to heart that he trusted me enough to feel that I would handle such an investigation with the utmost discretion. But, all things considered, I wasn't sure that I could trust myself as much.

"I can recommend someone—" I offered as a goodwill gesture.

"Don't do me any favors," Carter muttered irritably as he turned toward the door, gave me a final heated glare, and vanished much the way he had appeared.

I slumped back down into my chair, angry that he had put us both in an unenviable position. In truth, things had not been all that great for us even before the other woman entered the picture. Carter's obsession with getting ahead at all costs and his insistence on meticulousness in every aspect of our lives clashed heavily with my somewhat lower aspirations and lack of perfect order in my life. And our differences over when children should become part of the picture hadn't helped matters either.

The final straw came when I learned of Carter's affair and the reality that he didn't really seem to give a damn that the cat was out of the bag. It was more like a big relief to him. And when confronted with the option of me or the other woman, he was unable or unwilling to make what I believed to be the intelligent choice.

I sought to hold my ground where it concerned my ex. It had been over between us for a long time. I owed him nothing but the painful memories of days gone by. Neither of us had even pretended to be friends once our relationship had officially ceased. (I even turned down a generous divorce settlement, preferring to leave the marriage with only what I brought to it. At the time, it seemed like only a clean break could allow me to regain my dignity.) What was the point when we had gone too far beyond friendship to go back?

As far as I was concerned, that overused cliché applied perfectly when I thought of Carter Delaney. He had made his own damned bed and now had to lay in it—but not with me!

* * *

The privilege of sharing bed space with me in the post Carter Delaney era currently belonged to Ridge Larsen. A homicide detective for the Honolulu Police Department, Ridge had transferred from the Portland Police Bureau in Oregon just after I had gone into early retirement. He was forty, divorced, and handsome in his own rough-hewn, square-jawed way with crafty blue eyes, a shaven bald head, a thick dark moustache, and six foot three inches of solid muscle.

Ridge and I had been dating for the past six months. I wouldn't exactly call what we had serious, insofar as my

322

wanting him to put a ring on my finger. Being on my own for some time, I had become extremely possessive of my independence and privacy and was in no hurry to share my space with anyone on a permanent basis. Ridge seemed to understand and fully accept this, being of the same mind after a disastrous marriage, which probably accounted for half of why we seemed to work so well together.

The other half was that he tolerated my infrequent but not very pretty mood swings, knew when to leave me alone, was a great cook, and an even better lover.

An added fringe benefit of having Ridge around was that he came in handy during those not so rare occasions when I needed official snooping or able-bodied assistance in the every day and sometimes dangerous world of private investigations.

"I've never had the pleasure of meeting the current Mrs. Carter Delaney," hummed Ridge in bed, his strong arm holding me close to his taut body, "but from what I've heard, the former prosecutor's wife is hot stuff."

I jammed my elbow into his ribs and watched him wince. "I wouldn't know about that," I said tartly. "And now is *definitely* not the time for you to fantasize about my ex-husband's wife."

The afterglow of making love for the past hour was dimming quickly.

Ridge groaned. "I wouldn't dream of fantasizing about anyone but you these days." He planted a nice kiss on my lips. I enjoyed the taste of him. "I only go for pouty ones with long blonde hair and a smokin' hot body."

I soaked in the compliment and felt my annoyance beginning to wane.

Ridge sat up and asked nonchalantly: "So are you going to take the case?"

I looked at him dumbfounded while partially covering myself with a satin sheet, as if he hadn't already gotten a bird's eye view of every inch of me. "What case?"

"Delaney versus Delaney," he said cutely. "Sounds like pretty routine stuff to me." He grinned. "Let's face it, it took guts for him to come to you of all people for help."

I couldn't believe my ears. "Give me a break! Guts or not, why the hell would I want to find out for poor Carter if his wife is fooling around on him?"

"What are you afraid of?" Ridge asked.

"I'm not afraid of anything," I insisted. Except for maybe not being in full control of my own life at all times, I thought. But I knew it didn't work that way in the real world. We were all victims of circumstances for which we often had little to no control.

Ridge eyed me suspiciously. "You don't still have the hots for your ex, do you?"

I stared at his chest, then into his eyes, rolling mine. "What do you think?" He gave me that look all men have— the one that says they need to hear the words of reassurance. "No, I'm *not* still hung up on Carter Delaney," I said with an edge to my voice. "You of all people should know that, Ridge. I don't make a habit of sleeping with one person while fantasizing about another—" I hoped that would erase all doubts.

It didn't.

"Prove it," Ridge challenged me, "if only to yourself and maybe to Delaney. Take his case just as you would any other client. After all, it's just business, right?" He twisted his lips and added: "Who knows, you might even find it therapeutic."

I sneered at him. "Thanks for the advice, Dr. Phil."

He grinned crookedly. "Just wait till you get my bill. I don't come cheap."

I could vouch for that, as his expensive tastes included having a sometimes difficult girlfriend.

Reluctantly, I climbed out of his king-sized bed and gathered up my clothes that were scattered about the floor as if a tornado had passed through.

"What are you doing?" Ridge asked with a frown.

"I'm going home," I told him.

"Why? I hope it wasn't anything I said or didn't say."

I slid into my jeans and zipped them. "It wasn't. I have to feed my dog—"

He got out of bed. "Can't it wait—maybe for a couple of hours?"

"No," I said. "Ollie starts to get antsy when he goes practically all day without eating." I looked around, but couldn't find my cami, which seemed to work to Ridge's advantage.

He came up behind me and wrapped massive arms around my waist. "Are you sure you aren't just a little pissed at me?"

I wriggled out of his arms and gave him a sincere look. "There's nothing to be pissed about."

At least not with you, I told myself, reserving that for my ex at the moment.

Ridge looked relieved. "Good. I just don't want you to throw away Delaney's money for all the wrong reasons."

He was starting to press his luck and my patience.

I sighed and told him: "This may come as a surprise to you, but what's wrong for one person may be totally right for another—"

So maybe I was a little pissed at Ridge for seeming to represent the typical male in sizing up the situation. It was as if there was no room in the scheme of things for emotional baggage or ethical principles where it concerned making money. I wasn't sure I bought into that or if he really did.

I found my top, which had somehow ended up beneath Ridge's black denims. He gathered up his clothing.

"Any chance we can start the night over?" he asked lamely.

I couldn't help but smile at the thought. "Don't ask more of yourself than you're capable of delivering."

"Try me," he dared.

Though a repeat performance was pretty damn tempting, I grinned and said, "Isn't that what I just did?" while glancing

325

at the wrinkled bed coverings that betrayed the hot and heavy activity that had taken place there tonight.

"At least let me drive you home," Ridge offered.

"My car will get me there just as quickly," I said, and kissed him lightly on the mouth. "You can walk me to the door, though."

He grumbled and hugged me as we walked in step through his ranch style home on Keeaumoku Street in the Makiki section of Honolulu that wasn't far from my office.

I could never be upset with Ridge Larsen for very long. His intentions were usually anything but self-serving. Yet I couldn't help but wonder if by pushing me into this case, he was more motivated by his own insecurities than any self-doubts I may have had.

My instincts told me that both were likely to be tested before this thing was over.

Chapter Two

I left Ridge's house at eight o'clock, feeling a bit worn down for a day that had begun with Carter and ended with Ridge. At the moment, I was happy to be going to my own little piece of paradise, where I did my best thinking alone.

I had a one-year-old Subaru Forester that fit quite nicely into my current monthly payment budget. I drove to Waikiki, where I owned a nice house on a palm tree lined, dead-end street not far from the beach. I purchased the two-story plantation style home shortly after my divorce was finalized from an elderly couple who decided to move back to the mainland. It was my good fortune to be in the right place at the right time to get the property, which had been well maintained and reminded me of the home where I grew up on the island. My parents had been beach bums who island hopped before settling into Oahu and having me.

I could hear my dog barking when I pulled into the driveway. Ollie was a five-year-old German Shepherd, named after my late uncle who was as mean as a junkyard dog and ornery as ever. In fact, more often than not, Ollie was just the opposite—sweet and gentle as a lamb, as long as he was not provoked.

Opening the front door was all he needed to make me eat my thoughts, as Ollie literally attacked me. Okay, so it was just his way of playing and asking me "Where the hell have you been all day?" Or maybe "I'm hungry as a dog. What's for supper?"

We ended up wrestling for a few minutes before I turned on the ceiling fan in the living room, then fed Ollie his favorite dog food. He wanted more, but I wasn't about to let him get fat on me. That wouldn't help either of us.

After freshening up and changing into a sleeveless shirt and denim shorts, I allowed my sore feet some freedom from footwear, padding barefoot across the hardwood floor and into the kitchen. I made myself a salad and ate it with two slices of wheat bread and a glass of red wine. Ollie loved to hang out on the kitchen's cool ceramic tiles more than anywhere else in the house.

However, the kitchen floor still took second place to the backyard. When he began to grow restless, I got the picture, letting him out of the house to run around in our nice sized, fenced in yard. I joined Ollie a few minutes later and tossed a Frisbee around for him to chase, making sure he stayed clear of my vegetable garden.

Back inside, I watered the flamingo flowers, vanda orchids, and heart leaf philodendron I kept throughout the house, which helped give the place a Hawaiian botanical garden look.

By the time I was ready to call it a night, I had tucked Ollie in his basement hideaway, read a couple of chapters of a John Lescroart novel, and watched the news.

Before drifting off to dreamland, I had more or less decided that, for better or worse, I would take on the task of spying on the current wife of Carter Delaney. Business was business, I convinced myself, even if it happened to involve my ex-husband and his ex-mistress. I still hadn't decided if I wanted his suspicions to prove false or right on the money.

Only time would tell...

* * *

Read the entire MURDER IN HONOLULU, available in eBook, audio, and print. The book is also available in the MURDER IN HAWAII MYSTERIES 3-BOOK BUNDLE by R. Barri Flowers, in Kindle, Nook, iTunes, and Google.

# # #

ABOUT THE AUTHOR

R. Barri Flowers is the international bestselling author of mystery, suspense, and thriller fiction, as well as young adult novels.

Mysteries and thrillers include the Murder in Hawaii Mysteries bundle of Murder in Honolulu, Murder in Maui, and Seduced to Kill in Kauai; Before He Kills Again, Dark Streets of Whitechapel, Justice Served, Killer in The Woods, and Murdered in the Man Cave.

Teen fiction includes Count Dracula's Teenage Daughter, Ghost Girl in Shadow Bay, Out for Blood, Summer at Paradise Ranch, and Teen Ghost at Dead Lake.

The author's books can be found in audio, eBook, and print.

Follow R. Barri Flowers on Twitter, Facebook, Pinterest, Goodreads, Google+, LinkedIn, Booktrack, LibraryThing, iAuthor, and www.rbarriflowers.com